Book 1

a

novel

# WORLDS of DECEPTION

by

**Petra**

**Bossé**

Book and Cover Design by Vladimir Verano, Third Place Press

AUTHOR CONTACT:
WorldsofDeception@gmail.com

*ISBN: 978-0-9984699-0-4*

*This book is dedicated to all the readers who will travel into my imaginary world. I hope you enjoy the journey as much as I enjoyed creating it.*

# PROLOGUE

Earth Year - 2086

Director of Operations, Steve Reynolds, made his way hurriedly to the manufacturing level of the moon base Atlantis. It was early, so it surprised him how many people he passed in the narrow corridors. He always enjoyed the quiet, predawn hours, but today was obviously going to be different.

"Hey boss," Phil Jacobs, the base's production supervisor greeted him as he entered their small office.

"Morning, Phil. Seems to be a busy morning already."

"You noticed that too? Wonder what's going on?"

Steve held up the white tablet he carried. "Probably the unexpected communication from the International Space Station overnight."

"Really? Did they lift the blackout?"

"No. But evidently, Seattle Command felt this data was worth the breach."

"What is it?"

A big grin spread across Steve's face. "Well, from what little I know, this is going to make our benefactors extremely happy."

Twenty years ago, seven countries had come together to form a consortium, known as the United Alliance. A joint venture between the government and private sector, the Alliance had immediately set its sights on space exploration, and now 3500 men, women, and children lived in the underground moon base with a contract to build five interstellar spaceships. Three of which were currently in various stages of production.

"Seriously?"

"Yes. Seems our new alien friends, the Zantians, have given an extensive look at some of their technology, and this is the configuration for a new propulsion system. The communication didn't say much except that the science techs on Earth were able to do some preliminary conversions and are excited about the results. We'll need to convert the rest of the data, but if this is as powerful as they're saying, it will enhance our engines well beyond what the current specs call for."

"Is that even possible?"

Steve shrugged. "We'll have to wait and see. I have a meeting with the commander, and then I'm going to drop this off at the lab. Seems everyone's up early this morning, but I wanted to glance at last night's test results first."

"They're right here." Phil handed him the data collector. "I looked over them briefly, and everything's looking good. The seals held, and no air leaks were detected in the forward compartments. In another week, the robots can take over the rest of that section, and everyone else can move inside."

Steve took a cursory glance at the instrument. "Let's not rush it. I want to make sure those seals hold under the pressure."

"You're the boss, but I think the construction is sound, and we won't find any leakage. Functional tests are scheduled for the rest of the week, so that should give us a better idea how to proceed."

"Sounds good." He returned the collector. "The more data we have up front, the better. Call a meeting in an hour with all the crew leads and we'll dissect through this."

"Will do. How soon do you want to try the gravity generators? That part of the schedule is still open."

"Once the tests are conclusive, we'll install them and begin the phase-in." Steve saw the disappointment on the supervisor's face. "I know you're anxious to get this underway, Phil, but I want it right the first time, so we're going to go slow. They shouldn't give us too much trouble, though, since we have the lessons-learned from the station install to draw on."

"I know, but I'm anxious to get this moving. Two years we've worked on this project. Now it's all starting to come together, and if you're right about the engines…."

"Well, let's see what our lab guys say before we get all excited." Steve headed to the door.

"Don't let McGregor talk you into cutting any more corners, okay," Phil called after him lightheartedly.

"Ha, someone has to pretend to be concerned about the cost of things around here."

David McGregor sat at his desk as Steve entered after a short knock.

"Hey, why is everyone up so early this morning?" Steve quipped.

"Sadly, I've been up half the night," Dave said frowning, then motioned for the tall man to take a seat. "I take it you got the files that were sent up?"

"Right here," Steve held up the tablet. "Is this really worth breaking radio silence? What else did the ISS say?"

"General Feinberg authorized the transmission, so I assume it was. He only attached a brief note, saying we needed to safeguard that data because things were breaking down with the Zantians. That they were throwing unreasonable demands into the negotiations."

"What kind of demands?"

"He didn't say. Only that the President and the Alliance want this data hidden, so we're not to download it onto the mainframe. It seems a lot of risks were taken to get it here. He also implied that once this crisis is over, they'll take it back and do their own conversions."

"But not until we test it first."

"Well, I'm not sure—"

"I'll be damned if we're going to hold on to some new technology that will advance our engine capabilities, and just sit on it until the military asks for it back. I thought we were partners in all of this?"

Dave smiled. "I knew you'd feel that way. That's why I had the data sent to you first. I figured those wheels of yours would be on overdrive once you saw what it was. And yes, we're partners ... but only up to a certain point, I'm sure."

"Well, I'm going to pretend we didn't have this conversation. I'll tell the techs to scrub through it offline, ASAP."

"And let's keep this quiet for now too. Until we know exactly how valuable it is."

"Agreed." Steve looked thoughtful for a moment. "I guess we shouldn't be surprised that our first alien encounter isn't turning out to be this great thing after all."

"Doesn't seem that way. The Earth Government was formed so quickly, that I'm sure no one considered what would happen if the Zantians weren't as friendly as they appeared."

"Very true. And suddenly I don't trust this data. Maybe this information is incomplete, and they dangled it under our nose to make themselves look sincere, but in reality, it'll never amount to much. I'm afraid we're going to waste a lot of time on this."

"Let the lab figure it out before we jump to any conclusions. How did last night's test go?"

"I only took a brief look at the results. We've got a meeting in an hour, so I'll have a better idea after that."

"Keep me informed."

"My dad is going to kill me when he finds out I've skipped school again," sixteen-year-old Becca Reynolds said, looking purposefully at her friend Jamie Adams across her family's kitchen table. "Showing up for school once in a while might keep both of us from getting into trouble on a regular basis."

His soft blue eyes looked at her pleadingly. "Come on Becca; it's the end of the semester, and there are no exams today. Since when do you object to a trip to the tower?"

"Don't look at me that way. It's not going to work." But she was only giving him a hard time. Usually, she was the one who suggested skipping classes so they could sneak up to the observation room and look out over North America when it was in view. "However, since you asked so nicely," she chuckled, "how can I say no?"

He smiled, got to his feet and reached for her hand. "Well, then let's go before we miss it."

Twenty minutes later, the two teenagers sat in oversized padded chairs facing floor-to-ceiling windows which gave an unobstructed view of planet Earth below. It was an unusually clear day, with only a few visible pockets of scattered cloud cover.

"I wish we could come up here every morning." Jamie mused.

"Well, let's enjoy this while we can since we'll be grounded for the rest of the week."

Jamie tossed a wadded food wrapper at her which she easily avoided. Retrieving it from the floor, she turned to throw it back, but Jamie was moving toward the window.

"What is it?"

"I'm not sure. I thought I saw something."

"Like what?" she asked skeptically.

"I don't know. It looked like a flash of some sort."

"A flash? What kind of flash can you see from up here?" Becca walked up next to him.

"Look, there's another one, but it's over there this time." He indicated to the right.

"Is it a storm? Lightning maybe? Everything looks so peaceful."

Jamie activated one of the room's three high-powered telescopes and aimed it in the direction of the last flash.

"See anything?" Becca powered on one of the others and focused it in the direction Jamie had pointed.

"Not at the moment, but—"

"What in the world…!" Becca gasped as something moved across her view. She looked over the top of the telescope and stumbled back. A light gray vessel, triangular in shape, with countless armaments protruding from the hull, eased slowly from around the moon to their left. The ship was huge, and it seemed to take forever before its six large engines came into view.

Becca buried her face into Jamie's shoulder as the thick glass window vibrated from the powerful jet blast. As he pulled her tight against him, Becca waited for the glass to shatter, wondering how long it would take for them to die.

But soon the shuddering stopped. With a look of horror, the couple watched as ten additional ships, identical to the first, flew side-by-side on a trajectory toward Earth.

"Do you think they saw us?" Her voice quavered as she clung to him.

"They don't seem interested in us."

They went back to the telescopes and observed as each vessel took a separate course toward their home-world and positioned itself in orbit. Four stayed within their vantage point, while the other seven moved around the planet. After a few minutes, as if choreographed, tiny black objects emerged from below the mammoth vessels and scattered like an army of ants before disappearing into the atmosphere.

"I've got to call my dad!" Becca grabbed her bag and removed her vidphone. She punched in four digits, and silently prayed he would answer; if he were at the construction site, it would go directly to voicemail. Luckily, within several seconds, her father's face appeared on the small screen.

"Becca? Aren't you supposed to be in school?" Steve asked suspiciously.

"Dad, thank God," she said ignoring his disapproving look. "Jamie and I are in the observation tower."

"Becca! How many times have I told you—?"

"Dad, please, this is important!" She raised her voice hoping he would recognize her urgency. "I need you to come up here."

"Becca, I don't have time—"

"Please Dad, something is happening to Earth. Ships—"

"What are you talking about? You—"

"I need you up here, now!" She suddenly realized tears were running down her cheeks. *Great*, she thought, *we're in a crisis, and I'm falling apart!*

Seeing the tears on his daughter's face sent a chill down Steve's spine. From the day she was born, Becca had been a strong-willed child and never prone to emotional outbursts unless she was in serious trouble.

"I'll be right there." He disconnected.

"What's wrong?" Phil asked coming up next to him.

"I don't know. But Becca's in a panic and that concerns me."

Steve pushed a few buttons on his phone and waited for the subway engineer to answer. "Dan, I have an emergency in the tower, how soon can you route a car to the main terminal?"

"Hold on, I'll check," Dan said. Within a few seconds, he was back. "I can have one there in about three minutes."

"Perfect. Thanks, Dan." He turned to Phil. "Let's go."

The two men entered the small subway terminal just as the car came into view. They jumped on, and Steve set the destination code. Once the car moved into the tunnel at its leisurely pace, the director grabbed the overhead handrail and leaned his head against the cool glass.

"Are you going to tell me what's going on?"

"I have no idea. Becca and Jamie are in the observation tower…don't say it…I know." Steve often voiced frustration that she constantly skipped classes. "She said something's happening on Earth…said something about ships."

"What does she mean 'something's happening on Earth'? Must be something pretty big to see from here. Was she talking about Zantian ships?"

"Not sure. But like I said, she's never been one to get emotional. When she does, it's time to pay attention."

When the two men burst through the tower door, they found Becca and Jamie standing in front of the observation window holding each other tightly. Seeing her father, Becca ran weeping into his arms. As he comforted his daughter, Steve's heart sank when he saw the stricken look on Jamie's face as he moved closer to the window. Steve reached over and squeezed the boy's shoulder reassuringly.

"Earth is in trouble, Dad," Becca said woefully.

Steve was always awed by the sight of Earth. From here he could make out the oceans and continents, but today something was wrong; the southern portion of the European continent looked covered in a thick haze. He knew immediately that this phenomenon wasn't weather related. He had seen two massive hurricanes rotate over the ocean last year, and a huge storm cell over North America once—but this was something completely different.

Clouds, whether lazily gliding across the sky or violently swirling in an angry rage, still formed a cohesive unit. Steve looked through a telescope for a closer look. What presented itself below was like the pictures of a massive wildfire in western Canada the ISS took last year—not a natural occurrence he was sure. Searching the fogged area for a clue, something in the distance caught his attention: a flash from the west coast of North America, where the sun wasn't up yet. Turning just in time to see another one, Steve imagined the smoke thickened—but knew that was impossible.

"How long has this been going on?"

"It started about an hour ago," Jamie said. "When Becca and I came up here it was clear. The flashes began just before we saw eleven large ships head toward Earth."

"Zantian ships?"

"I don't think so. They didn't look like the ones on the newsfeeds. These were scary, like porcupines, but with weapons instead of quills. You should be able to see them in orbit."

Steve and Phil searched with the telescopes until they both spotted the orbiting behemoths.

"They were so close, Dad," Becca whispered still visibly shaken, "we could have reached out and touched one. What's happening on Earth, Dad? Does all the haze mean it's under attack?" A tear slipped down her cheek.

He pulled her close. "I wish I knew, baby. But Earth can take care of itself. All countries have a great military."

"Can we contact Seattle?"

"Becca, you know we can't. We still have to maintain radio silence."

"Steve, look," Phil said still looking through one of the telescopes. The Director of Operations adjusted his scope just as two of the triangular ships altered course and disappeared around the planet. But before he could comment, the vidphone in his pocket buzzed. He activated the viewscreen to find Commander McGregor.

"Steve, the ISS just came into communication range and sent an emergency transmission. I need you in my office. Now."

"Is this about what's happening on Earth?"

"Yes. How did you know?"

"I'm in the observation tower. What's going on?"

"There's a serious problem. I'll explain when you get here."

"I'll be there as fast as I can." He withdrew the phone's earpiece and inserted the small nub in his ear. He motioned for Phil to do the same. "Phil, stay here and monitor what's going on down there. Let me know if anything changes. Kids, let's go."

"But Dad—!"

"Don't argue with me. I want both of you home."

Back in the main terminal, Steve instructed the teenagers to go directly to their own living quarters and then ran to the commander's office.

"What's going on, Dave?" Steve demanded as he entered the office without knocking.

"Earth sent a message through the ISS saying they were under attack by the Zantians. But before the transmission could complete, the Earth-link went down."

"What do you mean went down? Did the system crash?"

"No, it just shut off. If it had crashed, we would still be able to trace a connection even if we couldn't access it. Our internal network is still up and running, but our connection to Earth is…gone."

"Which means something happened on their end." Steve collapsed into a chair in front of the commander's desk, realizing the implication.

"Yes, that's exactly what it means."

"What else did they say?" Steve asked running his hands through his hair.

"Only that negotiations had broken down, and the Zantians are pulling out."

"What! Is this because of the unreasonable demands they were making?"

"Yes. That was the last chilling thing that came through. It seems the Zantians wanted to trade technology for people."

"Oh my God!" Steve felt his stomach drop. "And they obviously had a backup plan if they didn't get what they wanted." He told Dave what they had seen from the tower.

The base commander blanched.

Steve touched his ear. "Phil, any changes?"

"No, things are pretty much the same, except the haze is spreading and getting thicker. I can hardly make out landmasses anymore, even with the scopes."

"Have you seen any flashes in space?"

"No, only on the planet so far. Why?"

"The ISS was sending a transmission when the Earth-link went down. That means something happened to Seattle Command, so I wanted to make sure the station is still there. It should be in visual range soon."

"I'll give you a buzz when I see it… hopefully. There are thirty people on that station. If they've lost their connection…."

"Then there is little hope for them in the long run."

"Well, hopefully, this craziness won't last long," Phil said.

"Let's hope. Keep your eyes open."

"Oh, trust me, they're open." Phil ended the connection.

"So what do you want to do?" Steve looked at Dave questioningly.

"I have no idea," Dave said with obvious distress. "Maybe we should break radio silence and contact Earth, find out what's going on. They'll tell us what to do."

"Even if we could, it's the last thing we should do. The Alliance went to great lengths to keep this base a secret. Now when Earth seems to be under attack is not the time to announce our presence. We can't help them, no matter how much you might want to. I think the only thing we can do now is to protect ourselves."

"Do you think those ships saw us?"

"I don't know. Ever since our order to maintain radio silence, we've also been keeping the outside lighting to a minimum. I was just getting out of my meeting when Becca called, so we're a little behind schedule, otherwise more people would have seen those ships. But, I'm sure they've been hovering somewhere nearby, waiting for the Zantians' signal. From what Becca and Jamie said, the warships flew right over us. If they wanted to destroy us, they had the perfect opportunity."

Dave pondered this information for a moment. "We need to get everyone inside and shut down all external systems. Everything. If they do come back, maybe they won't detect our internal power signature."

"That's a big if, but worth a try. We'll only be able to stay on minimal power for about a week, though, then the generators will need to be recharged." Steve reminded him.

"I know. Hopefully, this will all be over by then. I'll make the broadcast and get everyone inside."

Steve rose and moved to the door, but turned back before exiting.

"We need to prepare for the worst. That means accepting the possibility that we may never hear from Earth. If the rest of world is going through the same thing we saw, then Seattle Command may not be in a position to contact us or get the link back up. And with the link gone, we're completely on our own.

"I think during this next week, we need to take stock of our resources and make some long-term plans." Steve paused as the severity of his words sunk in, then added sadly, "it's a good thing they intended this facility to be self-sustaining."

The Atlantis commander grimaced and gave Steve a defeated nod.

"And let's pray that the Zantians truly aren't interested in us."

# PART 1

Zantia

Earth Year - 2197

# CHAPTER 1

# House of Alrack

Leea stood over the chopping board, her knife plowing through crispy orange and purple stalks with a silent vengeance, as she tried to control her temper. Although Marik stood several feet behind her, she sensed his breath on the back of her neck and no matter how much she tried she couldn't shake the feeling.

"You're making a mess, Leea," Marik said with a touch of irritation as he eyed pieces falling to the floor. "If you keep this up, there won't be enough left for the meal. I don't have time to get more from the greenhouse."

"And why not?" She turned and glared at him. "It's not like you do anything else around here anyway."

"Leea, ignore him," her sister Julia said from the other side of the kitchen. "He's just goading you."

Resigned, Leea continued her task but quickly lost focus on what she was doing. Instead, she envisioned ways to get rid of the nuisance behind her, as she often did of late. If she let her imagination turn to the bizarre, she would picture the fruit and vegetable stalks in the mansion's greenhouse coming to life and swallowing him whole. But of course, they would find him a bitter pill to swallow, spit him out, and she would be stuck with him again. She often thought of creative ways to use her knife, but would shutter that he could bring her to such violent thoughts. She just wanted him to leave her alone—for good.

"Leea!"

Julia's cry brought her back to reality. "What?!" But then immediately noticed what made her call out—Leea had missed a carrot and snagged a finger, and now blood dripped on the cutting board. Julia quickly tossed her a small towel, which she precariously wrapped around the oozing digit.

Marik came around to see what happened but kept his distance. "Are you kidding me?" he exclaimed, throwing his hands in the air. "Now I'll have to go collect the whole lot again. What's wrong with you?"

"You're what's wrong with me!" she yelled, thrusting the sharp knife in his direction and feeling a brief moment of satisfaction as he took a step back. "Why can't you leave me alone? I don't need your every-five-minute commentary, and I don't care if you have to collect the whole lot ten times. Not My Problem!"

"LEEA!" Everyone froze at the sound of Lauranna's voice. The tall, statuesque Zantian had come into the room unnoticed.

The kitchen where they worked was part of the ruling House of Alrack, the home of the most powerful family on the planet Zantia. Lauranna was the matron of the house, and her mate Jarock was the city's leader as well as the head of the planetary ruling Council. Although Lauranna managed the working staff with a light hand, she drew the line at conflicts; she insisted on harmonious surroundings.

All of the working staff was Human, their ancestors having been abducted from Earth more than a century earlier, and were scattered about the planet, providing whatever services the Zantians required. They didn't have a bad life on this world, but not free to come and go as they pleased.

"Marik, go and replenish the produce," the matron instructed him while concentrating her focus on Leea.

"Leea, tend to your finger, and then you are excused from the rest of the morning. Maybe you can contemplate your actions here."

Leea drew her lips into a thin line but nodded. Arguing with Lauranna would only make things worse. Realizing she still held the knife, the young woman gently laid it down and left the kitchen.

Marik paused at the greenhouse door, watching as she left the room. His momentary smirk went unnoticed.

"I wish you would reconsider." Lauranna took a sip from a tall, thin glass, eyeing her son Yaran over the rim.

"I've never spent time with your father, so why would he want my help now?"

"Because you know your way around the shipping requirements, and it will only be for a few months."

"I'm familiar with them here, in Alrack, not in Calthena. Why are you pushing this?" Yaran asked, swirling the dark liquid in his glass. But he didn't need to ask, because he knew exactly why this *opportunity* to spend time at his mother's childhood home had arisen.

Lauranna lowered her gray eyes and tucked a wayward strand of dark hair behind her ear. "Your father is getting impatient."

"He's always impatient."

"This is serious, Yaran. He has a responsibility and an image to maintain. Your crossover is less than three months away. Other ruling house children are well positioned to take on what is expected of them by now. You—"

"I, on the other hand, have failed to live up to any of my father's expectations. A good son would have found a mate to ensure the continued bloodline, completely taken over the family business, and would be striving to become the less-than-likable leader of the Council."

Yaran rarely voiced these sentiments, especially to his mother. She was, after all, obligated to follow certain rules and he could never fault her for that. And he, being their son, also fell under those obligations whether he liked them or not. He ran a hand through his short black hair in frustration.

Lauranna's glare told him he'd crossed the line. She drained the remainder of the golden liquid from her glass and set it aside. "It wouldn't hurt for you to make this effort. The time away would do you some good. You might meet new people... you never know."

*Yes, there it is,* he thought. Her not-so-subtle attempt to, once again, remind him that time was running out to abide by the Zantian tradition of being mated, or at least promised, by the crossover—age thirty.

He had three months left. He wouldn't make it.

"By the way, there was another incident today between Leea and Marik. I'm at the point where I'll need to separate them permanently."

"Why can't you just send Marik back where he came from?"

"That's not my decision to make. Your father brought him here."

"Then he should send him back since that worker can't seem to stay out of trouble."

"Well, that's not exactly how it went today...."

Leea sat in her favorite spot—on an old wooden bench underneath an ancient Jala tree, watching the sunset. There was no breeze today, which meant the stifling heat would linger, but the tree's long yellow fronds hung low, providing welcome shade.

Where she sat edged on a bluff and as far as the eye could see was nothing but a flat landscape of dark red soil, simply known as the Red Desert, which merged with an aqua sky at the horizon. The only thing that interrupted the level scene were the Alrack Mountains to her right, whose white peaks seemed forever lost in a never dissipating bank of clouds over the range.

Far below, toward the base of the foothills, Leea could make out one of the villages as well as the outskirts of the city nestled just beyond. The only indication of a larger metropolis was the occasional departure of a cargo ship heading for space, or standard shuttle traffic flying to some unknown destination on the planet.

Undoing the clip that held up her long auburn hair, Leea shook out the wavy locks and closed her green eyes. She enjoyed being outside right before sunset, where she could relish the warmth without wearing the protective robe needed during hot Zantian days, and took advantage of this as often as she could.

Concentrating on the surrounding silence, she recalled the day's events. Hardly one day passed anymore without some turmoil involving Marik. *When will this end?* she thought dismally, then let out a frustrated sigh.

As if on cue, two hands came to rest on her shoulders and gently massaged her tight muscles. A little more pressure and a moan involuntarily escaped her lips; this was exactly what she needed. When a hand pushed her hair aside, and soft lips brushed against her neck, her groan was instinctive.

When the kneading stopped, she looked up appreciatively into large expressive eyes and noticed the clouded expression clearly visible on the golden-brown face. She smiled, not needing to ask for an explanation. "I didn't think you'd make it today. But I'm so glad you did." She rotated her shoulders.

"I didn't think I would either," Yaran said, sitting down next to her, "but Jarock left for some crisis in the city and Lauranna wanted to retire to her sitting room for a while."

"And now I get the pleasure of your company." She leaned up and kissed him lightly.

"Uh huh."

Leea sat up and faced the handsome man. His Zantian features were not unlike the Human ones she saw in the mirror. He had a long angular face, with high cheekbones and a strong chin, but there was one distinctive difference—his eyes. All Zantians had round, steel-gray eyes, with irises slightly larger than their Human counterparts. Depending on emotion they had the ability to vary in color. They could change to a coal black, and grow slightly in size, during intense anger, or appear almost translucent, and smaller, during times of extreme happiness or pleasure; Leea could attest to the latter. Yaran's irises were presently a little darker than normal, telling her he was mildly upset. This characteristic was easily controlled with little effort, and some found it proper to do so, but Leea loved that Yaran never masked his feelings from her.

"You're upset with me."

Yaran drew in a deep breath and mumbled something in Zantian that she couldn't quite make out, which was never a good sign, as he always claimed it was easier to express displeasure with more familiar words. Her only consolation was how much she loved hearing him speak his native language. When he spoke in hers, English, something his ancestors had mastered during their short, destructive visit to Earth, his voice was a soothing baritone. But when he spoke Zantian, the tone rose several octaves, and each syllable sounded like part of a musical scale.

He shook his head. "Leea, why do you do this to yourself?" he whispered as if keeping his voice low would somehow calm him.

"Ah … I assumed your mother would tell you what happened today. I'm sorry. I couldn't help myself. Marik was annoying me all morning, and I just couldn't take it anymore. I certainly wouldn't have yelled at him like that had I seen Lauranna standing there. But I don't understand why I was the only one she reprimanded. She didn't say anything to him, and he started it." Leea looked down at her hands for a moment and then chuckled.

"What could possibly be funny?"

"I'm actually lucky, you know. My first instinct was to throw a knife at him. I had it in my hand."

"Oh my," he groaned. "The price for that action would be more than I could save you from." He ran a hand through his hair. When he was frustrated, as he clearly was now, he had a tendency to run his fingers repeatedly through the thick mass, setting the neatly combed strands askew.

"By *price*, you mean she would have told your father?"

"Yes, exactly. And we don't want to give Jarock any more reasons to be upset with you."

"I'm sorry I keep making things difficult." She turned her gaze out over the desert.

Yaran gently brushed a long strand of hair away from her lightly freckled face. "I just worry about you," he said softly. "We both know that workers can be sent away never to return. I would be devastated if that ever happened to you."

Leea instantly thought of her father, who had been sent to the mines when she was two years old and died in an accident there less than a year later. The primary source of export on this planet was mining, and male workers were often sent to labor there, either to replace lost workers or due to increased production. Many men died there—her father being one of the unlucky ones to perish young. It was against council law to send women to the mines, but they could be relocated to another city and lost forever.

"Don't worry about me, Yaran," Leea muttered. "I'll try to be good…at least for a while."

Yaran groaned loudly, but with a sideways glance, she watched as the corners of his mouth tilted slightly upward. He could never stay upset for long.

"What time do you have to go back?"

"I can stay awhile."

"Good." Leea snuggled closer to him, closed her eyes and listened to the silence around them. For her, there was nothing better than sitting in that isolated place with the man she loved.

But their relationship was strictly forbidden. Zantians were a stoic, sometimes socially backward race, governed by deeply rooted laws and traditions that frowned on ruling house children, especially sons, mating outside the ruling circle, much less outside the species. Yaran should have already found his future match, but his heart belonged to her—as hers did to him.

She knew with certainty that his father, the Desolk—as the head of a ruling house was called—would send her away without hesitation if he discovered that their childhood friendship had grown into love. So, they spent as much time as they could away from the house, never discussing whether they believed these tactics fooled anyone. But they had made a pact many years ago never to worry about what the future held. Instead, they would take each day as it came, and be happy with the time they had together.

They sat for a while quietly conversing until Yaran slowly rose, unfolding his six-foot-eight frame—an average height for a Zantian male—and tousled her hair. "I need to go. Mother wants me to play for her tonight."

"What's on the playlist?" She rose to stand with him, the top of her head just barely past his chin.

"Not sure. She's been requesting some of the exotic instruments lately. I've needed to do a little practicing."

"You?" she declared with mock surprise. "You can play any one of those without even trying. In fact, they play for you, not the other way around."

He smiled and ran a finger down the slope of her slightly upturned nose. "So you always say. Are you coming back with me?"

"No. I'm going stay a little longer." She reached up and laid a hand on his cheek. "I'm sorry," she said with regret.

"There is nothing to be sorry about, my love. I'm not upset with you. I'm irritated because you have to endure this nonsense with Marik while I'm powerless to do anything about it." He sighed. "That troublemaker seems to be taking a lot of liberties lately and then making sure the blame falls on you. Please be careful. Don't let him get to you. My mother is a patient woman, but she has her limits."

"I know, but it's easier said than done."

Yaran chuckled softly. "For you, I have no doubt. But you should try…for me."

"For you, *A'rinBientS'aan*, anything."

Zantians spoke to the workers in English because Human vocal cords had difficulty forming the complicated alien reverberations for any length of time. Although Leea understood a good deal, her attempts to repeat the words were usually met with muted chuckles from Yaran. The placement of accents and inflections always left her tongue-tied.

The phrase *A'rinBientS'aan* loosely translated meant 'my life's joy.' She had practiced endlessly to perfect every syllable of this Zantian endearment because Yaran *was* what gave her life joy, and she wanted to express it to him in his own language.

With one finger, he tilted her chin up and touched his lips to hers. At first, his kiss was soft and gentle, then slowly grew more demanding until Leea reluctantly pushed him away.

"Um…remember…you have to go," she said a bit breathless.

Yaran smiled, and then spoke the Zantian phrase he always did when they parted; *Er'ShaltMee'Sarn*, which meant 'keep my heart safe.'

"Always," she replied warmly.

Leea watched him go, gave one final wave before he disappeared around a curve in the path, and then returned to the bench. At twenty-five years old, she had lived in this house all her life, as had her parents and grandparents before her. A brief sadness came over her when she thought of her grandmother who had passed away almost three years earlier, leaving Leea with no immediate family—her mother having lost her battle with depression a few years after her father's mining accident.

She had Julia, but they weren't sisters by blood, only raised as such. After her mother had died, Julia's parents had treated her as one of their own, including her in most of their family activities. Despite a seven-year age difference, the two girls had always been close, and never considered themselves as anything but family.

Sitting upright, Leea tried to shake the glum thoughts from her mind. Dwelling on the past was never her favorite way to spend time, but sometimes it crept up on her unexpectedly. 'What's gone is gone; never let the past keep you from living today,' her grandmother had always said. These were words she tried to live by, never dwelling on how Humans came to this planet, or the cards fate had dealt them. Although city workers were treated fair and allowed a limited amount of freedom, in the end, they served the Zantians—nothing more.

She lived her life in service to the ruling family as a prep cook. She didn't hate the job. To her, slicing and dicing could sometimes be therapeutic, but several scars on her hands proved that wielding a chopping knife was not her forte.

If it were her choice, she would rather be in the hangar with Jeffrey, tinkering with the machinery, but that wasn't a task performed by women. At twelve, Leea had wandered into the head mechanic's domain one day and was fascinated by watching him work on one of the shuttle engines. After that, he encouraged her to come by, often letting her help, and teaching her to use basic tools, claiming they were things every girl should know. Although she didn't visit him much anymore, she would sometimes go if she'd had a difficult day. Fiddling with machine parts was safer than brandishing cutlery, as this morning's episode had proven again.

Moving nearer to the edge of the bluff, she looked up at the mountains as the last of the sun's glow disappeared. At that moment, before the light vanished, it seemed as if the summits reached out through the clouds, not wanting to let it go. Then, seemingly from one instant to the next, daylight was replaced with a bright starry sky, in which one of Zantia's three moons hung in its full round form overhead.

With an appreciative sigh, Leea turned away and took the now illuminated path back to the house. At night, bright lights built into the building's structure made it visible from all points in the city, and no matter how many times she came upon it, the magnificence of the place always took her breath away. With its sixty-foot high walls and three protruding wings, it was a formidable presence.

The building's three-story framework was constructed of composite steel; an alloy that contained a biological element, making it strong yet moldable and impervious to the heat. The rest was transitioning glass which served a dual purpose; it lightened or darkened, effectively keeping out Zantia's oppressive sun, as well as being a solar collector, providing power and allowing the house to maintain a comfortable inside temperature. Most of the buildings on Zantia were made of these materials because they also stood up best to the harsh, arid environment.

Each of Zantia's one hundred cities had a ruling family whose house stood in the center as its focal point, and in most cases sat at a higher elevation so it could be seen from anywhere. In Alrack, the house stood on a hill with the villages spread out below and the city beyond resting in the shadow of the mountains.

Leea stood for a moment at the manor's kitchen door before opening it. Life always seemed so much simpler outside these walls, which sometimes made her reluctant to enter. But it would be quiet now with all the chores done. Yaran would be with his mother in the music room, located in the art wing, and the workers would be relaxing before retiring to their rooms. It wasn't a hard life, but day in and day out it was the same—something Leea wasn't sure she could endure for the rest of her life.

"Out with him again?"

Leea hesitated as she crossed the threshold, hearing the arrogant voice of the biggest thorn in her side—Marik. *Hadn't he done enough today?* She debated turning around and going back out but knew from experience he would only find another opportunity to annoy her.

Marik had come to the house about a year earlier and taken an instant liking to her. He spent the first several months trying to charm her and seemed exasperated that she showed no interest in him. Even if she hadn't been in love with Yaran, she despised Marik. He was obnoxious, much too impressed with himself, and the main reason she got into trouble these days.

He was a year younger than her, the same height, with short blond hair and light blue eyes. She had to admit he was attractive, but she couldn't understand why his complete focus was always on her since there were two other women in the house about their age who might have welcomed his advances.

Ignoring him, she took the stairs up to the sleeping quarters but felt Marik right on her heels.

"Why do you waste your time with that guy? You know nothing will ever come of it," Marik said sarcastically, following her down the hall.

Stopping in front of her bedroom door, she turned and sneered at him. "Leave me alone Marik. Why don't you go find Marta? I'm sure she's more on your level." Marta was Julia's eight-year-old daughter, who for some reason adored Marik.

"This will only end badly for you," he sneered back at her.

"I'm sure everything will if you have anything to say about it." She slammed the door in his face.

"I certainly do have something to say about it," Marik muttered as he turned away. "You two think you're so clever... if you only knew."

He retraced his steps and made his way to the workers' common-room on the first floor. Entering the large area, he spotted Julia reading in an overstuffed chair by the window. Julia was thirty-two years old, petite, with short brown hair, and large brown eyes that seemed wise beyond their years. Marik sank into the chair next to her, scowling at no one in particular.

"Let me guess. You've been talking to Leea," Julia observed with a snicker.

"Yeah, I ran into *Her Highness* a few minutes ago," he snarled.

"You know, if you wouldn't bicker with her about everything—"

"I don't."

"Really? What do you call what happened this morning? You were constantly nagging her for no reason."

"Why are you blaming me for that? She talks to me like I'm a child, and it irritates me. It wasn't my fault she started yelling as Lauranna walked in." As much as he tried, Marik couldn't hold back a grin.

"And you had no problem letting her take the reprimand, knowing full well you were as much to blame."

"I take no responsibility for her outburst."

Julia shook her head. "If you didn't always come on so strong, you two might get along."

"That'll never happen. As long as she's involved with the *golden boy*, nothing will ever change."

"Marik, for the hundredth time, let it go," Julia laid a friendly hand on his arm. "You're not doing yourself any good getting all worked up over their relationship, and it's not going to change anything."

"They think they're so discreet, and that someday everything will change. The Desolk will never allow his son to be involved with a Human, so why even bother?"

"First of all, what they do is none of your business. And at the risk of repeating myself—again—let it go. Whatever Yaran's parents know, or don't know, is nothing for you to worry about. When the day comes, Leea and Yaran will deal with the consequences. But I'm sure Lauranna won't do anything to upset her son, so you never know how it'll all end up."

"Yeah, he is definitely a mama's boy. Which is so weird for a Zantian."

"Their families are complicated, and things they do seem strange to us."

"Never thought I'd hear you making excuses for them, after what they've done to your family."

"This is not about me. It's about your obsession with Leea."

"I'm not obsessed with her! I just don't understand what she sees in that guy. Why can't she let him go and be done with it and move on?"

Julia groaned and got to her feet. "It's late, Marik, and I'm tired." She gave him a sad smile and left the room.

"I'm going to need to come up with something," he said quietly. "This is about my future, and if things go bad for me, I'll make sure they go bad for her too."

For the next few weeks, life in the House of Alrack followed a normal routine. The Desolk was preoccupied with a planetary crisis, so was gone for days at a time, often taking Yaran with him.

When her mate was away for an extended time, Lauranna often took the opportunity to visit her family in Calthena. To the workers, this was like a vacation. It meant sleeping in, and a limited work schedule. Greta, Lauranna's personal aide, was always in charge when she was away, but Greta never enforced strict rules, as long as the basics were done.

"Let's go into the city today," Julia proposed one morning after a late meal. "We haven't been there in a while, and I think shopping will be fun."

"That sounds like a great idea."

Julia smiled widely. "I thought you'd agree, so I already asked Jeffrey if he'd take us."

Jeffrey was not only the head mechanic but also occasional chauffeur and Julia's father-in-law. When the family was away, Jeffrey happily gave any of the workers a ride into the city so they wouldn't have to make the hour-long walk in the heat.

"I want to stop at Qwenell's art studio, and see if she has any more of those little glass flowers."

"And I'm sure my little niece will want to visit the sweet shop."

Julia chuckled. "Marta wouldn't go with us if it weren't for the promise of sweets, even though they'll ruin her appetite for days."

"They usually ruin mine too," Leea said with a broad grin, "but I wouldn't give them up either."

An hour later, they were on their way to the city's central shopping district. As the shuttle made its way through the village, they admired the city skyline ahead as they always did which was the creative result of Zantian architects. Spires, towers, crescents, along with rectangles and pentagons blended into a cohesive configuration of living, office and retail space.

Several blocks away, was a multi-level hangar and two ten-story apartment buildings with units mostly owned by local business owners. Several of the upper floors had plush units reserved for visiting city leaders if it was inconvenient to stay in the house on the hill. Yaran's family also had an apartment there, on one of the top floors, for those times when night shipments needed to be monitored.

In the villages, where most Zantian citizens lived, homes were the typical steel and glass, three stories tall at most, and designed to blend well with the adjacent city.

"You have everything you need?" Jeffrey asked as he dropped them off.

"Yup," Julia answered. She held up the purchasing card they were allowed to use for small items, and the comlink to call him for pick-up.

From there, it was a five-minute walk, so they secured their protective robes and quickly made their way toward the main boulevard.

"Where should we start?" Julia asked as they crossed the street. At this end, the buildings were mostly single story structures, housing shops, and restaurants.

"Wherever you want. I'm not looking for anything special, so let's start at Qwenell's."

"Can we start at the sweet shop?" Marta asked, eyes bright with anticipation.

"No, we can't," Julia scolded with a smile. "We'll stop there after the midday meal." The little dark-haired girl with the bright dimpled cheeks gave her mother a sad face, which made both adults laugh.

They spent the next two hours wandering around, making small purchases as they went. Julia bought several of the glass flowers she wanted, and Leea acquired another small picture for her wall. Zantians love of art extended to their ability to create it, and looking at the intricate pieces of jewelry and beautiful artwork, it was easy to recognize their skill.

As the women always did when they were in the city, they headed for a restaurant called Man's for the midday meal. Man's was a small eatery which served Humans exclusively. The owner was a Zantian named Fortal, who greeted them by name when they entered.

"What can I get you, ladies, today? The usual?" he asked once they sat with menus in front of them.

"How do you always remember what our usual is?"

"Leea, there are no other women on this planet as beautiful as you three. How could I possibly forget?"

They all giggled and then placed their food orders. Fortal employed only Humans and claimed his restaurant served 'Earth authentic' cuisine. Of course, none of them knew how authentic it really was, but enjoyed Fortal's version of hamburgers, pasta dishes, or fish anyway, while pretending to be on that other planet, light years away. And Earth authentic or not, no meal was ever complete without a piece of Man's chocolate cake, over which all three of them salivated.

An hour later, pleasantly full, they were back on the street, ready to return home.

"Are we going to the sweet shop now?" Marta asked excitedly.

"You still have room for sweets?" Julia joked.

"No. But I need some for later."

"You're impossible," Julia kissed the top of her daughter's head.

"I don't believe it!" Leea said staring down the street ahead of them.

Julia followed her gaze and saw Marik. "What's he doing here? Did he know we were going shopping?"

"I told him," Marta said, looking up shyly at her mother. "I passed him in the hall before we left and he asked where we were going. Did I do something wrong?"

"No, of course not," Julia and Leea reassured her simultaneously.

"Do you think he's seen us?" Leea asked quietly.

"Hard to say. He's looking in every shop like he's searching for something."

"Most likely me. I'm in no mood to run into him. Quick, let's go down that alley." Leea indicated a small nearby passageway that provided rear access to several of the buildings. They moved into the shadows as far as the walkway would take them, hoping that from this vantage point, they would see Marik when he passed by.

"Do you think he's stalking me?"

"You seem to be his only focus lately, like an obsession."

"Spying for the Desolk, I'm sure," Leea chuckled, trying to lighten the mood. "He probably documents my every move then makes daily reports."

"The Desolk probably gives him early morning assignments, tells him what to do, and say."

"No wonder he repeats himself so much." They both laughed.

After several minutes, they still hadn't seen him.

"We must have missed him," Leea said. "Let's go back."

Turning to leave, they were startled as someone emerged from a nearby doorway. All three took several backward steps and Julia pushed Marta behind her. The figure was small, a little shorter than Julia, and wore a loose fitting black robe with a hood that completely covered its face. The only visible parts of its body were wrinkled hands with long thin fingers. It made no threatening movements and stopped a few steps in front of Leea, who stopped her retreat, suddenly knowing it meant them no harm. It took another step toward her, extending a gnarled hand with the palm up.

"Leea," Julia exclaimed quietly behind her.

"It's not going to hurt us."

"How do you know?" she whispered.

"I'm not sure...I just do."

In the alien's palm lay a bright blue crystal, about two inches long, with an irregular oval shape.

"It's beautiful, what is it?" Leea asked.

Again, she seemed to know the other's thoughts; it wanted her to take the crystal, and keep it safe until someone came and asked for it. It wasn't a voice she heard, but an instant knowledge. When Leea hesitated, the stranger took her hand and placed the stone in her palm, then closed its hand over hers. Instantly, a rush of thoughts raced through her mind that she couldn't seem to grasp, and then just as quickly they were gone. The alien let her go, hesitated a moment, then retreated through the doorway.

Leea stood in stunned silence, not knowing what to do. After a moment, shaking off the strange encounter, she stepped to the door where the small figure had passed through and tried the door release—locked.

Scrutinizing the entry, she searched for another way to open it but then noticed the locking mechanism at the bottom. This door could only be opened from the outside. How did the alien come through from the inside? Had they actually seen the door open, or just assumed it had?

Leea jumped when she felt a hand on her arm.

"Sorry. Are you all right?" Julia's voice was heavy with concern. "What was that all about?"

"I'm not sure. It wanted me to take this and keep it safe," she said, showing Julia the blue rock.

"I didn't hear it say anything."

"I don't think it did, but I sensed what it wanted."

Julia's eyes widened, and she removed the comlink from her pocket, grabbed Leea's arm, and pulled her back toward the street. "We need to get out of here."

"What about the sweet shop?" Marta asked, sounding disappointed.

"We can stop on our way back to meet grandpa, but you'll need to decide fast."

"I will, I promise!"

# CHAPTER 2

# Marik

Trying to make sense of what they'd seen in the alley, the two women rode back to the house in silence. Jeffery didn't seem to notice their solemn mood as he chatted happily with Marta, who couldn't wait to show him her colorful sticks and baubles from the sweet shop.

Once back in her room, Leea took out the blue crystal for a closer look. What made her wonder, was where on the planet Zantia could you find such a beautiful rock? While local jewelers created pieces using gems the mines extracted, Leea couldn't recall ever seeing anything made with this brilliant color blue.

Remembering the alien's desperation that she keeps it safe, Leea moved to the only logical place. She retrieved a small metal container from the top shelf of the wardrobe and set it gingerly on the table as if it were a breakable object.

Leea hated this box, yet treasured it at the same time.

Closing her eyes, she visualized the contents: a hairbrush, a book of poetry—a family heirloom passed down for generations—her mother's wedding band, and a holo-ring. These four meager items were the only things that connected her to the parents she had barely known.

Releasing the lid, a musty smell escaped. She had never opened the poetry book, afraid of damaging it, but she liked the smell and feel of the leather binding under her fingertips. She picked up the holo-ring and rolled the clear glass imager between two fingers before laying it in her palm. The base glowed, waiting for activation.

Studying the piece for a moment, she recalled the five holographic images stored there. Her parents' wedding day, and another one of them in a happier moment. Leea as a baby with her father, and as a toddler with her mother. And her favorite: with both parents smiling down at their nine-month-old daughter, and she, looking up adoringly at her father. In the video mode, the red-haired man, with green eyes much like her own, would reach down and swing her high above his head while she giggled uncontrollably. With a heavy heart, Leea returned the holo, along with the blue rock to the box, reclosed it, and returned it to its rightful place out of sight on the top shelf.

It was relatively early, but fatigue washed over her. Chores still needed to be finished in the kitchen, but no amount of exhaustion was going to prevent her evening visit to the bluff.


As usual, the bench was deserted, and for that Leea was always grateful. Most of the workers didn't understand her obsession with this place and preferred the common-room or one of the few establishments in the village where Humans were allowed. But for Leea, this spot allowed her to wind down, and it brought her closer to Yaran when he was away.

Deep in thought with the diminishing sun warming her face, she jumped as something touched her shoulder.

"Yaran!" In two steps, her arms were around his neck. "When did you get home? I wasn't expecting you today. Oh, I've missed you!"

"Slow down, my love!" he laughed, pulling her close, and kissed her. "I've missed you too. We got back about half an hour ago."

"How long are you staying this time?"

"I think the business trips are over for a while. We've been halfway around the planet, and everything has been arranged and discussed that needs to be, so for now, we're home—I am, anyway."

"I'm so glad you came to find me."

"I told Jarock that my head was full of business matters, and I wanted time alone." He gave her a sly smile. "Of course, I knew you'd be here." He lifted her chin and kissed her again.

Marik watched the lovers from the shadows and shuddered. Not because of the passion with which Human and Zantian embraced each other, but because of the knowledge that his plan would never work—never could have worked. Anger rose from within and threatened to explode, but he pushed it back into place. As a young boy, he had learned to master his ire, while living under the rule of a tyrant in Emborie. But as he grew older, the memories wanted to control him, and with each passing year the struggles to keep them in place grew harder.

He closed his eyes and tried to push away the old recollections of abuse, but it was too late, they had already flooded his mind. He mentally clawed at them, trying to shred the unpleasantness that was his past, but the visions seemed to go hand in hand with the anger, overtaking his will. He turned and hit the back of his head against the boulder he stood behind—and then again, a little harder, smiling. Pain always won out over the memories.

He let the tingling in his head subside then returned to the scene he'd come to watch. The Desolk had brought him here for one purpose, and he had assured the old man he could make Leea forget about Yaran. He had the charm; he knew he did. It had gotten him here, hadn't it? It had ensured his survival during the worst of times and brought him to a better life in the House of Emborie. But soon learning that that life would be short lived, and the mines would be his next stop, he charmed his way here, with a new promise to escape the inevitable.

The Alrack leader had given him a year, which was almost up, and observing this passionate reunion reaffirmed again that no matter how hard he tried, it wouldn't change a thing. He would have to come up with a different plan because he wasn't going to let her ruin the future he deserved—at least not without a fight.

Once the sun disappeared, Leea and Yaran left the bluff and made their way to the gardens, which were lit after dark just like the house. Each plot was filled with small trees and shrubs, and even some flowers that were indigenous to Zantia, and equally as drab.

Brightening this mixture, however, were flowers imported from off-world along with the soil to grow them. Velvety petals of red, long stems of tiny sun-kissed yellow flutes, and clusters of deep blue fronds sprouted as if they belonged. These plants were meticulously cared for, and kept under special cooling and light-filtering pavilions to shield them from the harsh rays of the sun, most managing to survive.

While most of the planet's ruling houses also had gardens, one thing distinguished Alrack from the others: a small stream that followed the trails. Water was as precious a commodity as anything else mined on this mostly arid world, but here it flowed freely, proving that power could make anything happen.

"Jeffrey told me that you and Julia went into the city today," Yaran said as they walked hand in hand.

"We decided we needed to get away, and shopping sounded like fun. We haven't been to the city in a while, and you weren't expected back until tomorrow.

So, we bought a few things, ate at Man's. There was one moment of unpleasantness, though."

"Oh?"

"We had just left Man's and noticed Marik wandering around."

"Marik?"

"I don't know what he was doing there, but we hurried in between two buildings, so he didn't see us. Once he passed, we called Jeffrey and came back."

She looked away and was glad for the low lighting. She didn't want to tell him about their encounter with the stranger in the alley. Something inside her told her not to say anything, and it felt right to listen to that inner voice. She would tell him—just not today.

"I don't like the way Marik always shows up around you. Maybe I should talk to him?"

"And say what? Leave my lover alone." She chuckled. "Not sure that's a good idea."

"But it might be fun," Yaran smiled slyly.

"Please let's change the subject. How was your trip?"

"The same as always: incredibly boring council meeting, inspecting some of the warehouses, and then lots of tedious conversations over too-long meals."

"Meals with eligible women," she added, trying to keep her voice cheery. She had no official claim to Yaran, and most likely never would. But knowing that his father always paired him up with Zantian women during their time away, gave her the usual knot in the pit of her stomach.

He sighed. "Yes, that too."

"So, tell me about them." This was a game she insisted on playing, hoping it would make the inevitable easier.

"Well, the one in Berland had stringy hair and crooked teeth, and the one in Feintig limped and had an unsightly growth on her face."

Leea snickered and hugged his arm. "She was obviously the pretty one." While she was never sure, she always suspected that the worse Yaran described their imaginary flaws, the more attractive they must have been.

"If you like that sort of thing," he said quietly, his lips drawn in a thin line.

"It's okay if you think they're pretty."

"I'd rather not think about them at all."

"You know you'll have to choose someday. Your crossover is less than two months away; decisions will have to be made." She felt his arm muscles tense and hugged him tighter. "Let's see, your choices will be, to name a few: crooked teeth, an unsightly facial growth, sickeningly green hair and crossed eyes, or, my personal favorite…five inches taller than you with feet the size of cargo ships, who wanted nothing more than to arm wrestle."

He laughed softly and seemed to relax.

"Even though I doubt Zantians arm wrestle," she added with slight amusement.

"No, I don't suppose we do, but she had the physique for it." Yaran patted her hand that rested on his arm. "I would appreciate it if you didn't try and help my father in his endeavors to fix me up, as you always say."

"But why not? If I'm going to have to give you up someday, wouldn't you rather I helped you find the perfect mate? Make sure she meets with my approval?"

"That's not funny."

Leea sighed. "No. I guess not. But in reality, like in the Earth fairytale Cinderella, where at the stroke of midnight the beautiful princess turns back into the servant she is, you will turn into the prince you were born to be when you reach your thirtieth birthday."

Leea often imagined that day. In her mind, his birthday represented a large magical wall. When they reached it, he would be able to pass through but she wouldn't—forcing him to leave her behind. And as that day grew closer the knot in her stomach grew exponentially.

"I'm no prince," he said, stopping to pull her into an embrace, "nor do I ever want to be."

"You will always be my prince and nothing will ever change that."

He gently kissed her full lips. "You know what? I have an idea on how to get away from all these depressing topics. Come."

"Where are we going?" she asked as they hurried along the path.

"You'll see." When they reached the art wing, Yaran pulled her in through the rear door and led her down the long hallway to the music room, which was filled with dozens of instruments arranged by type. Some with playing surfaces almost beyond the reach of Yaran's outstretched arms, to something so small it needed a stylus to operate. This was his favorite place.

As they passed through the arched doorway, keyed instruments sat straight ahead, which included a grand piano from Earth, a *honire* from the planet Karba, which had five short rows of clear glass keys, and a *choU* from a planet Yaran couldn't remember. She had only seen him play the *choU* once, which hung vertically on the wall and had two dozen keys that lit up when you touched them. He claimed its sound was too intense, and the flashing lights too disorienting. The other pieces in this area fell somewhere in between.

In other parts of the large room stood, or lay; wind, stringed, and percussion instruments, as well as a few that only played in water and one that would only operate over fire, and he could play every single one.

Taking her hand, Yaran moved to the piano and pulled her down on the bench beside him. "So, what do you want to hear?"

"Are you sure this is a good idea? Your mother won't show up unexpectedly, will she?"

"Okay, a cheery song it is." He winked at her and activated the screen in front of him, selected the instrument he was playing, and then began to scroll through the titles once they appeared. "Here's one." Activating the title, the musical notes appeared. He poised his hands over the ivory keys, but Leea stopped him with a hand on his arm.

"Are you sure this is a good idea?"

"And what if my mother does come in here? You and I have been friends almost our whole lives. What can she say if she sees us here?"

"Probably nothing," Leea said quietly.

"Exactly… nothing. So let me play for you."

She looked into his eyes and smiled. "I would love that."

Over an hour later they stood at the kitchen door. "Thank you, Yaran," Leea said sliding her arms around his waist. "It's been a long time since you've played for me like that. I loved it."

"I will make it a point of doing it more often."

"I'll hold you to it." She kissed him. "I better go. I love you."

"I love you too. *Er'ShaltMee'Sarn*."

"Always."

Leea finished her chores and made her way to the common-room which was down the hall from the kitchen. The evening had revitalized her, so she decided to visit with her friends for a while. The room was 'L' shaped, with the workers' dining area to the left and straight ahead a lounge. A dozen overstuffed chairs were arranged in two separate circles with a low table in the middle, and several smaller seats sat against the back wall. Julia and a few other women played cards at one of the tables.

"Hello there," Julia said as Leea sank into the chair next to her. "I thought you'd already gone to bed."

"No. I was walking in the gardens, listening to music," she replied, blushing.

"Ah! Not alone, I take it?" Soft giggles echoed around the circle. Julia leaned over and whispered loudly. "We saw he was back."

Leea's face flushed as she turned her attention to the activity on the table. Her relationship with Yaran was no secret among the workers, and while many didn't understand the attraction, they did understand the need for discretion, and never mentioned it outside this room.

As the games ended, the others excused themselves until Leea and Julia were alone.

"So, tell me about the big reunion," Julia demanded. "I want details!" She stared at Leea, eyebrows raised, drumming her fingers on the table.

"Funny, funny. I'm not telling you anything," Leea replied with mock indignation.

"Oh come on! I live vicariously through your love life; I need my daily fix."

"I hate to break it to you, but I have no love life, except in my dreams."

Julia groaned. "Please. You two generate more heat than the valley below. The rest of us should be so lucky."

"You are lucky…you have a husband."

"Who I only see four days a month."

Leea smiled slyly. "Then you should know how these reunions work."

"You're ignoring my question."

"What are sisters for?" They both laughed.

"Did you tell him about what happened in the city today?" Julia asked in a serious tone.

"No"

"Why not?"

Leea shrugged. "I don't know. It still seems so unreal, and I didn't want him to worry. So for now, let's just keep this to ourselves, okay?"

"I haven't mentioned it to anyone, so if that's what you want…okay."

"Thanks. I'll tell him eventually, just not now."

Julia got to her feet. "Well, I should get going too. I need to make sure Marta isn't sleep walking through the halls and terrifying the royalty."

They both snickered. When they had read about royalty on Earth in their school books, they had quickly put members of the Zantian ruling houses in the same category. Leea playfully referred to Yaran as her prince, even though his people had no such titles.

"Okay, you go rescue the innocent. I'll clean up here before I turn in."

"Thanks. I love you." Julia gave Leea a big hug.

"I love you too."

Leea collected the cards and several games left in the lounge. With her arms full, she rounded the corner to the storage closet in the dining area, and almost dropped the bundle.

Marik sat in the back corner.

"I thought she'd never leave," he said with a menacing tone, sending a chill down her spine.

As calmly as she could, Leea put the games away, ignoring her instinct to flee.

"We should talk."

"I can't imagine what we have to talk about. Or do you want to get me in more trouble?" Leea straightened things on the shelves, shifting them from one corner to the other, hoping he would go away.

"You don't really think your little secret is an actual…secret, do you? You're not fooling anyone."

"What are you talking about? If you're trying to irritate me, you're doing a great job."

"I've been watching you, you know."

Her irritation was instantly replaced with apprehension, and she spun to face him. "What?"

"You and him…sitting on that bench as if you were the only two people around. But let me tell you—everyone knows."

"Everybody knows what?"

"About you cavorting with the golden boy."

"And how would you know what everyone else knows?" Leea hoped he didn't notice the tremor in her voice.

"Well, that's my secret. One that I would share with you if you were…cooperative."

"With you?" Leea snickered loudly but felt a touch of hysteria setting in. "You're delusional if you think that will ever happen."

With two steps, Marik stood in front of her, eyes narrowed in an intimidating glare that Leea couldn't bring herself to look away from. Her heart pounded in her chest. She had never been afraid of Marik, but her blood ran cold as his face took on a crazed look, and before she could react, he grabbed her arm, digging his fingers into her flesh.

"Let go of me!" Leea met his gaze with her own icy stare.

"What's wrong with you? I just want to talk?"

"As usual, it's you. LET GO OF ME!" Leea tried wrenching her arm away, but Marik's grip held fast.

"You have no idea what you're doing, do you?" he asked, moving closer.

"Whatever I'm doing is none of your business!"

Leea tried to take a step back, but he quickly wrapped an arm around her waist and pulled her against his body. Grabbing a handful of her hair, he yanked her head back and kissed her roughly. She pushed against his chest, but he was too strong, and her resistance only made him clutch tighter. Leea's mind raced. How could she get away from him?

Panic gripped her, followed by desperation, and only one thing come to mind. Leea brought her knee up into his groin as hard as she could. Unfortunately, Marik held her too tightly for the full effect, but it was enough that he groaned and loosened his grip. She pushed him away and scrambled for the door—but he recovered swiftly.

Knocking over a table, decorations clattering to the floor, Marik grabbed her hair, and yanked her back. Leea landed hard on the floor, which forced the air from her lungs. Disoriented, and before her brain could form a clear thought, he was on top of her, pinning her arms together above her head. She attempted to scream while she struggled, but couldn't pull in enough air.

Marik snickered. "Go ahead…scream. Who do you think is going to hear you? Mama's boy? One nice thing about this house, it has sound proof walls."

"Please don't do this," she begged, tears slipping from the corner of her eyes.

Surprisingly, his expression softened. "You should have done what you were supposed to," he said almost mournfully. "This all could have been so much easier." The sardonic smile returned. "So you have no one to blame for this but yourself. I intend to get the reward I was promised, one way or another."

He forced a knee between her legs as Leea continued to struggle, trying to shake him off. Her head was spinning, and Marik's weight made it impossible for her to fill her lungs fully, but she managed to seethe, "Get off me!" She cried out as his fingers dug into her wrists.

"Is this how you like it…rough? I didn't think Zantians liked that kind of thing. Maybe I'm wrong. But we can do this any way you like." He lowered his head and tried to kiss her again, but she quickly turned away—then regretted the instinctive reaction. Her stomach turned as his tongue forged a wet path from her cheek to the base of her neck where her tears had flowed. His hot breath against her skin grew ragged, and he tried to force her legs further apart but groaned in frustration as she continued to struggle.

"Well, let's do this slowly then, I'm in no hurry." Taking both her wrists in one hand, he cupped her left breast. "I've often fantasized about how they would feel." He massaged languorously and flashed a wicked smile. "There's a lot more here than I envisioned. The last woman I was with had very little … it was disappointing. I bet they look even better than they feel."

Moaning, he reached between them and ripped open the front of her shirt then became distracted as he concentrated on pulling her bra out of the way. His weight shifted, and his grip on her hands relaxed, allowing her left arm to slip free. Frantically, she reached out—searching. Lights brightened behind her eyes from the lack of oxygen and bile rose in her throat as he gripped her bare breast. Just then she felt something round and smooth—the flower vase from the table he'd knocked over. It wasn't big, but it was heavy.

With all her strength, Leea swung as hard as she could. The vase connected with the side of Marik's head. He cried out and started to roll away. Finally relieved of his weight, she pushed him away and struck harder. Without a moment's hesitation, Leea scrambled to her feet and bolted out the door. She didn't bother to worry if her attacker was hurt. At that moment, she hoped he was dead.

Stumbling into her room, she secured the door and leaned against it, fearful Marik had managed to follow. "Lights off!" she commanded the automatic lighting. Still fighting for air, Leea wrapped her arms around her stomach and slid to the floor, letting her sobs come.

When the tears finally diminished, her first instinct was to find Yaran, but she was afraid of his reaction. He would cause a scene—rightfully so—but she didn't want that. She could go to Lauranna, but the matron hated conflicts and would most likely do nothing but would then, of course, tell the Desolk. The last thing Leea wanted was to deal with Yaran's father. The Desolk wouldn't care that Marik attacked her, only that once again she was involved. Tears welled in her eyes anew, but she wiped them away impatiently. What she needed was Julia.

With an arm around her sister, Julia listened in stunned silence. "I am so sorry," she finally said. "I shouldn't have left you there."

"It's not your fault. We didn't see him come in."

"What are you going to do?"

"I have no idea."

"I'm sure Yaran will."

"I'm not telling him."

"What do you mean, you're not telling him?" Julia said incredulously. "Leea, you have to!"

"NO! Do you know what he'll do?"

"Of course. He adores you, so he'll be furious and make Marik pay for what he did."

"Exactly. And what do you think is going to happen if Yaran gets in the middle of this?"

Julia frowned. "The Desolk won't be happy."

"Which will cause even more tension between them," Leea said mournfully. "And how will Yaran explain any action he takes against Marik?"

"The Desolk wouldn't condone an attack like this, not against anyone."

"I'm sure he wouldn't, but it isn't just anyone… it's me. Marik made sure we were alone, so it'll be another incident where it's his word against mine. And that seems to be his game lately."

"But you have to do something. You can't let him get away with this."

"I think that's what he's counting on. I hit him pretty hard, so he's going to have quite a lump on his head. If I make a scene, he'll play the victim. And again I'll be to blame."

Julia sighed. "So you're just going to let it go?"

"As much as I would like nothing more than to smash his head in even harder, I have to." Leea leaned over and rested her forehead in the palm of her hands. "I'm so tired of all this, Julia. I want things to go back to the way they were before he came."

"I know you do." Julia gently rubbed her back. "But you shouldn't deal with this alone."

"I have you."

"Yes, you do. But I know you'd be happier with Yaran."

"That's not possible right now. And you need to promise me that you won't say anything… not to anyone."

"Fine. But I have a bad feeling about this. Marik has been incredibly annoying recently, but he's never been violent. Something's changed. You really should reconsider and tell Yaran. When he finds out about this, and he will, he'll be angry with you, and rightfully so."

"I'll make him understand. But not today."

The tiny woman grimaced and slightly shook her head, but it was evident Leea had made up her mind. They sat for a while and then Julia walked her sister back to her room. She hugged her reassuringly and told her to try and get some rest. Once the door closed, instead of going back to her room, Julia made her way in the opposite direction and down the stairs. Leea was trying to be rational about this whole situation, and that worried her. She was clearly in shock and needed the one person who could truly help her.

Julia took the long hallway past the common-room, looking in briefly but finding it empty. When the corridor turned left, she rapped lightly on the first door to the right. After a second knock, a groggy Yaran opened the door.

"Julia? What's wrong?"

"There's been an incident between Leea and Marik. She needs you."

He turned away, leaving the door ajar. In less than a minute he reappeared, hastily dressed and his hair smoothed with a quick finger-comb. As they made their way hurriedly to the workers' living quarters, Julia told him what had happened.

"I wish she would have come to me," he said sadly, more to himself.

Julia held him back. "She's afraid of what you might do, and that she'll be blamed for causing trouble again."

"But he attacked her," he hissed angrily.

"Yes, he did. But how many times has Marik been able to make things seem like her fault lately?"

"I won't let that happen."

Julia looked up at him and grimaced. "And what do you think is worse than being blamed for what Marik did? It's having you get in the middle."

Yaran pressed his lips together and inhaled a calming breath.

"No one really knows what Marik's role is here. Leea and I joke about him being a spy for your father, but what if that's true to some extent?"

"That's ridiculous."

"Is it?"

Yaran turned away. "I think that's a discussion for another day. Thank you, Julia, for coming to get me."

"You're welcome. I promised her I wouldn't tell you, but if it were the other way around, she would want to know."

Yaran gave her an appreciative smile then tapped lightly on Leea's door. "Leea, it's me, please open up," he pleaded quietly.

When the door finally opened, he quickly moved in and closed it behind him. Immediately, he gathered her into his arms and stroked her hair, telling her everything would be all right as she clutched at him and wept.

"Did he hurt you?" he asked cautiously when her sobs finally quieted.

"No. I got away first." She looked into his dark eyes. "I'm sorry I didn't come to you."

He stroked her puffy red cheeks and smiled reassuringly. "I understand your need to talk to Julia first. She explained your reasoning. But you know I love you, so I wish you would trust me to do the right thing." With an arm around her waist, Yaran led her to the bed, where they both sat on the edge.

"I trust you implicitly, and you know that. But this time, you need to trust me."

"I'll talk to my mother. She'll—"

"No. I don't want you to do that."

"But—"

"No." She smiled at him adoringly. "You have no idea how much I love you for wanting to protect me. You always have. But this time, I need to do it my way."

"I won't let him get away with this."

"Well, for now, I'm asking you to. This will just be another incident of my word against his, and I don't want you to try and fix it. That won't be good for either of us. Promise me you won't interfere."

Yaran pressed his lips together and then sighed. "Okay. I'll stay out of it … for now."

"Thank you." She attempted a smile and kissed him lightly. "I'm so glad you're here."

He pulled her into an embrace but said nothing.

She snuggled close to him, feeling safe in the comfort of his arms. "Will you stay with me?"

He pulled back and looked into her sad emerald eyes. "My love, you may have coerced me into silence, but under no circumstances am I leaving you."

"What can I do for you, Marik?" Jarock asked, irritation rapidly surfacing. Dawn was barely visible through the window, so it was too early in the morning to listen to Marik's complaints. He never imagined that a Human could be so infuriating. Jarock had often wondered this past year how he let himself be talked into this scheme, and why he thought the girl would so quickly change her affections away from Yaran. Not with this Human she wouldn't.

"Leea tried to kill me last night," Marik blurted matter-of-factly.

"What?" The Desolk looked at him confused. As much as he disliked the girl's influence over his son, he never thought her capable of violence. He must have misunderstood.

"We were in the common-room," Marik explained, "and she hit me over the head with a vase." He turned his head to show a lump and large purple bruise.

"Why would she do that? What did you do?"

"I was just trying to talk to her. She came in late after spending the evening with Yaran, and when I approached her, she got mad and hit me."

Jarock's irritation increased. It was no secret that women considered Yaran a handsome man, and being the son of the council leader, he could certainly have anyone he wanted. So, the Desolk always arranged meals with eligible Zantian women when they were away on business, hoping Yaran would appreciate the possibilities. But instead, he went running to that girl again—he should have known. He silently fumed, but then an idea surfaced. Maybe this could work to his advantage.

Quickly, he brought his anger in check and asked with false concern. "Did anyone see this happen?"

"No, we were alone."

He was positive the girl would never allow herself to be alone with this troublesome man, but that didn't matter; this was an opportunity he could not pass up. "Thank you for bringing this to my attention, I will take care of it." He indicated that Marik was dismissed.

"What are you going to do?" Marik wasn't letting himself be brushed off so quickly.

"How I handle the working staff is none of your concern."

"What does this do to our agreement?"

Jarock glowered at him. "I will honor our agreement as long as you keep all this to yourself."

"I won't tell anyone," Marik promised, trying to hide a smile.

"See that you don't."

Leea woke up exhausted. Laying in Yaran's arms during the night had made her feel safe, but every time she drifted off to sleep Marik's self-satisfied smirk would wake her with a start. Yaran tried his best to comfort her, but in the end, the restlessness kept both of them from getting any rest.

Her head throbbed as she sat up, and her chest ached slightly so she made her way slowly to the washroom to ready herself for another dull day. Red puffy eyes and flushed cheeks stared back at her from the mirror, and no amount of cold water lessened the effect. She studied her arms, surprised not to find any bruises.

Her upper arm was sore where is fingers had dug in, but there was nothing but a slight bit of redness.

Yaran walked her to the common-room and kissed her lightly, promising to meet her as soon as her chores were complete. Although he promised not to interfere at the moment, he said that under no circumstances would he allow her to be alone until he could deal with Marik. She had given him a frustrated sigh but knew there would be no compromise.

Blindly she ate the same bland cereal and fruit the workers served themselves every morning and then headed to the kitchen. Crossing the threshold, she froze— just inside stood Lauranna and the Desolk. The house leader eyed her sharply, and Leea instantly knew they were waiting for her.

"You will follow me," he said in a chilling tone. Leea looked to Lauranna, but Yaran's mother looked away—no conflicts for her.

The Desolk led her down the main hallway and motioned her inside the library, indicating she stop just inside the ten-foot high arched doorway as if her presence could contaminate the space. Except for the cleaning staff, workers weren't allowed in this room, but unbeknownst to him, she had visited here many times. Yaran often brought her here when his parents were away so she could admire the objects that had originated from her home-world.

Dutifully she stood and surveyed her surroundings. The room was set into a corner of the house, and had four unequal walls, giving it a skewed look. With fifteen-foot high ceilings, it was far more cluttered than the rest of the almost minimalistic manor. The wall opposite her was floor-to-ceiling glass and overlooked the city below, but was currently obscured behind thick draperies. Window coverings weren't required in Zantian homes since the transitioning glass could be manually adjusted to lighten and darken as needed. But in this room, they were added as extra protection for the ancient and fragile contents.

All the remaining walls were covered with eight-foot high shelves, containing books and artifacts from many parts of the universe. From the top of the shelves to the ceiling hung an eclectic assortment of artwork, some from Earth, and others from places the Zantians had dealt with. The paintings from Earth were a mixture of landscapes, seascapes, flowers, or endless night skies. Leea's favorite showed a stormy gray sky overlooking high ocean swells crashing onto a beach.

She could make little sense of the remaining artwork. Empty squares protruded from the wall at odd angles, along with mounds that looked like dirt. Some things were shaped in waves with moving imagery, which always made her dizzy if she looked at them too long.

Among the hundreds of books and datapads that lined the shelves was a section written in several Earth languages including English. Leea had read many of them. Yaran would bring them to her, one at a time, and she devoured every single volume. She had read novels, memoirs, and historical accounts, which she felt gave her a better understanding of the planet she came from, and its struggles.

But aside from the books, what fascinated her most were the artifacts resting on glass shelves to her right. Most of the cases were open, and Yaran had allowed her to hold some of the delicate pieces, many acquired through trade, and others, like those from Earth, stolen. However, two enclosed cabinets, standing in the center of the bank, always drew her attention first, as they did today.

In the narrowest cabinet stood more than a dozen round pieces, the largest about the size of her fist, the smallest no bigger than a pebble from the garden. Each piece was a different color, from the brightest blue to the palest yellow. They had a soft consistency and occasionally rotated in their bowl-shaped stand. Yaran called them *telling stones*. They were voice-activated holographic projectors of which you could ask a question, and it would show you your answer or recite a favorite story.

Yaran had demonstrated this for her once. Quietly, he had removed an emerald green orb, about a half inch in diameter, and set it on the nearby table then spoken a few words in an unknown language. The ball started to spin. Without warning, a bright flash caused Leea to cover her eyes. When she reopened them, the orb had transformed into a mist about a foot across. It swirled in place, emitting soft rhythmic tones. The sounds made little sense to her, but Yaran explained that it was reciting a children's story. When finished, it returned to its original shape, awaiting the next command. The projectors were extremely sensitive, so the case they rested in was constructed of soundproof glass to keep them from randomly activating.

The most amazing piece in the Desolk's collection was in the second cabinet, hovering about three inches above the large center shelf. Stark white and about the size of her forearm, its entire exterior was covered in tiny facets. These features shifted, seemingly at random, to form symbols that Leea equated to ancient Earth hieroglyphs. As the exterior rearranged itself, soft blue light emitted from within, illuminating around random tile groupings.

It had evidently been discovered on a deserted planet several centuries ago. Extensive tests had been performed to determine its purpose, but it was impenetrable to any of the Zantian probes. Yaran didn't believe this story, saying he thought there was more to it, but had no proof to the contrary. So there it hovered, with a seemingly eternal supply of power, telling a story no one could understand, but mesmerizing anyone who came within visual range.

The Desolk stood between the long drapery panels looking out through the glass. Leea wondered if he was contemplating what to say to her, or if he'd forgotten she was there. She didn't mind. His deliberate indifference allowed her to prepare mentally for the unpleasantness that was about to descend upon her. This would be her first reprimand by the Desolk. That task was always carried out by Lauranna, so Leea knew that what was about to be said would be extremely distasteful.

She assumed this had to do with Marik, which gave her a horrible feeling in the pit of her stomach. The decision to see what he would do first seemed to have been the wrong choice—one she would now have to live with.

As if sensing her unease, the house leader turned and walked as far as the seating area in the center of the room. He studied her for a moment before he spoke. "I am aware of the incident yesterday evening between you and Marik."

Leea felt her blood run cold.

"The conflicts between the two of you have been brought to my attention on numerous occasions, but I was more than a little disturbed when Marik told me you attacked him."

"What?!" Leea cried in disbelief.

"Do you deny this?" His sarcastic tone and raised eyebrows told her he wasn't going to believe anything she said.

"Of course, I deny it. He attacked me first. I was defending myself." The words came out faster than she intended, revealing her desperation.

"This is not the story he—"

"Of course, it isn't, he's a liar!"

"Did anyone witness this?"

Dejectedly, she shook her head. "No. He made sure we were alone."

"Well, unfortunately, he's the one with a lump on his head. And since there were no witnesses, who do you expect me to believe?" He paused for a beat. "I cannot allow someone with violent tendencies to live under my roof. This leaves me no alternative but to move you to another city."

Leea was stunned. Her stomach went into a freefall, and she didn't know how to make it stop. This was her worst nightmare come true. "I don't suppose there is anything I can say to make you change your mind?" she choked out.

"No, there is not." He lowered his voice but glared at her intently. "You are a distraction in this house, and I believe it's better for all concerned that you move on. As you well know, my son's crossover is but weeks away, and then he will be required to assume certain responsibilities. His infatuation with you, while I'm sure entertaining for him, will no longer fit into his life." He smiled contemptuously. "And yes, to be clear, whatever you thought you were hiding, you were not."

She swallowed hard as her stomach started to churn, and dug her nails into her palms to keep from screaming. He was using this incident with Marik to get rid of her—to finally have a reason to separate her from Yaran. No matter what she said, nothing would change his mind.

"It will take several days to make the arrangements," he continued. "So, except for your duties, I'm confining you to your room."

"Confined to my room! Why?"

Jarock studied her for a moment. "We certainly don't want another incident, do we?"

Leea could tell he was enjoying this, making her uncomfortable, but what could she say? Not a thing. Her shoulders slumped in defeat.

He waved his hand across the top of the table and a moment later, David, his personal assistant, entered. David was a few years older than Leea, and the brother of Julia's husband Tim. The sadness in David's eyes told her he knew what was happening. She looked away as she felt tears stinging her eyes and dug her nails deeper—under no circumstances would she let the Desolk see her cry.

"David will escort you back to your room. I will allow you a few moments to collect yourself, and then you are to return to your duties. If you are planning anymore... confrontations with Marik, I will have you confined to your room permanently."

Without another word, Leea followed David out of the library.

"I'm so sorry," he whispered when they reached her door. "I wish there was something I could do."

The tears that had been threatening to spill constricted her throat. Unsuccessfully, she tried to give David a smile, then mouthed a "thank you," and walked through the door.

Once inside, Leea looked around her sparsely furnished room: a bed, a bedside table, a wardrobe opposite, and in the corner, a small table with two chairs. Artwork that had belonged to her grandmother decorated iridescent white walls. One window overlooking the greenhouse, and a door leading to the washroom completed her home.

Leea was numb. She prayed this was a bad dream and willed herself to wake up, but knew deep down this was all too real. She sat on the edge of the bed, the feeling of despair overwhelming her. Unable to sit upright, she curled herself up as tightly as she could, letting the sobs take over.

What was she going to do? This place held a century's worth of memories of her family. How could she leave them behind? And Yaran... could she survive never seeing him again? Her grandmother's passing had been the most painful time in her life and some days she wondered how she had ever made it through. If it hadn't been for Yaran, she wasn't sure she would have. Who was going to help her with this? Who was she going to turn to when the pain of loss made it hard to breathe? Who would hold her and tell her everything would be all right?

No one.

In a new environment, she questioned if there would be time to grieve, time to adjust, or to let the pain subside. Could she live through that? Did she want to? She startled at the last thought. Was this how her mother had felt all the time? Would the pain in her heart eventually take over so that giving up on life would be her only relief? Hurriedly, she pushed the notion away. No, she would always have hope. Even in the worst of times, for her, there was always a light somewhere on the horizon.

"How can you do this?" Yaran demanded as he burst into his father's office.

Yaran saw an older reflection of himself when he looked at his seventy-one-year-old father: same height, same golden-brown skin tone, and same defined bone structure. The only significant difference was that Jarock wore his hair in the long, cumbersome braid of his generation. A quizzical look flashed across the older man's face but quickly disappeared, and he let out a sigh.

"Yaran, I can do whatever I want in my house and with my staff."

"Leea did nothing wrong!" Yaran shouted, barely able to control his anger. "Marik attacked her. She was only defending herself."

"Is that what she told you?" Jarock's eyebrows rose in mock surprise. "Unfortunately, it's her word against his, and he's the one with the injury, so whom do you suggest I believe?"

"Leea has lived here her whole life, Marik only a year. How could you take his word over hers?"

"As I see it, Marik brought out the worst in that girl, along with her tendency for violence. You should—"

"I can't believe what I'm hearing! You will believe anything that discredits her, and you're using this incident as an excuse to send her away. Was this your plan all along? If your protégé couldn't come between us, you'd find a way to accuse her of something she didn't do?"

The city leader glared at his son. "I don't have to develop some elaborate plot if I want to relocate our workers. You seem to have forgotten one crucial fact: I am the head of this house and all of its responsibilities. Since you show no interest in assuming any of these, you have no say in the decisions I make.

"But to be clear, whatever I do, I do for the benefit of this family, and our life-long traditions. The sad thing is, if you followed the path of our people and didn't associate with off-worlders, we wouldn't be here.

"You are my son, the only one who can carry this family forward, which means becoming Desolk one day. I will do whatever I have to, to ensure that happens. You need to live up to what is expected of you, Yaran. It's time you find a mate and carry on the traditions set forth by the ruling ancestors. If the only way I can make you take on those responsibilities is to take away your distractions, then so be it."

"And you think this scheme of yours is suddenly going to make me into your definition of the perfect son?" Yaran laughed humorlessly. "Well, I'm afraid you've wasted your time. You can't force me to be something I don't want to be."

"We'll see about that, won't we?" Jarock made a dismissive gesture. Now... I tire of this conversation. My decision about the girl is final. There is nothing you or your mother can do to change my mind."

Yaran glared another moment but knew further argument was futile. "This isn't over," he promised and exited the office.

Yaran entered the bright open space of the atrium located in the center of the house, gratefully finding it empty. Humans spent time in this room during the mid-day rest period, which was still several hours away, and most took advantage of the opportunity. Tiles inlaid along the base of the walls emitted cool, moist air into the room, providing a comfortable atmosphere while keeping the heat from the sun above the glass ceiling at bay. Leea called time spent here her spa time, saying her skin felt rejuvenated after an hour.

Lauranna often enjoyed her midday tea here as well, yet Yaran's father rarely crossed the threshold, claiming the area frivolous. Only when the monthly council meeting was held in Alrack—once a year—was the wall opened to combine the atrium with the dining room, a design feature he then showcased with pride.

Yaran felt the cool breezes envelop him, but they could do nothing to douse the flames churning in the pit of his stomach. This was like nothing he'd ever felt before, but something deeper, something he couldn't put a word to which scared him.

He had wanted to tell Jarock that sending Leea away wouldn't make him stop loving her, or stop him from finding her—no matter where she went. But Yaran saw no point in escalating an already tense situation until he knew what was going to happen. However, as his father had so eloquently stated—no matter what the leader decided to do, there was nothing Yaran could do about it.

Behind an opulent fountain, he slumped onto a bench next to a miniature Jala tree, hoping the droopy yellow fronds would obscure him should anyone enter. He lowered his head and ran both hands through his hair. What confused him most was why his mother had failed to mention Leea's summons by Jarock during their morning meal. He had wanted desperately to tell her what had happened the night before but had respected Leea's wishes to stay silent for the time being. But now he suspected that she already knew about the incident.

While Lauranna insisted on maintaining a regular routine, and would have assured him Leea was fine, she should have told him and given him the opportunity to stand between the woman he loved and his father's ridiculous accusations. David had found him after the meal and said Leea needed him. When he finally held her in his arms and felt the wracking sobs convulse her body again, he knew he had failed her. He had told her everything would be all right, but now it was worse than either of them had imagined.

Yaran stood with purpose. Right now he needed to be with the woman he loved—and then he would find Marik.

# CHAPTER 3

# Decisions

Through the greenhouse's glass ceiling, stars began to wane with the approaching dawn. Planting beds arranged perpendicular to the outside walls, teemed with herbs, berries, and vegetables, and sweet smells from various fruit trees permeated the warm space—but the lone occupant failed to notice.

Yaran sat quietly, partially obscured by the work table, unsuccessfully trying to calm his demeanor as he waited for Marik to collect the produce for the day's menu. He hadn't wanted to leave Leea, who had slept fitfully in his arms again, but when she finally calmed, he slipped out silently. As much as he dreaded this inevitable confrontation, putting it off for even one day would ensure his own sleepless nights.

The kitchen door opened, and Yaran drew in a calming breath as Marik entered and placed two containers on the opposite end of the workbench. He retrieved gardening tools from underneath, not noticing Yaran right away, but after a moment, as if sensing another presence, he stopped and turned.

"What do you want?" he asked with irritation. "I'm busy."

"Oh, I'm sure you know why I'm here." Yaran rose slowly, stretching to his full height, and moved so he could look down at the worker.

"No, actually I don't. Are you here to see where Leea tried to bash my head in?" While Marik tried to act calm, his voice betrayed his trepidation.

Yaran pulled in another deep breath and with one hand, grabbed Marik by the front of his shirt, and lifted him so only his toes touched the ground.

"You tried to rape her, you miserable … !" He let the rest of it fall away. Zantians didn't curse, as their language had no such words. Although the Human language did, workers in the house didn't use them, so Yaran found it difficult to articulate an appropriate phrase. At the moment he wished he could. Instead, he twisted his fist and pushed his knuckles into Marik's throat, causing him to gasp.

Marik grabbed at Yaran's hand and tried unsuccessfully to loosen the grip. "I don't know what she told you, but she hit me—"

"Stop wasting my time with your lies! I'm not going to let you get away with what you did to her." Yaran forcefully pushed him away. The worker's back hit hard against the work table, and he stumbled but managed to stay upright. With one long stride, the Zantian loomed over him again, the distress in Marik's eyes giving him a moment of satisfaction. "Unless you want something worse, you are going to tell my father that you attacked Leea, and she only defended herself against you."

Marik moved a few steps away. "And why would I do that? The Desolk already made up his mind who he wants to believe, and acted accordingly."

"And explain to me exactly why he would believe you?"

Marik shrugged and retreated several more hesitant steps. "How should I know?"

Yaran balled his fists. "Did he bring you here to come between us?"

"I have no idea what you're talking about."

"Of course, you do." Yaran narrowed the distance between them and Marik's jaw visibly tightened. "You made a deal with my father. What was it?"

"I think you're imagining things. Maybe you should stop listening—."

"Is there a problem here?" Lauranna asked softly from the doorway.

Yaran sighed with frustration. He completely forgot that his mother also came here first thing in the morning to get herbs for her tea.

Noticing Yaran's hesitation, a big grin spread across Marik's face. "Is there a problem here?" he mimicked sarcastically, his courage returning.

"No…no problem," Yaran assured her. He started to turn but stopped. "Oh wait…there is one more thing."

In one swift motion, he balled his fist and swung as hard as he could. Marik, seeming to sense what was coming, began to turn but wasn't fast enough. Yaran's large fist connected with the other man's face and he felt bone crushing under his knuckles.

The force of the blow sent Marik crashing into several flowering trees before ending up sprawled on the floor. Somewhere in the distance, Yaran heard his name called, but ignored it as he moved to stand over the groaning heap. He cringed inwardly at the amount of blood gushing from Marik's nose and saw that his left eye was already swollen shut, but then an involuntary smile spread across the tall Zantian's face.

Crouching, he whispered. "Be glad my mother was here to save you or you wouldn't have been so lucky." He left Marik where he lay, kissed his mother lightly on the cheek as he passed, ignoring her shocked expression, and sauntered out.

Humming softly, Yaran concentrated on the colored graph dancing across a six-foot screen in front of him while his fingers effortlessly glided across a hundred-key panel. As his hands manipulated the keys, the bars of the graph changed height and color until an upper piece moved to the top of the screen where it blended into a rhythmic wave. The pulse of the wave corresponded with tones resonating from wall speakers, which produced an enchanting melody that changed with each additional piece.

Happy with what he'd just created, Yaran gave the command to stop. He then spread his arms and brought them together quickly over the console which simultaneously collapsed the image on the screen like a deck of cards. One final downward motion and everything went dark.

"That was beautiful."

Startled, he swiveled to find Julia leaning against the doorframe. "I've been working on this piece for almost six months," he explained wryly, "but could never get the tones quite how I wanted them. Today of all days, the inspiration seems to be flowing nonstop." He motioned Julia to a nearby chair while he completed shutting down the synthesizer. "Is it rest period already?"

"Actually, the rest period is almost over," Julia said, taking the offered chair. "The house is quite abuzz over what you did to Marik."

"Oh?"

"They had to call the doctor, and once he examined our resident trouble-maker, he immediately had him taken to the med-center. You not only broke his nose in two places but also shattered his left eye socket. Doc said he could have easily repaired the nose, but the eye socket will need a day of regeneration. Marik might have to stay a day or two longer, depending on any actual eye damage." Julia laughed.

"What?"

She shook her head while trying to suppress a mischievous grin. "It was about four years ago, I think you were away at the time, when Tim was home. He was running around with Marta, and she learned the hard way that her elbow was not as resilient as the wall."

"Ouch." He pulled another chair over and sat down.

"She had to wear a regeneration cast for two days, and did nothing but complain about how tight it was, and how her elbow continuously tingled. They claim those micro-lasers are painless as they're doing their job, but not according to my daughter. Of course, she was five and very dramatic."

"So why were you laughing?"

"I'm hoping they put a nice tight cast around Marik's face. Maybe the lasers could make some adjustment to his brain."

Yaran chuckled.

"How does your hand feel?"

He looked down at his right hand and flexed his fingers a few times. "A little sore, but not too bad. The healing spray took care of the few abrasions, and the soreness won't last long."

"Ah yes, Zantian bones of steel."

"Our bones are not as brittle as a Human's, but they are breakable just the same."

"Well, all I can say is Marik deserved exactly what you gave him."

Yaran fell silent as he considered her words. Instinctively, he ran a hand through his hair. "I could easily have killed him. At the time I thought I wanted to," he confessed. "If my mother hadn't walked in … ."

She laid a reassuring hand on his arm. "Nobody is blaming you. What he did to Leea is unforgivable."

"Yes, it is. I bet my father is upset over what I did to his protégée. Is he looking for me to explain?"

"No, the Desolk left right after they called the doctor. Didn't even stay to hear the prognosis. We were told later he would be gone for a few days."

"A few days? I wonder if he changed his mind about sending Leea away."

"Well … that's actually why I came. I heard something I thought you should know. Your father told Leea yesterday morning that it would take a few days to make arrangements for her. Well, he hasn't contacted any of the other cities yet."

"Then that's good news."

"I don't think so. While he hasn't talked to any of the city leaders, he has contacted several of the mine administrators."

"How can you be sure?"

"Your father doesn't make a big effort to keep things secret. He must think when he speaks Zantian no Human knows what he's saying. But some know more than they let on."

"But mine administrators? We don't send women to the mines. It's against council law."

"Are you sure about that? Could your father hate Leea so much that he would break those laws? As the head of the Council he can do whatever he wants, right?"

He shrugged. "I would like to believe he wouldn't go to such lengths, but it's probably just wishful thinking. This whole thing with Marik makes little sense to me…."

"I would like to believe that too, but there's one more thing. Your mother relieved Leea of her duties this morning and turned them over to someone else. Said Leea didn't need to come back after the rest period. And consider this; the Desolk wants her away from you, he's not going to take the chance you'll go looking for her."

"We don't know that for sure." Yaran's voice rose with irritation.

Julia grimaced. "We have to assume he brought Marik here to come between you; what happened yesterday is probably proof of that. I'm not sure what went wrong, but something made Marik believe attacking Leea was the only way to ensure his reward. Marik has been unusually strange these last few weeks. His time must have been running out." Julia lowered her voice and glanced furtively toward the door. "If what I believe is true, I have a way to help her."

"Help her how?"

"Have you ever heard of the escape network?"

"Uh… I've heard of it, but they're just stories."

"What stories have you heard?"

Yaran lowered his voice to match hers. "Supposedly, Zantians help workers escape off-world."

"But you don't think that's likely?"

"I know there are Zantians who believe our forefathers were wrong for what they did to other races. Still, I can't imagine anyone going to such elaborate lengths to defy our laws."

"Sometimes, to right a wrong, you have to start with small steps. Your father wants nothing more than to return to the old ways, and you know this. And that's the reason the network is necessary," she persisted softly.

"And you think this network can help Leea?"

"If your father is out there right now, making arrangements to defy council law about women in the mines, then I will do everything in my power to give her other options."

"And you think I wouldn't? Don't you think I want what's best for her?"

"Of course, you do. I know that more than anyone. But like Leea, you are too emotional and probably hope this will all just go away. Leea is my little sister, blood relation or not, and I don't want to lose her. But I would rather see her leave this place and be happy, than think of what lies ahead if she stays."

"And go where?"

"From what I understand, there are agreements with some of the trading planets who have taken escapees. I have a contact who might be able to get her off this planet before your father can make his arrangements."

The realization of what Julia was saying sunk it. He sat back hard in the chair, suddenly overwhelmed. "I'll think of something else. I'll reason with him. My mother—"

"Your father isn't going to listen to reason. I'm sure you've already tried. And your mother has most likely lost her influence over him on the subject of Leea. We might only have a day or so before she's gone. Are you willing to let her face that uncertain fate?"

"And how is this option any more certain?" Yaran blurted, his voice raised.

Trying to calm the situation, Julia lowered her voice again. "Obviously, I don't know what lies on the other end, but my source says there is nothing to fear."

"Who is this *source*?"

"I can't tell you, but I trust this person implicitly."

"I'll need to talk to Leea. Since we're deciding her fate, she should have some say in it."

"Agreed, but let me talk to her first. Let me be the one to give Leea her options."

Yaran hesitated. "Okay. But if she resists your plan, I will stand by her choice."

"Fair enough."

Leea opened the door to find Julia. She let her sister inside but was unable to completely hide her disappointment.

"I'm sorry it's only me," Julia apologized, giving Leea a hug.

"No, I am glad you're here. It was just—"

"I know, and don't worry, he'll be here in a little while. He went to talk to Lauranna. But the truth is, I wanted to talk to you first."

"About what?"

Julia repeated her conversation with Yaran, explaining what she'd learned about the Desolk's plan, the network, and the difficult decision that lay ahead.

When she finished, Leea took a moment to collect her thoughts; her pain was evident.

"So, my choices are to wait and see what the Desolk has planned, and possibly end up in a mine where no woman has ever been sent, or, put my trust in a network no one knows much about?"

"This is a horrible situation. I wish there were a better choice." Julia said.

"What does Yaran think?" Leea asked after a brief hesitation.

"He wants to find a different alternative. That's why I wanted to talk to you first. Yaran doesn't believe the Desolk would be this devious. So I wanted to tell you the facts of what is most likely going to happen before he can convince you everything will be all right."

"Yaran would never do anything to hurt me."

"Of course, he wouldn't. But he also believes reasonable solutions can always be found. I think there's more of his mother in him than he realizes." Leea managed a smile at Julia's attempt to lighten the mood. "The Desolk has gone to great, although strange, lengths to come between the two of you. Since he's decided to believe Marik about what happened, he won't back down now, or it would make him look weak." Julia put an arm around Leea's shoulders. "In the end, this has to be your decision. But you can't take too long to decide…tomorrow at the latest. I'll find out later today a more definite plan on how the escape will work."

Leea stared at the tile floor searching as if a magical solution were somewhere etched on the white surface. She couldn't believe the turn her life had taken in barely a day and a half, and was still holding out hope this was all a dream, and she would soon wake up. But of course, this was all too real.

She was seventeen years old the first time she had told Yaran she loved him, and even as he had joyfully accepted her words, she knew deep down that someday she would have to let him go. Over the years, she'd convinced herself she was prepared for the inevitable outcome of their forbidden relationship and that the years they had had together would somehow sustain her. But now she realized how utterly ridiculous that was. She loved him. Loved him with every fiber of her being. And now she was faced with two choices: one where she would most likely never see him again, and the other that she might not live through.

"What should I do?" she asked dejectedly.

Julia shook her head. "I can't make that decision for you, but I can tell you what I would do. The Desolk desperately wants you out of this house, obviously at any cost. He blames you for Yaran rejecting his responsibilities, even though we all know a lot of it was his mother's doing. For that reason alone, I would expect the Desolk to do everything in his power to make sure nothing spoils his plans to remove you from his son's life. As hard as it will be for everyone, I would choose the option which would allow me to make my own decisions on the life I want to lead."

"I thought you'd never come." Leea slid her arms around Yaran's waist and pulled him close.

"I went to see Lauranna and ask if she would talk to Jarock again."

"And?" She led them to the seating area, where they sat holding hands across the small table.

"She said she'd try, but that she talked to him before he left and he was adamant about his decision. She said she tried to make him understand how losing you would disrupt the flow of the household." He smiled grimly.

"Then why did she relieve me of my duties?"

"She wanted to give us the opportunity to spend some time together, in case you truly had to leave." Yaran shook his head. "My mother is quite the mystery. She also wanted me to tell you you're no longer restricted to your room."

"I'm so confused," Leea moaned, resting her head on their joined hands.

"You talked to Julia."

"Yes, she was here."

"I think her proposal is somewhat hasty. We don't know anything about this network, and it could be much worse than what awaits you here." He squeezed her hands. "I will find you, no matter where my father sends you. I won't rest until I do, and in the meantime, I'll find a safe place for you."

Leea saw the determination in Yaran's eyes and understood exactly what Julia had tried to tell her. If she stayed on Zantia, he would exhaust every minute searching for her, but to what end? Since the Desolk had gone to such lengths to get rid of her, how would he react if Yaran still rejected his responsibilities? It would put an even bigger rift between them.

She was sure the leader would have someone watching her, and at the first sign of Yaran, what would he do? Get rid of her? Permanently? Then use her as an example of what happens if you go against him. Yaran needed to do what his family expected of him, and he would never fulfill that destiny unless he were free of her.

"I'll go with Julia's plan," she whispered, choking back tears.

"What? Why?" He looked at her in disbelief.

"It's what needs to be done…for both of us. Your father will never send me to a place where you can find me, and we both know that. What that means for me, I don't want to know."

"I won't let him defy our laws!"

Leea pulled on what was left of her emotional reserves, slid from the chair and moved to kneel in front of the man she loved. She pulled his hands to her face and nestled her cheek into his palm, then willed her voice to steady.

"I love you so much, sometimes it hurts." Her voice cracked, but she brought it in check. "But we both knew this day would come. You have a destiny to fulfill, and it never included me. We may have spent years loving each other and pretending otherwise, but deep down, we both knew this day was inevitable."

"But—"

Leea gently put a finger to his lips while tears welled in her eyes. "We were never guaranteed a future, only a limited number of days, and that limit has run out. I love you more than life itself, Yaran, and I will feel the same until the day I die, but you know you have to let me go. In order for both of us to move on with the life we were supposed to lead, I can't hide anywhere on this planet." Leea got to her feet and turned her back to him, not sure she could continue. She believed with her head what she was telling him, but her heart was self-destructing.

He walked up behind her, slipping his arms around her waist, and whispered. "Are you sure this is what you want?"

"Yes." Leea was glad he couldn't see her face because it would contradict her statement. "I would also like to get out of this room, go to our favorite place and enjoy the sunset. We can wait there for Julia to bring us any news."


Dusk had come and gone but neither Leea nor Yaran seemed to notice. The two lovers sat on the bench, eyes closed, holding each other in a tight embrace, so the small figure approaching went unnoticed until she stood in front of them, startling the couple.

"I'm sorry," Julia said quietly.

"Do you have news?" Leea asked apprehensively.

"There is no easy way to say this… I got word from my contact. There is a cargo ship leaving for Dekarra at four o'clock tomorrow morning."

Leea clutched at Yaran's arm as they both sat upright. "In six hours?!"

"I am so sorry."

"Why Dekarra?" Yaran asked.

"I understand they're sympathetic to us and have gladly taken anyone we've sent them. And because they're our closest neighbor…if you consider four weeks' space travel close."

"There are a dozen ships that travel to Dekarra. Why does it have to be tonight?"

"There are only a few on the entire planet equipped to take escaping workers. They were designed for that purpose and have a crew member taking care of all the details. My source said we are lucky there's one in Alrack, and they were willing to take her on such short notice."

"What do we have to do?"

Yaran brought Leea a travel bag and offered to help her pack, but she asked him to give her some time alone, so he took the opportunity to find some answers. Entering his father's office, he didn't know what he expected to find but was sure what he sought was here. He activated the large terminal and studied the display. An abundance of data covered the screen, and he suddenly felt at a loss on where to begin.

"Can I help you find something?"

Startled, Yaran looked up to find David. He didn't have time to think up a plausible excuse, so he decided on the truth. "I'm looking for something that will tell me if Jarock is really planning on sending Leea to the mines. Julia told me he made calls to several mine administrators. I assume she got that information from you. Do you know what was said?"

David closed the door behind him. "Julia had a feeling you would want to talk to me. My Zantian is fair, so I understand quite a bit."

"Does my father still record all his conversations?"

"Yes, that's standard procedure. And he also records his personal ones."

"Really? Can you access them?"

"They're protected, and he's the only one who can open them. Even if I tried, unauthorized attempts are recorded."

"There's no other way?"

David pressed his lips together before answering. "You realize if your father finds out I helped you, he'll send me to the mines faster than I can blink?"

"I promise you he won't find out. I'm only looking for information to help Leea."

David hesitated a moment then moved to the terminal as Yaran stepped away. "There are several backups. I should be able to access the messages there without detection." David worked the terminal, touching and swiping the screen now and then for what seemed like forever. Finally, he raised his hands and stepped back.

"I retrieved the communications in question, and they're ready for you. I'll be back shortly to shut everything down."

"Thank you."

"This is for Leea. If anyone can help her, you can."

Yaran sat down and activated the first message. There were very few pleasant-ries or explanations before Jarock came to the point.

"I have a worker I need to remove from my house as soon as possible. Before I talk to your Desolk, I wanted to check if you have a place for the worker."

"Is there trouble with this one?" the administrator asked.

"The trouble is on a personal level, so it shouldn't affect any working ability."

The administrator wouldn't give a definite answer, suggesting Jarock contact the city leader. The other two messages went pretty much the same. At no point did he mention Leea by name, but who else could he mean? A worker he needed to get rid of for personal reasons—it had to be her.

Leea looked at her meager belonging and realized she didn't have much she wanted to take. Not knowing if her drab clothing would be appropriate, she only packed what was necessary. She added her datapad, along with its solar charger, making sure it was fully charged, and silently hoped her new home had plenty of sunshine. She collected several of her grandmother's books and removed two things from the wall. This left one final item: her mother's box.

Pulling it from the shelf, Leea sat on the bed but didn't open it. She rarely did, and now wasn't the time to add anything more to her emotional plate. But sitting there with it resting on her knees opened a floodgate of memories which she was rescued from by a soft knock on the door. Without waiting for *come in*, Julia entered carrying a small wrapped bundle.

She joined Leea on the bed and handed it to her. "Here, I brought you something."

Leea took out a white shirt with black piping and black, carved buttons. She pulled the fabric to her face and inhaled the scent she loved. "Where did you get this?"

"From the laundry. I thought you should take it with you. When Tim's away, I can't sleep unless I'm wearing one of his shirts. I thought this might help you for a while."

"Thank you," she whispered. Carefully, she rewrapped it and tucked it in her bag.

"What are you doing?" Julia asked, looking at the box on Leea's lap.

"Trying to decide if I should take this." She ran her hands over the smooth lid.

"Why wouldn't you? It's the only thing you have left of your parents."

"I know, but if I actually had any memory of them, it might hold some value to me."

"Leea, you don't mean that. You're upset. It's understandable."

With a sigh, Leea added the box to her bag, then met Julia's sad gaze. "Is this truly my only option?"

"I would never have suggested this if I didn't believe you'd be better off away from here. David was there the other morning when Marik came to see the Desolk. He didn't hear their conversation, but after the two had talked, David said Marik was very smug, and the Desolk seemed almost happy."

"Did you talk to Yaran?"

"Yes, I did. He has all the information he needs to get you away safely."

"I've packed what little I'm going to take, so I guess I'm ready."

"I'm sorry," Julia whispered, tears welling up in her eyes.

"I know. But this is all my fault. If—"

"None of this is your fault! You can't—"

"Yes, I can. I love a man who I knew could never be mine."

"It's not that simple."

"Of course, it is. I always knew this day would come, and yet ... and yet I didn't care. And the tragedy is, he would do anything for me, and follow me wherever I go if I stay here."

"That's why you agreed to this."

"Yes." Tears flowed down Leea's cheeks. "We made a pact, years ago, to be happy with the time fate allowed us. But when he came here earlier, I saw the determination in his eyes. He would defy his legacy again, and find me no matter what. I can't let that happen. Fate has decided we shouldn't be together anymore, and we should listen."

"That's easier said than done when you're in love."

"Yes, it is. But I'm not going to let loving me ruin his life ... he's better off without me."

"You don't really believe that?"

"I have to. For my own sanity, I have to."

"I'm going to miss you, little sister." Julia's pulled Leea into a tight embrace.

"This won't be forever, you know. I have to believe that too."

They held each other and sobbed as they said their goodbyes. Once Julia left, Leea curled up on the bed. She was emotionally drained and couldn't keep her eyes open any longer, so she let them close.

It seemed like only a moment when she felt a hand on her shoulder and looked up into Yaran's mournful expression. Remaining on her side, she straightened her legs and, without a word, he lay down beside her, enclosing her in his arms.

"I'm sorry, my love, I tried to come sooner."

"I know."

Tears blurred her vision, but she didn't want to cry anymore or spend these last hours worrying about what tomorrow would bring. She wanted to be with the man she loved and not waste one minute of the time they had left. Reaching up, she ran a hand through his hair and noticed his eyes starting to moisten.

"No," she said, stretching to kiss each eye, tasting their salty tears. "Remember our pact: we will enjoy every moment we have, no matter what." She got up on her knees and cupped his face. "I won't be sad for the last hours we have left. I'll have the rest of my life for that." She slid her hands under his shirt and drew in a quick breath. "Make love to me. Let's pretend for the next few hours there's no one in this world but the two of us, and tomorrow will never come."

Yaran looked lovingly into her eyes then pulled her down to him.

# CHAPTER 4

# Escape

The occupants of the House of Alrack slept as Yaran and Leea stepped out into the warm night. Entering the hanger through a side door, they hastily made their way to the four vehicles parked by the bay door where Yaran chose his personal air-shuttle, standing last in the row. He said he would have rather taken the smaller ground shuttle, thinking it less conspicuous, but there were no straight roads to the airfield, and time was of the essence since they had waited until the last possible moment.

Once aboard, Yaran busied himself with the controls while Leea remained outside to take one last look at the familiar surroundings. At the workbench, she picked up the diagnostic scanner Jeffery had taught her how to use and was tempted to put it in her pocket as a keepsake, but laid it back in its designated spot, not wanting anyone to be blamed for the missing tool. She ran a hand over the familiar surfaces but knew it was only a ploy to avoid the inevitable.

The vertical-lift engines were primed, and their low rumble indicated the shuttle was ready. Taking a deep breath, she stepped into the vehicle and secured the door. Neither said a word—there was nothing left to say. While their love-making had been a distraction for a time, the reality of the situation hovered just below the surface, and they finally broke down, promising each other the impossible through blinding tears. Now, they were both physically and emotionally exhausted, and Leea just wanted it all to be over.

Effortlessly, Yaran manipulated the controls until the vehicle cleared the hangar, and brought them airborne. Leea looked around to catch one last glimpse of the house, marveling at how imposing it looked from the air. Would she miss the confines of this place? It would depend on what awaited at the other end of her journey.

"What do you think will happen when they find I'm gone? Will they try to look for me?" Leea asked, still watching the house as it receded into the distance.

"They'll have no idea where to start."

"Your father will know you helped me."

"I'm sure he will, but it won't matter."

Leea released the seat latch and swiveled to face him. "Come with me, Yaran," she pleaded.

"That's not possible."

"Why?"

He looked at her with a pained expression. "Leea, you know this story. My people have traveled the stars for centuries, and in that time, we've made many enemies. What allies we did have, most have betrayed us, so it's no longer safe for us to roam the galaxies. Now we stay here, protected in a self-constructed bubble to keep our enemies at bay. As you know, we only travel to a few planets to keep our trade going. If I were to leave this world, I would not be welcome anywhere, even to those with whom we do business."

"I'm sure that's not true. You've told me many times that a large number of Zantians want to make amends for the past. I'm sure people on other worlds won't hold you responsible for the decisions your ancestors made. Your people will have to try someday. The energy field can't last forever."

"And maybe we will someday. But right now, the damage we've done makes that impossible."

"I still think—"

He reached over and laid a hand on her knee and massaged gently. "It is not meant to be, my love, no matter how much we might want it."

Seeing the sadness in his eyes, she let it go.

"What can you tell me about the Dekarrans?"

"Unfortunately not much, except that they are obsessively secretive."

"Secretive?"

"No one has ever seen a Dekarran, and we've traded with them for almost a century."

"I don't understand. How do you negotiate with them?"

"They keep themselves concealed under robes during any discussion. The items we trade are loaded and unloaded strictly by them while the Zantian crew is kept isolated."

"And this is a place I'm supposed to be safe?"

"We've never had a problem with them," Yaran reassured her. "I'm certain there is a logical reason why they don't reveal themselves."

"Well, too late to worry about it now."

Leea looked out the windshield to catch a glimpse of the city. From the air at night, it was more impressive than the house on the hill, seeming comfortable under the protection of the Alrack Mountains. She didn't know if it was an optical illusion or by design, but the city lights seemed to twinkle as if mimicking the stars above. It was a beautiful view, one she hoped to see again someday.

Yaran landed the shuttle in an isolated area, saying they would walk the remaining half mile to the airfield's security barrier. Once they disembarked, he took out a small triangular instrument, made a few adjustments until a green light appeared in the center.

"What is that?" she asked as he tucked it back into his pocket.

"A scanner. It'll tell us exactly where the barrier is."

"Did you get that from Julia?"

"Yes. Julia gave me a few things."

Yaran removed a mini light from the shuttle and manipulated the lens until a wide beam illuminated their path, then clipped it to the front pocket of his shirt. He picked up Leea's bag, took her hand in his other, and they made their way over the rugged terrain.

"What happens once we're at the airfield?" she asked as they walked.

"We need to make contact with a man in the office building. That's all Julia told me. I wish we didn't—"

"So do I," she interrupted, afraid of what he was going to say. "But there's no turning back now."

"I know. But it doesn't make this any easier."

They continued in silence until the instrument in Yaran's pocket made short beeps. Retrieving it, he stopped and studied the screen, where now a yellow light blinked brightly.

"We're here?" Leea asked nervously, studying the strange readout with him.

"Yes. It should be a few feet ahead." Yaran made an adjustment, took several more steps until the screen brightened, and a holographic image of the field appeared ahead. "I'm going to interrupt the field's power. Once it's down, we'll have three seconds to cross."

"Three seconds!"

"That's all. When power to the barrier is interrupted, it takes three seconds to recycle. If a full connection isn't made in that time, it sets off the alarm in the guard-center."

"And what happens if we don't make it through in time? Does the field electrocute us?"

Yaran chuckled softly. "No. It's a deterrent, nothing more. Only designed to shock, not kill."

"A deterrent for what?"

"Workers have attempted to stow away on the cargo ships before. Not so much anymore, but there was a time when the barrier was necessary."

He moved them closer to the invisible field and swiped a finger across the projection. The light around the small screen flashed for a few seconds then beeped as the image of the barrier disappeared. With a hand at her back, Yaran gently pushed Leea through. Before she completed her third step, the hairs on her arms stood up, and she assumed the energy field had reactivated behind them.

Continuing, they soon found themselves on a small rise overlooking a cluster of buildings with a well-lit perimeter.

"Our destination is the building closest to us," Yaran said pointing to a three-story structure with only a few lighted windows. "The large building beyond that is the terminal itself."

"Are those the cargo ships?" Leea indicated three large vessels parked on the opposite side of the compound.

"Yes. One of them must be yours," he said sadly, then they continued down the shallow incline. "We have to go around back and through the door closest to the terminal. Once inside, we're to look for an artificial red tree on the ground floor. It will be next to the room we're looking for."

A short time later, they crossed the threshold and found themselves facing three deserted hallways. They went to the right, which eventually led to another exit. Several short hallways branched off along the way, but there was no red tree, so they returned to the main entrance.

Next, they took the center hall which quickly came to a dead-end. With a sigh of frustration, Yaran led Leea down the remaining corridor, where they made their way slowly, looking down more adjacent aisles, but still no red tree. Approaching another intersection, voices could be heard coming from around a corner up ahead. Yaran quickly tried several nearby doors until he found one open, and then pulled Leea into the dark refuge.

Certainly, he could go wherever he wanted. But what plausible reason would the son of the Desolk and a kitchen worker have to be at the airfield in the middle of the night? Not that anyone would question him, but word might make it back to his father, and once Leea was discovered missing, it would prove that Yaran had helped her. Leea slipped her arms around his waist and laid her head against his shoulder, momentarily relishing the feeling of safety. Instinctively, he wrapped his arms protectively around her and kissed her forehead.

Two figures in animated conversation suddenly stopped outside their hiding place. Not sure if they were visible through the window, Yaran pulled them further into the empty office.

"They're arguing over a woman," he whispered. "She seems to be a coworker."

One of the Zantian men leaned against the door, rattling the glass, but after another moment, laughter ensued, and the two men walked away.

Yaran chuckled. "They came to the conclusion that she wasn't worth their efforts." When their voices faded, he opened the door, carefully checking both ways before motioning Leea to follow.

They rounded the corner at the end of the main hall, and about ten yards away stood a tall red object. As they neared, the silliness of the shiny piece became evident, and they stood a moment gazing with raised eyebrows. It had a six-inch diameter trunk that stood floor-to-ceiling against one wall. At the top were large bushy leaves attached to the ceiling, almost reaching across to the opposite wall, and some were pressed behind it, all in bright red. It stood next to the only door along the wall.

"I guess this is where we go in." With a grip on Leea's hand, he eyed the door hesitantly before stepping through.

Inside was a large office with six work-desks. The room was deserted, but lights at one desk indicated someone should be nearby. Recessed into the opposite wall was an enormous screen, showing the three cargo ships they had seen outside, and next to each was a scrolling readout.

"Are we too late?" Leea asked nervously.

"No. We should be right on time."

"May I help you?"

Startled, they spun around to find a Zantian male entering through a door to their left.

"I am looking for a supervisor called Mearos," Yaran said in a shaky voice.

The man studied them for a moment. "I am Mearos," he said, closing the door behind him. He was a couple of inches shorter than Yaran with a lighter complexion and softer facial features. But one thing made it hard not to stare—his piercing blue eyes—an anomaly for a Zantian.

"We were sent by the guardian and request passage to the mountain top," Yaran said.

His words made no sense to Leea, and she suspected it was a code phrase. The Zantian walked around them and took the seat behind the illuminated desk.

Immediately, the surface powered on. Data scrolled across a vertical screen, which the supervisor swiped away before returning his attention to his visitors.

"Did the guardian provide a token?" he asked.

Yaran retrieved a data-cube from his pocket and handed it over. Mearos laid the object in front of the translucent screen and information instantly scrolled across. The Zantian studied it intently, and for a brief moment, a grimace pulled on his lips.

Leea's heart beat loudly in her chest. What if something was wrong with the information? What if this was a trap to catch people like her trying to escape?

The supervisor rose and wordlessly motioned the couple into the adjoining room that contained wall-to-wall cabinets. He closed the door behind them and went to the far corner where he opened the top door of the nearest cupboard and removed a small tube from behind the upper lip of the frame. He twisted the piece, and when it began to glow he scanned them with an up and down motion. Seeming satisfied after a second pass, he closed the cabinet door.

"I am sorry for all the mystery," Mearos addressed Yaran, "but we can't be too careful. We've never had a house member ask for our help before. Typically, the workers find their way to me with the aid of an outside contact, and then I take them on alone. But I've been requested to allow you to accompany us further."

"Requested by whom?" Yaran asked, puzzled.

Mearos shrugged. "Truly, I don't know. But I have confidence the request would not have been made unless you can be trusted to keep what you see here to yourself."

"Thank you," Yaran whispered, putting an arm around Leea's shoulders.

Mearos slid into a small space between the high storage sections and inserted the rod at the back. Soon, the closest cabinet rotated away, revealing a door which slid open without a sound. Stepping through, they found themselves in a narrow, dimly lit corridor with another door at the opposite end. The warm space smelled stale as if the air circulators didn't reach here. As they moved away, the door closed automatically, and Leea assumed the storage cabinet also moved back into position.

"The door up ahead leads into a tunnel," Mearos explained, "which will take us under the tarmac and directly to the cargo ship."

Using the rod again, Mearos opened the second door, which revealed a long narrow staircase, and he motioned for them to go first. At the bottom, lights automatically illuminated a stiflingly hot passageway that seemed to go on forever.

"When they first built this airfield, hundreds of years ago, these tunnels were put in to provide maintenance access to the ships," Mearos explained conversationally. "Eventually, the maintenance hangar was built and the tunnels abandoned.

Several decades ago, at the beginning of the escape network, this passage was re-opened with the help of sympathizers."

"I don't understand how this network has remained undetected all these years," Yaran interjected.

"This isn't used often, once a year at most. The last guest to come through here was almost three years ago. You are Yaran, correct?"

"Yes."

"I don't know what brings you here, but I'm sure this was the last resort...it always is. I assure you this will be perfectly safe for her," he said, indicating toward Leea.

But she had stopped listening. Instead, she concentrated on the sound of their footfalls against the stone floor—knowing each stride brought her closer to the one thing she feared most: being without the man she loved. Her dread of the impending finale made tears well in her eyes, but she hurriedly blinked them away. *Keep it together. In a few short minutes, this will all be over.*

They climbed the next staircase to a small landing, where a retractable hatch was visible above their heads. Mearos inserted the scanner into an instrument panel affixed to the wall.

"I'm making sure the area above is clear," he explained. "This was part of the original tunnel design to prevent the hatch from opening under a ship, or as some-one was walking by. At one time there were warning lights outside, but those were removed long ago. This ship's cargo is already loaded so it should be clear."

After a quick check, the hatch slid back, and a short set of steps leading to the tarmac appeared. A loading ramp, about ten yards away, still extended from the enormous ship. Four external engines, two above the large cargo opening and two further forward on either side, protruded from a ribbed, black hull.

The door over the ramp was partially lowered, but enough clearance remained for them to slip under easily. Inside, they made their way between large containers before entering the ship's storage area. Shelves against the walls held containers Leea recognized as food essentials.

Mearos walked into the area and stopped in front of a blank wall and inserted the rod into a hidden location. An outline of a door appeared then slid back to reveal a small room beyond. They stepped inside and soft light illuminated the sterile space. The painted white room contained a cot, an old work-desk, a chair, and a door on the far wall was presumably a washroom.

"I can only give you a few minutes," Mearos said, starting for the door. "Then I need to take Yaran back before we take off."

"We? You're coming too?" Leea said surprised.

"Yes. I'm the captain," he said, a soft smile crossing his face. "Just a few minutes," he repeated, and partially closed the door behind him.

They stared at each other for a moment, seeming at a loss on what to do, but then quickly fell into each other's arms. Yaran held her so tight she almost couldn't breathe, but Leea didn't mind. She would give anything to feel his crushing embrace forever.

"I love you, Yaran." Tears spilled over and refused to stop. She reached up and cupped his face, looking deeply into his dark, tear-filled eyes. "No amount of time will ever make me stop loving you."

"I will find you," he promised with a trembling voice. "Somehow we will find a way to be together again, no matter how long that takes." Leea slipped her arms around his neck, and they shared a passionate kiss.

"Thank you for loving me," he finally said leaning back to take in her face. "And thank you for giving me the incredible joy of loving you in return."

Desperately, Leea clung to him, not knowing if she could ever let go. She knew this would be difficult, if not impossible. But she had only prepared herself for her own sorrow and not his. "You are my *A'rinBientS'aan*, and you always will be. But this is not the end for us. I believe that with all my heart."

He kissed her again, lingering a long moment. "I... I have to go," he whispered. "Live well, my love. *Er'ShaltMee'Sarn*."

"Always...." Leea clutched at his shirt.

His jaw visibly clenched as he gently pushed her away and retreated out the door without looking back.

As the entrance slid closed between them, Leea's first instinct was to pound on it and make it open, but calling him back would change nothing and only prolong their agony.

Immediately, she realized how much she'd underestimated the pain—it was as if her insides were being ripped out. The painful sobs she'd been trying to suppress since they'd left the house would no longer be silent, and they gripped her heart like a vise. A loud ringing sounded in her ears, and her field of vision began to narrow. She scrambled to find the edge of the cot and sat down, lowering her head between her knees and willing herself to breathe. As the air finally found its way back into her lungs she lay back and curled up as tight as she could, and for the third time in as many days let the sobs overtake her.

Leea emerged from the fog to the sound of someone calling her name. She looked up to find Mearos standing over her, reaffirming that the nightmare was real.

"I'm sorry to wake you."

She wanted to tell him it was all right, but her voice wouldn't work.

"Yaran made it safely back outside the airfield perimeter."

She eased into a sitting position and wiped at her cheeks, but said nothing.

"I just wanted to let you know that we will be taking off shortly. I won't be able to come back down here until after we've left the solar system. Can I get you anything?"

She shook her head but then forced herself to answer. "I'll be okay. It's been a long night. I'm going to try and sleep."

"That sounds like a good idea. I left you some water and fruit." Mearos pointed to items he had set into recessed holders of the work-desk.

"Thank you. Can I ask a question?"

"Of course."

"Do all the people you've helped live on Dekarra?"

"Since I only make deliveries there, I assume so."

"Is it truly safe?"

He smiled wearily. "Yes, of that I'm certain."

Jarock sat overlooking the brightly lit cityscape from the family apartment. He took a long drink of the strong brown liquid then exhaled forcefully as if blowing out a flame.

He checked the time. Right on cue, the small communications console chirped beside him, and he activated it without looking at the screen.

"The plan is in motion. Everything is arranged," said the familiar voice.

A smile crossed Jarock's lips, and he disconnected the link without responding. He got to his feet, lifted the glass as if to salute, and downed the rest of the contents.

# CHAPTER 5

# Lauranna

Yaran sat in his shuttle, head resting against the instrument panel. As a distraction, he listened to the sound of his shallow breathing, being careful not to let any random thoughts rise to the surface. Nausea gripped his insides, so he concentrated on each labored breath as it went in and out, hoping to settle his stomach. He wasn't sure how long he'd been there, as time seemed irrelevant, but at some point, he heard the deep rumble of the departing cargo ship.

"Pull yourself together," he reprimanded himself, trying to raise his head. The effort made the cabin spin, so he decided against it, but after a few minutes, he drew in a deep breath and sat back then waited for the world to settle. Opening his eyes, he saw the beginning of the sunrise, and quickly closed them again. He didn't care what time it was; as far as he was concerned, he would sit here until the pain went away. A cloud of despair enveloped him but his exhaustion triumphed, and he welcomed unconsciousness.

Loud tapping noises brought him back to reality. He was trying to escape something in the mist, but couldn't remember what and rationalized it was probably a good thing. The tapping noise again. He opened his eyes and stared into the face of a Zantian man wearing a security uniform.

"Are you all right?" the guard asked once Yaran managed to find the window release.

Was he all right? And then it all came rushing back—Leea. He took temporary control of his emotions and stammered, "Yes, I had trouble with the engine, must have fallen asleep, sorry."

"No problem, but you can't stay here. If you need help with—"

"No, it's fine now. I'll be on my way." He started the engine and was airborne almost before the guard could step out of the way.

At home, Yaran maneuvered the shuttle back into the hanger, grateful the area was empty. He thought about using the outside entrance to his room, but that would take him through the gardens, and he wasn't ready for the memories the walk would evoke. Since it was early, he hoped to slip quietly through the front door.

But that would have been too much to ask.

"Yaran? Are you just now getting home?" Lauranna called from her sitting room adjacent to the large foyer.

"Should have gone through the kitchen," he grumbled quietly.

Yaran entered his mother's sanctuary, not surprised to find her with an ancient tome on her lap. Hundreds of books, datapads, telling stones, story orbs, and other forms of alien literature filled the shelves around the room.

Zantians had the ability to decipher most alien languages, which is what made them good traders—they weren't easily fooled by those races attempting to take advantage. Lauranna was especially gifted in this process. She could interpret the meaning of words through sounds. Once the alien context was understood, and a few keywords memorized, she found it easy to comprehend the language structure; this applied not only to the verbal but the written as well.

"I had trouble with the shuttle and accidently fell asleep. I'm sorry." He reused the same story he'd told the security guard, hoping it wouldn't sound like the lie it was.

"Hungry?" she asked. "The morning meal should be ready soon."

So like his mother, no probing questions. "No, thank you. I'm not feeling well, and just want to lie down."

"Wait. Before you go, sit with me for a moment." Lauranna motioned to the chair next to her.

The last thing Yaran wanted at this moment was pleasant bantering with his mother. Although he loved her dearly, she could be tiresome at times. Her mental energy continually needed to be released, and Yaran was usually her first target.

If tradition didn't frown upon a Desolk's mate spending time away from the home, Lauranna would have made an excellent teacher. She had a photographic memory, so retained everything she read, and wanted nothing more than to share her newfound knowledge with anyone who would listen.

"If you don't mind, Mother," he said calmly, kissing the top of her head, "maybe later. My head is splitting."

She chuckled softly but rested a hand on his arm. "Please, I only want a quick word. Don't worry. I won't subject you to a story-telling this early in the morning."

Resigned, he settled in next to her. "What's on your mind?"

"I want to apologize for your father. He's been too hard on Leea lately."

"Mother, it's—"

"No, let me finish. I know he disapproves of your friendship, but he had no right to take Marik's side in this latest incident."

"Mother…please," Yaran groaned softly, his mind racing. He'd forgotten that she had released Leea from her duties, so no one had noticed her absence yet.

"I'm not making excuses for him, but he has had a lot on his mind these days. There's still some unrest at the mines, but that's no excuse for the way he lashed out at her. But you know—"

"What's going on in the mines?" Yaran hoped to change the subject.

"Oh, I'm not sure, but he and your uncle Toref have been spending a lot of time going over the data logs. He typically doesn't discuss these matters with me, and I don't ask. But I'm sure that's why he's been a little short tempered lately, and well. You know, Leea can over—"

"Mother…please!"

"I told you I would talk to him when he returns. I'm not sure I can change his mind, but as I mentioned before, losing Leea will significantly disrupt things, since Marik is indisposed as well."

"But you already dismissed her from her duties."

"I shouldn't have been so hasty with my decision. Jarock is going to be away for another two days, so I'll reinstate her. Tell her to be patient."

"Okay, I will tell her when I see her." Yaran got to his feet. "I really am tired… if you don't mind…."

"Certainly. I apologize for keeping you. Oh, and make sure Jeffrey checks the shuttle." Lauranna smiled at her son wryly. "I don't want you to get stranded again."

"Of course." He made his way down the hall, desperately wanting to close his eyes and make the pounding in his head cease.

"Yaran?" a soft voice said behind him.

He turned to find Julia.

She stopped and studied him for a moment. "I take it by the look on your face everything went as planned?"

Yaran nodded.

"I'm sorry, Yaran, so truly sorry. How long do you think it'll take before Leea's absence is noticed?"

"Not long. Mother wants her to return to her duties. But right now she's engrossed in one of her books."

"Well, hopefully, it's a long one." Julia started to turn away but stopped. "Oh, in case you're interested, Marik will be staying at the med-center a few more days. It seems there is some extensive damage to his eye, and they're not even sure they can save it."

Yaran pursed his lips. "I'm only sorry I didn't give him a matching pair."

Hoping for no more distractions, he hurried to his room and closed the door behind him, then dropped onto his large bed and let exhaustion overtake him.

*Yaran walked alone down the halls of a ship. Echoing footsteps and voices resonated in the distance, but no matter how many junctions he crossed, he encountered nothing but empty passages. Rounding another corner, he saw Leea at the far end standing next to a small, faceless figure. She beckoned for him to follow. He ran as fast as he could but they seemed to pull further and further away. He called her name as they disappeared around a bend. Following, Yaran stopped short—the stranger stood alone in front of him. Before he could retreat, a gnarled hand grabbed his wrist, holding tight against his struggles.*

*"Find the crystal cave," a mystical voice instructed him.*

*"Where is Leea?"*

*"Leea is safe, but it is imperative you find the crystal cave."*

*The dream shifted and Yaran stood in the center of a long rectangular room with bright blue walls. At the far end stood a rectangular platform, upon which lay the faceless figure. Yaran approached the dais. As he looked down at the lifeless body, the ancient hand grabbed his wrist again. This time, Yaran didn't move.*

*"The answers you seek lie within the blue walls."*

*The partition behind the bed disappeared. In the distance, Leea stood along with a small figure dressed in green. She looked over at him, smiled, and gave a wave.*

Yaran came awake drenched in sweat, calling Leea's name. Sitting up, he shook his head to clear the fog and attempted to calm his breathing. He rarely dreamed, so the intensity of this one shook him to the core. It seemed so real—so vivid. He rubbed his wrist, still feeling the pressure of the alien's hand around it. The reference to a crystal cave puzzled him. There were hundreds of caves in the mountain range. He had visited a few during his education years but never heard of one made of crystal.

"It was a dream, nothing more," he reassured himself.

He started to lie down again when he heard voices in the hall. He recognized his mother's, who surprisingly seemed agitated, but couldn't make out who she was talking to. Yaran's first instinct was to see what the problem was, but he didn't want to face anyone, so decided to let her deal with it on her own. However, the choice to get involved was made for him with a knock on the door.

"Yaran? Are you there?"

"Yes, come in," he called with a deep sigh but remained seated on the bed.

Lauranna entered, closing the door behind her. From the look on her face, he knew something was wrong and got to his feet.

At sixty-seven, Lauranna was considered, by many, to be a strikingly beautiful woman. She was slightly shorter than him, slender, and had an oval face with soft features. Her light-brown complexion was flawless and for as long as he could remember she had worn her dark, wavy hair a few inches below her shoulders. Her eyes were normally a lighter, radiant shade of gray, which Yaran always attributed to her self-prescribed serene life, and never letting her emotions rule—except at this moment.

"What's wrong?" he asked impatiently.

"Where is Leea?"

"I haven't seen her this morning,"

"She's gone, Yaran. No one has seen her since yesterday, and some of her things are missing." The pitch of her voice rose.

"What do you mean—missing?"

"I sent Julia to her room. When she came back, she said Leea wasn't there, and neither were some of her things."

Yaran looked at his mother but said nothing.

"What do you know about this?"

"Why do you think I know anything? I haven't seen Leea since I got back, and that's the truth."

"But you know where she is?"

"I don't—"

"Yaran, I'm in no mood for games. Leea would never leave without you knowing about it. So where did she go?"

Yaran could never lie to his mother. "I have no idea where Leea is…exactly. But yes, she's gone, and she won't be back."

Lauranna studied him for a moment. He watched as her expression softened, then she laid a gentle hand on his arm. "Is she somewhere safe?"

"I believe so."

She pulled her son into an embrace. "Be happy for her, Yaran." She kissed him gently on the cheek and then left without another word.

No longer feeling the need to sleep, Yaran paced the floor, trying to make sense of his life, and the clear path laid out for him.

Zantian rule dictated that at age fifteen, children born into affluence enter a transition phase to bolster their academic achievements. While they were taught certain things at home during their younger years, the transition marked the beginning of a rigorous educational schedule. Girls participated in all the same basic studies, but boys took a different path, concentrating heavily on business.

The period started with the separation from family to remove all distractions and allow the teachings to have the desired effect. The theory was that emotional attachments clouded judgment, and a true Zantian leader, whether in government or business, relied heavily on unwavering negotiation techniques that could only be taught with no outside influences.

The separation typically lasted five years, depending on individual progress. The children were moved to another city, where they lived in outlying villages with a temporary caregiver. At that home, they received most of their schooling and some with specialized instructors in the city.

But Lauranna didn't believe in the antiquated rule and decided her son would receive his education at home. Strangely, no one fought her decision. To make up for not sending Yaran away, she made him study hard, leaving little time for outside interests except for his music. Yaran never wondered what he might have missed by remaining isolated in Alrack, and now it seemed he should have.

Because of Yaran's unconventional upbringing, by age twenty-one, Jarock insisted he take on certain business responsibilities, mostly centered on the shipping end. He was more than capable, and willing, to help in the city office, but the Desolk demanded more. Jarock attempted to instill interest in council business, requiring his son to accompany him to meetings, whether away, or in Alrack.

With his thirtieth birthday—the crossover—looming ahead, these gatherings only reinforced Yaran's resolve that he wanted no part of planetary leadership. He didn't want to create rules that others were required to follow without question, or to have endless discussions about the current state of their trade.

The House of Alrack had led the Council for generations, and Jarock had no intention of letting the position fall to another family. Therefore, he pushed Yaran continually, hoping his son would eventually develop interest, along with not-so-subtle reminders that the future of Alrack rested with him. But Yaran detested all those things his father held dear: overseeing the mines; ruling their city and the Council; maintaining a stiff household with someone he chose because it was expected of him.

Yaran's reluctance to embrace the leadership path was well known in the ruling circle, and he assumed the other council members were positioning themselves for a future takeover while they waited to see what their leader's son would eventually do. He should probably feel guilty about the inevitable change in Alrack's status…but he didn't.

The events of the last few days made him realize that life was unpredictable and could change in an instant, for which he was ill-prepared. He was hesitant to admit that he never envisioned his future any different than it had been all these years; his music, and Leea. Now, he didn't recognize the path that lay ahead and it frightened him. As the son of the council leader, all doorways were open to him, but which ones he would actually cross, remained to be seen.

Julia brought Yaran's evening meal and informed him Lauranna would be dining in her room. This surprised him. His mother was adamant about meal times— all family members must be present. But he was relieved that she was letting him have this time alone.

When he finished the few bites he could manage, Yaran felt the walls closing in on him and had the sudden urge to be outside. The setting sun cast long shadows over his room's private terrace as he stepped outside, but he didn't linger. He made his way to the gardens, and wandered aimlessly along the path, recalling his walk with Leea only a few days earlier. She had made light of their impossible future, and he acted as if nothing would ever change. He sighed.

Without paying attention to where he was going, Yaran soon found himself approaching the bluff. Up ahead he spotted the Jala tree and felt an instant pull. This had been Leea's special place, and he immediately sensed her presence. He stopped and closed his eyes, seeing her there on the bench, auburn hair flowing down her back, looking out at the landscape beyond. He had often asked her what she saw there, and she always answered, "Peace."

As he continued, Yaran's heart momentarily skipped a beat as he noticed someone sitting there, but then recognized Julia. His first instinct was not to disturb her, but he found he wanted the company and hoped she wouldn't mind the intrusion. He quietly sat down beside her. She turned her head slightly, glanced up, but said nothing. Silently they drew strength from the other's presence.

"Do you think she's scared?" Julia asked after a few minutes.

"I'm sure she is, but I believe she'll be okay."

"You really think so?"

Yaran described the events at the airfield, telling her about meeting Mearos, and what the Zantian captain had said about the network.

"Does he know what happens to them once they get there?"

"No. He said he trusts the person who takes them from the ship but didn't go into details. He reassured me several times that Leea would be safe, and not to worry. And I must say, I believed him."

"Did he tell you anything about what life is like on Dekarra?"

"No, about that he was vague. And I was in no frame of mind to push him for more information."

"Where is Dekarra from here?"

Yaran searched the sky for a moment then pointed above the mountains. "In the Haster constellation, which is that six-point cluster looking as if it's touching the highest peak. Dekarra's star is the furthest point on the bottom right."

Julia adjusted her position to face him. "I'm sorry this happened," she said softly. "I know how much you loved each other."

"I know this isn't easy for you either."

"No, it isn't. It would be easier if I knew for sure she was okay… safe. But it's better than thinking about what could have happened to her here." Julia smiled warily. "Leea truly believes we'll all see each other again."

"I will always hope for that too, for as long as I live."

"I will too." Julia got to her feet. "It's getting late. I should get back to Marta."

"I'm going to stay a while."

She laid a hand on his shoulder. "We'll get through this. I know it doesn't seem like it at the moment, but we will."

# CHAPTER 6

# Goodbye

The image of Leea on the cargo ship, already millions of miles away, kept Yaran awake for hours. As he tossed and turned, rehashing the events of the last several days, it brought him to one inevitable conclusion: his future no longer belonged in this house.

As much as he would miss his mother, he could no longer occupy the same space as the two men who conspired against him. He had no idea what he was going to do, but leaving was certain. He couldn't stay in the city apartment since Jarock used it occasionally for late night business. He might be welcome in Calthena, but had never spent much time there, so it would probably be awkward. He would sleep in the shuttle, as uncomfortable as that might be, if he needed to.

But first, he needed to tell his mother. He didn't know if she would try and talk him out of it, but his mind was made up, and he hoped, in the end, she would understand. He felt they were both victims of his father's schemes, but she had an obligation to stay—he did not.

"Yaran, I'm happy to see you this morning," she smiled up at him as he entered her sitting room.

"Good morning, Mother." He sank into the chair next to her.

"How are you feeling?"

"All right." Suddenly, all his well-prepared words were gone, but one thing he needed to ask. "Did you know why Marik was brought here?"

Lauranna frowned and set the pad she held aside. "I'm sorry this situation ended up the way it did. There should have been a better way to handle it."

"So you knew?" he said in disbelief.

"Yes, I did. But not to what lengths Marik would go. If I had, I would never have tolerated him." She drew in a deep breath. "Your father has been unhappy about your friendship with Leea for years. He asked me many times to talk sense into you…his words…but I refused. I always told him you would eventually make the right decisions."

"You really believed that?"

"At one time I did. I truly thought you two were just friends…more like brother and sister, so your friendship never worried me, until one day the playful moments between you were gone, and you stopped talking about her. I thought maybe you had a falling-out, but then recognized a different kind of emotion in your eyes—love. I knew then it was too late, but kept that to myself, waiting to see what would happen." Lauranna leaned back, looking up at the high ceiling reflectively.

"I should have sent you away when you reached your transition year. But I couldn't bear the thought of you living among strangers and not seeing you for years." She paused for a moment. "I'm sorry, Yaran, the mistake was mine, and your father's for not insisting—"

"None of this is your fault!"

"Yes, it is. I wanted nothing more than to make you happy, and your father indulged me. I should never have used his love for me to manipulate our long-held traditions to get my way."

Hearing his mother speak about the love of his father was new to Yaran. His parents never openly showed affection, so he often wondered if they actually cared for each other, or were only mated out of convenience. He reached across and took her hands. "Thank you for not sending me away. I've learned more from you than anyone else could have taught me, and it made me a better person."

"What do you plan to do?" she asked with a shaky voice.

"The only thing I can do: leave. With everything that's happened in the last few days, I can't stay here anymore."

A look of sadness crossed Lauranna's face, but she nodded. "I was afraid you might make that choice." She sighed. "This house seems to generate so many sad memories."

"This isn't goodbye. Just because I can't live here, doesn't mean we won't see each other. I'll come by every chance I get."

"Where will you go?"

"I'm not sure yet, but as soon as I do, I'll let you know."

"Are you certain this is what you want?" she asked wistfully.

"No, this is not what I want at all, but there's no other alternative. I'll never be able to move on as long as I'm in the same house with Jarock and Marik."

"I'm not sure what your father plans on doing with Marik now. No one will be happy with what he did to Leea. She was well liked, and the other workers won't take kindly to his deception."

"Well, that's his problem. And Jarock has no one to blame but himself."

"Yaran, I understand you're angry, and you have every right to be, but your father did what he thought was best, right or wrong."

"I'm sure somewhere in the recesses of his mind he believes that, but I don't."

Lauranna smiled wearily. "When will you leave?"

Yaran looked at her sadly. "Today."

"Can I hear you play one more time?"

"Of course."

Selecting her favorite pieces, Yaran played until it was time for the midday meal.

At the dining table, mother and son sat across from each other in relative silence, both saddened that the end of the day was fast approaching. Yaran absent-mindedly stirred his soup without taking a single spoonful. Lauranna studied him, trying not to think about how lonely her days were going to be once he was gone. She understood his reasoning, but at the same time wished they could all find a peaceful solution to the current problem. Maybe once a little time passed, Yaran would reconsider this hasty decision. This was, after all, his home.

Just as they were finishing, Julia entered and approached the table to address Lauranna. "The Desolk has returned. Would you like me to set a place for him?"

"Yes, Julia, thank you."

Yaran scrambled to his feet as if the chair had caught fire. "Julia, you can remove my dishes. I'm finished. Excuse me, Mother, I have things to prepare in my room."

Lauranna refilled her teacup from the sideboard then reflected on her mate. Jarock hadn't always been the stern, unyielding man leadership had turned him into. She had been attracted to him from the moment they met, and knew he felt the same about her, but she'd kept him at arm's length for over a year. She smiled at the memory of how he had relentlessly pursued her. While her love for him had never wavered over the years, she often longed for the younger Jarock, the one who would go out of his way to make her smile. But all that changed with his parents' death, which forced him to take over the role as council leader much too early.

Now, he ran his family, his business, and the planet's leadership with a single-mindedness that sometimes scared her, and the only thing his efforts accomplished was to drive everyone away. She loved him regardless, but some days it seemed too much. In all their years together, she could not recall a time when she had been this angry with him. His continued inflexibility was now forcing their only child to separate himself from his family—and for what?

"Lauranna," Jarock beamed as he entered the dining room. He kissed her gently before picking up his dish. "I was hoping I would make it in time for the meal. I'm so glad I did." Jarock filled his bowl, and then took his seat at the head of the table.

"How was your trip?" she asked, pushing her half-empty bowl away.

"It went well. Toref and I spent long hours going over accounts again, and I think our problems are resolved, at least for the moment."

"Good."

"How are things here?"

"Things were a little…complicated after you left," she said with a grimace.

"You could have contacted me."

"When you rushed out, you said it was an emergency. I'm not going to interrupt you for household matters. I can handle the staff without your iron fist."

"I know you can." A smile pulled at the corners of Jarock's mouth. "Have things uncomplicated themselves?"

"Marik is in the med-center."

His smile widened. "I assumed as much when I saw him. I must say, I was impressed that Yaran took the initiative to put Marik in his place. I didn't think he had it in him."

"You pushed him too far, Jarock."

His smile disappeared. "It needed to be done. It was long overdue. I made arrangements for the girl to leave first thing in the morning, and then this matter can be closed."

"You honestly think it's that simple?" Lauranna glared at her mate.

"It should be."

"Where do you plan to send her?"

"No reason for you to know. Then there will be no temptation for you to tell our son."

"Well, you can cancel your arrangements."

"I am not changing my decision to send her away." He said sternly, picking up a piece of bread and breaking it in half.

"She's gone."

Jarock's hand stopped halfway to his mouth. "What do you mean, she's gone?"

"She left sometime during the night."

Dark eyes glared in anger. "And Yaran helped her of course?"

"He has no idea where she is."

"He's lying."

"What difference does it make? You wanted her gone. She's gone. I guess you can be happy now." Her voice dripped with sarcasm. He looked at her with an almost guilty expression. She knew that look. He was hiding something. "What did you do?"

The Desolk's stoic demeanor returned. "What was completely within my right to do."

Yaran entered his father's office, having been summoned by David.

"I don't suppose there is any point asking where she is?" Jarock said accusatorily.

"I don't know," Yaran answered curtly.

"Are you really going to stick with the lie you told your mother?"

"It's not a lie. But I did help ensure she was protected from whatever you had planned."

"I have no idea what you're talking about."

"Really? Now who's lying? Why don't you tell me where you were planning to send her?"

The Desolk studied him a moment before answering. "Somewhere where her influence could no longer affect you?"

"Her influence?! Is that what you think our relationship was all about; so she could influence me? To what end? Reject my responsibilities? Give her an easier life?"

"That's ridiculous. Rejecting your responsibilities was your own doing, for sure. But then you've never had to follow what's required. For that, I blame your mother."

"Don't you dare blame her! She—"

Jarock raised a hand to silence him. "Your mother had her own ideas about your upbringing, and I indulged her. So I'm partly to blame. But as far as being involved with one of our workers, that's all on you. And it's unconscionable for someone in your position. And then aiding in her escape makes it even worse."

Yaran studied his father in confusion. "Why do you care? You wanted her gone; now she's gone. Why does that anger you?"

"It doesn't," he said forcefully. "What I'm not happy about, is the possibility of you running after her."

"Well, you can rest assured. I made sure she was out of your reach, which put her out of mine."

Jarock flashed a winning smile. "Good, now you can finally concentrate on your crossover without hindrance."

"Do you seriously think this changes anything? I am not interested in what you, or anyone else, expects of me. I have the right to live my life as I see fit."

"No, actually you don't. You see—"

"I'm leaving…for good," Yaran blurted, suddenly tired of trying to make his father understand.

"Really? And where would you go?"

"It doesn't matter, just as long as it's away from here. And away from your influence and schemes."

The older man's expression changed to dark amusement. "As much as you'd like to think you can leave and never look back, you can't. There is a world out there you're not prepared for. Not to mention, you enjoy the comforts of this house too much. How will you spend endless hours with your music, or walk in the privacy of our gardens, if you leave?"

"And what good are all those luxuries if they depend on you dictating my life? None of this," Yaran spread his arms for emphasis, "is worth that."

"Don't be ridiculous. In time, you will forget that girl. Your crossover is just a month away. Once that day comes, your focus will change."

"You refuse to hear anything I say, so let me be clear: I will *never* embrace your way of life. I'm not interested in your traditions, or these responsibilities you think I'll accept simply because I've reached the appropriate age. And to be perfectly clear…again…, you took from me the one thing I cared about most, and for that, I will never forgive you. You can take your title, your Council, and find someone else to give them to."

Yaran started for the door but then turned back. "What did you promise Marik for trying to come between Leea and me?"

"I don't know what you're talking about."

Yaran leaned over and placed both hands flat on the desktop. "Of course, you do," he insisted through clenched teeth. "That worker has been much too confident these past months. Almost as if he knew there wouldn't be any consequences for his actions. Which means he was expecting some personal gain."

"I don't make deals with anyone, least of all Humans."

"Normally I would agree. But since you took his word over Leea's when he attacked her—and you know he did—it proves my point."

"That's ridiculous."

"What I'm actually asking is, what was my unhappiness worth to you?"

"You're overreacting!"

"I don't think so." Yaran made a dismissive gesture. "Now I tire of this conversation. Goodbye, Jarock."

Yaran stood in front of the small house owned by his father's younger brother, Toref. His uncle had retreated from the luxurious living of the family estate after the death of his mate, Cassa, five years ago, finding the memories there too painful.

When she suddenly took ill, and the healers couldn't determine a cause, Toref had dedicated every moment to her. She was supposed to stay indoors and rest, but Cassa refused. Instead, she and Toref traveled around the planet for nearly a year, visiting with family and friends until she was finally too weak to move. After that, he carried her to the gardens every day, and it was there that she died quietly in his arms, taking the light in Toref's eyes with her.

They hadn't been blessed with children, and after her death, the healers surmised it was her illness which kept her from conceiving. Now, his only focus was running the mines, and he seemed to have pushed everything, and everyone, else into the background. All this made Yaran wonder if he should have come. He didn't want to intrude on his uncle's solitude, but what else was he to do? He needed help, and Toref was the only one he thought might offer it.

Yaran hadn't seen much of his uncle since he'd moved here and suddenly realized how much he missed the gentle giant. "Gentle" because he was always the peacemaker; "giant" because, although the strong family resemblance included Toref, he was taller and broader than both his brother and nephew.

His house was much like those in the surrounding area: single story, with four twenty-foot floor-to-ceiling glass panels, separated by black steel beams. In the center, a ten-foot white door and a flat roof that angled upward toward the front. It was strategically located on the edge of the western village, between the airfield and family offices. Although Toref managed all four Alrack mines, he spent most of his time in the city, so it made sense to live close by.

He knocked on the door.

"Yaran!" Toref greeted him wide-eyed. "Come in."

"I'm sorry for coming unannounced."

"Don't apologize. You are always welcome, even if unexpected. It's been a long time since you've been here."

"And for that, I also apologize. I should have visited more often."

"Now that the apologies are out of the way," Toref smiled, "tell me what brings you here? I'm pleased to see the son of my brother, but I can tell by your troubled look that something's wrong."

Toref led the way into the large, sparsely furnished living room: a sofa, two chairs, and a small table sat in the middle of the room. A few paintings, similar to ones hanging in his father's home, adorned the walls, and one cabinet, filled to overflowing, stood in the far corner.

"Have a seat."

Toref took a well-worn chair while Yaran sat across from him on an almost unused sofa.

"Do you keep up with things at the house?" Yaran asked.

"No. When I see Jarock, I always ask about you and your mother, but other than that, we don't discuss domestic issues. We went over mine reports most of the day yesterday, but he didn't say anything to me. What's happened?"

Yaran recapped the events of the last few days, stopping short of revealing Leea's escape.

Toref frowned. "So, you're saying that my brother, your father, brought Marik from the House of Emborie, to make trouble for Leea?"

It seemed a rhetorical question, but Yaran nodded.

Toref flashed a bemused smile. "The special connection between you and Leea did not go unnoticed…not by anyone, I'm afraid. Cassa noticed the change in your relationship, and we both watched, with humor, I might add, as you two tried so hard to hide the obvious. It surprised us that Jarock allowed this, but I'm sure that was because of your mother's influence."

Yaran looked away with embarrassment and shook his head. "And we thought we were so clever. In our defense, once we realized our true feelings, we knew it was imperative to keep it a secret. I don't think either one of us considered that by then it was already too late." Yaran chuckled. "Did Cassa tell you she surprised us in the greenhouse once?"

"Yes, she did," Toref grinned. "She wasn't positive it was you, but we were pretty sure. Who else would be hiding in there?"

Yaran shook his head with renewed humiliation.

"I knew Jarock would eventually intervene," Toref admitted, "try to put a stop to it. But I had no idea he would go to these lengths. I am sorry for that. How is Leea doing?"

This was the question Yaran dreaded answering.

Toref sensed his hesitation. "What aren't you telling me?"

"That she … that Leea is no longer on Zantia."

"Really?"

Yaran went to the window and looked out. He was about to lie to a man he respected, and couldn't quite bring himself to look him in the eye.

"When I learned of the possibility that Jarock might send her to the mines, and not to another city, I knew I had to do something. I had heard about the escape network, so I contacted someone who made arrangements to send Leea off-world."

"Who did you contact?"

"I'd rather not say. I don't want to make trouble for anyone." He returned to the sofa.

"And you believe this network to be real, and let them take Leea away? How do you know these people can be trusted? How do you know it wasn't a trap?"

Yaran wasn't prepared for the reprimand or the sudden chill it sent through him. "I … I trust the people who gave me the information," he declared nervously. "I can't give you any details, but I'm certain Leea is in good hands."

"I'm sorry. I didn't mean to upset you. You did what you had to. I'm just not sure I could let the woman I love go off alone."

"Sadly, accompanying her was not possible." Yaran sighed. "Maybe we should have been more open with our relationship?"

"What? No. Don't think that." Toref vigorously shook his head. "All that would have accomplished was to get Leea sent away sooner." He inhaled deeply. "You can't forget why Humans are here. We may not keep those in the city locked up, unlike the mine workers, but they are far from free to do as they please. Ironically, they've lasted much longer than other races we've brought here and even managed to make a life for themselves, but they are still here to serve. Zantians are not ready for that dynamic to change. Especially not in the House of Alrack."

"Do you take advantage of their services?"

"A Human woman comes twice a week to clean, but that's all."

"Have you heard of the network?"

"Oh, I think everyone's heard the rumors, but I think most people believe it's just that … rumor."

"That's what I thought at first too, but it is very real, I can assure you."

"Well, I'm sure there are many things out there we know nothing about... which is a good thing," Toref smiled. "So, this brings me back to my original question; what brings you here? You didn't stop by just to bring me up to date on my brother's latest escapades."

Yaran took a deep breath and ran his hands through his black hair. "After what's happened in the last several days, I can't stay in that house anymore. I wish I could, but I can't be around Jarock and Marik."

"I understand. You're welcome to stay here if you like. I have an extra bedroom, and it's yours for as long as you need it."

"Are you sure?"

"Of course, I'm sure. You're family, where else would you go?"

"Thank you," Yaran said with relief. "But I want to contribute and help you in any way I can. I need something to keep my mind occupied."

"No problem there, but you may not like what I'm going to suggest."

"Oh?"

"There is plenty of work in the mines, as production is on the rise. Things are a bit hectic now, so your help would be welcome. I know this wouldn't be your first choice, but I guarantee it will keep you busy."

"Thank you, that's exactly what I need." Yaran chuckled sarcastically. "Won't my father be proud that his wayward son is finally doing what is expected of him?" He then leaned forward and laid his head in his hands.

"Is everything all right?" the older man asked with concern.

"I miss her, Toref." Despair had returned. "I had no idea this would hurt so much. Leea is the love of my life, my best friend. We could talk about everything and nothing or just sit silently taking comfort in each other's presence. How am I going to survive without her?"

Toref joined him on the sofa and laid a hand on his shoulder. "Eventually, it will get better. Trust me. This is something I know a great deal about."

# CHAPTER 7

# The Voyage

The first few days on the ship passed in a blur as Leea's sobs came and went. The emotional pain cycling nonstop through her body demanded attention, and she was powerless to ignore it. Now, at the end of day five, the well of tears was dry, along with her ability to sleep.

Twice a day Mearos brought her meals. Each time, he attempted to engage her in conversation, which she wasn't yet ready for, and sensing this, quickly withdrew, leaving her to the despair. Despite her inner turmoil, Leea decided she liked the ship's captain.

Tossing and turning on the cot, she almost wished for the volatility of the previous nights to return, where she had merely passed out from exhaustion. *It's time to let go and accept this new chapter of my life.* She told herself this over and over again. If only it were that easy—if only she didn't miss Yaran so much.

An idea came to mind just as troubled sleep claimed her and in the morning, she thought it through to fruition. She would document her life on Zantia, just like the memoirs she had read from the Desolk's library. Not that she expected anyone to be interested in her life, but this would give her something to do for the next few weeks as well as make those she loved feel closer.

She didn't want to use the voice input on her datapad but key it in instead. Since her small device would be cumbersome, she decided to ask Mearos if he had an extra one to fit the work-desk. Manual documenting would also ensure she got off the cot every day, which might keep her sane as sanity seemed in short supply at the moment.

A knock on the door announced Mearos bringing her morning meal. She was seated on the cot, legs crossed, back propped against the bulkhead with a pillow, reading on her pad. He wouldn't have heard a reply if she gave one because the room was soundproof, but he always waited before entering, giving her a moment to collect herself if she needed it.

He looked at her quizzically for a moment as he set a covered tray on the desk. "Good morning. You seem different today."

"Better or worse?" she asked lightheartedly.

"Ah, almost a smile. You must be feeling better."

"I do. Not great, but better."

"Small steps, Leea, small steps."

"That's easier said than done, I'm afraid."

"I understand." Mearos turned to go. "Hopefully, every day forward will see an improvement."

"I hope so too. Can you stay a few minutes?"

"Yes, I have a few minutes." He pulled the desk chair over and took a seat.

Leea studied her benefactor. Since Zantians lived longer than Humans, it was sometimes hard to approximate an age, but she guessed him to be between forty and fifty. He had a genuine smile which caused tiny crinkles around his blue eyes that she desperately wanted to ask about, but didn't want to be rude.

"What?" Mearos interrupted her observations.

"I am so sorry," Leea gasped, mortified to be caught openly staring at him, then quickly said, "do you mind if I ask you some questions?"

"Ask away."

"Do all escaping workers stay in this room?"

"Yes."

"Has anyone ever been discovered here?"

"No. Each ship is scanned before leaving the ground. This not only ensures the correct cargo is loaded, but also that there is nothing that doesn't belong. This room has a special shielding which is impervious to any of the Zantian equipment. What's outside the door is just extra storage, and non-perishable provisions. So, no reason for anyone to come down here, except once or twice a week."

"Can I ask a favor?"

"Of course."

"I want to document my life on Zantia. This will help me put things in perspective, as well as keep me busy during this voyage."

"That sounds like an interesting idea."

"I brought a datapad," she held hers up, "but it's not compatible with the work-desk. I was hoping you might have an extra one I could use while I'm here."

Mearos thought a moment. "I'm sure we have one. We keep spares on hand. I assume the desk works, but not that I've tried it."

"That would be great."

He rose. "I'll see what I can find and bring it with the evening meal."

As promised, Mearos brought a datapad and a power pack for the desk that evening. He installed the pack, made sure the pad worked and then left her alone. After she had eaten, Leea set to the task before her. Deactivating the automatic voice feature, a virtual keyboard appeared and she configured it to English. After several tries, she finally found the words to begin.

*When Life Made Sense*

*I've always wondered if the recollections I have of my mother, Kathryn, are real or simply dreams I've confused with memories. I recall a tall woman with light brown hair and sad hazel eyes.*

*My most vivid memory is of her holding me after I'd fallen and skinned my knees. I couldn't have been older than four. What I was running to, or away from, I don't recall, but down I went on all fours into the dirt. The recollection is too vague to feel the pain, but I do remember crying out, and then familiar arms lifting me. She held me close, and whispered in my ear, "Mommy will make it all better."*

*She takes me into the big house, washes my hands and knees, applies a healing spray then sits and rocks me back and forth humming a melody I've long forgotten.*

*I'm sure I loved her, and I'm sure I was happy. Although the scene is fuzzy, I still remember the feeling as she took care of me: safe. Nothing could hurt me as long as she was there.*

*I was five, almost six when she died, but it's a day I've blocked from my mind. When I was old enough to understand, Grandma told me I was the one who found her… in the bathtub with her wrists slit. She must have known I'd be the one to find her, so she staged her death in a way that wouldn't upset me. The faucet was along the long wall, with the drain at the narrow end, so she positioned herself sideways in the tub, her hands tucked under her head and over the drain. The water ran slowly, washing away the blood as it pumped from her body. How considerate of her. My grandmother said I came to her room, and casually told her Mommy was asleep in the bathtub and wouldn't wake up.*

*Once I realized my mother was gone, I cried for days, but then resigned myself that she would never come back and rarely mentioned her again. The truth is, I thought about her a lot, wondering where she had gone. But when I saw how her death upset my grandmother, I kept the wonderings to myself, not wanting to add to her pain.*

*There was a time as I grew older that I resented her for leaving, but then came to understand it had nothing to do with me, and eventually forgave her. Today, I'm sad to think she was in so much agony that she felt leaving this life, and me behind, was her only option. I regret never having the opportunity to know her, but my biggest sorrow is that she never had the chance to know me. Maybe if she had hung on a little longer, I could have helped her.*

*Unfortunately, I don't remember my father, Roger, at all. He was sent to work in the mines when I was barely two and died shortly after that. His death was the reason my mother lost hope. Apparently, she had always suffered from depression, and my father was the one thing she counted on for survival and without him, she couldn't find a way to go on.*

*History lessons taught us that when the people of Earth were first brought to Zantia, many died by suicide, but as time passed, people found reasons to live again. Humans rarely took their own lives anymore, choosing instead to ensure our race survives, probably because Zantians came to realize that granting some fundamental freedoms gave us hope. Our captors also allowed us to study our planet's history, so it was easier to believe survival was possible.*

Leea paused and let the words she'd just keyed sink in. Did her race truly want to survive? She hoped so. Humans didn't know what was left on Earth, and if the Zantians did, they wouldn't say. So, if her species wanted to rebuild, the Humans on Zantia needed to endure for as long as it took until they could regain their independence.

*My mother's death left me with only my grandmother, Sara. Although she was my only true family, others took me under their wings. Julia is seven years older than me and was always like my big sister. From the time I could walk, I followed her everywhere. Some of my favorite childhood memories include Julia—playing with her, reading with her, and lots of laughter.*

*Julia's mom tried her best to be like a mother to me, including me in most things Julia did. She was our teacher and our caregiver, and I loved her, but at the end of the day, I always wanted Grandma. She was the one who tucked me into bed at night, held me when I was sad and chased the monsters from my dreams.*

When Leea finished the first segment, she felt exhausted and laid her head down on the table. Reliving the past wasn't as easy as she thought it would be. She was suddenly heartsick over her mother's death—an emotion she hadn't felt in a long time.

She did have to admit, though, that it felt good to put it all into words. Focusing on the memories, happy or sad, brought them close enough to touch, which made her anxious to continue. She yawned. The writing would have to wait until tomorrow. She powered off the pad, got ready for bed, and was asleep soon after her head hit the pillow.

The next morning, Leea woke up feeling more rested than she had in over a week. She washed and dressed, and finished just in time for Mearos to arrive with the morning meal.

"You look relaxed today, you must have slept well," he observed.

"I spent all evening writing and completely forgot about the time until my brain was exhausted. Sleep came easily."

"I'm glad. So the datapad worked well?"

"Perfectly. Thanks again for bringing it."

"Before we land, I'll bring you a data-cube. I'm not sure if you'll need one, but just in case."

"That would be great. It'll be easier to transfer the file to a cube instead of my pad."

"We have plenty of them laying around. Once you leave the ship, I'll wipe the pad clean and return it to storage. No one will be the wiser."

She thanked him again, and Mearos returned to his duties.

*The first time I ever spoke to Yaran was the day of my mother's remembrance. Zantians don't bury their dead, they believe when you die you're simply gone, so they see no reason to preserve what no longer exists. Bodies, Zantian, and Human alike are cremated and the ashes discarded.*

*Dr. Benjamin, who lived in the city's worker-complex, also doubled as the minister and presided over my mother's service. I had seen Doc a few times as a child, but never in the capacity of a minister. Religious services were held in the compound, but we had never attended one because work schedules wouldn't allow it.*

*All remembrances took place at the bluff with the entire Human staff in attendance. I don't remember the words Doc spoke that day, only the sad faces looming around me. Many of the women, including my grandmother, shed silent tears as they honored Kathryn's life. When the formal service ended,*

*Grandma took a thin, delicate glass container which held her daughter's ashes and threw it over the edge into the abyss where it shattered on impact, scattering the contents to the wind.*

*After that, people gathered around, expressing their sympathies, but I soon lost interest and wandered away, leaving my grandmother to deal with the adults. I hadn't seen Julia in a while and went to find her. As I started along the path, I noticed Yaran standing a short distance ahead, partially obscured by a scraggly bush.*

*I passed him every day in the house and had to admit he fascinated me. Zantians as a whole are not a boisterous race, but Yaran seemed exceptionally reserved which often made me wonder what he was thinking. The adults who lived there, as well as those who visited, rarely acknowledged Human workers unless they needed something. But Yaran was different. He always treated us with respect, said "please" and "thank you," and, much to his father's disapproval sometimes took his dishes to the kitchen.*

*At times I felt that he was watching me, but assumed it was just my imagination. He would tell me years later that he did seek me out, especially after my mother's death because he had appointed himself my protector.*

*That day on the path, all I wanted was to be his friend because he was always alone. I knew he had just passed his eleventh birthday, and often wondered if he had any friends. As I headed toward him, he quickly left his hiding place and started to leave. At his young age, he was already an attractive boy, foreshadowing the handsome man he would become. His hair was long, tied at the nape of his neck like his father's, something he would change after his transition year.*

*"Don't go," I called to him. "It's okay if you stay."*

*He stopped and turned but remained silent.*

*"I'm going to go find Julia. Do you want to come along?"*

*He studied me a moment, then flashed a smile. "I'm not allowed," he said and hurried back to the house.*

Leea sat back as a big grin lit her face. After twenty years, that memory was still clear in her mind. Yaran's smile had made the sadness of the day seem a little more bearable. Years later, after they became close friends, she had thanked him for the momentary reprieve.

*After that, I became more aware of Yaran and went out of my way to see him. Looking back now, I was acting like a young girl completely infatuated* with an older boy—which, of course, I was. Even Julia noticed and became irritated with me about it on more than one occasion.

Almost five years after my mother's death, we were out studying plants for one of our lessons, and on our way back from the gardens, I saw Yaran leave the house.

"I want to go back outside," I told Julia as nonchalantly as I could, once we'd put our things away.

"Why?"

"I just do."

"You saw Yaran leave, and now you want to go see where he went," she said with an accusatory tone.

"No! That's not it at all."

"Well, I don't want to, so if you want to follow him, be my guest." She stomped off.

I stood there not knowing what to do. I did want to see where Yaran had gone, but I didn't want Julia to be mad at me so I decided I would take a quick walk outside. Maybe he was already back, and it wouldn't matter.

I took the path into the gardens, which at that time of day were shadowed by the house, and soon realized it had been a bad idea. I never ventured into the gardens alone because the shadows scared me. I hadn't seen Yaran, and the stillness of the place was making me jumpy, so when I reached the end of the first path, I decided to go back.

I turned around and screamed. Yaran stood a few yards behind me.

He startled. "I'm sorry, I didn't mean to frighten you," he apologized.

"Are you following me?" I snapped, not wanting him to get the idea I was actually following him.

"No," he answered, shocked at the accusation. "I saw you come in here. I was wondering where you were going, that's all."

"Well, I planned on going for a walk but changed my mind." I pushed past him, mortified at my foolishness.

"Don't go. It's okay if you stay."

Involuntarily, I smiled, remembering the words I'd said to him that day at my mother's remembrance. I turned but continued to step backward, "I'm not allowed," I stated with a big grin, and ran back to the house.

After that day, we sought opportunities to expand our conversations, and by the time I turned fourteen, a special friendship had blossomed between us.

"So how are the memoirs coming along?" Mearos asked as they sat eating at the work-desk. A few days after she'd started her story, he had brought an extra chair along with his own meal and now spent time with her most evenings.

"Better than I expected. But I think I spend more time daydreaming about events than actually writing them down."

"So, tell me something about your life in the ruling house."

"What would you like to know? My life was fairly commonplace. When you work every day and are pretty much confined to the house, not a whole lot of exciting things happen."

"Oh come on, from what little I know about you, you don't strike me as someone who always plays by the rules. You were in love with the Desolk's son. That alone is anything but ordinary."

"True enough," Leea chuckled. "But our relationship was more like a game of hide-and-seek. We were always hiding from prying eyes."

"Keeping something like that a secret couldn't have been easy. Did you ever get caught?"

"No, but we came close a few times. Once by his aunt in the greenhouse, once by his father in the library, and another time by a worker." She sighed. "It's amazing how in such a big house with so few people there is no place to be alone… except in our rooms, of course." Leea lowered her eyes and blushed.

Mearos visibly struggled to suppress a grin. "What was your favorite place in the house?"

"I loved the atrium. It's a large room in the center of the house where an abundance of plants and small trees grow. It's open all the way through the buildings three stories to a glass ceiling.

"The air was filtered into the room through a cooling system and then through specially designed tiles along the base of the wall that somehow produced moisture. The effect was like a cool sunny day, and the humidity is what it must feel like to sit be a lake. I'm not sure how it all worked, but we all loved it. The staff was allowed time in there to lounge in the many chairs and benches during our afternoon rest period.

"But the most breathtaking room was the library." Leea described the paintings, the bookshelves, and the various artifacts including those in the two enclosed cabinets.

"Sounds like a remarkable collection."

"Oh, it is. I find it hard to imagine the people who created such beautiful things…even harder to believe such places actually exist."

"Not every place is like Zantia. Each planet out there is unique."

"Have you been to other worlds?"

"No. Unfortunately, my travels only take me to Dekarra. Maybe someday I'll get a chance to visit other places."

Leea looked down at her hands. "Will I like it there?" she asked hesitantly.

"I'm not supposed to tell you anything about their world. The Dekarrans want that honor for themselves. But I guarantee you that everything will be all right."

They sat quietly for a moment.

"How long have you been captain of this ship?" Leea asked.

"A little over fifteen years."

"Did you start right after crossover?"

A strange look passed briefly across Mearos's face. "Strict adherence to crossover is only practiced by the children of families in higher positions. The concept was created for them. Ordinary people aren't quite so stringent about it. I finished my education by the time I was twenty-two, including my pilot training. I had a few odd jobs but came to Alrack because an opportunity presented itself. I became copilot to an aging captain, and once I knew my way around, the job was mine. I've been doing this run ever since."

"What's the size of your crew?"

"Only six: me, my co-pilot, a navigator, a systems specialist, and two crewmen who monitor the cargo. This is our standard crew size unless we're carrying nothing but volatile cargo, in which case I'll add an extra man or two."

"Who prepares the food?"

"We do our own cooking and cleaning, which some days can be good, some days bad," he chuckled.

Leea raised her eyebrows.

"This is not a glamorous job. Running cargo can be dangerous, dirty, and honestly…boring."

"Do you have women crew members?"

"I can't imagine any woman wanting this kind of life. I've heard of a few ships where the mate of a crewman travels along, but none that flies out of Alrack."

"Do you have a mate?"

Mearos paused reflectively. "No. I came close once."

"I'm sorry."

"It was years ago," he said sadly, but continued. "Selane and I had talked about mating, but one day I returned from my cargo run, and she was gone. She left me a message saying she was leaving to be with family but didn't say when she would return. I made two more runs before I finally had to admit to myself she wasn't coming back."

"I am so sorry."

"The worst part was not knowing exactly why she left. It made it hard to move on. But, as I said, that was a long time ago."

"Did you ever go looking for her?"

"I considered it. Thought maybe something happened to her. But the truth was, I didn't know she had any family. She had told me her parents were gone and that she didn't have any siblings. So, I had no idea where to start."

Leea's heart went out to him. "And you never found anyone else?"

"No. Being the captain of a cargo ship makes it hard to have a relationship with someone unless they enjoy spending a lot of time alone. Not many women want that."

"Well, don't give up, I'm sure someday you'll find the right person."

"I'm happy to see optimism returning," he said lightheartedly. "I can assure you, if the right woman comes along, I won't send her away."

# CHAPTER 8

# End of a Journey

*I* don't remember exactly when I fell in love with Yaran. It wasn't a bolt of lightning that struck me one day, rather the sudden realization that I couldn't imagine my life without him. He had been away with the Desolk for two weeks, and my heart ached every day at not seeing him. I finally had to admit that what I had always insisted was friendship, had grown into something much more. I was seventeen, and strangely, that revelation scared me.

When he returned, I was still trying to come to terms with my feelings, so I shut him out which made things tense between us because I knew I was hurting him. When I confided in Julia, she laughed and asked what took me so long to figure it out. But once she realized I was truly confused about what to do, we spent many long hours talking, and me crying. Finally, she convinced me not to worry about what the future held. I should tell him how I felt and let fate take care of the rest. So, I followed her advice.

I had avoided Yaran for a little over a week by taking on extra duties and then claiming to be too tired. A couple of days I claimed to be ill. I hated deceiving him, and even worse, I hated the expression on his face every time I made another excuse.

But then the day came when I couldn't take it anymore. As always, Yaran was in the music room during our afternoon rest period, so I made my way through the garden toward the wing's side entrance. I heard him playing as I approached, and hesitated before entering.

In all the years Yaran and I had been friends, I had told him everything, and shared my innermost feelings and fears without hesitation. But there I stood, so nervous because I was about to tell my longtime friend that I not only loved him but was in love with him. It should have been the easiest thing in the world, but I could barely breathe at the thought of saying those words.

Gathering my courage, I silently entered, stopping in the small foyer. A door to the left went into the art room, and an archway straight ahead led to the music hall where Yaran stood in front of the choU, an instrument I had never seen him play before. His hands flew over vertically-aligned round keys, brightening in different colors as he touched them. He also played a piece I didn't recognize—the tone angry and the rhythm intense, making me wonder if it was being fueled by his emotions.

His eyes were closed, and there was no mistaking the tightness in his jaw, but I gathered the remnants of my courage and passed through the entry, moving to stand just out of his field of vision. I wasn't sure if he sensed my presence, or had seen me enter, but his hands suddenly stopped.

"Did you just come to listen, or is there something you need to say?" he asked without turning.

The pain and anger in his voice startled me, and I took an involuntary step back. Had I gone too far? I wanted to turn and run, but of course, I couldn't because I had come to say something. I took a few steps further into the room.

"I'm sorry that I've been so distant lately. I've had a lot on my mind."

"And now, after avoiding me for a week, you feel you can talk to me again?" He came toward me, stopping a few feet away, his dark eyes searching my face.

"I… I deserve that. But I had a decision to make, and I… I didn't know how to deal with it. I needed to think… without distraction. Again, I'm sorry."

"What decision would you need to make that you couldn't discuss with me?" He took a few steps closer, his tone softening. "I thought we told each other everything."

"We did… do, but this was something… something I had to work out for myself. I had to be sure before I said anything."

"Sure about what?"

"That my feelings for you have changed." I knew the minute I spoke those words that they were all wrong. By the expression that crossed Yaran's face, I knew he'd misunderstood.

"That's not what I meant!" I quickly closed the distance between us and grabbed both his arms and looked into his eyes. "Yes, my feelings for you have changed. It seems I've finally realized that I… that I'm… in love with you." The last words were barely above a whisper.

At first, I thought I'd spoken too softly, and he hadn't heard. Confusion crossed his face. I was about to repeat myself when he pulled me into his arms and kissed me. Yaran had often kissed my forehead or cheek, but this was a *sensation I wasn't prepared for. At first, our lips barely touched, and then the pressure intensified. If my heart had been beating fast before, now it was ready to explode. The feeling of being in Yaran's arms, with his lips pressing against mine, was the most incredible thing I'd ever felt. I never wanted it to end.*

Leea pushed the chair back and lowered her head to the desktop. Tears dripped onto the hard surface as she tried to control her sobs. She closed her eyes, imagining Yaran's kiss—sometimes as gentle as a warm breeze, other times hard, demanding, wanting more. How was she going to make it through the rest of her life knowing she might never feel that again?

"I will feel it again," she declared forcefully. "I will!" She whisked the tears away, took a quick break, and repositioned herself at the desk.

*When our lips finally parted, we stood in the middle of the room, our arms unwilling to let the other go. "Why didn't you tell me this sooner?" Yaran whispered.*

*"I only found out last week," I chuckled.*

*He chuckled as well, then leaned back and tilted my chin. A smile now brightened his face, and his eyes had lightened. My heart warmed at the transformation, but it still beat strongly with anticipation.*

*"I have waited a long time for this day," he said almost absentmindedly, then seeing my confusion, he laughed. "In case you hadn't noticed, I fell in love with you on the day of your mother's remembrance."*

*"What?"*

*"On a day which should have been the saddest of your life, you went out of your way to include me—someone who had no business intruding."*

*I stared at him in disbelief. "You may be older than me, but you couldn't have felt that way back then."*

*"Oh, but I did. I sensed that day on the path that you were different from anyone I would ever meet, and someone I wanted to know. And as we got to know each other, I knew I wanted you in my life…forever."*

*After that, the hardest part was keeping our feelings to ourselves.*

"How are you feeling today?" Mearos asked as he did every day while they sat eating at the work-desk.

"You know, you ask me that every day, and I always say I'm fine, but today I'm not doing so well."

"In what way?"

"Well, I've had a headache for a couple of days although it's nothing serious. It comes and goes. Also, I'm feeling a bit sluggish. It was hard getting up this morning."

"You should have told me. There is a reason I ask every day."

"There is?"

"I apologize for not giving you this sooner." He pulled a flat container, five inches' square, from his shirt pocket, and handed it to her. Inside were two compartments, one filled with crushed white leaves, and the other with a fine red powder.

"What are they?"

"Herbs. Add a pinch of the white leaves to your morning tea. They are mildly sweet and will help with the headache. The red powder is flavorless. Mix it sometime during the day with water. They will help with the sluggishness."

"Is there something wrong with me?"

"Oh no. The atmospheric pressure and gravity are slightly higher on Dekarra. Once we're out of the Zantian solar system, we slowly start to adjust the ship so that by the time we reach our destination we've adjusted to their environment. There, the doctors will be able to give you something more permanent to help with the change."

"I'm going to have to take medication the rest of my life?"

Mearos chuckled. "Everyone reacts differently, so you'll have to wait and see. But it shouldn't be anything to worry about."

They sat in silence for a few minutes, continuing their meal.

"Doesn't anyone miss you when you're down here?"

"No. My policy has always been to eat by myself. We have a tradition of eating together on the first and last night of the journey, but other than that, I eat in my quarters. It's mostly because it gives me time to update the logs and just relax a bit."

"I don't want to cause you any trouble. Don't feel obligated to keep me company."

He smiled. "I'm not here out of obligation. Most of the men who've stayed in this room welcomed the solitude. And the rules state, I'm to limit my interaction with the escapees to bringing meals. But to be honest, I felt I needed to make an exception with you."

"Why?"

"The others were here because they wanted to be, you were not. You were so distraught when you came aboard so I couldn't bring myself to leave you alone until I knew you'd be all right. Now that I do, I find I've come to enjoy our daily conversations."

Leea studied him for a moment. "Thank you. Do you really think I'll be okay?"

"I do. You are stronger than you think. But if you'd rather I didn't stay, you need to tell me."

"No. I enjoy your company as well. I'm not used to being by myself. At first, I wanted to be, but being alone gives me too much time to dwell on things. Between this," she gestured to the work-desk, "and your visits, I think I'll make it through this journey in one piece."

"I have no doubt you will."

Leea finished her meal and leaned back. "Tell me what you do all day on this ship of yours?"

"Oh, it's pretty boring."

"You've mentioned that before, but I don't believe it. You travel across space every few months. I can't imagine you would if it were boring."

"No, I suppose not," he said between mouthfuls. "But by most people's standards, it is. On the flight between Zantia to Dekarra, there is a lot more to do than on the return trip. The cargo needs to be checked several times a day. Some containers are under pressure, and those numbers need to be kept constant. Any number of things can bring them out of balance which would be catastrophic if that's not caught in time. Some of the containers emit a gas which has to be vented into space, so those levels are monitored. Of course, we have instrumentation for all that, but once a day I insist on manual checks as well."

"Why?"

"If you could look outside and see the ship hurtling through space, you would probably think nothing can harm us. But that's not entirely accurate. Many things are floating out there that could penetrate the hull."

"Gr... great," Leea stammered, wide-eyed.

Mearos chuckled. "Not to worry, the space around us is continuously analyzed and the checks I insist upon are for those things our instruments might miss... not that that has ever happened. We always scan for the obvious: meteor showers, comets. But mostly we're interested in unexpected things: debris, shockwaves, radiation spikes, things like that. The ship is protected from small elements by a special electrically charged coating on the hull. But our instruments have a limited range, so we also have remote sensors which scout the way for us."

"Remote sensors?"

"Useful little inventions. Once we leave the planet's orbit, we launch a dozen of them ahead of us. They are about two feet in diameter and travel faster than the ship. During our four-week journey, they gain about two days' time on us. They each take a slightly different route and regularly send data back. If they transmit something that doesn't look right, we can concentrate our efforts in that direction, and take appropriate action."

"Has there ever been a problem?"

"Only once. We were on our way back to Zantia when four of the sensors started to malfunction. We were instantly on edge. We slowed the ship, and slightly altered our course, but weren't able to completely avoid what I can only describe as a dust storm moving at an incredible speed.

"Some unknown object out there must have experienced a catastrophic event which totally destroyed it. If we hadn't had the advanced warning, we would have hit the cloud head-on, and it most likely would have pulverized us as well."

Leea stared at him wide eyed.

"It was incredible, though. We were pretty close to the Zantian system and had a full view of the sun. As we bounced along the edge, the light from behind made the dust particles sparkle in different colors. We were able to get some remarkable images of the phenomenon."

"Well, as exciting as that sounds, I'm happy to make this trip as uneventful as possible."

Mearos smiled. "I will try to accommodate as best I can."


*Leea ran through the garden trying to get away. She turned and saw Yaran chasing her, and giggled. Just then, her foot caught something on the ground, and she went down on all fours. The fall didn't hurt, but she started to cry. Two strong arms picked her up and held her close, making her feel safe. He began humming a familiar tune, and she relaxed.*

*Suddenly, he was gone, and she was alone in the house walking cautiously down the hall until a familiar door loomed ahead. She was about to enter when it opened, and Yaran stepped out, closing it behind him and blocking her entrance.*

*"You can't go in there, Leea," he said.*

*"But I need to." She tried to push past him.*

*"You're not safe in there."*

*"You have to let me see." She tried to push past him again, but he held her in place. "No!" she screamed, "I have to go in! Please, I have to go in!"*

*As she struggled, he again hummed the tune. "It's important to keep you safe. I won't let anything happen to you." She relaxed into him and let him lead her away.*

Leea came awake with a start and sat up, trying to clear her head. *These writings must be affecting me more than I thought,* she rationalized. She couldn't be sure, but the room seemed to be about her mother. That episode in her life had been buried in the depths of her subconscious for twenty years, and she wasn't ready for that to change. The last thing she needed was something else to be sad about.

She took a drink of water and tucked herself back into bed, hoping Yaran would visit her again.

*It had been six months since I stood in the music room and declared my love for Yaran. While we found moments to share a few passionate kisses and caresses, our time alone had been limited due to his busy schedule. But we realized from these brief encounters that we wanted more—our bodies demanded it.*

*I confided in Julia one day, then the proud mother of one-month-old Marta, about my growing feelings. With a big smile, she admitted having noticed the subtle yet telling glances between us. When I told her we wanted desperately to be together—physically—she did her sisterly duty and told me what I might expect on the first night, and then took me to see Dr. Benjamin, who assured me I was healthy in every way.*

*Because it's an easier process, men on Zantian are responsible for birth control. A painless injection once every three months ensures there were no unwanted pregnancies. A few weeks before our first night together, Yaran told me, with a sly smile, that he'd visited the medical facility. I didn't need to ask why, but I remember feeling my cheeks warm and Yaran's resulting laughter, followed by a passionate kiss.*

*"That's not nice," I'd chastised him lightheartedly, trying to catch my breath. But all he did was flash the playful smile which always melted my heart.*

*We had made specific plans on how we wanted our first night to be, which included waking up together in the morning. This, of course, would require his family to be away. On those infrequent times when everyone was gone, and Yaran was able to stay home, he never required the staff to fix a morning meal for him, preferring to make something for himself instead, which meant none of the workers needed to get up early.*

*So we waited patiently, or not so patiently until the day finally came.*

*The monthly council meeting was being held in Calthena, and the Desolk planned to be there for several days. Since it was her childhood home, Lauranna accompanied him to visit her family, and Toref and Cassa left for an overnight stay with friends. During our evening meal, I told Grandma I would be staying the night with Julia, which I often did, especially since Marta was born, and Julia, of course, knew where I would be.*

*My heart beat wildly with anticipation as I stood outside the door of the man I longed for, imagining the night to come. I took a deep breath and knocked softly. The door opened immediately, and my pulse quickened at the sight of him. Soft exotic music played in the background, but I quickly drowned it out and focused on him. Without saying a word, or taking my eyes from his, I walked into his arms.*

*We shared a passionate kiss until we were both panting for air. He let his mouth travel to the base of my neck, and one hand down my back, pulling me tightly to him. I moaned softly at the feel of his body.*

*After a long moment, Yaran scooped me up and carried me to his large bed, gently lowering us down where, between passionate kisses, we managed to shed our clothes. Feeling his naked body against mine for the first time was the most sensuous thing I'd ever felt—even to this day—and it made my head spin. We were then completely lost in the discovery of each other, sometimes awkward and clumsy, but never uncertain, until we found our own special rhythm.*

*When it was impossible for either of us to wait any longer, our bodies gently but urgently joined. That incredible feeling made me forget the world around us: the separate lives we led, and the fact that our forbidden love could someday be in jeopardy. I was completely lost in my love for him, and right then nothing else mattered. When the crescendo of our union abated, we clung to each other in awe, never wanting to let go.*

*"I want to stay here with you forever," I professed a short time later, contentedly wrapped in his arms.*

*He kissed my forehead. "Nothing would make me happier. But I'm not sure I could ever be happier than I am at this moment."*

*We made love twice more that night, never finding the time to sleep. One thing we discovered through that amazing experience was that we were truly meant to be together. We had both opened our heart, body, and soul and let the other ease in completely as if it were the most natural thing in the world.*

*As the sun began to rise, Yaran left me snuggled in his soft blankets and made us a wonderful meal, which we ate leisurely in the shade on his private terrace. My grandmother had often used the word soulmate when she spoke of my grandfather. I finally understood what that meant.*

Leea sat back as tears blurred her vision. Regardless of the forbidden nature of their relationship, she knew without a shadow of a doubt that Yaran was her soulmate and that she was intended to spend the rest of her life with him. A sob escaped as her hands covered her face. Unable to continue, the grieving woman blindly found the cot and let the sorrow run its course.

She questioned her eagerness to document the life she'd left behind, never considering the amount of pain and loss it would bring to the surface. But as the tears subsided, Leea vowed to continue. She rationalized that one day she'd be able to read through these and marvel at the life she once had.

"How would you like to get out of this room?" Mearos asked during the evening meal, three days before reaching Dekarra.

"Um … sure. Where would we go?"

"I'd like to surprise you."

"Okay," she agreed hesitantly.

"Wonderful. I'll be back after the crew starts the sleep period."

As promised, he returned about four hours later looking conspiratorial. "Ready?"

"Yes."

He slid the door open, let her cross into the storage area, and resealed it behind them. Over two dozen containers, each six feet wide and ten feet high, lined the walls on each side, locked into place along a floor rail. Lighted control panels were attached to the first half, showing several green or yellow flashing lights and text scrolling across narrow displays, some giving an occasional beep. Three of the boxes on her right had a large tube protruding from the top which disappeared through the bulkhead.

"These are all full," Mearos explained. "The ones with the large duct at the top hold volatile substances which are strictly monitored; their gasses vented into space at regulated intervals."

On her left, a wide area divided the containers from a half dozen others.

"These over here are empty," Mearos indicated the separate group. "We import more from Dekarra than we export, so we always bring empty ones with us. There is also a smaller hold at the forward end of the ship. This way." He guided her into the short corridor between the containers, which ended at a passenger door with a large porthole.

"I thought, since we are out here in deep space, you might want to see what it looks like." Mearos stepped aside and motioned her to the entry.

Leea gingerly approached, stopping about a foot away. She craned her neck to see through the thick glass.

"You can move closer," Mearos chuckled. "The door is secure. There's no chance it will open."

Leea rested her hands on each side of the window and leaned into the glass, expecting to find vast empty space with lots of stars like she saw in the Alrack night sky. But what presented itself was entirely different. Against the black backdrop, the stars appeared three times the size she was used to, and there seemed to be a hundred times as many. In some areas, the light of the suns completely blocked the dark void.

"It's so bright," she said with wonder.

"The sky looks completely different when you're not viewing it through an atmosphere. I waited until today to bring you here because we can now see the Irlin Nebulae, which will be visible until we reach the Dekarran solar system. Look to your left."

The dense cloud of the large nebulae loomed brightly ahead. It was interlaced with vibrant blues and greens alongside reds and purples. The center of the mass was a white swirl with a half dozen tendrils extending in all directions to the outside edge. Within the entire phenomenon, sprinkled randomly, were several twinkling stars.

"It's beautiful," Leea whispered, mesmerized.

"Keep watching. One more surprise. It might take a few minutes."

Leea concentrated on the colorful display, marveling at how something so stunning could exist in the spatial void. After a short time, one of the cloud's arms started to change to a muted red, the color slowly spreading upward.

"Now, concentrate on the bottom corner."

Barely visible, the arm seemed to eject a stream of red, much like a solar flare shooting from the surface of a sun. It was only visible for a moment before dissipating.

"What was that?"

"We have no idea. The first time we encountered it, one of our remote sensors picked it up, and we thought it might be an exploding star. Over the years, we've discovered it happens at regular intervals, so it's a mystery. But it is spectacular to see in person. It would be interesting to get a closer view, but Zantians aren't much for exploration."

"Thank you for showing me this. No wonder you enjoy making this trip." Hesitantly, she stepped back and faced him. "I never imagined what amazing things might be out here, away from the drabness of Zantia."

"It's a vast universe, Leea. Everywhere you go is different…this is just one of those places."

She took one last glimpse before turning away. "Thank you, again."

A Zantian crewman stepped from the shadows and watched as the captain closed the hatch behind him at the top of the stairs. A smile played on his lips but didn't quite form. He walked to the empty wall Mearos had just passed through, and rested a hand on the cold steel. The outline of the door appeared, but he quickly moved away.

"Not today."

Instead, he made his way to the porthole and placed his hands on both sides of the window as Leea had done, but without looking out. A barely noticeable flutter crossed his eyes, and in one imperceptible motion, the figure's features rearranged themselves, and the tall man was replaced by the figure of Leea. It stepped back, looked at its female hands, turning them over and over, and then observed the reflection in the glass. The duplicate moved its head side to side, running fingers through the auburn hair, pulling at the long curls.

"Well," a whispery voice said, and then smiled, "this just might be useful."

The form of the Zantian crewman returned and made its way to the forward staircase.

As the final days passed, Leea continued to write about her life, trying to capture the memorable moments. Many made her laugh, but in the end, most made her cry as she realized they were now all part of a past she would forever long for. She hoped the Dekarrans were nice people and would allow her to live a quiet life. All she wanted was to find a way to fulfill the promise she made to herself—to one-day return to Yaran.

The day before landing, Mearos brought her a new data-cube. The white, glass object wasn't actually a square, but a two-inch rounded rectangle with a flat bottom. It not only held data but some models could also be used as a voice and/or video recorder. Leea laid the cube on the work-desk, and once the pad recognized it, she pushed a button on the screen to copy all files from the pad.

She ate her last evening meal alone since Mearos was following his tradition of eating with his crew. But, she preferred it that way since her mind was racing with thoughts about what the next day would bring, and she doubted she'd be good company. She had become accustomed to her solitary life on board the ship and almost viewed the upcoming change as an intrusion.

"We will be arriving shortly," Mearos said, bringing her morning meal earlier than usual. "How are you feeling? You look a little pale this morning. Are the herbs working?"

"They're working fine. It's just nerves. I'll be glad to get off this ship, though. I'm looking forward to breathing some fresh air."

Mearos laughed. "No matter how many of these trips I've made, I, too, look forward to something besides recycled air." His expression turned somber. "After we land, you will need to wait until the cargo is unloaded. Then someone will come for you."

"Someone?"

"My part in your journey is over." He tried to give her a reassuring smile. "From here on, the Dekarrans will take care of you."

Panic flashed in Leea's eyes. Noticing, Mearos placed both hands on her shoulders.

"There is nothing to fear. You will have a good life here."

"I'll survive, of that I'm sure. But what would have made my life good, I left on Zantia."

"You told me once that your grandmother always said never to let the past keep you from living today. I'd hate to think you're not going to listen to her advice."

"Oh, I'll live my life as best I can. I have to. Otherwise, all of this will have been for nothing."

"I have no doubt you will. Live well, Leea."

She threw her arms around his neck catching him off guard, and he hesitantly returned the embrace. After a few seconds, she stepped back, eyes glistening with tears. "Thank you for everything. Your kindness made these weeks bearable."

"You are welcome." He flashed a crooked smile. "I will always think of this as one of my most memorable trips."

"Should you ever see Yaran … ?" Leea lowered her eyes, blushing.

"I'll tell him you made it safely."

With renewed grief, Leea watched the door seal behind him. Mearos was her last link to the world she left behind, and while she wasn't ready to let that go, she was relieved to have the goodbyes finally over.

Hoping to stop the shaking which was slowly overtaking her body, Leea paced in the small space. She didn't know what was worse: the waiting, or the fear of what would happen once the waiting was over. After a few minutes, the pacing seemed a fruitless effort, so she lay down on the cot and closed her eyes.

She slowly became aware of the silence. Gone was the low hum of the engines, which had been a constant background noise these past weeks. They had landed. Carefully, she opened her eyes and blinked a few times to clear her vision. She sensed the presence before she saw it—an unidentifiable figure standing just inside the doorway. Mearos had told her to expect someone, but she wasn't prepared for the fear that immediately gripped her. The captain had reassured her she would be safe, and there was no reason to doubt him, but suddenly facing this stranger—this alien—was overwhelming.

Fear turned to panic as the figure slowly started toward her—its head and body completely covered in a long brown robe.

"Please don't be afraid. I won't harm you." A soothing female voice spoke her language, so Leea instantly relaxed. She sat up facing the alien woman.

"My name is Bettina. I'm here to introduce you to your new home."

"Why are you dressed like that?"

"We keep our identity a secret until we know it's safe to reveal it."

"You don't feel safe with me?"

The woman chuckled. "I feel perfectly safe with you, Leea." Reaching into the folds of her robe, she pulled out a similar one, handing it to the new arrival. "Please, put this on." Leea took the garment while Bettina offered an explanation. "We conceal our identities from the Zantians for protection. I must conceal yours for the same reason."

Leea guessed the alien to be Julia's size—a little over five feet—but she couldn't determine anything else under the billowing garment. Once her own robe was on and fastened, Bettina reached up and adjusted the hood, making sure she was fully covered. The strange fabric allowed her to see out without obstruction, but looking at Bettina, she couldn't see in. When everything seemed to her liking, the escort took Leea's arm and guided her into the cargo area.

"My bag—" Leea looked around.

"Don't worry. I had Mearos take it to a protected area. We'll get it later."

They ascended to the ship's main deck and moved along a narrow corridor until they reached an open door leading to an enclosed walkway. Leea could see the terminal on the other side and paused before stepping out. Beyond this short access bridge awaited her new life, and crossing the threshold would seal her fate. The finality of the next step terrified her, but there was no turning back, and no other choice. So, with one foot in front of the other, she reluctantly entered the next chapter of her life.

Mearos stayed out of sight and watched as Bettina led Leea away. He would miss her. Even under all her sadness, an interesting woman lay underneath whom he wished he could have gotten to know better. He envied Yaran the love she felt for him and truly hoped the couple would one day find their way back together. His experience with the pain of heartbreak made him sympathetic to their predicament.

He was glad he'd ignored the rules and spent time with her. At first, he'd made the exception because he worried about how she would handle the long isolation. But after the first week, he found he enjoyed their visits. He'd taken the chance she wouldn't ask too many questions, which she didn't, seeming happier to cling to what was left behind instead of worrying about what lay ahead.

His one real regret was that he hadn't been able to be truthful with her. Truthful about Dekarra and its people, about himself, but most of all, about the room where she'd just spent four weeks. Although he wanted to share more, in the end, the secrets stayed hidden—as they always did.

"Are Zantians allowed over here?" Leea asked Bettina as they stepped into a large area with unadorned white walls. The lobby had three open doorways leading to other rooms, but no windows.

"The crew can use this level of the terminal. There is a lounge, a bathroom with real showers, and we provide their meals. But they are not allowed anywhere else."

"So once we leave this floor, we no longer have to wear these robes?"

"We've had incidents where Zantians tried to roam into other areas, so as long as a Zantian ship is on our world, we keep ourselves covered here at the airfield."

Bettina guided her to an elevator halfway down an adjacent hall, which took them to an underground parking area. Cool air seeped through the fabric of the cover-up, and she involuntarily shivered.

"Are you all right?" the Dekarran asked.

"Yes."

"Let's get you to a more comfortable place so we can talk." She laid a gentle hand against Leea's back and guided her to a small white vehicle where another hooded figure sat on the left side of the front seat looking out the only window. It was smaller than a Zantian shuttle—fitting only four people—and shaped like an elongated dome. Four wheels and no visible engines told her it was only for ground transportation.

When both women were settled in the back seat, a glass panel rose between them and the driver. As the vehicle silently motored away, the divider faded to black.

They rode in relative silence until they reached what Bettina called the Inn. Parking underground again, they took an elevator to the sixth level where Leea was ushered into a room about the size of hers in Alrack. The absence of windows immediately caught her attention, and she wondered what the small alien woman was trying to hide.

"I'll leave you here to rest a bit. I'm sure you would like to clean up after your long trip in that small room."

"Yes, I would!"

Bettina showed her how the facilities worked so she could take a much-needed shower, and then quietly closed the door, leaving her alone. Out of curiosity, Leea tried the handle—locked.

Removing the robe, she laid it carefully over a chair in the corner and entered the washroom. For the first time in weeks, she took a good look at herself in a large mirror.

"You look terrible," she scolded the face looking back at her. Although the hidden room on the ship had had an adequate washing station, it did not allow for a bath or laundry. Everything needed to be washed in the sink, and the daily water supply was limited.

After spending longer than needed under the welcoming cascade of warm water and lathering twice with pleasantly fragrant soap, Leea wrapped herself in a large white bathrobe that hung behind the door and scanned her surroundings. She didn't remember seeing it on entering, but her travel bag sat on the large bed centered on one wall, opposite a low wooden cabinet with six drawers. A small desk with two chairs and a comfortable looking armchair near the entry completed the room. Clothing draped over the large chair wasn't there before either. Someone had apparently come in while she was in the shower.

On top of the cabinet stood a music player, similar to the ones used in Alrack. Pushing the start button, she watched unfamiliar titles scroll across the screen. She started the player and let it choose the tunes at random. The melodies were different, but she liked them.

She dressed in the oversized clothes: lightweight tan pants with a drawstring waist and a blue short-sleeved button shirt. Then, she sat down in the plush chair and waited. In what seemed like only a few minutes, there was a knock on the door, and the hooded figure of Bettina entered.

"I hope you've had a chance to freshen up?" she asked.

"Yes I did, thank you," Leea smiled. "The shower was extremely welcome."

"I can imagine. I'm also glad you found the clothes."

"Thank you again. They're a little big, but they're clean."

"Since we've only had men come off the cargo ship, these are all I have stored here."

"Don't apologize. They're fine."

"I'm sorry I'm still dressed like this. I want to reveal myself to you slowly, so I don't frighten you."

"I think that's what frightens me the most."

"I understand." Slowly Bettina pulled the hood away from her head, revealing short white-blonde hair, aqua blue eyes, and a reassuring smile.

"As you can see, Leea, you have nothing to fear from us. We are from Earth, just like you."

# PART 2

Dekarra

Earth Year - 2197

## CHAPTER 9

# New Haven

eea was stunned. Of all the things she had imagined, this wasn't one of them. From Earth? How was that possible?

"But how…?" she finally managed to say.

"I'm sorry for the shock. There's never an easy way to do that." Bettina removed her robe and pulled over a padded desk chair. She was in her mid to late thirties, smaller than Julia, although about the same height.

"Are you really Human? I mean…I don't doubt it…it's just that…I have so many questions I don't know where to begin."

Bettina flashed a reassuring smile. "Okay, let me answer the easy ones first. Yes, we are from Earth. Our ancestors came here a few years after the Zantian attack."

"How did you get here?"

"The people who came to this planet were from Earth's moon base, Atlantis. The Atlantis Project was a combined effort of a group called the United Alliance to build the first interstellar spaceships. Two years into the construction phase, the Zantians made first contact. If the aliens were aware of the efforts on the moon, no one ever knew, but those managing the project wanted to minimize the chances of discovery, so they ordered a communications blackout.

"When negotiations on Earth began to deteriorate, someone took a chance and sent the location of the alien's world, along with copied plans for a new propulsion system, to the base. That effort made it possible for them to come here. After the Zantian attack, the colonists quickly finished three of the ships while planning a trip to find their abducted kinsmen. They found this planet on the way, and knowing they were only a solar system away, decided to build a new home here, realizing that returning to Earth would be impossible."

"And now you take in escaping workers…one by one."

Bettina pursed her lips. "One day we will find a way to rescue them all. Until then, this is the best we can do." She rose from her chair. "Come. Let me show you our world. We'll have plenty of time to talk later."

The tiny woman moved to the far corner, where she activated a hidden screen. Making a quick input, the adjacent wall slowly became transparent, the reverse of what the dividing panel in the Dekarran vehicle had done. Another swipe and half the wall slid noiselessly to one side. Leea was confused by the darkness outside and reacted instantly as cool air enveloped her. She shivered, involuntarily hugging her arms and taking a step back.

"I'm so sorry," Bettina apologized. "I forgot the temperatures here are much cooler than on Zantia. I'll be right back." She left the room, returning after a few moments and handed Leea a sweater. "We keep a storage closet down the hall," she explained.

Slipping on the soft blue garment, warmth returned, and she moved cautiously to the door. "Is it always dark this early?"

Bettina chuckled. "Actually, it's late evening here. The cargo ship keeps to the Zantian time cycle, so upon arrival, it was morning for you, but here it was already evening."

"I wish Mearos had told me."

"We prefer that the ship's captain not share information about Dekarra. This way I can introduce myself to you when I think you're ready. He told you about the atmosphere and gravity, but only out of necessity."

The newcomer marveled at the sight that welcomed her. As far as the eye could see were tall buildings illuminated by hundreds of lighted windows. From the edge of the balcony, she looked down to a four-lane road with vehicles traveling in an orderly fashion, and wide sidewalks on both sides where people milled about against illuminated storefronts. She wished for daylight so she could see it all better.

"What is this city called?"

"It was christened New Haven. They believed it was a port in the storm, and provided a new beginning for them."

"Yes, I suppose it was." Now that the fear about the Dekarrans was gone, renewed sorrow gripped her. *Oh Yaran, I wish you were here. This is nothing like I imagined.* "Could we go in and just talk for a while? Unless you need to leave."

"No, my schedule is free until everything for you has been arranged. Come, we'll make ourselves comfortable inside and leave the door open to let in the evening air. I'll order up some tea and a light meal for you."

"That would be wonderful."

"So why did the Atlantis colonists come here? What were they hoping to accomplish?" Leea asked once the food arrived. Realizing she wasn't hungry, she set the sandwich aside for later but welcomed the warmth of the tea.

"At the time, they planned to rescue their people from the Zantians. But the long voyage took more out of them than they expected, and once here, they realized their simple plan would never work."

"And in over a hundred years that idea has been abandoned?"

"Not abandoned…merely postponed. We don't have the armaments or troops to launch such an offensive. We have an excellent history museum where everything is documented in much greater detail. But of course, it is limited to what the moon colonists knew. What actually brought on the attack, and abductions, is still a mystery."

Leea lowered her head and said shyly, "I know a little bit about what happened on Earth."

"You do?"

"The history of how we came to Zantia has also been carefully documented, but in stories passed down from one generation to the next. My great-great grandfather was an aide to the prime minister of a place called New Zealand. The prime minister was a member of the newly formed Earth Government, so he had firsthand knowledge of the negotiations."

Bettina looked at her excitedly. "I always hoped that one day someone would come with answers, but never believed it would happen."

"I don't know a lot, but I can tell you what I do know. The Zantians refused to negotiate with any one nation, so a new Earth Government was formed. It was difficult to bring the separate governments together in such a short time, but most everyone wanted what the aliens were willing to give. And what they were asking for in return seemed so minimal."

"Seeds for everything that grew on Earth, claiming nothing grew naturally on their planet." Bettina volunteered.

"Yes, and that's true. Indigenous plants on Zantia have very little nutritional value. But that's not the only thing they wanted. They are lovers of art and literature and proclaim themselves the only ones who can truly understand their beauty. At some point in the negotiations, Zantians started upping their demands. The seeds were easy, but when it came to the art, they demanded originals, not copies."

"That's crazy!"

"Not from their standpoint. And that's when things on Earth took a turn for the worse. While the government debated their current demands, the Zantians threw in a new request—they also wanted people. They explained that, because of their limited population, many tasks on their world went unfulfilled, so they needed people willing to work. The negotiators said they would ask for volunteers, but that was all they could do. The aliens threatened to call off the entire deal if Earth didn't agree to all of their terms. After a few days of private discussion, the delegates unanimously said no.

"And that's when they decided to destroy Earth? Eleven other ships hid somewhere nearby, apparently waiting for the final word."

"Eleven ships? Are you sure? Abducted Humans were brought on four overcrowded transports. The Zantians have verified that much."

"Well, maybe they're lying. But I guess it doesn't matter. Do you know how many were taken?"

"No, I don't think anyone does. Many Humans died during the long voyage, but I think thousands were dispersed throughout the cities and mines. Many couldn't adjust to the new world. Suicide was widespread in the first years, but slowly the abductees learned to adjust. I believe the Zantians learned to adjust to us and have tried to make our lives reasonably comfortable."

"You don't honestly believe that?" Bettina said in disbelief. "You've never talked to those who spent their entire lives in the mines; there's nothing *comfortable* about it at all."

Leea lowered her head and sighed. "I'm sorry, you're right. I do know how working the mines affects people and tears families apart."

"I'm sorry too. I didn't mean to suggest you didn't. I realize you're only telling the story as it was told to you. But you have to understand, because of your unique relationship with them, you probably have a different view of who the Zantians really are."

"I'm sure you're right. But you should know, many Zantians don't agree with what their ancestors did. Otherwise, I wouldn't be here."

"True enough. Maybe someday they'll all change. But until that happens, the people of Earth are being forced to work in horrible conditions against their will."

They sat a little while longer before Bettina got to her feet. "Well, I think we've talked enough for one night." She smiled. "It will take a few days for you to get used to the time change, but try and get some sleep anyway. I will be bringing the doctor tomorrow to start your examinations."

"Thank you for everything."

"You're welcome. Everything will be all right, Leea. It'll just take some time."

"I know."


Dawn brightened a teal blue sky as Leea watched the sleeping city come to life below her sixth-floor balcony. Unable to get much rest, she'd stepped outside and now marveled at the world around her, but also the unimaginable phenomenon of white clouds passing overhead. Clouds never reached Alrack, dissipating as soon they escaped the grip of the mountain range, but here they hung free and lazy like fluffy white pillows.

Sipping from a steaming cup of tea that Bettina had shown her how to make, using a small appliance in the washroom, she leaned over the railing and ignored the fluttering in her stomach. It wasn't because of the height. She had looked over the edge of the bluff many times, even sat at the rim with her feet dangling over. But this was an alien world, and as the sights and sounds began wafting up, they made her nervous.

Leea took in her surroundings and felt she could explain what she saw in one word—colorful. Compared to the drab landscape and glass and steel buildings of Alrack, any place might have fit that description, but New Haven had to be an extreme. Red and green trees alternately lined the four-lane road below, and sprouting bushes of varying colors edged the walkways.

As fascinating as the plant life was, the buildings themselves were equally unique. Most were square towers, the tallest one within her vantage point had thirty-six floors. They looked to be constructed of colored concrete and glass, and Leea turned to run a hand over the blue wall behind her, confirming her suspicion. Other colors alternating randomly along the avenue were, green, red, yellow or white.

As the morning progressed, the world unfolded. More and more people made their way along the sidewalks, and cars—still moving orderly—began clogging the roadway.

A fluttering sound interrupted her concentration. Turning, she watched as a bird landed on the iron railing a few feet away, seeming undisturbed by her presence. The creature's face, breast, and clawed feet were a shiny black, offset by yellow and blue feathers that crowned its head and flowed to the tip of its long tail, hanging about a foot past the rail. They both studied each other with interest. After a moment, as if to show off its magnificence, the animal spread its wings to their full five-foot span and fluttered a few inches in the air. Leea chuckled, stepping back in amazement.

"Well, I'll be …." Bettina said from the doorway.

"It's a bird, right?" Leea asked excitedly.

"Yes."

"Are they always this friendly?"

The Dekarran paused. "Sometimes. But these are … different."

"Different how?"

"They're not just any birds. We call them greeters. It's not their official name, of course, but what they do." Bettina stepped back inside, and Leea reluctantly followed.

"I don't understand."

Hesitantly, Bettina looked out where the bird still sat eyeing them but then smiled. "There are things on this planet that are still a mystery. Greeters are birds who we've always assumed were attracted to newborns. Here in New Haven, as well as in other Dekarran cities, there are designated birthing centers. When some children are born, a young bird will land on the newborn's windowsill as if claiming the infant as its own.

"Greeters don't usually interact with people, but seemingly stay close by. Something as simple as a scrapped knee will bring them about quickly. But seeing it with you means it's not babies ... it's new life. New life to the planet." She smiled, the apprehension from a moment ago gone. "This is exciting. Our historians will want to talk to you about your knowledge of what happened on Earth, but the science community will look at this as another breakthrough."

"Really?"

"Oh yes. Everyone gets excited at any little advancement to understand the planet we live on. I'm going to inform our military leader tomorrow and let him decided what to do. The military and science community work closely together," she explained seeing Leea's confusion.

"So everyone on Dekarra has a greeter?"

"No, only some children attract them—another of this planet's mysteries. Some people are superstitious, saying greeters bring good luck."

"Do you have one?"

Bettina briefly pressed her lips together. "No. I find the whole issue ridiculous. They're just silly birds that people have spun some mystical meaning around."

For the next six days, Leea spent as much time as she could on the balcony, watching the world go about its daily routine. A doctor came every other day, performing new scans to determine if she had any pathogens or viruses harmful to the environment. The female physician assured her it was for her own protection as well as others. New medication took away the residual fatigue and headaches, and the doctor said it would take about six months or so for her body to completely adapt. Having adjusted to the local time, and slightly longer days, Leea was getting anxious to leave her confinement.

She and Bettina spent hours talking, and Leea couldn't get enough of the stories the Dekarran shared with her. Most were about the struggles Humans experienced after their arrival here, but they all fascinated her. In return, Leea talked about life in Alrack and her family. Bettina asked a lot of questions about the Zantian Council and military structure, but most Leea couldn't answer.

The greeter visited every morning but flew away once Bettina arrived. It would sit perched close by, watching as she observed the world around them. She always had the urge to reach out and touch the creature, wanting to feel its feathers, but couldn't quite muster the courage.

"Hello!" Bettina called from the front door.

"I'm out here!"

"How's the view today?" The tiny blond woman stepped cautiously onto the balcony and leaned on the balustrade.

"Magnificent, as usual," Leea replied and reluctantly turned away from the view.

"I have good news for you."

"You do?"

"The doctor has given you a clean bill of health, living arrangements have been made, so you are free to leave."

"When?" Leea was unable to contain her excitement.

"First thing in the morning, but if you like, we could take a short walk outside now."

"Are you sure?"

"Yes. But keep in mind, it is the weekend, so there'll be more people out there today."

"That's okay."

Twenty minutes later, the two women walked out onto the streets of New Haven. From six floors up, Leea had witnessed the activity but quickly realized that many of the sounds never reached her. Now they assaulted her senses. Cars swooshed by quietly except for the occasional screeching tires, or loud honking. Music drifted onto the sidewalk from nearby open doorways, along with loud, cheerful voices. Conversations resonated from all directions and were almost disorienting.

She moved closer to the building trying not to get caught in the stream of pedestrians after a group of young girls, chattering wildly and screeching with laughter, almost pulled her with them as they ambled by.

She took in the people—people like her—Human. They came in all shapes, sizes, and colors, most dressed in bright colors, some of which she didn't even know the name. Couples, young and old, walked hand in hand, which accentuated her sadness, but she quickly pushed it away.

Unfamiliar food smells permeated all around forming unique aromas. This was far more emotional than she had expected. Did she really belong here? At the moment, she wasn't so sure. With renewed courage, Leea made her way toward an outside seating area, full of people enjoying the sunny afternoon.

Having kept her distance, Bettina now fell into step with her. "Are you all right?"

Leea wiped a tear away. "I don't know," she answered. "I'm a little overwhelmed."

"I'm sure that's to be expected."

"Sixteen Humans live in the House of Alrack, and probably several hundred more throughout the city. Seeing this," she gestured in front of her, "is something I never imagined. And you know what the worst thing is? I feel guilty for being here in this beautiful place while those I love will always wonder what happened to me."

Bettina stopped and pulled Leea back to face her. "There is nothing for you to feel guilty about. You wouldn't be here if they hadn't forced you to leave. The ones you left behind, the ones you love, they would understand."

"I'm sure they would, but that doesn't make it any easier."

They continued their walk.

"Did Earth look like this?" Leea asked.

"As far as I know, it was very similar. The people who settled here wanted to make it as Earth-like as possible."

"What an amazing place that must have been." The outside world started to close in, and Leea suddenly feared it might crush her. "Can we go back? I can't believe I'm saying this, but this is all I can handle at the moment."

"Of course. We'll do this as slowly as you need."

Light filtered through the window when Leea woke up the next morning. Knowing she would never get back to sleep, she got up, packed her meager belongings, and stood on the balcony one last time. Her feathered friend didn't visit, which disappointed her, but she hoped Bettina's explanation was correct, and it would find her no matter where she ended up.

Bettina brought a light breakfast for each of them, and when they finished, she led them to the rear exit of the Inn where they got into a small black car, and Bettina guided it into the flow of traffic.

"How long will it take to get there?"

"About half an hour. Unfortunately, this is a busy time of day with everyone back at work today, which slows down traffic."

"People drive into the city every day for their job?"

"Yes, many people do."

"Will I be getting a job?"

"Of course. You'll be required to pay your expenses just like everyone else."

"Do you know what I'll be doing?" Leea asked apprehensively.

"No, not yet. I have a few ideas, but there's still time before we need to decide."

Eventually, the number of cars and people diminished. Tall city buildings were replaced with boarded up, single-story structures.

"This was the original settlement the colonists built," Bettina explained. "They lived here for many years while building the city. As soon as areas were livable, they moved there, then started on the residential area we're headed to. It was a slow process, but they were determined to make it work."

"And by the look of New Haven, I'd say they did. Is this old settlement empty?"

"Most of it. Some of it's used for military storage."

Just beyond the old township, they crested a small hill, and the road took a sharp turn to the left. Leea inhaled sharply as a large body of water emerged on their right, with the mountain range rising behind it.

Bettina smiled at her passenger. "That's Lake Bridges, named after the man who first discovered it. Zantia doesn't have lakes or oceans, does it?"

"It has a few lakes, but Alrack bordered a desert, so it didn't have one. I've only seen this in books, and I have to say, pictures don't come close to the real thing. Can we stop?"

"We'll come back in a few days. Right now we should get you settled."

Leea didn't take her eyes off the expanse of blue until it disappeared through the trees. Fields soon appeared to their left and Bettina explained those were some of the farmlands. Seemingly around the next bend, rows of small houses came into view, nestled within tree lines.

"This is a quiet neighborhood, so I think you'll like it," Bettina said as they made their way slowly along several streets. Finally, she stopped in front of a yellow, single-story dwelling. "Here we are. Welcome to your new home."

Stepping out of the car, Leea studied the small residence. It was light yellow with a green door and three windows. A wooden porch ran the entire length and was outlined with small plants, some in the early stages of bloom. A red stone walkway, two large trees with black bark and yellow fluted leaves, and a small patch of light green grass completed the front of the house.

Leea bent down to touch the lawn. "It's soft," she exclaimed.

"Grass on Dekarra is supposedly softer than what they had on Earth," Bettina explained. "It looks similar but feels different… or so the texts say."

She tried to take it all in, but the view behind the house drew her attention away—trees. As far as the eye could see in either direction, treetops seemed to touch the sky.

"This is the edge of the city limits," Bettina said. "There is nothing beyond here except forest lands and mountains." She pointed to the right where crags through a break in the trees could be seen.

"Is it safe to go in there?"

"Yes, of course, but I wouldn't advise it until you're familiar with the area. I wouldn't want you to get lost. There are several marked trails that start from the road, so as long as you stay on one of those you should be fine."

"Wonderful."

They stepped through the front door and directly into a furnished living room that had a fresh smell as if it had just been cleaned. A worn brown sofa, two mismatched chairs, a low table, and an empty bookcase filled the small space. An arched doorway attached to a half-wall led into a small dining area, and beyond that, through another arched opening was the kitchen. A short hallway went to the right where three doors stood open.

By Zantian standards this house was tiny. The homes in the Alrack village were, at a minimum, three times the size as this one, but to her it was huge. After living in a single room most of her life, she couldn't believe all this space was for her. And not just the house itself, but the outside as well.

"Are you sure this is for me?"

"Yes, it is. I hope you like it?"

"I like it a lot." Leea sank onto one of the dining chairs. "How am I ever going to repay you for this?"

"For right now, you need some time to adjust, and as I mentioned before, I'm working on a job for you. Once you start that, you'll be able to contribute just like everyone else."

"Will we still see each other then?" she asked apprehensively.

"Of course. I've enjoyed our talks, and hope they continue." Bettina gave her a crooked smile. "The sofa looks comfortable. How about I stay here tonight and head back in the morning?"

"I'd like that. Not sure I'm ready to be in this quiet place alone. But I feel like I've taken up enough of your time already."

"It's been no problem at all."

They spent the rest of the afternoon walking the quiet neighborhood. Bettina pointed out the trailheads she'd mentioned, and Leea felt excited at the thought of exploring there one day soon. The Dekarran then left for a short time to get an overnight bag and dinner for them, and then answered many more questions about this new world.

Tired after her long day and yearning for sleep, Leea looked at her new bed. It was twice the size of the one she'd left behind, but she wasn't sure she wanted to lie on it. Suddenly, the permanence of her situation became a reality. She had known when she boarded the cargo ship that it would be temporary. When she had entered the Inn, she also knew it would only be for a short time. But this was permanent. Here, she might spend the rest of her life, and she feared that slipping under the soft-looking covers would seal her future.

With trembling hands, she dug through her travel bag until she found the object of her search—Yaran's shirt. She hadn't touched it during her voyage, knowing it would be too much to bear, but now she needed it. She pulled the fabric to her face and inhaled deeply. She would never wear it, hoping the scent of the man who had would remain longer if it didn't mingle with hers. The tears were automatic. Unwillingly, she sunk to the bed, clutching Yaran's shirt to her chest and wept.

The next two days Leea spent getting used to her surroundings. She familiarized herself with everything in her new home, amazed at everything it contained. The house had two bedrooms, one set up as an office, with a small desk and data terminal—or computer, as Bettina called it. She continued to explore the immediate area outside and was grateful that there weren't many people around during the day who might want to welcome her to the area. She wasn't ready for the questions she was sure her neighbors would ask.

On the third day, Bettina took her to the lake. The experience of walking slowly through the warm, grainy sand and then feeling the cool water up to her knees was exhilarating. And while it would be exciting to go there every day, apprehension would keep her from venturing too far into the water, which she mentioned to Bettina on their way back.

"Thanks for bringing me here. I think I could come here every day."

"Yes, this is a popular place. I promise we'll come back again."

"I was surprised to see so many people here. On a work day."

Bettina chuckled. "Not everyone works a standard shift. Some jobs require odd hours. During the summer months, you'll find a lot of activity at this beach. But on weekends, you'll never find a place to park; it's almost wall to wall people."

"Not sure I could deal with that right now. And as much as I liked the water, it was hard to look at the people swimming, even little children. To me it's scary."

Bettina chuckled. "Well, after you get settled, you should look into swimming lessons. They have them for all ages."

"I'll consider that," Leea said with little enthusiasm.

"When we get back to the house, I'm going to introduce you to your neighbor, Mary Sullivan. She's a widow whose husband died about ten years ago. I think you'll like her, and I'll feel better that you know someone close by."

The house next door was similar to hers in style except white with a bright blue door that opened as they approached. Mary was an average-height black woman in her fifties, with short curly hair touched with gray, and large brown eyes. She smiled brightly as they approached.

"Bettina, how nice to see you," she said cheerfully. "And you must be Leea. I'm so happy to finally meet you." Mary took Leea's extended hand and clasped it in both of hers.

"It's nice to meet you too, Mary."

"Come in. I'm just getting ready for some afternoon tea."

"We don't want to intrude," Bettina said, "I just wanted to bring Leea over to meet you."

"Don't be silly. I'd love the company."

Mary led them into the house and said since it was such a warm day they should have their tea, which turned out to be iced, in the back yard. Seated in the shade of a tall tree, they talked about their families. Mary had one daughter who lived with her husband and two children on the other side of the city where they owned a grocery. Before they knew it, an hour had passed, and Bettina said they should go. With a promise to stay in touch, the women said their goodbyes.

"Thank you for introducing me to Mary. She instantly felt like family. It will also be nice to have a neighbor who knows about me," Leea said as they walked back to her house.

"I knew you'd like her. And I know she'll be discreet." They stopped at the bottom of Leea's walkway. "I've known Mary for many years, not well, but we've had the occasion to talk now and then. She always struck me as a cheerful person. That's why, when I found this house was available, I thought it would be perfect for you."

"Thank you again."

"You are welcome. Well, unfortunately, there are some things I need to take care of in the city, so I have to head back. But I will see you tomorrow. I'll be by early."

"It was a fun day. I think I'm starting to feel a little more relaxed."

"That's good. I hope it gets easier as time goes on."

"Me too."

The next morning, Leea stood at her back door looking out over the tree-lined backyard waiting for Bettina to arrive. She loved the view. The immense forest stood as a giant wall blocking out the rest of the world for all the houses on this side of the street. Between each yard, stood two or three smaller trees, giving a little privacy but not separating the properties completely. Leea had walked to the edge of the dense foliage several times, and each time what lay beyond had called for her to step inside, but each time she'd resisted. It didn't frighten her. Actually, the thought of stepping among the giants excited her, but she wasn't ready for that much exploration yet. So, instead, she had simply looked into the darkness beyond and listened to the sounds of rustling branches and animal conversations.

Her greeter had appeared the second day after her arrival, and she'd been happy to see it, almost like a visit from an old friend. After that, it had stayed out of sight except when she stood at the edge of the woods. Then, it would suddenly appear, landing on a low branch nearby.

"Do you want me to go in?" she had asked it once and then smiled as it studied her with its intense black eyes, remaining noncommittal.

"Are you going to keep me from going in, or show me the way once I'm inside?" In response, her feathered friend had spread its yellow and blue wings, flapped them languorously, but then returned to scrutinizing her.

"Well, I'm not sure what that means," she'd said, "guess I'll find out once I step through." She had then laughed softly. "I'm talking to a bird as if expecting an answer. What a crazy world this is."

After a brief knock, the front door opened, and Bettina stepped in. "Sorry I'm late, traffic was horrible this morning."

"That's all right." Leea reluctantly turned away and joined her friend in the living room.

"I have good news," Bettina said with a big smile. "I found you a job."

"You did?"

"Yes. There's an opening in the Research Laboratory. It's nothing exciting. You'd be mostly running errands and keeping records."

"Wow, I was expecting a cooking job or something like that."

"Oh no, I'm sure you've had enough of that on Zantia. I think you should try something new."

"I'd like that. When do I start?"

"On Monday. So, I thought we would take care of all your registrations today."

The rest of the morning was spent answering endless questions. Everywhere they went, people asked for full name and birthdate. Of course, Leea knew when she was born, but in Zantian time. The Birth Information Center, their first stop, although not happy, accepted her best guess.

Next, she needed to pick a last name. She didn't know much about her father's family since he wasn't born in Alrack, so she chose one from her mother's side. From her family history, her grandparents who were abducted from Earth were Beverly and George Dennison, so that was the name she chose. After they'd satisfied all the agencies, Bettina suggested lunch.

"Tired?" she asked while they waited for their food at a local restaurant.

"No, just a little overwhelmed. There is so much involved in getting a new life."

"Yes, bureaucracy can be overwhelming, but you'll get used to it…we all do. So, I thought after we eat we would go to the labs and take a look around?"

"We can do that?"

"Sure. You'll need a security pass for work, so might as well get that today too."

"Do you work in that building?"

"No. I do freelance work."

"What does that mean?"

Bettina hesitated, then said, "I have certain specialties that people hire me to do. If a job sounds interesting, I do whatever they tell me to do. If not, I can say no."

"Such as?"

"Oh, a lot of different things. Like right now, my job is to take care of you."

"Someone hired you to do that?"

"Of course." Bettina got to her feet. "Excuse me. I need to visit the ladies room."

Leea watched the tiny, impeccably dressed woman walk toward the rear of the restaurant in confusion. She had never wondered how Bettina came to take her off the cargo ship. And it shouldn't surprise her that others knew Zantians sometimes brought more than just cargo. She certainly had more questions now but assumed Bettina's hasty retreat to the washroom meant this particular conversation was over. She would approach it another time.

"How am I going to get to work?" Leea asked once Bettina returned.

"At first, you'll go with Mary. She works for Admiral Shaw, who is our highest military leader. His office is in the same building. She takes the bus, so after a while, you'll be able to make the trip on your own."

"Perfect."

After finishing their meal, they drove the short distance to the research lab, a red, twenty-six-story building Leea had seen from her room at the Inn. They stopped at the security office where she was issued an access card, then to the twenty-fifth floor to say hello to Mary. They talked for a few minutes then made their way to the tenth floor. Her boss was out, so after a quick look around they left. Instead of heading home, Bettina suggested a shopping trip. Knowing the few items she'd brought wouldn't fit into this colorful world, Leea was grateful for the offer.

As with everything else she'd experienced on this planet, shopping was another eye opening experience. Never having had to worry about fashion, the choice of what to wear was almost overwhelming, but with Bettina's help, appropriate items were added to her wardrobe. Now Leea hoped the next few days would pass quickly. She was anxious to start.

As the dark heavens gave way to the approaching sun, Leea sat outside on a lounge chair with her new best friend: coffee. Mary had introduced her to this the day after they'd met, explaining it was the Human drink of choice.

*How have I lived my entire life without this wonderful beverage?*

She sipped the hot liquid slowly, inhaling the aroma of the steam while watching the rising sun brighten the sky. As it did every day, one of Dekarra's three moons preceded the sun as if announcing its arrival. And just as the sentinel moon declared, the bright yellow orb cleared the mountains and began to appear through the treetops.

Looking up, Leea was disappointed to see a clear blue sky as the day began to brighten. These last few days, she had enjoyed studying the clouds as they glided overhead, and always managed to find something familiar within the formations. Resigned, she laid back in the chaise and closed her eyes, balancing the coffee cup in both hands on her lap.

In two days these quiet mornings would be replaced with getting ready for her new job. On one hand, she was happy to finally be doing something useful, but on the other, the thought of going into the big city, being around a lot of people, somehow scared her. How would people react toward her once they knew where she came from? Bettina said her boss knew, although not under what circumstances, and sharing further information would be up to her. She hoped people would be understanding.

Bright light warmed her face as she opened her eyes and realized she'd fallen asleep. The cup in her hands was cold, and she was amazed it hadn't slipped from her grasp. In spite of the warm sun, a chill made her wrap her sweater tighter around as she sat up and set the cup on the ground. She ran both hands through her hair, twisting it together at the nape of her neck while taking one last look around. Movement within the tree-line caught her attention, and she could barely make out a dark figure obscured by the shadows.

Someone was watching her.

Her first instinct was to flee into the house, but her legs wouldn't obey their order to move. She could do nothing but watch as the stranger began to emerge from the forest.

# CHAPTER 10

# Mines

Sluggishly, Yaran sat up on the side of the bed and slowly massaged his temples before pulling his fingers through his hair. *Another restless night—will they ever end?*

Four weeks had passed since he moved in with Toref, and he had yet to get one peaceful night's sleep. When he finally did drift off, the dreams wouldn't let his mind rest. He couldn't remember most of them, but the turmoil they created was evident upon waking. The only dream he did remember—vividly—was the old man in the blue crystal room, urging Yaran to find him. He didn't understand the meaning, or even if there was one. What he did know was that total exhaustion would soon take him if he couldn't find a way to turn off the thoughts that plagued him.

One week ago, he had quietly celebrated his crossover with Toref and found it ironic that as much as he'd struggled against it, he was exactly where tradition dictated he should be—working in the family's business. So far the work had been limited to the city office, getting familiar with mine protocols, only to discover that the task ahead didn't seem as unpleasant as he'd expected. And now, the day had come to take over one of the four Alrack mines.

Toref admitted that after Cassa's death he wanted nothing more than to bury himself in the work, but now found it all exhausting and looked forward to the help. But his uncle wanted him to start slowly and come to terms with the emotional upheaval his life had gone through. Yaran thought of the old Earth adage 'time heals all wounds,' and decided it must not apply to him—time had only made the pain worse. Every waking moment was filled with thoughts of Leea. Not to mention the unimaginable regret over letting her go. It was like torture. She would be on Dekarra now, and Yaran made himself imagine that she'd found a better place than the one she'd left behind.

Losing Leea, being betrayed by his father, learning about the escape network and wondering what other secrets this world might hold was more than Yaran could handle some days. And as much as he tried to make sense of it all, it was a useless effort that gave him one sleepless night after another.

Getting to his feet, Yaran rubbed his face with both hands, feeling the stubble—he hadn't shaved in days. He briefly thought about letting it grow, but quickly decided against it. His hair grew slow, and he felt the upkeep was something he didn't want to deal with, so he headed for the washroom. Reluctantly, he looked at his reflection, something he wished he could avoid because the face that stared back frightened him. He had lost weight. His already prominent cheekbones were now more pronounced, giving him an almost skeletal look, and his skin had taken on an ashen tone. The constant dark eyes indicated the unhappiness and anger that still dwelled within.

"Where will it all end?" he asked mournfully. But the stranger in the mirror only looked back with sad eyes.

"Good morning," Toref said as Yaran walked into the kitchen and took a seat at the dining table. "How did you sleep? Or do I need to ask?"

"About the same, I'm afraid."

"You really should think about taking a sleeping aid. You're going to fall over one of these days."

"I know. I just hate the feeling sleeping aids give me the next day."

"Better than finding yourself face down in a med-center. They will certainly notify Jarock if that happens. Not sure you want that."

"Thanks, a little scare tactic should help," Yaran smiled. "What's new for the morning meal?"

"Unfortunately, just the usual. How would you like your cooked grains this morning, plain or with fruit? Tea?"

"Yes to the tea. Fruit would be nice. And thanks for waiting on me … again."

"My pleasure. It's going to be a busy day today. I want you to be well nourished—just wish you were well rested too."

"Maybe the change in work will help. Sitting behind a desk these last few weeks hasn't been too exciting."

"Getting involved in mine operations will certainly be more exciting, but be careful what you wish for. There will be unique challenges."

"Which is exactly what I need."

"Are you sure you're ready for this?" Toref's voice took on a serious tone. "You can wait a while longer."

"No, I'm ready. I have memorized every procedure and protocol possible. There is nothing more I can learn, short of doing it myself." Yaran paused for a moment. "I need a change and something else to occupy my mind." He ran his hands through his thick damp hair and sighed. "I'm so tired. Not just from the lack of sleep, but from the constant thoughts going through my head that I can't turn off. I'll never stop thinking about Leea, but at some point, the worry and the regret should go away. I keep telling myself it'll get better, but it doesn't. I'm not sure what else I'm supposed to do."

Toref walked up and laid his hands on Yaran shoulders. "I know it's hard to believe right now, but it will get better. Eventually, the pain will be replaced with manageable thoughts. One day you'll find yourself laughing at a happy memory, and realize that life does go on. I can't tell you how long it will take, but I can guarantee it will happen, it'll just take a little more patience."

Yaran looked up and attempted a weak smile. "Thanks, Toref, I appreciate the words. I always thought I was the most patient person in the world, but sadly, in this last month, I've realized even I have my limits."

Toref chuckled and patted him on the back. "You'll be ok. I'm sure of it."

After a short stop at the city office, the two men made their way to the west mine. Alrack mines were designated by location: north, south, east, and west, making it the only city on the planet with four. An abundance of ore and minerals were found within the mountain range and under the Red Desert which also made it the major planetary exporter. Even the dark red soil had properties they extracted to produce spices and some medicines.

Because of the surface's oppressive heat, most of the planet's mines were built underground, except for the produce and protein farms which were protected in other ways. Toref oversaw all four of the city's mines and warehouses, which included production schedules, resources, and shipments for export and import distribution. Except for imports, Yaran would take on the responsibilities of the west mine—the largest of the four. Zantian administrators oversaw day to day operations while Human foremen led the individual working teams.

A few miles outside the city limits, the road narrowed and took a sharp turn, sending them out into the desert. As they neared their destination, the only thing visible in any direction were hundreds of windmills and an array of solar collectors. All buildings on this planet produced their own energy through solar grids built into the transitioning glass, which the underground mines didn't have, so they relied on energy farms.

As their vehicle came over the last small rise, several large stone structures, blending in with the surrounding desert, came into view. The one closest to them housed administrative offices, Zantian and Human sleeping quarters, and the main entrance into the vast expanse below. Attached to the rear was a large covered area, where workers could spend time outside, and just beyond there, stood two large depots. Train cars were loaded below and brought into the stations with an elevator system where they were then secured and placed on high-speed trains bound for the city.

"Nervous?" Toref asked as he guided the shuttle next to the main entrance.

"No."

"Good. By the way, I talked to Jarock early this morning. He is leaving on an off-world trip next week."

"Off-world? Why?"

"Seems there are some delicate negotiations taking place on Karba, and he decided to handle it himself."

"I didn't know he took on negotiations personally. It must be important."

"He didn't say much about it. But I believe he's using this as an opportunity to get away for a while."

"Well, good. I'm glad he's leaving." Yaran's mood instantly darkened.

"You should know this whole situation is hard for him too."

"He has no one to blame but himself," was all Yaran managed to say as he stepped out of the vehicle.

Walking through large double doors, they were greeted by, Cashon, the administrator. He was an older man who walked slightly stooped and whose braided hair was almost entirely white. According to Toref, he had been in charge of this mine since before he and Jarock were born, which was another reason he wanted Yaran here—the day to day operations were getting to be too much for the aging Zantian, even though he refused to admit it.

"Welcome."

"Good morning Cashon," Toref greeted in return, giving him a respectful nod. "Is everything set up as I requested?"

"Yes, of course," Cashon exclaimed with a touch of irritation. "Yaran's office is ready, all site information has been downloaded to his terminal, and the foremen are waiting in the outer office."

Toref smiled and patted the much shorter man on the back. "I never doubted you for a minute."

Cashon looked up at Toref and scowled lightheartedly.

"Thank you, Cashon, I appreciate you getting everything ready for me," Yaran added. He had dealt with the administrator often over the years when he'd helped with shipping schedules in the city office and found the man to be a bit of a curmudgeon. "I'm going to need all the help I can get until I learn my way around."

"I'm sure you won't have any trouble."

Yaran smiled appreciatively. "Well, I suppose we should go to my office and not keep the foremen waiting any longer than necessary."

Toref led the way down a back hallway, and the three men entered the spacious bureau through a side door. A large desk stood in the center of the room, supporting several data terminals. On the right-hand corner sat a shallow metal box filled with red soil. Two dozen pieces of raw and processed ore lay nestled on top.

"Mining samples?" Yaran asked, picking up a black rock and running his thumb over the smooth surface.

"I like being reminded of what our city produces every day, so I thought you might too."

Yaran picked up several pieces, feeling the rough, raw textures or smoothly processed surfaces. One piece, a blue crystal, seemed out of place. He held it in his hand, studying the glow it seemed to emit from within. "Where do we mine this?" he asked.

Toref studied it confused. "We don't. I'm not sure how that got there."

"Well, it's interesting." Returning it to the box, the vivid dreams of the pleading alien flashed through his mind. *Find the blue crystal cave.* The walls in his visions could have been made with these crystals—even in the dream, they seemed to glow. He suddenly felt an odd sense that there was more to his nighttime visitor than he was willing to believe.

"The foremen will brief you on the day's activities," Cashon informed Yaran. "There is a meeting every morning to go over the daily schedule, and with your permission, I will continue to run these until you become more familiar with the operations."

"Absolutely," Yaran exclaimed with relief. "Please keep to your regular routine. I will let you know, when and if I want to handle anything myself."

"Cashon runs things effectively," Toref added, "I'm sure you'll find his help invaluable."

"I'm sure I will," he agreed, smiling. "So, shall we bring the foremen in and not disrupt their day any longer?"

"Excellent idea," Toref agreed.

Yaran stood in front of the desk as seven men entered the office. Toref made brief introductions, then he and Cashon left him to get acquainted on his own.

They were of varying ages, and as different in size and coloring as any seven men could be. Toref hadn't told him much about them, saying he wanted Yaran to form his own opinions, but he wished his uncle had mentioned one thing—one of the foremen was Tim, Julia's husband.

Yaran didn't know Tim well and had only spoken to him on rare occasions when Tim had performed maintenance on his shuttle. He was a slender man, about five-foot-eight with blond hair. Stray strands fell over his forehead, which he seemed to brush involuntarily out of his face at regular intervals. A closely trimmed beard gave him a rugged look and masked the boyish features Yaran remembered. He took a deep breath and returned his focus to the task at hand.

Chairs had been set up for the men and Yaran motioned for them to take a seat, then made room on the desk to sit instead of using the chair behind it. They reintroduced themselves, explained which tunnel they managed, and brought Yaran up to speed on the daily status. Except for Tim, each man was in charge of a specific tunnel. Tim was foreman of the maintenance crew in the processing plant, because, like his father, he could do amazing things with machinery.

After an hour, Yaran felt he had enough information to keep busy for the rest of the day and dismissed them, except for Tim, whom he asked to stay a few minutes longer. When the others were gone, Yaran took a seat previously occupied by a large man with a long blond ponytail. Yaran knew the size, and somewhat scowling look would be enough to keep anyone in line, which made him chuckle softly.

"What's funny?" Tim asked.

"I'm sorry. I was thinking about the man who sat here. I'm sure he has no trouble keeping things on track."

Tim chuckled in return. "Dennis is not as mean as he looks. He's actually a nice guy once you get to know him."

"Does he have a family?" Yaran asked quietly.

"No. Tran is the only other foreman with a family. They live in the city complex. His wife works for one of the larger galleries."

"Does he go home and see them?"

"Yes, all the foremen are allowed time away. The tunnels shut down once a month on a rotating schedule to service the equipment, and it's during that time that the foremen can leave the site."

Yaran sat back. "First off, I'd like to say I'm sorry that we've never had the opportunity to get to know each other. I consider Julia a friend, so I feel we should have."

"She feels the same about you. But don't apologize. My time at the house is limited, so I want to make the most of it with my family."

Yaran smiled warily. "I understand. The reason I wanted you to stay is that I'd like to ask a favor. Since I'm taking over the operations here, I want to learn how to interact with the other foremen and not just be an extension of the administrator. I truly want to know how things are run, and who runs them. From the little we all spoke, I got the impression everyone has a great respect for Toref, and I don't want to do anything to upset that."

"I will admit, some of the men are worried. Everyone is wondering if you have your own agenda."

"No agenda except to learn all I can."

"We're all treated well here, thanks to your uncle. I know some of the other cities have their troubles, but things in Alrack run pretty smooth overall. I can certainly help you learn about the other foremen, but what about Cashon?"

"I doubt the administrator cares much about interacting with the workers and will be of no help in that regard."

"Probably not. Although he treats us well, that's most likely because Toref wants it that way. Other than that, he keeps his distance."

"He's been here a long time, so I'm sure there's a lot of old ideals lingering there."

"I'm sure you're right."

They sat quietly for a moment, before the foreman said, "I'm sorry about Leea. How are you holding up?"

Yaran grimaced. "I'm all right, just taking it day by day."

"Julia is still pretty upset too."

"I think the hardest thing is not knowing. Did she make it? Is she safe? Happy?"

"She's safe," Tim said cautiously. "You have to believe that. These escapes have been happening for years. The cargo ship captains make sure it all goes smoothly."

'How can you be so sure?"

"So I've heard," he said hesitantly. "The escape network is well known in certain circles. Since the foremen aren't cut off from the outside world, a few discreetly placed questions can yield lots of information."

"You told Julia about the network?"

Tim fidgeted in his chair and repeatedly swiped at the hair falling over his forehead. "Yes, I did…some time ago. When things started coming apart for Leea, she had my brother contact me, and I told him what he needed to do."

"Well, I'm not going to pretend I understand how all that works, but thank you for helping her, from whatever my father was planning. But right now I just want to get settled and learn my way around."

"I'm sure you'll do fine. Just remember you're not alone here. We all work together to make this operation run smoothly."

"Thank you, I appreciate that. So, you don't mind if I rely on you for a while?"

"No, not at all," Tim assured him with a smile.

"And please reassure the other men that I'm not here to change anything. I want everything to stay as it is. If anything, I'd like to make things better. How many workers here have families?"

"I don't know. There aren't any on my crew."

"Well, I'll find out as I learn my way around. I have never understood the need to take these men away from those they love," Yaran mumbled absentmindedly. "If I'm going to change anything, it's going to be to give the workers who have families more time at home."

Tim looked at him in surprise. "Cashon won't be happy."

Yaran got to his feet. "He may not be happy, but what can he say? Toref has turned the responsibility of this mine over to me. Cashon should have no reason to complain as long as it doesn't disrupt the work schedule, and I'll make sure it doesn't." He smiled. "And, I'm going to implement my first new order right away."

Tim also rose and studied him questioningly.

"My father is leaving for an extended trip in a week. He'll likely be gone a few months. During that time, I'm going to arrange for you, and Tran, to spend more time with your families, as well as more time off for the other foremen … if they want it."

"I'm not sure what to say, except … thank you. But what will your mother say if I start showing up at the house more often?"

Yaran heard the hope in his voice. "Probably nothing. You have to remember that she's the one who defied Zantian tradition so I wouldn't be sent away for my transition training. She doesn't believe in splitting up families."

"Good point. Thank you again, this means a lot to me."

"Just keep in mind that once my father returns, things will need to go back to the way they were."

"I know, and I will make the best of every extra moment."


Yaran walked off the elevator onto a metal walkway with Toref and Cashon. He had been to this level only once before, when his father had brought him here as a young boy, hoping to spark his interest in mining. The sight of the immense cavern was more spectacular than he remembered. It was circular, about fifteen hundred feet in diameter, and eight hundred feet from floor-to-ceiling. Twelve massive support columns, equally spaced in a circle, held the rock and soil of the desert above their heads.

The processing plant took up the space between the columns, its top at eye level to the walkway—four hundred feet up. Protruding from the top were four, twenty-foot diameter tubes that disappeared into the rock ceiling. Three continually bringing in fresh air, and the fourth, surface soil for processing. More than two dozen fifty-foot fans were built into the ceiling, continuously exhausting air.

"Impressive, isn't it?" Toref stated, leaning over the railing next to his nephew. The walkway wrapped around the entire space and supported five bridges to the processor. "As many times as I've seen it, I still have to stop and take in the view."

"Yes, it is amazing," Yaran agreed.

Looking below, Yaran could see six rail tracks at ground level going from the processor and disappearing into the individual mining tunnels. Full cars brought raw ore from the excavation sites to the plant, which then separated out minerals, precious metals, and extracted natural gasses. Some of the material was processed further, and then everything was transported along three elevated rails that led to the massive elevators.

"This is our livelihood," Toref stated proudly. "This is what we're good at. Other Zantians have their art forms. Well, this is ours, the art of making something useful out of rocks and dirt."

"A form of art. Hmmm …." Yaran pondered the idea. "I guess that's something I never considered."

"We are a world of artists, each in our own way. No matter what path we take, we can all be proud of our accomplishments." He laid a hand on Yaran's shoulder and gave him a big smile. "You too will learn to be proud of this new art form you are venturing into."

Yaran raised his eyebrows and smiled in return. "I think you might be overselling it." They all laughed.

Yaran stayed at the mine that week, sleeping in the small bedroom adjacent to the office so he could familiarize himself with all the minute details, even those that came up in the middle of the night. Every morning he attended Cashon's meeting and quickly decided the administrator should continue to run them. During the meetings, he sat to the side taking notes on his datapad. He would chuckle silently when he realized he couldn't go about his day without it. Having studied all the processes and procedures didn't quite prepare him for the actual daily routine, so he was creating his own summaries to track each tunnel's schedule.

To learn more about the operations, each morning Yaran selected a foreman and observed him during a day's work. He chose Tim first, hoping word would spread that he wasn't there to interfere, only to learn. This seemed to work, as most of the men seemed relaxed during his visit with them.

He enjoyed the day in the processing plant, fascinated by how precisely the minerals were separated and then transformed, by compression or extraction, into something completely different. But he had to admit he didn't enjoy the days in the tunnels as much. He now understood why Humans objected to working in the sometimes dangerous environment day after day. It was something he could never do.

While their process of mining was precise, and the extraction of elements left much of the surrounding area intact, it was still dirty, musty, and stiflingly hot. He also discovered that he was a bit claustrophobic and longed for each day to be over so he could leave the confined spaces.

The days were exhausting, but finally awarded Yaran the one thing he longed for—uninterrupted sleep.

On his last overnight stay in the office, Yaran was finishing his entries in the evening when the blue crystal, gleaming among the rest of the ore, caught his attention. Picking it up, he sat back and studied it. Everything else laying on the tray he had seen, in one form or another over the past week. So why was this here? Toref said he didn't know how it ended up in the tray, but where did it come from? *Find the blue crystal cave*, resonated in his mind. The dream had eluded him this week, for which he was grateful.

Yaran returned to the terminal and scrolled through the system until he found the individual mining servers, and then opened them one by one. He did a quick scan through invoices, schedules, even worker lists, not sure what he was looking for, but didn't find anything out of the ordinary. He opened all four simultaneously and compared them side by side. About to give up, something struck him as odd.

He reopened each worker list and moved through the individual information concurrently again until he found what had caught his attention—a folder in the east mine called Imports. *This is an odd place to log an import*, he thought, *maybe it's here by mistake*. Zantia imported many things, but those were documented in warehouse reports and to his knowledge, nothing they imported was used in the mines. And why would it be in the worker files?

Opening the errant folder, he found it contained one unnamed file. Attempting to open it, he received a return message; 'access restricted.' The terminals on his desk were coded to his specific DNA, so nothing should deny him access. Puzzled, he checked the file's history, surprised to find it was last opened over a year ago, and only three times previously: ten years, twenty-three years, and sixty-three years.

Pulling the file to the forefront, Yaran attempted to open it again but to no avail. What could be in an import file that was designated restricted? Another thought came to mind: was it a coincidence that Toref insisted on managing the imports himself? This definitely sparked his interest. He decided to ask his uncle for a tour of the other mines and see if he could determine what mystery the east one might hold.

Nine days after Yaran assumed his new responsibilities, Toref informed him that Jarock had left Zantia. This was the news he had been waiting for... it was time to go home.

# CHAPTER 11

# Going Home

Yaran eased his shuttle into the hangar and angled it into its designated spot and then took in the familiar space for a moment—it felt good to be home.

"You're sure this is going to be okay?" Tim asked for the tenth time.

Yaran smiled at him. "It will be fine, I promise. Jarock is well on his way to Karba and Lauranna won't object, so don't worry."

"Does she know we're coming?"

"No, I wanted to surprise her."

Tim looked at him and shook his head.

They disembarked and made their way along the side of the house. Yaran wanted to make a side-trip before going in, so at the kitchen entrance, Tim went in alone.

Yaran felt Leea's presence grow with every step that brought him closer to her favorite place. As the yellow fronds of the Jala tree came into view, the emotion of losing her welled up in his chest, making each step more difficult, but he continued. Surprised, he found the bench occupied and instantly recognized Julia and Marta. Marta noticed him first, alerting her mother.

"Yaran!" Julia and Marta got to their feet to greet him. "It's so good to see you."

"It's good to see you both of you too. Marta, I think you've grown a foot since I last saw you."

"I'm going to be nine soon," she said proudly.

"Ah, almost a young woman," he said with mock seriousness.

"No! I'm just a kid."

"But one of the smartest kids I know." Yaran sat on the bench and leaned forward. "Can I tell you a secret?"

"Sure," she agreed, a little uneasy.

Yaran motioned her closer, and he whispered quietly in her ear. Marta's eyes grew round and her two dimples deepened with a broad smile, but Yaran quickly put a finger to his lips before she could say anything.

"Really?"

Yaran nodded, and she turned to her mother. "Can I go back to the house?"

"Sure," Julia said skeptically. "What did you say to her?"

"Nothing. A little secret between us for the moment. Is it all right if she goes back? We'll follow in a moment."

"Yes, of course, you can go." Julia narrowed her eyes at Yaran. "What are you up to?"

"I'll tell you in a minute, but I was hoping we could talk for a bit."

"Okay, go on Marta, I'll be there soon."

Marta hugged her mother and ran toward the house. They watched the dark-haired girl until she was out of sight, and then returned to the bench.

"How are you doing?" she asked Yaran cautiously.

"I'm okay I suppose. I'm living a life I don't recognize, but I'm finding it not as difficult as I imagined it would be."

"This house hasn't been the same without you. The routine hasn't changed, but it's almost like living in a mausoleum."

"A mausoleum?"

"A place where dead people are kept."

"I see."

"Your parents hardly say one word to each other anymore. The workers are afraid to say anything around them, so things are almost spooky quiet."

Yaran was silent for a moment. "It saddens me that this situation has had such an adverse effect on everyone. I do miss it here, but under the circumstances ...."

"I understand completely. Where are you staying?"

"At my uncle Toref's. He's teaching me the ways of the family business, ironically. I'm managing one of the mines now. And while it's not what I want to be doing, it keeps me busy so that I don't have to dwell on ... other things."

"I'm glad. Did you hear Marik is gone?"

"No." Yaran looked at her with surprise. "I talk to my mother regularly, but she hasn't mentioned it. What happened?"

"Evidently we were wrong about your father's intentions. The calls he made to the mine administrators were for Marik, not Leea. Jarock sent him back to Emborie shortly after he recovered from his ... injury."

"What? We sent Leea away for nothing?"

"No! Sending her away was the right thing to do." Julia sighed heavily. "I'm not sure how to tell you this, but the Desolk's plan for Leea was to send her off-world."

"Off-world to where?"

"Not sure. Your father was pretty angry that Leea disappeared on her own. We speculate that this trip to Karba had something to do with that. What little David could piece together, and we've made up the rest, is that the Council has some agreement with Karba that goes beyond the mineral trade."

"You think his quick departure is because of Leea's disappearance?"

She shrugged. "David said the Desolk was very secretive about his communications before he left and David briefly saw a comm module he'd never seen before. And, there was no official correspondence that led to this trip. That alone doesn't mean anything, but his anger about Leea's disappearance was irrational. He wanted her gone, so he should have been happy when she was. And then this trip came up." She shrugged again. "But like I said, a lot is speculation."

"Well, it doesn't matter, does it? Leea escaped my father's plan, whatever it was."

"Agreed."

"And Marik is where he's supposed to be; somewhere he can't cause any more trouble."

"Also agree. Were you aware he followed Leea around everywhere?"

"She told me he admitted something like that during his … attack on her."

"I guess all the time. Around the house and even here."

Yaran shuddered.

"He followed us to the city that day."

"Leea told me about that too."

Julia hesitated. "There is one thing she didn't tell you about."

"Oh?"

"We had an encounter with … uh … a strange … person."

"What do you mean, strange?"

"We had just left Man's and were heading to our next stop when Leea spotted Marik. We hurried between two buildings to avoid him and waited at the far end of the alley, hoping he wouldn't see us. After a few minutes, we thought we'd missed him and started to leave when a small figure, not quite my height, came through one of the side doors. It wore a long hooded robe so we couldn't tell what it looked like."

Yaran thought for a moment. "Dekarrans wear robes to hide their appearance, but there aren't any on Zantia, and I never heard they were such small people."

"It was all very strange, and I have to say, I was more than a little scared. It focused on Leea, and she just stood there and let the alien put something in her hand. It never said a word, but Leea knew exactly what it wanted."

"Really? What did it give her?"

"It reached out a wrinkled hand and gave her a stone…wanted her to take it."

"What kind of stone?"

"It was more like a crystal, about the size of my thumb…blue, I think."

A chill run down Yaran's spine. "What was she supposed to do with it?"

"Keep it until someone asked for it."

"And that was it?"

"Yes, as far as I know."

"What did she do with it?"

"I don't know. She put it in her pocket, and I never saw it again."

Yaran seemed thoughtful for a moment. "I wonder why she didn't tell me."

"She said she didn't want you to worry. She thought you had enough going on at the time, being away with the Desolk so much, and didn't want to add to it."

He smiled knowingly. "Sounds like something she would say."

Julia lowered her head and let out a sigh. "With everything else that happened that day, the whole incident was forgotten."

*Could this be related to my dreams?* Yaran reflected silently. *Julia said this person had an old hand and gave Leea a blue crystal. That can't be a coincidence.*

"I take it you haven't seen your mother yet?"

"No. I wanted to come here first. Of course, I didn't know you were going to be here, but I'm glad we had a chance to talk. How are my mother and father, other than the silence?"

"We don't see much of the Desolk most days. He and your mother still share meals together, but other than that, he mostly stays closed up in his office. David said this trip seemed to be the first thing to excite him in quite a while."

"I'm also excited he took this trip, and I plan to make the most of his absence, especially now that Marik is gone."

"So, what did you say to my daughter that had her running off so quickly?"

Yaran smiled at her sheepishly. "I hope you won't be upset with me."

"Why would I be?"

"I brought Tim back with me."

"What!" Julia jumped to her feet. "And you're just telling me this now?"

"I am sorry. I took the opportunity for us to talk and give Marta a little time alone with her father."

She threw her arms around his neck and gave him a big hug. "You're forgiven!"

Yaran rose from the bench. "Well, let's go back to the house. It seems we both have a family reunion waiting for us."

Entering through the kitchen, Julia hurried up the stairs, and Yaran made his way through the house toward his mother's sitting room where he stopped in the doorway. Lauranna sat in her favorite chair, feet propped up on an ottoman, engrossed in a data reader laying in her lap. Seeing her there made Yaran realize how much he truly missed her.

"Hello Mother," he said quietly.

She jumped at hearing his voice. "Yaran! You're home." She rose and walked into her son's embrace.

"I've missed you," Yaran said.

"I've missed you too," she whispered.

Yaran released her and took a step back. "I'm sorry I haven't come to see you sooner."

"I hoped with enough time you would."

"I'm not here to stay, Mother. Once Jarock returns, I'll go back to Toref's."

"I know, but let's not discuss that now. How are you doing?"

"I'm fine. Nothing much has changed since our conversation a few days ago."

"That's good to hear."

"Something I should tell you, though; Tim came with me today. I hope you don't mind if he visits his family more often these next few months?"

"No, not at all." A smile played on her face. "I've never agreed with the philosophy of splitting up families, so I'm proud that you thought of bringing him."

"I've earned a great respect for Tim. He had been a great help to me at the mine. The workers, for the most part, have been respectful, but some try to push the boundaries. Since I made the decision to take a hands-on approach...unprecedented, or so I'm told...Tim has helped with that adjustment."

Lauranna smiled. "Having Tim here for more than his normal visit will be refreshing. Julia and Marta will be ecstatic."

"Yes, they will."

In the following months, life fell into a pleasant routine for Yaran in the House of Alrack. Several days a week he worked in the mine office and one or two days at the city office. On the days spent at the mine, he stayed with Toref, or in his office bedroom. The rest of the week he slept in his old room.

Lauranna was elated to have her son home again. They would spend time in her sitting room where Yaran would share his day, and Lauranna would extol her latest discovery from the literary shelves. Yaran had little interest in the literary tales of other cultures, but listening to his mother recall some story or event she had discovered now intrigued him. He had forgotten what a great storyteller she was.

An equal amount of time was spent in the music room, where he played and spent some time composing. After the evening meal they would walk the loop through the gardens and on a few occasions, he was able to entice her to sit awhile on the bench under the Jala tree.

"You and Leea spent a lot of time here, didn't you?" she asked on one such occasion.

"Yes, this was her favorite spot. She came here almost every day."

After a brief hesitation, she asked, "Can you tell me where she went?"

Yaran took a deep breath. He suspected this question would eventually come up, but he hadn't decided what he would tell her. He didn't want to shatter any of her innocent perceptions.

Lauranna noticed his hesitation. "It's all right if you can't. I understand if you need to keep it a secret."

Yaran arranged his thoughts before he answered. "There is an underground organization who feel we are unreasonable in our treatment of mine workers and have secretly helped some of those in trouble. This group found out about Leea's impending exile, and offered her the opportunity to go to a safe location of their choosing."

Without really lying, Yaran felt he had explained it as best he could. He cut a glance at his mother, wanting to gauge her reaction, and noticed an interesting expression: relief. Did she know more than she let on? He decided to leave that question for another time.

As Yaran had planned, he asked Toref one day to take him on a tour of the other mines, and he happily agreed. Their first stop was the north mine which employed only three dozen workers because the extraction process was completely automated. Nestled in the mountain foothills, this facility had approximately thirty shafts cut deep into the rock at any one time, extracting deposits of precious stones and metals.

The tunnels were small, about twice the circumference of an average man, burrowed by specialized machinery that could pinpoint the exact location of the desired element and extract it with little effort. When the tunneling machine finished removing what it could or had reached its one-mile maximum distance, the shaft was resealed with rock and the device moved to a new location. Since these elements were time-consuming to remove, only about a dozen shafts completed per year, the rewards were left for Zantian artists, whose creations proved the effort worthwhile.

Next, they viewed the south mine, the furthest from the city, located under the rocky extension of the mountain range. This facility mirrored the west mine in many aspects, only on a smaller scale; the cavern was about half the size and only had four tunnels. The mine's yield was strictly for export, which meant the ore went through minimal conversion in their processing plant, and the rest left to the city refineries. The administrator gave them a full tour, proudly displaying some of their techniques, then invited them to an evening meal which they eagerly accepted.

"Last stop, east mine," Yaran stated once they were back in the shuttle.

"I think we should call it a day since it will be dark by the time we get up there. And also because the south and east mines are run by the same administrator." Toref chuckled. "Since we just left him, he can't be in both places at once, right?"

Yaran joined in the humor but didn't believe for a moment that darkness was the reason Toref steered them back toward home. He didn't want to think his uncle would intentionally lie to him, but he was apparently trying to keep him from seeing something there. Yaran vowed to make his own way to the mountain facility as soon as the opportunity presented itself.

Yaran walked into his home office late one evening and saw the message light flashing on the communication console. He activated the reconnect and a moment later Toref's face came up on the screen.

"Sorry I wasn't here when you called. Lauranna and I were out in the gardens."

"Hopefully, it was a nice walk," Toref said smiling. "I was calling because I need you to take Tim to Emborie tomorrow."

"Of course. Why?"

"They've been doing maintenance on their machinery and are having some trouble. Tim has helped them before, so he's familiar with their equipment. I told them you would be there first thing in the morning."

"If anyone can help them, Tim can."

"Thank you Yaran, I appreciate it. They would have sent someone to get him at the mine, but I didn't see any reason for you to go there first."

"No, it's fine, I can take him. I'll be in the city tomorrow, so I'll see you for the evening meal." Yaran was about to disconnect when he noticed Toref hesitate. "Something else?"

"I received a communication from Jarock's ship. He is expected back on Zantia in about two weeks."

"Two weeks," Yaran muttered. "Well, we knew he would be back eventually."

Before dawn the next morning, Yaran and Tim were on their way to Emborie.

"Toref told me you've helped out in Emborie before?"

"Yes, four or five times."

"Always for repair work?"

"Yes. They have several men who do the maintenance, but the machinery is old, and so are some of the mechanics."

Yaran chuckled. Then with a somber tone, he broke the news. "Toref told me my father is on his way back. He'll be here in about two weeks."

Tim took a deep breath and sighed. "Well, we knew this was temporary."

"Yes, we did. It just seems the time has gone by so fast."

"Yes, it has."

"I've been contemplating an idea, but I didn't want to say anything before I knew it would work."

"What kind of idea?"

"This depends on Julia's okay of course, but I want to move her and Marta into the city. The warehouses are shorthanded due to the current increase in production. Since some of the staffing is now my responsibility, I would like to have her start work there in a couple of weeks. I already checked, and a family apartment is available in the workers' complex, which might be good for Marta to meet children her own age."

Tim looked skeptical. "What about your mother?"

"I talked to her about this yesterday."

"Really? She's okay with it?"

"It's hard for me to admit, but I can easily make her see my point of view. Not with any evil intentions, of course, but if I really want something, she has a hard time saying no."

Tim roared with laughter. "I think everyone already knew that."

"Very funny. But seriously, the house isn't going to miss one more worker. Leea was replaced, and Marik didn't do much. It didn't take long for her to see through my request, by the way, and knew exactly why I chose Julia, but she was agreeable to the idea."

"And the Desolk?"

"Women are in charge of the household staff, so it's her decision. I doubt he'll even notice."

"Your father isn't stupid."

"No, he's not," Yaran smiled slyly. "That's why I've asked Lauranna to let Julia leave before he returns."

"I don't know how to thank you."

"No need. I would do more if I could. You and Julia should discuss this and let me know if it's something you want to do. It would mean starting over."

"If we can see each other more, I don't think there's anything to think about."

"Good. Then it's settled."

The shuttle landed near the entrance to one of Emborie's two mines, which was close to the main house. They were met in the reception area by Administrator Graeden. Tim gave him a quick greeting and then hurried through the building.

"Hopefully, we can return Tim later this evening," the administrator said, letting out a sigh. "One of these days we'll replace that old machinery, and these requests for his assistance will no longer be necessary. But until then, we appreciate the help."

"We are happy to assist."

"I don't believe you've been in our mine before, have you, Yaran?"

"No, this is the first time." He had met Graeden on several previous visits to the main house. Haliel, Emborie's city leader, was his father's closest friend, and the families visited each other often. Graeden had worked in Emborie about as long as Cashon had worked in Alrack, and was considered more like a family member than merely an administrator.

"If you would like a tour, I would be more than happy to show you around."

"Thank you for the offer, Graeden, but maybe some other time. I have some business with the Desolk, and then need to return to Alrack."

"I'm sorry, the Desolk is away at the moment. Is it urgent?"

"No. It was more of a courtesy call, but maybe you can help."

"I will try."

"I was hoping to speak to one of your workers."

"Which one?" Graeden asked surprised.

"Marik. He was recently transferred from Alrack."

Graeden turned toward a nearby desk, and without having to ask, the guard seated there touched the terminal screen. "There's been no update on his status today," the Zantian informed them. "Should I contact the foreman?"

"Yes. Ask him to join us here in the reception area."

"Right away." After a minute on the communication link, the guard added, "The foreman will be here in about fifteen minutes."

After getting both of them a cup of tea, Graeden moved to the nearby seating area. "May I ask why you want to see that particular worker?" he asked once they were settled.

"I need to clarify a few things with him. I want to hear his side of an incident that happened in Alrack. I promise I won't keep him."

"I'm not sure Marik is going to be much help to you. We sent him to tunnel 15, which was obviously a mistake because he spends much of his time in isolation. It seems he can't stay out of trouble."

"I guess some things never change. What's in tunnel 15?"

"It goes down to the underground river where the bio-extraction is performed for the steel."

"I understand it's a dangerous process?"

"Unfortunately, it is. The extracted element is quite unstable until transferred to a containment unit. We continually improve on the process, but there is still a short time where it's unprotected. We have lost several workers who were careless, but obviously, Marik has found a way around that," Graeden said with some sarcasm.

"You know him?"

"Oh yes. He worked in the main house for several years before going to Alrack. And trust me, Marik made himself known to everyone."

"Well, it was the same in Alrack. That worker has a knack for causing trouble."

"So I understand. That's why he was sent back here, although I think they should have sent him to the other side of the planet."

"Or maybe off the planet."

With a slight creak, the lift door opened, and an older Human with red hair and a graying beard, both in desperate need of a trim, headed in their direction. The two Zantian men rose. He was tall for a Human, only a few inches shorter than Yaran, with an athletic build, which was typical for many mine workers.

He stopped a few feet away at the edge of the seating area, and without the formality of an introduction, the administrator asked about Marik.

"Roger, is it possible to have a word with Marik? Would that interfere with his duties?"

"Unfortunately, he's in solitary confinement again. He still can't seem to stay out of trouble."

Yaran took a few steps closer, wanting to ask a question, but stopped when the man's bright green eyes looked at him.

The foreman's face flushed as he turned to the administrator and said nervously, "Marik being on my crew is more trouble than it's worth, I'm afraid. I'm lucky if I can get three days of work out of him in a week. And his antics distract the others."

Yaran barely heard the comment as his heart begin to race. Familiarity washed over him as he looked closer at the foreman. It was the eyes. He had looked into those same green eyes almost every day for the last twenty years.

And then the man's name registered—Roger. This was Leea's father.

# CHAPTER 12

# Morodons

A familiar feeling came over Leea as the stranger took a few steps past the tree-line into the sunlight. A quiet chuckle escaped her lips when she saw it wore a long hooded robe. *Why is everyone on this planet trying to hide under a cape?* she thought.

"Hello," she called out hesitantly, getting up from the lounge.

Suddenly, in her mind's eye, she was back in Alrack, standing in the darkened alley. She watched as the hooded figure stepped from the doorway, reached out with an aged hand and placed a blue crystal into hers, and then the feeling of desperation coursing through her mind as the alien clutched her hand.

The mysterious figure reclaimed her attention. It wanted to know if she had the object from Zantia.

"Yes, I do. It's in my bag in the house. I'll get it for you."

Before she could turn, the alien held her back. The gift was meant for their clan leader only. She would need appropriate clothing, along with food and water to make the long trip.

Leea stopped short. "You want me to go with you? Where?"

The figure indicated through the trees.

"You want me to go with you into the woods?" Although she feigned concern, the truth was, she felt no fear at all. If anything, the prominent emotion was curiosity. But before she could dissect the sentiment any further, her greeter landed on the edge of the lounge. It eyed her for a moment then flew to the trees and perched itself on a branch above her visitor.

"Do not be afraid," a distinctive voice now spoke in her mind. "No harm will come to you." The greeter spread its wings as if to confirm the promise.

"O… Okay. Give me a few minutes to get some things together." Hurrying into the house, she went straight to the bedroom closet and pulled down the travel bag stowed on the top shelf. She removed her mother's box, opened it, and took out the small stone. *Was it just a coincidence that I put this in here, or did the hooded figure in Alrack have something to do with it?* Leea dismissed the notion.

Quickly, she dressed, packed a few bottles of water and some meal bars into a new rucksack, and secured it to her back. Reaching for the door release, she hesitated. "I must be crazy." She shook her head, took a deep breath, and stepped back into the morning sunlight.

They walked through the trees at a constant pace, with Leea about twenty feet behind the barely five-foot figure. Although the guide never turned to make sure she was still following, she had the distinct impression the mysterious being was keeping pace with her instead of the other way around.

The woods were astonishing. Trees so tall, it was hard to define where they ended, and the sky began. Smooth, glass-like trunks—whose circumference she couldn't begin to estimate—brown branches and pale neon-green pleated leaves merged well with the cloudless teal blue sky. The whole environment made her feel incredibly small. Several varieties of shorter but equally impressive trees stood among the giants.

One, in particular, made her smile. It had no leaves but was covered in two-to-three inch soft black quills that swayed lightly in the breeze. Extending a hand, Leea cautiously approached. But before her palm could make contact, ten sets of glowing green eyes appeared through the black fleece, followed by five tiny white, pointy-eared smiling faces. She jumped back. Before deciding if she wanted to investigate further, five long pink tongues jutted from the cute little features, one sliming her jacket with sticky goo, and then the tree erupted into chatter. Looking up the trunk, and across the branches, she realized it wasn't a breeze that caused the quills to sway, but the movement of hundreds of the tiny creatures—curious faces protruded everywhere. She had disturbed their home. It was time to move on.

Examining each new species as she walked, her guide, as expected, kept pace. From the white nubby tree to the small purple fuzzy bush, everything invited further study. She knew some of the foliage was bioluminescent because she'd seen their glow through the trees at night. Concentrating on the unique life around her, she hoped the stranger would keep her from touching anything harmful.

It had been unnerving the first few days, listening to the forest noise from her open back door. Now, she wanted to stop, close her eyes, and take in the sounds that assaulted her senses. At the House of Alrack, the world was still, with the exception of light winds on the bluff rustling the Jala tree branches, or the occasional ship flying over the city, there was nothing to disturb the silence.

Here, deep within the canopy, everything was alive. All creatures, down to the smallest, whether chirping, tweeting, snorting, or screeching in the distance, wanted to be heard, and the newcomer wanted to listen to them all. Several times she had to stop short as something small, or not-so-small, slithered or walked across her path—all as curious about her as she was about them.

After about an hour, fatigue started to set in. The trek they took followed no designated path, but went straight through the trees, which required a lot of stepping over roots and rocks, as well as an occasional steep incline. Although the medication was helping her body adjust to the Dekarran environment, the increased exertion was taking a toll on her systems.

They eventually entered a clearing, and the guide motioned to a fallen log laying in the sun, and she understood she was supposed to sit and rest. The alien walked ahead and stood just inside the tree-line.

"Don't you need to rest? Eat something?" As expected, silence remained.

She drank a bottle of water and ate one of the bars, which re-energized her, then leaned back on the log and raised her face to the sun. The cooler temperatures were enjoyable and allowed for a sense of freedom she had never known, but at times she missed the oppressive heat, and how it would envelop her like a warm blanket.

After a few quiet minutes, chirping sounds caught her attention. Looking up, she spotted her feathered companion but was surprised to see it wasn't alone. Another bird sat by its side on a high branch, this one more colorful, no doubt belonging to her guide. Four wings fluttered—it was time to go. Repacking her bag, she headed out of the clearing.

In the next hour, the terrain remained the same except for an increased incline. Leea slowed her pace, and on occasion needed to stop a moment to catch her breath and take a drink. She regretted not bringing more water. A few minutes after another short rest in a smaller clearing, the trees opened up to reveal a wide, rushing river that curved its way through the now visible mountain.

Turning upriver, they soon came to a suspension bridge that crossed the water at a narrow point. Three stone steps led up to a large rock platform that supported bound wooden slats, and two nearby trees were used to anchor the roped sides.

"Is this thing safe?" she asked rhetorically.

With ease, her guide started across. Under its small frame, the bridge seemed fixed as the figure moved carefully over the boards. Making sure her bag was secure, she climbed the three steps, waiting until the escort was halfway, then gripped the handholds, and cautiously stepped onto the first plank. It felt sturdy, and looking ahead, they all seemed intact. Taking a few steps, she found it took no effort to keep her balance and continued.

At the halfway point she stopped and looked down at the rushing water, clutching tighter as the bridge slightly swayed under her feet. The sound was deafening. A large rock below, protruding through the swell, caused the water to plume upward, soaking her pants and making her hope they would reach their destination soon.

"I need a rest," she panted, sinking to the stone steps of the opposite platform. Her guide waited for her a short distance away, having taken up its usual position within the trees.

Once their procession continued, the foliage started too thin and was soon replaced by a rockier terrain. A narrow path materialized, making the pace easier for which Leea was extremely grateful. Switchback curves caused her to lose sight of her guide every few minutes, but walking faster to keep up was impossible; her legs were sore, and she was now finding it difficult to catch her breath.

"Please slow down, I can't keep up!"

After a few more bends a straightaway appeared, but up ahead the trail was empty.

Irritation set in.

"Great!" she called laboriously. "Did you bring me all the way up here just to abandon me? Where are you?" Leea scoured the area for signs of her greeter, but couldn't find it. *And what help would a bird be anyway?* she thought sarcastically.

Moving slowly along, movement on the right caught her attention. Although the uphill pathway stayed close to the rock-face, occasionally a small drop-off appeared between the two. At the base of one such valley, her guide waited patiently next to an outcropping of bushes. Leea hesitated briefly but saw no option but to follow, so careful not to slip, made her way down the incline. The alien waved a hand across the rock wall behind the foliage and an outline of an arch appeared. Almost instantaneously the wall dissolved, revealing a cavity inside.

Leea stared in astonishment. "How did you do that?"

As if it hadn't heard, the small figured stepped aside and indicated she should go first. Resigned, Leea leaned down to clear the entry and found herself in a long, narrow space with blue glass-like walls and a high ceiling. As the entry rematerialized behind them, light seemed to exude from the walls and negated the fact that she should be standing in a dark cave. Gently touching the glass surface, she found that although it looked smooth, it had a textured feel, and emitted a low level of heat.

"This is amazing." Leea looked down at the alien and smiled.

With one hand, the hood was pulled back, revealing a bald head, light brown eyes, and nondescript facial features, making it impossible to guess if it were male or female.

The alien spoke in a monotone voice, but this time not in her head. "My name is Tellia, and I apologize for the oddity of our encounter. It is imperative that we are not seen, but I will let someone else explain." Tellia smiled and motioned her through a low archway at the far end of the narrow foyer.

If Leea thought the small entry was fascinating, the sight that greeted her next took her breath away. She stood at the top of a stairway leading down into an immense oval cavern. The blue walls continued throughout the large expanse, and the air was warm with a sweet herbal scent. The steps ahead were made of large carved rock, and connected at the bottom with an intricate stone floor—more than half of which was taken up by a colorful design.

A bright yellow circle was the largest piece. Seeming to lay on top, was an elongated triangle filled with small multi-colored stones with the narrow point protruding outside the sphere. Each of the three sides had a different color: red, green, and dark brown. At the center of the design was another circle, this one a lighter brown. Connecting the inner circle to the narrowest side of the triangle were two curved blue lines.

Her guide waited as Leea took in the surroundings but now urged her to make her way down.

"If you would please wait, our clan leader will be here to welcome you shortly," Tellia said once they stood on the cavern floor.

"May I look around?"

"Yes, of course. This is our gathering place. Feel free to enjoy our home." The alien gave Leea a brief nod and was gone.

Around the walls were several arched doorways twice the height of the previous ones that seemed to be hallways. The colors of the floor design, as well as the design itself, were repeated along the blue surface but on a much smaller scale and Leea couldn't resist walking around, tracing the intricate carvings with her fingers.

"They are the keepers of our history."

Startled, Leea turned to find a new member of the mysterious race wearing a dark green robe with a small replica of the floor pattern hanging around her neck. Like Tellia, gender was impossible to decipher. This person was shorter than the guide, and just as bald, but had one distinctive difference—its age—it seemed ancient. It had a weathered bronze complexion, with deep lines across its face. Nestled among the grooves were profound amber eyes with tiny flecks of bright orange. As the incandescent light played off them, they sparkled like embers of a fire while radiating soft warmth. Leea felt extremely comfortable as the eyes took her in, and knew she had nothing to fear.

"I don't understand," Leea said, embarrassed to be staring.

The alien pointed at the floor's center. "We call it *remdalar*, which simply means 'that which sustains us,' and symbolizes our connection with the world around. The yellow circle represents our sun and the light that we need for energy. The triangle signifies all that grows, the different colors defining the variety this world has to offer. The circle in the middle indicates our planet; the ground beneath our feet where we are free to roam. The blue curves denote the air and water we need to survive. The arrangement of the planet, water, and air signify the people who are allowed to flourish here. The *remdalar* intertwines the pieces to convey how all aspects of life are connected and depend on each other."

"It's beautiful."

"Come, there is much to talk about." Gently, the small figure took Leea's hand and guided her to a smaller room along one of the hallways. This space was bare, with the exception of uncomfortable-looking furniture in a far corner. The material mimicked the surrounding walls and Leea braced herself for the hard surface. But once seated, the chair gently molded to her body.

"Interesting," Leea observed, running her hands along the sides. It was solid but as comfortable as any cushioned furniture she'd ever sat on.

"The material makeup of the crystal allows for versatile uses."

Leea pondered that information but remained silent.

"I am happy you have come to visit us."

"I didn't think I had a choice."

"The choice was always yours, but I am glad you came."

Leea smiled warily. "I don't mean to be rude, but who are you? I thought that except for Humans this planet is uninhabited."

"First, let me introduce myself. My name is Nethas, and my people are called Morodon. We would not have revealed ourselves so soon, but you carry something my people have waited a long time for."

"Oh! Of course!" Leea retrieved the blue stone from her pocket, only then noticing it mimicked her surroundings. "What is it?"

"A message crystal."

Nethas took the offered object, then gripped Leea's hand. Momentarily displaced, visions of the alley and the gnarled hand that had placed the rock in hers flashed through her mind. Julia and Marta occupied her peripheral vision, and Nethas stood to the side watching the scene play out.

*What am I supposed to do with this?* Leea had silently asked.

The answer had flowed effortlessly through her mind. *"Put this in a sacred place until and the rightful owner comes for it. Do not be afraid."*

Then the alien seemed to turn toward Nethas. *"We have done our best to give you as much information as we can. Unfortunately, we are losing our will as many of our voices are dying. Protect yourselves."*

Startled, Leea pulled back. "It was talking to you. How…?"

"Forgive me; I did not mean to intrude on your memories. And I apologize for the brief message he imbedded in your mind."

"That's okay. It was just…unexpected. I remember an odd feeling when he touched me, but thought it was my imagination. Did you know him?"

"No," the alien said, seeming disappointed. "We had never met."

"How long have you lived on this planet?"

"This world is several billion years old. Our species came to life not long after."

At this Leea could only stare wide-eyed. "Do…do the Humans know you're here? Live here in this cave?"

"Some do, but not where we live."

"I… I don't understand."

"We are a reclusive race. Our clans live in mountain caves, such as this one, on several continents. We once moved freely beyond these walls. But long ago, Zantians came to plunder our world. After many years, when traditional conventions and reasonable negotiations failed, we had no choice but to give the impression that we contaminated our home and fled."

Once again Leea stared wide eyed. "You can do that?"

"We do what needs to be done to protect ourselves."

"Then why are there Morodons on Zantia? How did they find you?"

"We let our guard down, and they returned. However, this time, they did not want to destroy us, they wanted to trade for our people. A handful of brave citizens volunteered, and that is the last we heard from them."

"Why did they take them?"

"What you think you know about the Zantians is only a fraction of who they really are. Many of their own kind are unaware of the secrets they hold."

"I know their history."

Nethas shook her head. "Unfortunately, you only know what they want you to know."

"Of that, I have no doubt."

"Before the Humans arrived here, I saw the visions change again. An end to the tyranny was within reach, but keeping ourselves concealed was imperative for the positive outcome."

"But you said some knew you were here?"

"Yes. Protecting our anonymity has been … somewhat unsuccessful. Humans can be quite clever. We have managed to keep our caves hidden, but we are in constant peril when we venture outside."

"So that's why Tellia always stayed in the trees."

Nethas nodded.

"Do they want to do you harm?"

"No."

"You said you saw the danger before the Humans came? How old are you?"

"We are a long-lived race. I am over three hundred of your years. Life expectancy should grant me fifty to seventy-five more."

"Wow," was Leea's only immediate response, but then she quickly asked, "I still don't understand when you said you saw? And what the visions are?"

"I am a seer. I see what the future brings."

Leea paused with renewed amazement. "That's how you knew I would be on Dekarra?"

"What I see are fluid images of events to come. With each choice you make, you move toward one thing and leave something else behind. As a seer, I can interpret the signs of what will happen, and what might. To answer your question, yes, I knew you would be here. Not you specifically, but someone from a faraway place that would set this world on a different path."

"Because of me?" Leea looked at Nethas incredulously. "Because of the message I brought? Maybe it's one of the other men who've come here?"

"I have not seen anyone else arriving here."

"I don't understand. Others have come here before me."

"That is possible. But I would not see them unless they had some effect on our environment, as I have seen with you."

Leea needed to clear her head. She rose from the chair and approached the nearest wall, instantly admiring one of the recessed carvings. The *remdalar* in the main hall was stone, the one around Nethas's neck looked to be metal, but the ones along the walls were glass, fused with their colorful pattern into the crystal. Interspersed were other symbols, each incorporating some part of the main design.

"They are the keepers of our history."

Leea jumped. "What does that mean?"

"Each carving represents a major occurrence in our past. We can access them and relive a part, or the entire event."

"How does it work?"

Nethas waved a hand in front of the nearest carving. An opening appeared in the center, and she reached a hand inside. The colors of the design started to emerge from the wall in streams of light, enveloping the small alien. Hues brightened, and a low hum resonated. Shades accentuated and seemed to separate then regroup, producing a new color. Within a few seconds, Nethas was completely engulfed in sparkling light. Leea took a few steps back, not sure what she was seeing.

Then, as quickly as the display started, it disappeared.

"The story glyphs interact with our body chemistry," Nethas explained, stepping back. "What you discerned as light is actually energy which produces the connection to the past event inscribed in the carving."

"That was incredible. If I put my hand in there, would the same thing happen?"

Nethas chuckled. "No, it would not be possible. Human chemistry is quite different from ours."

"Is this entire cavern made of crystal?"

"Most of it, yes. Our history teaches us that we draw our power from the crystal, which draws its energy from the world around. Without this element, we would most likely die."

"You really believe that?"

Nethas smiled. "We all have a source from which we draw inner strength. For some species, it is a physical thing you can touch, like ours. For others, like Humans, it is mystical. In the end, the belief keeps us moving forward, as it should." Nethas led them back to the seating area.

"Can I ask one more question?"

"You may ask as many as you like."

Leea lowered her head, crimson rising in her cheeks. "I mean no offense, but are you male or female?"

Nethas laughed softly. "No offense taken. Considering our appearance, it is a reasonable question. We are born asexual, meaning we have no established gender. However, we do take on the role of one or the other eventually. For example, I am considered female. The guide, who brought you here, Tellia, is also female."

"How do you have children?" Leea blurted, her cheeks brightening more.

"Not in a manner familiar to you. Our bodies possess all the necessary components to produce a child when we choose. Since our life span is many centuries longer than yours, and right now our accommodations are restricted, the need to reproduce is limited. We would quickly overrun our home otherwise."

Leea couldn't imagine such a way of life. Thoughts of her relationships with other people flooded her mind. Without a doubt those connections helped mold her into the person she was. Her grandmother and Julia; the family with whom she shared happy times, and who had sustained her during the sad ones. Her cheeks warmed as she thought of intimate moments with Yaran, and the unbreakable bond that existed between them, born out of love. Did the Morodons experience any of these things?

"We are all family here," Nethas said as if sensing her confusion. "Special relationships are formed, but not exclusive ones like in your society. We have no need, or longing, for such associations. When children are born, they are raised by the clan as a whole."

"Have you had a child?"

"Yes. I have given birth to one child who has chosen the gender of male. He is with a clan on another continent."

Nethas rose from her chair and moved to the wall. Waving her hand, a small drawer appeared from where she retrieved what looked like a necklace

"I would like to give you something before you return. Do not be afraid." Nethas took Leea's hand and placed a round yellow pendant, about an inch and a half in diameter, in her palm and closed her fingers around it. The hard object slowly began to warm in her fist. As the heat intensified, Leea tried to open her hand, but Nethas held it shut.

"It will not hurt you. Keep your hand closed a few more moments."

A burning sensation shot up her arm, and Leea groaned loudly. At that moment, the heat diminished and Nethas released her. Gingerly opening her fist, Leea examined her palm and found no visible burns, not even a red mark.

Leea ran a finger over the still-warm glassy surface. "What is it?"

"It is called *jarkut*. It represents a part of the *remdalar*, and possesses the ability to remove obstacles you may encounter."

"I will need this because…?"

"I believe it could be invaluable at times."

"How does it work?"

Nethas stood and hung the chain around Leea's neck. "Hold the amulet in your fist and project your wishes on the nearest person or object. It has limitations, of course, but will easily open a door or make someone regard you in a positive light."

"Can anyone use this?"

"No. The *jarkut* bonded with you as it heated in your hand, so only you can control it." Nethas touched Leea's shoulder. "Believe in its powers, and it can help you. But beware of those over whom the *jarkut* has no power."

"I don't understand…"

"You will in time. There will be challenges ahead, so I offer you this small item to assist you in the fulfillment of your journey."

"Can you tell me what all that means?"

"I cannot influence any decisions you are going to make. You need to live your life as it is meant to evolve. Do not second-guess your actions."

"I'll try."

Leea retrieved her bag and stepped away from the seating area. *What a beautiful, yet strange, alien place this is.* "Will I see you again?"

"I will not summon you, but if you need something from me, the greeter will show you the way."

"The greeter will…?"

"Yes, the greeter has chosen you, and, therefore, can help you…also in a limited capacity, of course."

Leea looked down at the small alien with the wise, amber eyes, gave her a weak smile and shook her head. "I'm not sure I'll ever understand."

"I have every confidence that someday you will."

"Will the guide take me back?"

"Tellia will take you as far as the bridge, and then the greeter will guide you the rest of the way."

Leea could only shake her head again.

Nethas walked Leea back to the entrance, where Tellia waited with her water bottles refilled and extra food. Leea repacked her bag and turned before stepping through the portal. "Can I ask one more question?"

Nethas smiled and nodded.

"Can your visions tell me if I will see those I love on Zantia again?"

Nethas shook her head. "As I said before, the visions do not work that way. But let me give you some advice. Never give up hope. As long as you have that, all possibilities exist."

"I will always have hope," Leea assured her softly.

Nethas watched as Leea and Tellia disappeared up the embankment and re-sealed the entry. It was hard to imagine that the presence of this young Human could bring about the change the Morodons sought for so long. The trigger had not been revealed, but the signs indicated it would happen soon.

She had been intentionally vague with Leea. There was no point in telling her the true nature of the visions, or the reason for her people on Zantia because it would only overwhelm her. The greeter had sensed her influence the moment she landed, so Nethas saw no reason to doubt the truth. Now, they needed to proceed with caution. Once the visions were substantiated, she would speak to Leea again, of that she was certain.

Nethas made her way to the viewing room. Once she viewed the communiqué from Zantia, she would connect with the other caves and share the information with everyone. That way, there would be no hesitation when the time came. The news from Zantia would play heavily in the coming effort.

Nethas hoped the elder who sacrificed his life reestablishing this connection would have word about all those who had stepped forward that day long ago—including her son.

She also never lost hope.

## CHAPTER 13

# New Friends

Sitting at the kitchen table, Leea rested her hands around a hot cup of coffee. She normally opted for tea in the afternoon, but her mind reeled from her morning's discovery, so she wanted the comfort of the dark, aromatic liquid.

*The universe sure held some unique mysteries,* she thought as she pulled the *jarkut* from under her shirt. *This small inanimate object can help me remove obstacles. What does that really mean? And why would I need something like this?* Light emanated through the small glass sun as she held it up to the window, brightening it like the large orb outside.

"Nethas said to wrap my hand around it, and concentrate on what I wanted it to do," she said out loud. "Hmmm…"

She enclosed it in her fist and looked around her table, her gaze coming to rest on the salt shaker. She willed it to move. Nothing. She tightened her grip and tried again. Nothing.

"Okay, how is this supposed to work?"

*Concentrate,* her thoughts replied.

Leea closed her eyes, cleared her mind, and visualized the container. Ever so slightly, the *jarkut* warmed in her hand. Opening her eyes, she found the four-inch glass bottle hovering about an inch off the table. Startled, she let the mysterious talisman slip from her grasp. Instantly, the suspended container dropped with a clang and rolled across the table.

She tucked the *jarkut* back under her shirt, righted the salt shaker and stepped away from the table, eyes wide. "Enough experimentation for one day."

Pouring a fresh cup of coffee, Leea went into the back yard to enjoy the waning afternoon. Walking the perimeter of her yard, she stepped into the trees where Tellia had stood that morning. She chuckled. *What a crazy world this is. What would*

*Yaran say if he could see me now?* The absentminded thought instantly changed her mood, so with a heavy heart, she slowly returned to the house.

Once she'd finished dinner and cleaned the kitchen, Leea retrieved the data-cube from her travel bag and retreated to the second bedroom. She had resisted continuing the writing, wanting to come to terms with her emotions first. The tears were slowly diminishing, which she attributed to Mary's many hours of patiently listening to her talk about her life, and the woman's comforting words that things would get better. Yaran still occupied most of her thoughts, but she found them easier to manage every day.

Settling into the desk chair, she powered on the datapad and waited for the file to upload. Bettina had shown her how to interface the two systems, and within a few seconds, a list of seven files appeared. Confused, she looked at the white rectangle, wondering if it was the wrong one, but another scan of the monitor showed the one she had titled 'When life made sense.'

Mearos had told her the portable storage device was new so she speculated these files must have been hidden somewhere on the pad. Since she had believed her story was the only one there, she'd used the quick-copy function, which would have pulled all files, even those not visible.

She scrutinized the list. Except for one that had a Zantian title, she couldn't decipher the rest because they were titled in a symbol-like font she didn't recognized. Opening the one in Zantian, it seemed to be a letter. Her comprehension of the written language wasn't good, but she recognized enough words to give her cause for concern.

The next three were blank except for a single, unfamiliar Zantian name at the top. The fifth looked like sets of numbers arranged in rows and columns along with a row of the unusual typeface. The last of the strange documents contained an entire page of the symbols, arranged exactly like the numbered file, in rows and columns.

What gave her pause was wondering what function in the language selection would produce such writing. She had played with the language fonts before but didn't remember anything even close to these. They were intricate in their design of lines and curves, but each one unique, none repeated. She wished she could show them to Mearos, especially since she surmised the letter was about the captain. But how could she get these to him? His cargo ship came every three months, so she had some time to figure it out.

The associate reviewed the video a second time, gaping as the salt shaker levitated in front of the auburn haired woman. He activated his comm-link.

"I have news about the new girl," he informed the person on the other end.

"Like what?"

"Early this morning she went outside before sunrise. After the sun came up, she rushed in, packed a bag and left. The elapsed time on the video said she was gone about six hours. But the interesting thing happened after she came back."

"Send it to me and wait while I take a look." Three minutes later the other came back online. "Interesting. They gave her a *jarkut*. I wonder why they think she'll need it. We should step up the surveillance."

"I could put a tracker on her."

"No. That's probably not necessary. The only reason I can think of as to why they contacted her, is because she had something, or some information they wanted. Which makes me wonder why she's really here. I doubt they'll take the chance to summon her again anytime soon. But this could be the break we've been hoping for, so just keep monitoring the feeds. We can be patient."

Leea prepared to enter the Dekarran workforce. She was used to working every day, but this would be different. On Zantia, she got up at the same time every morning, no exceptions, and went the short distance to the kitchen where the same tasks awaited her day after day. She had never questioned the duties her race performed for the Zantians; she was born to them, so they were a part of her life. Her parents and grandparents had done this without complaint, and she'd known her life would be no different.

But the lifestyle on Dekarra was completely alien to her. Yes, people here also did their tasks—jobs—but there was a definite separation between work and home. She looked forward to this new concept. Bettina had taken her to visit a small salon yesterday where she had sat uncomfortably while her hair and nails were pampered but had vehemently declined the offer to add color to either— much to Bettina's amusement.

She tried on the outfit she planned to wear on her first day: black slacks, a short-sleeved red and white shirt. Leea was pleased with her reflection and hoped her newness to this world wouldn't stand out.

*Leea ran giggling through the garden, trying to avoid the shrubs as they brushed against her legs. She turned and saw Yaran chasing her and giggled louder. Just then, her foot caught something on the ground, and she went down on all fours and started to cry. The tears weren't for her scraped knees, but for a sudden sense of loss that she couldn't immediately understand. Two strong arms picked her up and held her close, his touch making her feel safe. He began to hum a familiar tune, and she relaxed.*

*Suddenly, she was alone in the house walking cautiously down the hall until a familiar door loomed ahead. She was about to enter when it opened, and Yaran stepped out, closing it behind him and blocking her entrance.*

*"You can't go in there right now, Leea," Nethas said, suddenly standing beside her.*

*"But I need to." She tried to push past Yaran.*

*"You're not ready yet." The Morodon laid a hand on her arm.*

*"You have to let me see." She tried to shrug it off, but Nethas held her in place. "I need to go in! Please, I have to go in!"*

*As she struggled, Yaran pulled her close. "It's important to keep you safe. We won't let anything happen to you." She relaxed into him and let him lead her away.*

Leea woke with a jolt. That dream again, or should she call it a nightmare? Why did her subconscious continue to plague her with it? It was rarely the same, as certain details always changed. This time, Nethas was there, which made sense, given her recent encounter with the Morodon, but it also included Yaran. In fact, it was both of them trying to protect her, but from what? She appreciated their words of encouragement, but the once-weekly visit always seemed to center on the room where her mother died; one that no one in her dream would let her enter.

She sat up and did a mental calculation, knowing what the answer would be— it would soon be the twentieth anniversary of her mother's death. But the question remained: what did her mind want her to know? She wasn't sure if she welcomed that answer or feared it.

The bus ride to the city was eye-opening. The large vehicle motored silently along, weaving its way through populated areas, stopping about every few blocks to let on another one or two passengers who quickly found a seat. Some would pull out a reader while others settled back and closed their eyes hoping for a few more moments of rest before entering another day of work—or so she assumed.

The ride took about forty minutes. When the bus stopped near the lab complex, she, Mary, and eight other passengers disembarked. All ten headed in the same direction. Mary helped her through security then showed her to the office of her new boss, Kent Madigan. A receptionist informed them that he hadn't arrived yet, but Leea could wait for him in his office. Mary gave her a hug, wished her luck, and promised to return for her at the end of the day.

Leea set her bag on a chair in front of a small desk angled in a corner, but not wanting to sit, moved to the large window and looked out over the city. It was almost reminiscent of her stay at the Inn, which she could see if she leaned into the glass.

"Magnificent sight, isn't it?"

Startled, she spun around to find a slightly overweight, middle-aged man standing in the doorway. He was about five foot ten, with short, bright orange hair. He might have been an attractive man had it not been for the chill emanating from his ice-blue eyes and a facial expression that couldn't seem to hide a sense of displeasure. A feeling of dread came over her, and she hoped his scowl wasn't because of her.

"Yes, it is beautiful." Leea approached him, hand extended as was customary. "I'm Leea Dennison. I believe you are expecting me."

He reluctantly took her hand but released it quickly as their skin touched. "Yes, Bettina Reese arranged for your employment," he said with disinterest. "My name is Kent Madigan, and I will be your supervisor. You won't work for me directly, but in one of my offices." He seated himself behind the desk and powered on the computer, then concentrated on the screen, seeming to forget about her standing there.

Nervousness about starting this job surfaced. Bettina and Mary had assured her she would enjoy working here, but having looked into Kent Madigan's eyes, she wasn't so sure. He knew where she came from, and she feared his indifference meant he didn't approve. How would everyone else react to a stranger from an enemy world? Her nervousness increased.

After a minute, Leea was sure her new boss had forgotten about her. He rummaged in a drawer, made notations on the computer, did everything except look at her. She reached to pick up her bag, having made the decision to leave when he rose.

"Follow me."

Leaving the office, he walked past the reception desk, and into the open office area where she and Bettina had visited a week earlier which was already buzzing with activity. Once through the maze of workers, a short hallway brought them to an office with five desks. Except for a small one in the corner, all were occupied. Kent stopped and introduced her to the occupant of the first desk, Farrell Reynolds, and was gone. Leea still wasn't sure what to make of his attitude but decided not to worry about it. She turned her attention to the woman now standing in front of her.

Leea guessed they were about the same age. She was shorter by a few inches, with long, golden brown hair pulled straight back into a ponytail. Her features were plain, in a pretty sort of way, but what immediately stood out were her large blue eyes, and the widest, friendliest smile Leea had ever seen.

"I'm so glad to meet you finally!" Farrell's enthusiasm overshadowed her soft voice as she extended a hand.

"Thank you," Leea took the hand and appreciated the friendly grip.

"We've all been anxiously waiting for you to get here. We've talked about nothing else for a week."

Leea's smile faded. "Really?"

Farrell's eyes grew big. "I'm sorry! I didn't mean to offend you. I just meant… we've been so excited to meet you. We can't image how you've survived on Zantia all your life. Most of us have often wondered about the Humans there. How well they were doing, hoping they had survived—and here you are, somewhat of a miracle to us."

Leea cocked her head to one side, confused. "You know about me? I was told only Kent did."

Farrell clasped a hand to her mouth. "Oh my God… really?! Again, I am so sorry… wow… this introduction isn't going how I had envisioned." She sighed.

Leea smiled and laid a hand on her arm. "I don't mind. It's just that only Kent was supposed to know where I came from, and it would be up to me to share it with anyone else."

"Well, that was somebody's first mistake. He doesn't know how to keep a secret."

"I think I offended him."

"Oh, I doubt it. Kent is grumpy by nature. I think if he ever smiled his face would crack." Both women giggled. "And again I apologize. I wouldn't have said anything had I known."

"Don't apologize. Actually, I'm glad. I wasn't sure how I was going to answer questions about myself if no one knew where I came from. Now I don't have to worry about it."

"Well, thank you for letting me off so easy. But I still feel bad." Farrell gave her a sly smile. "I hope you won't mind a few questions, though, about your life on Zantia?"

"No, I don't mind. I've answered so many already that a few more won't matter."

"I promise I won't bombard you with too many. You'll have enough to deal with just getting familiar with things around here."

Farrell took Leea by the arm and introduced her to the remaining occupants of the office. The three men greeted her warmly, and her apprehension from earlier began to fade.

After a few minutes of polite conversation, Farrell led her out into the hallway. "How about I show you what we do around here before we get into the boring details?"

"I'd like that."

The lab facility consisted of the main twenty-six-floor structure, which they referred to as the 'tower', and two five-story buildings located across a rear court-yard. Farrell said there was also a hangar at the airfield strictly used for military purposes.

"The building over there," Farrell pointed to the five-story white structure to their right, "is where all Earth's history is stored. One day, when we have more time, I'll take you on a tour. The one on the left is where military research is done.

"The military occupies floors twenty through twenty-five of the tower, and the government has offices on the twenty-sixth, which is the top floor. The govern-ment has a whole complex down the street, but since they're involved in some of the research, they keep offices here too."

"What kind of research is done in the...tower?"

"Most of what we do involves energy, medical, electronic, things like that. There are a lot of discoveries made here every year, as there have been for the past century. Rumor has it that the research is going to outgrow these facilities in a few years, and we'll need to find a new place—there isn't enough room around us to expand. We'd like to stop trading with the Zantians someday, so the experiments continue."

"Does our job extend to the military facility?"

"No. They work on top secret stuff, so they keep their own records although we do make occasional deliveries. If you want to see what it looks like, I have a friend who works there, and if he has time, he can give us a tour of the public areas."

"That would be nice. A friend?"

"Yes, Jackson and I have known each other for many years. But around here, we're worlds apart. He's a test pilot, and I'm just an office girl."

"I'm sure you're more than just an office girl," Leea protested.

Farrell looked at her and smiled. "Thanks. I guess we all do our part, no matter what it is. Come on. Let's see if he's available. He's only here on Mondays, so this is perfect. The rest of the week, he's at the airfield, doing whatever test pilots do."

They entered the military facility on the opposite side of the building. A security station stood a few feet inside and looked minuscule in the vast atrium ahead. Farrell asked the female guard if Jackson Owens was available.

The receptionist pushed a button on her headset, and after a moment spoke into it in hushed tones.

Leaning toward Leea, Farrell whispered, "See, what did I tell you? Even a simple request must be kept top secret." Both women did their best to stifle a giggle.

After the brief conversation ended, the guard scanned their security badges. "Please take a seat in the waiting area," she said, "Captain Owens will be with you shortly."

Several white leather sofas and a dozen matching chairs stood in the center of the large area, surrounding a tall glass sculpture standing in the middle of a shallow pool filled with colorful fish. Bright light filtered in from five stories up through dozens of skylights. Large pieces of art adorned three walls, while the fourth was a divided glass barrier that separated the atrium from the rest of the building. The top three floors were visible through a clear portion, while a frosted part hid the bottom two.

"We call this area the party room." Farrell spread her arms out for emphasis. "Formal government and military functions are held here, and I understand they're quite elaborate."

"You've never been?"

"Oh no. Jackson has invited me a few times, but I never have anything to wear."

Leea's eyebrows shot up. "Really?" she said with a chuckle.

Farrell shrugged, and then pointed to the glass barrier. "What you see up there are the office floors, and the laboratories are on the bottom, which takes up the center part of this building. On the other end is an area about twice the size as this one where the military builds some of its secret projects. I don't know if you noticed, but there are no windows on that side…so no one can look in." She rolled her eyes then turned her attention to the muscular man approaching.

Farrell made introductions as they shook hands. Jackson's eyes softened as he looked at his friend; a look Leea recognized all too well. When he stepped closer, and inconspicuously brushed a hand against hers, Leea knew the couple was more than just friends.

"It's nice to meet you." He returned his focus to Leea. "Farrell has talked of little else since she heard you were joining her team."

"Don't say that," Farrell chided him, mortified. "She thought only Kent knew where she came from … and then me and my big mouth … ."

"Oh no. Well, I'm sorry, Leea. But that's Kent."

"So I gather. But it's all right really." Leea smiled and met his dark brown eyes, which were the same color as his short, neatly trimmed hair. He had a square face and a reserved smile that revealed dimpled cheeks.

"I'm showing Leea our facility, so, of course, this is part of the tour," Farrell smiled brightly at Jackson, who returned with a barely noticeable wink. "Since you're here today, I was hoping you could show her around."

"Absolutely. You're actually in luck. Nothing is going on here this week, so I can take you over to see the build area."

The trio walked up a nearby set of stairs to the third floor.

"For obvious reasons, we can't go to the lab floors, but it's boring anyway. Nothing but men and women in white coats hunched over microscopes and computers behind locked doors. I don't even know what goes on in half of those rooms."

They walked through a busy office area whose desk arrangements were similar to those in the tower building. Up another stairway, and down another hall, they found themselves in an observation room overlooking a vast space below. Five large platforms, twice as many portable ladders, forklifts, and several small cranes, were scattered across an otherwise empty floor.

"Can I ask what you build here?"

"We've done everything from weapons and personal armor to armored vehicles, as well as planes," he explained without hesitation.

"Planes? How do you get those out of here?"

"We do small planes or small models of larger ones that can be disassembled and moved to the airfield by truck where we reassemble them."

"And you fly those?"

"Oh yes, that's what I love. I give input on the designs from a pilot standpoint, and then test how my ideas work. Sometimes they do, sometimes they don't."

"Sounds like it can be dangerous work."

"It can be, but we take every precaution, and so far, no mishaps."

After giving a more detailed overview of some of their recent projects, Jackson took them to the first floor and stepped into a showroom where models of what he'd just described stood on display.

"Thank you for taking the time to show me around," Leea said once they were back at the main entrance. "I enjoyed it."

Jackson gave her a big smile. "My pleasure. Come again anytime."

"How did you meet Jackson?" Leea asked as they made their way back.

"We met in college. He was training to be a pilot, and I was studying engineering. After a year, I realized engineering wasn't for me, so I moved into an administrative field."

"College? Does everyone here go to college?"

"Most everyone. It's not a requirement, but most people choose to. Have you been told about our society yet?"

"The only two people I've met, Bettina Reese, who escorted me off the ship, and Mary Sullivan, my neighbor, have told me some things, but not everything, obviously. Bettina suggested I visit the history library."

"Hmmm..."

"Do you know Bettina?"

"Not personally, but I know who she is. She does occasional work for the admiral."

"Well, during our conversations, she was more interested in my history. But I guess I understand. According to her, I'm the first person to come here with information about the Humans on Zantia, so we focused on that."

Farrell furrowed her brow with a faraway look, then said, "how about I save you a trip to the library. Let's get together after work today, and we can swap stories. If you're interested, of course?"

"Yes, I'm definitely interested. But I came in on the bus with Mary, so I should go back home with her."

"No problem, I have an idea."

Once back in the office, Farrell showed Leea how to reach Mary on the phone, and let her explain their after-work plans. Farrell then offered both ladies a ride home. Mary seemed genuinely excited that Leea had made a new friend, and invited both women to her house for dinner, which they gladly accepted.

For the remaining hours of the workday, Farrell explained Leea's job responsibilities, trying not to overwhelm her with too much information. Files were stored in various forms and locations, but Leea felt sure she was up to the challenge.

Dinner consisted of fish, seasoned rice, and a green salad, along with pleasant conversation. For the first time in weeks, Leea didn't feel the constant sadness which had become her life. However, being with Farrell made her heart ache for Julia. There was a lot of similarity between the two women, which she knew she would appreciate eventually.

After dinner, they helped Mary with the dishes, and then all three moved into the small living room with coffee and a plate of cookies.

"Did you know Farrell is one of our little-known celebrities?" Mary asked Leea as they settled in.

Leea gave Farrell a questioning look. "You failed to mention you were famous?"

"I didn't know anyone in the tower knew."

"I'm not sure anyone does. But I paid attention in history class, so when I heard your name, I inquired." A blush could almost be detected under Mary's dark skin as she lowered her eyes. "I'm sorry for any intrusion."

"Don't apologize. I don't broadcast my past, but I don't hide it either."

"What are you talking about?" Leea asked.

"Farrell is a direct descendant of the person who first saw the Zantian attack on Earth."

"You are?"

Farrell smiled shyly. "Yes, my great-great-grandmother's name was Becca Reynolds. She and my great-great-grandfather Jamie—then boyfriend—had skipped classes one morning to spend time in the observation room of Earth's moon base Atlantis where they lived. They saw the attack begin, and alerted the colonists."

"It must have been a horrible time for them."

"It was. The Zantians were on Earth for less than a month, and completely changed the course of the entire planet, ending with an unprovoked attack. And those on the moon could do nothing but watch it happen."

Leea saw the sadness cross Farrell's face and knew with that statement she had summed up exactly what the Zantians had done to her people. "From what Bettina told me, the colonists never returned to Earth after the attack. Why?"

"People were afraid. They tried to make contact, but with no luck. They watched for signs of life, but the lights never came back on, so they stayed away. Remember, this was a colony with children, whose parents wanted nothing more than to keep them safe. A rumor started that the aliens had left some of their people behind to destroy what the ships hadn't. There was never any evidence, but once fear takes hold, it's hard to squelch without concrete proof to the contrary.

"The last message they received from Earth, which was right after the attack started, told them the Zantians were abducting people, and there was a great dread it could happen to them. So, after more than a month, the decision was made to finish the ships already under construction, and then head for the stars to find the abductees. They had the Zantians' location, and the new propulsion data that was smuggled to them earlier, so the decision was easy. In the year it took to complete three of the five ships, they still hoped for some communication, but it never happened. I would like to think that once the ships left to come here, the people who remained did make their way back to Earth and found that our world survived. They wouldn't have been able to endure on the moon indefinitely.

"The journey here took three years. Finding this uninhabited planet was a Godsend. At first, they were only going to replenish their food stores, but the long passage took more out of them than they expected and by a unanimous decision they settled here instead of making their way back; something they weren't even sure was possible. And they rationalized that it would be easier to bring the abductees here.

"So, while they started rebuilding their lives, they made trips to the Zantian system hoping to discover which of the eleven planets their people were on. Unfortunately, they never found it and soon gave up, wondering if the alien negotiators had given them the wrong location. They weren't aware that one of the Zantian cargo ships spotted them, and about two years after they arrived here, the enemy they pursued came knocking… so to speak. Camouflaging themselves, they were able to set up trade. It was still a stressful time, though, but eventually, they made it work."

"Didn't the Zantians recognize the language? English was what they spoke when they were on Earth, and we still speak it on Zantia."

"The colonists worried about that too, so many of them quickly learned Chinese. The country of China refused to take part in the new Earth Government, so the hope was that the Zantians weren't familiar with their language. Several people among the colonists spoke fluent Chinese and led the early negotiations. I understand they still use it today."

"There's a reason they couldn't find the right planet," Leea said. "The Zantians have gone to great lengths to hide from other races."

"Why?"

"They have made many enemies over the centuries and now hide behind a planetary shield to avoid any retaliation. Earth was one of the last worlds they coerced out of its treasures before turning themselves into an almost reclusive society."

"Did you tell this to Bettina?"

"Yes, but not in any great detail. After my first day, her interests were more about the Zantian culture: how many cities they have, how many Humans are in those cities, their interaction, and treatment of them… things of that nature. Unfortunately, most of her questions I couldn't answer."

"Maybe that's a good thing," Farrell mumbled.

# CHAPTER 14

# Atlantis's History

**"S**o you know everything that happened on the moon?" Leea asked.

"Yes. My grandmother, Becca, meticulously kept a journal ever since she was old enough to read and write. After the attack, she started keeping extensive accounts of the day-to-day turmoil, so we've gotten a different point of view from the official records. Teenagers have an interesting perspective on their surroundings.

"Becca's journals are an amazing collection of conversations and arguments between friends and neighbors. All the meetings were recorded, of course, but my grandmother stood on the sidelines and delved into how people were feeling. Eventually, they made her the official scribe, a responsibility she took seriously, even after they'd settled here.

"Her stories were also a source of entertainment for the long, arduous journey. Computers were linked between the ships, making it easy to share the weekly inventions of her imagination. She was incredibly creative, and could spin a tale around any subject. Jamie was a great artist and made sketches to go along with her articles. Together they made quite a team.

"Not knowing how long the voyage would take, everything had to be rationed. All three ships had a hydroponics garden which produced enough food, but the water was an issue. Can you imagine only being able to wash twice a week and no shower in three years? The first thing everyone did after setting foot here, was run into the lake."

"I can certainly imagine. There were no showers on the cargo ship I came on, but at least, I could wash every day. That was only four weeks, of course, but I understand. Do you have your grandmother's journals?"

"Oh no. They were deemed 'property of the people of New Haven' a long time ago. Some of the stories are on display at the Atlantis History Museum; the rest are kept in the Earth archives at the lab along with Jamie's sketches."

"She would have been an amazing person to know."

"She was. And full of life till the end."

"You knew her?" Leea's asked, surprised.

"Yes, she died sixteen years ago at the age of one hundred eleven."

"I didn't think Humans lived that long."

"Back on Earth they rarely did, but here, people are starting to live longer. One of the original Atlantis colonists lived to be one hundred fifteen, the longest on record so far."

"That's amazing."

"There is something about this planet. It seems no different from Earth: plants, animals, dirt, rocks, water. But there is a force here no one's been able to explain."

"Maybe they can't. Maybe it's just something that is."

"Maybe…."

"It must have been difficult for the colonists to rebuild their lives here."

"Yes, it was, but you need to remember that the Atlantis colony was self-sustaining. They had teachers and medical staff. Botanists and gardeners tended to fruit and vegetable gardens and were essential when they first arrived to determine what was edible. They brought a lot of seeds, and within a couple of years, along with the abundant wildlife, they had plenty to eat.

"The second most important group were the shipbuilders, who quickly constructed much-needed shelters. All the heavy machinery that was used to build the moon base was abandoned once the station was finished, so the colonists brought as much of it with them as they could. The equipment operated on solar power, and they also brought large solar collectors for the new settlement.

"Our ancestors arrived here with all the knowledge to create a society, all they needed were the resources. So, knowing their livelihood depended on it, they planned. And then slowly, they set their plan into motion—survival at all costs. Once the trade with Zantia started, they could accelerate the building of the city. Every year our manufacturing capabilities grow, and soon we won't need to import much anymore."

"New Haven is an amazing accomplishment."

"The colonists had their struggles, but they made it work. Without this planet, they would have all died."

Deep in thought, they sat quietly for a minute.

"I can fill in some of the blanks about what happened on Earth," Leea finally said.

Farrell arched her eyebrows. "You can?"

"Ironically, my great-great-grandfather, George, sat at the forefront during the Zantian negotiations. He met my great-great-grandmother, Beverly, on the ship after the abductions, and they were married there. People were kept in crowded rooms with limited facilities, and meager, twice-a-day meals. Their ship made three stops on their way to Zantia, presumably for provisions, but the Humans never left their rooms… not in the two years it took to get there."

"Oh, my God!"

"It took its toll on some, but most persevered."

Leea repeated the story she'd told Bettina on her first day. After another hour of questions, Farrell realized the time and said she needed to go.

"I'm sure by tomorrow I'll have a hundred more questions," Farrell smiled brightly, as she and Leea stood by Farrell's car. "I also think you need to sit down with one of our historians. I'm surprised Bettina hasn't suggested that already."

"She did, but she wanted me to get used to my new home first."

"Hmmm… Well, maybe she has a point there."


Farrell sat quietly behind the wheel of her blue compact car before powering it on.

What an exciting evening.

Most people of her generation hardly gave a second thought to Earth. Dekarra was the only home they knew, and most didn't see the point in longing for a place they would never see. But for Farrell, Earth was as much a part of her family as Dekarra—a legacy she could never leave behind, and she enjoyed the historical knowledge only she and her immediate family possessed. Becca's written accounts of that time were well known, but only those close to her, and a few historians had read them all.

Farrell hadn't been quite truthful with her new friends. She didn't lie, only left out the part that as Becca grew older, she became paranoid about her stories being lost or stolen, and made several copies. Her reason for the omission wasn't so much because of Leea—although she needed to be cautious of the planet's new arrival—but she didn't know Mary, and was always hesitant to share too much with people she didn't know.

Farrell powered on her car and entered the requested code. Once the systems light turned green, she guided the vehicle away from the curb and headed for home. A smile played on her lips as she remembered Jackson would be waiting for her. She suspected once she relayed the evening's conversation, neither would get much sleep.

"It's me," the associate said as his contact appeared on the small screen. "Good thing I followed the Dennison girl on her first day at work."

"What happened?"

"She came home with Farrell Reynolds."

"Really? That is interesting. What did they talk about?"

"Unfortunately, they went to the neighbor's, so I don't know. But they stayed for several hours, and the two women seemed quite friendly when Reynolds left."

"Well, too bad. Install a camera into the neighbor's house tomorrow. I'll make some inconspicuous inquiries with Mary, see how her neighbor is doing. Since we have the cameras, there's probably no point in you watching her during the week, but keep a lookout on the weekends."

"For how long?"

"As long as it takes. If there's any chance she can lead us to the alien's mountain home, we need to stick with her. We've never been this close before so I'm not going to let this slip by. The alien's trade-value is immeasurable, and I've recently found out not just to the Zantians."

The associate looked wide eyed. "How's that?"

"We'll give the surveillance a little time," the contact continued, ignoring his question. "If it takes too long… I'm sure we can come up with something more persuasive."

Eleven weeks after her arrival, Leea decided to find out when Mearos's cargo ship would return.

"Hi," Leea greeted Farrell as she entered the office on Monday morning.

"Hi yourself," Farrell replied, not looking up from her computer. "How was your weekend?"

"Quiet and uneventful, which was nice after the hectic week we had."

"I agree. My weekend was pretty much the same; spent time relaxing."

"That's good." Leea deposited her bag and jacket on her desk and returned to Farrell. "Say, can I ask you a favor?"

"Sure. One second, let me finish this." Farrell finished an entry and looked up with her usual warm, toothy smile. "What can I do for you this early in the morning?" Farrell held up an empty cup. "Coffee?"

"Yes, definitely that, but I was wondering if you could find out when the next Zantian cargo ship will be here?"

Farrell looked at her quizzically. "Why?"

"I was hoping you wouldn't ask," she said sheepishly.

"Okay, not even a hint?"

"I'd love to tell you, but at the moment, I'd rather not."

"Okay, but you know I'll lay awake nights wondering what you're up to."

They both laughed.

"All right," Farrell conceded, "but let me guess, you're looking for the one from Alrack?"

"Yes."

In a little over a minute, Farrell found the airfield's schedule. "The ship from Alrack is due in four days."

"And if I remember correctly, if it comes in on Friday that means it departs on Sunday."

Farrell verified the departure on her screen and nodded. "Early afternoon on Sunday."

"Wonderful. Can I ask you another favor?"

"Sure…."

"Can you take me to the airfield Sunday morning?"

"And you're still not going to tell me why?"

"Okay, the captain of the ship gave me something I want to return."

"That's it?"

"Yup, that's it."

"Well, I'm sure there's more to it, but of course, I'll take you." Farrell touched her computer screen. "I sent you the schedule. Call me on Saturday to remind me."

"Thanks, Farrell, you're a great friend, I really appreciate it. I'll tell you the whole story afterward."

"Sounds like a deal. Now, how about that coffee?"

"How long do you think you'll be?" Farrell asked.

They sat in her car a short distance from the terminal entrance. On the way to the airfield, Leea told Farrell the reason for her visit. "Probably not too long. I'm sure Mearos will be busy this close to takeoff, and I don't want to get him in trouble."

"Do you want to call me when you're done, or do you want me to wait?"

"I left my link at home. Not sure who Bettina thinks I'm going to call, so I rarely remember to take it with me."

Farrell chuckled. "No problem. I'll wait." She held up a datapad and smiled. "I came prepared. I'll pull into the parking garage."

"Thanks again, Farrell."

"No thanks necessary. Just go give the captain what you found."

"I'll come find you when I'm done."

Since Bettina had told her everyone at the airfield wore the concealing robe when a Zantian ship was docked, Leea adjusted her hood to make sure it covered her face. Approaching the automatic doors, she took a deep breath to steady her nerves before stepping inside. This terminal was strictly used for off-world traffic, so she didn't expect to find anyone and headed straight for the elevators on the other side of the room.

"Excuse me. Where are you going?"

Leea froze. To her left stood a security desk she completely overlooked.

*Now, what?* she thought and moved slowly toward the guard, whose robe hung over a nearby chair. This gave her pause. Had the cargo ship already left? She wasn't able to see it when Farrell drove into the airfield, but per the schedule, it wasn't due to depart for at least another two hours.

"I have business with the Zantian ship," she informed him, using her best authoritative voice.

"They're already preparing for departure. Can I see your identification?"

Leea blanched and was suddenly grateful for the hood. Not sure what to do, she brought a hand to her throat and felt the chain. The *jarkut*.

Now was a good a time as any to test it. She had practiced on inanimate objects with limited success—now for the most important test. If she failed, she wouldn't be able to get the mysterious files to Mearos, and he'd never know someone on his ship might be spying on him.

She clutched the amulet through the fabric of her robe and enclosed it in her fist. She'd never tried it this way, but what other choice did she have? Closing her eyes, she concentrated. *Let me pass*, she repeated over and over in her mind. Finally, the amulet started to warm, and she held her breath. Moment of truth.

Through the one-way fabric, Leea watched as the guard turned his attention to the computer.

"The ship will depart in one hour; you'd better hurry."

Not sure how long the *jarkut's* effects would last, Leea rushed to the elevator and willed the car to hurry. As the lift moved upward, Leea took in several deep breaths—her lungs felt as if they had been deprived of air for hours. When the car came to a stop, nothing happened. Again Leea wrapped her hand around the talisman and willed the door to open.

Mearos sat in his cramped cabin, finishing up some last minute log entries before he needed to ready the ship for takeoff. The last of the cargo had been loaded about an hour ago, and now he waited for the Cargo-master to do the security sweep. He detested keeping these logs. They weren't difficult, but he hated accounting for every minute of his day.

A welcome knock interrupted his grumblings. "Come in."

His longtime friend, and copilot, Pindac, stuck his head in. "Sorry to bother you, but one of the Dekarrans wants to speak to you."

"I thought our business with them was completed?"

"It is, as far as I know, but she said it was urgent. She's waiting up top."

Mearos made his way to the ship's entry door, located just past the flight deck. He assumed because Pindac said it was a female, that his visitor was Bettina. But Bettina was a short woman, and this Dekarran, standing just inside the doorway, was a head taller. This confused him since women generally didn't conduct business with the cargo ships.

"Can we talk privately?" a familiar voice spoke from behind the hood.

"Of course." Mearos led her into the flight deck and motioned for her to take a seat in the navigator's chair. The crew was busy so they should have a few minutes of privacy.

"Hello, Mearos." Leea pulled her hood back, giving him a sheepish grin.

"I thought I recognized that voice," he admitted, smiling. "But you are the last person I would have expected. How did you get up here?"

"I just walked in…no problem. I hope I didn't interrupt anything. I promise I'll only stay a minute."

"You didn't interrupt anything. I was catching up on some log entries. What brings you here? But first, let me ask. How are you?"

"I'm doing well. Things here are quite different than I expected, and pleasantly so. I've been made to feel welcome."

"I'm happy to hear that. You deserve it. So, what brings you here?"

"I came to bring you this." She pulled the data-cube from her pocket and handed it to him.

Confusion registered on Mearos's face. "You came all the way here to return this? I'm sure I said you could keep it."

"You did. But when I uploaded my file to my pad, I found several others."

"Why didn't you delete them?"

"I was going to, but then I looked at them. Except for one written in Zantian, they are all in an odd language. The one in Zantian is definitely about you, so I thought you should take a look."

"You sure it isn't one of my logs?"

"It could be, but why would one be on an old pad kept in the storage room; since you said the cube was new."

"Good point." Mearos looked down at the object in his hand and smiled. "Thank you…I think."

Leea reached over and laid a hand on his arm and said softly, "I will be forever grateful for the kindness you showed me. If this is something more than a misplaced log entry, then you should know about it."

Mearos laid a hand on top of hers and squeezed lightly. "Thank you, I appreciate the concern. And make no mistake, I enjoyed your company as well."

Leea smiled and lowered her eyes. "Can I ask you a question?"

"Of course."

She took a deep breath. "Have you seen Yaran? Do you know how he's doing?"

He gave her a sad smile. "No, I haven't seen him. But I heard he moved in with the Desolk's brother, Toref, and is now in charge of one of the mines."

"He is?" Leea's eyes grew wide. Then almost deflated, she added, "He must be so unhappy."

"Well, what little I know, he is doing a good job with the mine. The men there seem to have accepted him."

"Will you tell him I'm okay?" she asked pleadingly.

Mearos hesitated a moment. "Why don't you tell him yourself?"

"What do you mean?"

The captain returned the cube to her. "Record a message for him. I'll see that he gets it."

Leea contemplated the suggestion. "You really think I should?"

"Why not? You want to put his mind at ease, right?"

Leea jumped up from the chair and threw her arms around his neck, catching him by surprise. "Thank you so much. Once again, I'm in your debt!"

He returned the hug. "No thanks needed. Unfortunately, this cube will only do a voice recording, and I can only give you a few minutes."

"That's all I'll need."

He showed her how to use the recording option but before leaving the cockpit, he turned and said, "I would caution you not to reveal too much about your new home."

Leea narrowed her eyes at him questioningly but then nodded in understanding. In less than three minutes, she opened the door and handed the cube back to him. The look on her face told him it had been an emotional task, and he wondered if his suggestion had been a good idea. But she gave him a big smile, thanked him again, and left.

The two women spent the drive back to Leea's house in relative silence. When Leea had returned to the car, Farrell took one look at her, and cautiously asked, "Are you okay?"

Leea simply nodded, and Farrell didn't push for further explanation.

When they pulled up in front of the house, Farrell stopped her friend before she got out. "I'm here if you need to talk."

Leea smiled appreciatively. "Thank you. And thank you for the ride. I'm not sure what I'm feeling at the moment, so I need to get my thoughts together first. We'll talk tomorrow."

As Farrell drove away, Leea made her way slowly toward the house and stopped to admire the flower beds. She hunched down to get the last lingering scent of the bright purple flowers with the sunshine-yellow leaves, taking pleasure in their fruity aroma. Its neighboring companions, some with long white fluted buds, and some with red and blue velvety petals had all seen better days. The gloomy skies were taking its toll on these bright, aromatic blooms.

She had enjoyed cultivating her garden these last months. Now, as the colder weather approached, they'd soon go into hibernation. It saddened her to think these splashes of color would no longer adorn the outside of her small home, but she was assured they would return to their full vibrancy with the warmer weather next year.

She walked the length of the bed, caressing each remaining flower as she went as if saying goodbye. At the corner of the house stood a plant with stalks that reached her knees, called *Protectors*. Their thorny, purple-black leaves were a stark contrast to the large, fuzzy, pale pink blooms that grew from the top, forming a square about the size of a small pillow that looked equally as inviting. But Leea knew better. The fine tendrils of the blossoms were razor sharp, and would create painful scratches if they touched the skin. The plant was carnivorous, and with its pleasing scent, easily attracted small prey.

Leea had once watched as several insects got caught in the wisps, struggling to free themselves. The four corners slowly folded up as it gently pulled its victims into the center of the harmless looking flower.

What was equally fascinating was when the blooms died, they turned to gel as they lay on the ground, as if to prevent anyone from being hurt by them after death. Leea waved her hand across the top, only close enough to ruffle the deadly tendrils, but not touch.

"It is not wise to entice a meat eater with possible reward."

Startled, Leea jumped back, only then noticing the figure hidden in the shadows at the side of the house—Tellia.

"You scared me. What are you doing here?"

"I apologize. I did not mean to frighten you. I have come with a message." Tellia reached out and handed Leea a crystal, similar to the one she had brought from Zantia. "It is important the test captain receives this. Nethas wants you to deliver it as soon as possible."

"Jackson Owens?"

"Yes."

"Why me?"

"She did not say, only that it was imperative you get this to him."

Before Leea could ask another question, Tellia vanished back into the shadows.

Mearos forced himself to study the readouts as the diagnostic scanner relayed the status of each cargo container. Internal sensors checked the seals and the stability of the contents, and when the stasis fields were in place, returned a green light. This procedure was redundant to the external sensors, but necessary when dealing with perishable cargo. As each container's light changed, Mearos realized his attention hand wandered. He shook his head.

"Are you okay?" asked Pindac, obviously noticing the gesture.

"I'm fine," he reassured his friend. "Guess I'm a little tired today."

"Well, once we've cleared Dekarra's orbit, I can handle things here if you want to take a nap?"

Mearos raised his eyebrows and smiled. "A nap? I haven't taken a nap since I was three. But…I just might take you up on it."

The scanner beeped three times, indicating the diagnostic was complete, with no issues. Mearos set the scanner to continuous, and then inserted it into the control panel. In the case of a problem, alarm bells would chime.

Leaning back in his seat, he closed his eyes and waited for Pindac to finish running the last system diagnostics before takeoff. His mind wandered back to the real reason for his distraction—Leea. He had to admit; he had been happy to see her. The Dekarrans had established strict rules for transporting escapees. Now that Leea had re-established contact with him, and he had encouraged her to send a message to Yaran, he was breaking rules no one had even thought to make yet.

In the four weeks she spent on his ship, Leea had made him rethink his life, and brought to light what it was missing—someone to share it with. This, unfortunately, brought back memories of Selane. If he allowed himself to think about her, he would reluctantly admit that he still missed her. But he had come to terms with her leaving long ago and had managed to compartmentalize her memories. But he would always wonder if the decision to let her slip away without a fight was the right one.

"Hey, are you asleep over there?"

"No," Mearos answered without opening his eyes, welcoming Pindac's interruption. "I just wanted to see if you would take off without me."

"Like you would ever let that happen." Pindac laughed heartily. "Not to worry, I have no intention of taking over your job."

Mearos sat up and stretched his arms. "Trust me, some days you can have it."

"So what did your visitor want?"

"Oh," Mearos hesitated, "there was some confusion, on their part, as to the quantity in one of the containers. I needed to get the weight for her."

"I've never known them to send a woman up."

"She was just an office worker, guess the loaders had already left."

Mearos trusted his copilot implicitly. They had known each other long before they served together on this ship, but after what Leea told him, he thought it best to be careful how much he revealed until he had the chance to look at the files on the cube.

Well on their way to Zantia, Mearos powered up his personal datapad and waited for the files to appear. Once the upload was completed, he opened the new directory and found eight files: five titled in an unfamiliar script, one in Zantian, Leea's stories, and the voice message she had just added for Yaran. He was tempted to open the story file. He was curious about her past but then instantly ashamed at the thought of invading her privacy. He started to delete her writings, but decided against it; maybe Yaran would want to read them.

The first three files were blank, except for his senior officers' names: Pindac, Grys, his systems engineer, and Rilla, his navigator. He closed these, not knowing what to make of them.

The fourth looked like financial records, but for what he couldn't tell. There were columns with amounts, and what he assumed were dates, some in a receiving and some in a spending column. But the row that should have listed each entry's subject contained the same code as the title. He searched through the entire file for a code key, but couldn't find one.

Because they traded with different cultures, codes were often used, each specific to the trading planet. These symbols were not Dekarra's, so their presence on one of his pads was certainly a mystery. He closed this one as well. Once back on Zantia, he would verify their origin.

The fifth one was gibberish. Ten columns of the same ciphers as the financial records filled the screen. Was this a code, or a language? The thought gave him a start. Could someone on his ship be in league with alien race? He wasn't sure that was even possible, and if so, what would they be doing on his crew?

The last file was the one Leea thought he should see. Mearos quickly scanned through the writing and saw it was a copy of one of his logs, but with added commentary chronicling his movements. A sent verification stamp at the bottom indicated it was transmitted from the ship via the communications buoy about ten months ago. He rechecked the previous two and found the same stamp.

He leaned back and laced his fingers behind his head. What did all this mean?

# CHAPTER 15

# Reconnection

Leea stood at the side door of the lab's military facility contemplating whether going to see Jackson was a good idea. *Could this be a test,* she wondered? Nethas had told her never to second-guess any decisions, but at the moment, she couldn't help it.

"Well, here goes," she whispered as she entered the building. Her office made occasional deliveries here, so she doubted anyone would question her presence, but she didn't have access to the build area, so she wanted to get in and out quickly.

Hurriedly, she made her way along the deserted hallway until she stood in front of the restricted room's double doors. Pulling in a deep breath Leea withdrew her *jarkut* and wrapped her hand around it. Within a short moment, the talisman started to warm, and from experience, that meant it was working. A moment later one of the doors eased open a few inches.

Cautiously, she pushed through, and once inside, it closed automatically behind her. Several yards ahead stood a small, black, arrow-shaped aircraft with a single seat visible through the cockpit window. She reached up and ran a hand along its underbelly near the wing, marveling at the cold smoothness beneath her fingertips.

"What the hell are you doing here!?"

Startled, Leea spun around to find herself standing face to face with her boss, Kent Madigan.

"I asked you a question! What are you doing here, and how did you get in?" The anger in his voice made her take a step back, causing her to bump into the aircraft's landing gear.

"I'm just making a delivery, and as I came by the…the door was open, so I came in."

"You walked by, and the door was open?" The sarcasm oozed through his tone. "You can't lie any better than that? Those doors close automatically as soon as anyone passes through, and an alarm sounds if they don't close properly. Try again."

"Well, they were open. How else do you think I got in?" Laying a hand over the *jarkut* under her shirt, Leea concentrated on making Kent believe her. But instead, he became angrier.

He took a step closer to her. "Listen here you—"

"What's going on here?" Jackson Owens appeared through a side door.

"I caught this…girl here, spying." His voice calmed as he spoke to the pilot.

"Leea?" He looked at her puzzled.

"I… I have no idea what he's talking about. I came to make an early delivery. When I walked by, the door was open. I'm sorry, the plane caught my eye. I didn't mean any harm." She moved away from the craft, wanting more distance from the angry man.

Kent snorted.

"What? Again?" the captain said shaking his head. "I thought they fixed those doors."

Kent looked at both of them incredulously and then stomped off mumbling to himself. Leea breathed a sigh of relief when the door closed automatically behind him.

"Thank you. He really scared me, if you hadn't shown up—"

"How did you get in?"

"The door was—"

"No, I only said that because I could tell how frightened you were. I'm not a big fan of Kent's; I find him obnoxious, but there is nothing wrong with those doors."

Leea drew in a breath and stared at the floor. She couldn't possibly tell him the truth.

Jackson smiled. "Never mind, I don't want to know. Were you actually just walking by?"

"No," she admitted sheepishly. "I came to bring you something. And before you ask from whom, I can't say. But I was told it's important you get this as soon as possible." She retrieved the crystal from her pocket and handed it to him.

Jackson turned the object over in his hand, looking skeptical. "What is it?"

"I don't know. I assumed you would. I'm sorry, that's all I can tell you. But I think I should go before someone else finds me here." Without waiting for him to comment, she quickly exited.

Back at the office, Farrell told her Kent had come in angry for some reason, then said he would be gone the rest of the day. Leea hoped she would still have a job tomorrow.

As they got ready to leave that evening, Farrell asked, "how about dinner tonight?"

"Sure, sounds good."

"Great. Maxie's okay?"

"You know I can't say no to Maxie's," Leea admitted, rubbing her stomach. "But it's Monday, don't you have plans with Jackson?" Farrell often suggested dinner or a drink at Maxie's after work, it was popular with people from the research facility, but never when Jackson was at the lab, which she completely understood.

"I do, but he wants you to join us today."

Maxie's was a large restaurant with a large bar, almost filled to capacity today. Dark paneled walls gave the interior a cozy feel and the dark, heavy tables added to the ambiance. They made their way through to where Jackson already sat.

"Waiting long?" Farrell asked as she and Leea took their seats.

"Nope. I just got here myself. Hello, Leea, nice to see you today…again."

"Again?" Farrell raised her eyebrows.

"Leea didn't tell you she visited me this morning?"

"No." She glared at her dinner companions.

A waitress came to take their order. "Let's talk about this after we eat," Jackson suggested, opening his menu.

They finished their meal, and after the waitress cleared their plates, they sat back to enjoy a second glass of wine.

"Okay, now tell me about this visit today?"

"I'm surprised you made it through the whole meal without asking," he joked.

"It was hard, for sure. But now…out with it." With deliberate motion, she looked from one to the other.

Jackson relayed the events of the morning.

"No wonder Kent was in a snit. I'm surprised he even bothered to let me know he would be gone…again. Why did he come to see you?"

"I'm not sure. He said he was closing out some old files and found same data missing that he thought I might have. But before he could be more specific, we heard the door close. He hurried out of the office, and well, the rest you know."

"So Leea saved you from Kent's fishing expeditions?"

Jackson laughed, which accentuated his dimples. "Yes, I suppose she did."

"What kind of blue stone did you give him?" Farrell asked Leea.

Leea shrugged. "I have an idea what it was, but not a hundred percent sure."

"It was a message crystal."

"Did you know what it was when I gave it to you?"

"Not at first, but I had my suspicions. When I took a closer look I found the release, and up popped the message…so to speak."

"What did it say?" Farrell asked curiously.

"It said…and I quote, 'The time for revelation has come.'"

"And what does that mean?" Leea asked.

"I know exactly what it means. Time to go."

"Wait!" Leea laid a hand on his arm. "You know who gave me the stone, don't you?"

"Yes, of course."

"Care to explain?"

"If you'll be patient, we'd like to show you something first?"

"Do I have a choice?"

"No." He patted her hand reassuringly.

With Jackson at the wheel, they took the road toward the lake and parked a few blocks from the old township.

"We're going back to the settlement, but we have to go on foot," Jackson explained to Leea.

"Why are we going in there?"

"All questions will be answered soon."

They walked along a deserted gravel path, and Leea studied the small run-down wooden buildings standing close together, some had missing slats while others were partially collapsed. The small windows, now boarded up, had at one time been covered with shutters, some still hanging precariously on the walls.

Passing a square light pole, four equally spaced green lights on two sides caught Leea's attention. Each faced the next pole in line, and she surmised the complex was surrounded by an energy field. Within a few minutes, small trees and other foliage took up the space between the path and the invisible barrier.

Leaving the gravel walkway, Jackson headed into a darkened area where trees blocked the lamplight. Leea's heart skipped a beat when she noticed the device he pulled from his pocket. It was the same scanner Yaran had used to deactivate the energy field the day she left Alrack.

"I know what that is." Leea pointed to the instrument in his hand. "We're going through an energy barrier, aren't we?"

Surprise briefly crossed Jackson's face. "Yes. No one is allowed in the old complex without invitation, so we have other ways to get in." The last comment brought a smile to his face.

"Are you going to tell me what this is all about?"

"Not yet. If you know how this works, then you know we only have a few seconds to make it through before the field resets itself."

"Yes, I remember," Leea acknowledged quietly.

Once they'd safely passed, Jackson instructed her to stay close as they made their way under the cover of the trees to the nearest building. As they walked, he explained in hushed tones that the complex was patrolled by guards, so they needed to be careful.

Approaching the next building, Jackson stopped as the area ahead of them started to brighten and quickly motioned them around the corner. They were barely out of sight when intense light flooded the area where they had stood, then slowly faded away. Leea carefully peered around the edge and saw an open vehicle moving in the opposite direction.

"Why is this place so heavily guarded?" she whispered. "I thought it was abandoned?"

"Not quite," Farrell answered quietly. "The military uses this place for weapons storage."

"Weapons?"

"They build their weaponry in the southern continent," Jackson explained, "from personal arms to military grade munitions, then they are shipped and stored here. I've heard a lot of shipments have been coming in lately, so guards are on patrol twenty-four hours a day."

"Would people steal them?"

"Most people have no idea what they keep here. But the government leaders are a bit paranoid. Okay, the guards are gone. We need to get to that building over there." Jackson pointed to where Leea could barely make out a corner. "The only problem is…look there?" A narrow turret with several rotating spotlights stood at the end of a large courtyard to their left.

"That's a guard tower, and it's always manned. We will have to cross between the beams and hope we're not spotted."

"There's no other way around?" Leea asked nervously.

"Unfortunately no. Collapsed buildings block the courtyard at the other end, and there are none past the tower that we can move behind undetected. And where we entered the compound is the only blind spot around the whole perimeter, so we have to come this way."

Stealthily, they moved between two more buildings and now stood in front of the open square, their destination fifty feet away.

"Jackson, you and Leea go first. I'll follow once you're across."

"Sounds good. Leea, stay close behind me."

With the timing down, they took off in a stooped run, following the beam, and took momentary refuge behind a three-foot tall stone enclosure. Leea wanted to look over the wall but knew that was probably a bad idea. When the next beam passed, they ran and took cover in the shadow of a small shed.

"How often do you come here?"

"Once in a while," he offered. "Here comes Farrell."

Farrell broke into a run, also stopping behind the low wall. As she waited for the searchlight to pass again, a bright light focused on her from another direction; they hadn't noticed the patrol car returning.

"RUN!!" Jackson yelled.

He grabbed Leea's arm, and they ran down the closest alleyway, slowing only long enough for Farrell to catch up. All three turned the corner and ducked behind a stack of weather-beaten crates, just in time to avoid being seen by the next beam.

"Guess, we're going to do it this way," Jackson mumbled, reaching up and pressing a palm against the nearest wall. Immediately the section dissolved into an open archway, just like she'd seen Tellia do at the cave. He pushed the women ahead of him through the opening, which returned to its original form once they were inside. They stood a moment in total darkness catching their breath.

Jackson activated a small light, and they found themselves in a room about ten feet square with a door ahead. The abandoned space had an old, musty smell which made Leea instantly wrinkle her nose.

"How did you do that?" she asked.

"Patience," Jackson said. "We're almost there. This way."

Outside the small room, Leea could make out a narrow, stone stairway leading into a dark void below. Jackson led the way down, and they came to a long arched walkway carved into the earth.

"When the people from Atlantis first came here," Farrell said as they walked single file, "they discovered this system of thirty tunnels and decided to build the complex on top of it. Their original plan had been to be closer to the lake, but this place gave them somewhere to stay immediately.

"They lived down here for almost a year while the settlement above was being constructed. Several passageways branch off in different directions, but they all dead-end at some point. Many of them have rooms built out along the way which they assumed must have been previously occupied. However, no evidence of who was ever found."

"But you know who lived here, don't you?" Jackson had indeed indicated at the restaurant that they were familiar with the Morodons.

Before she could answer, Jackson stopped and placed a palm against the rock wall. Leea caught a glimpse of glowing blue. She wondered if it was a *jarkut*. The section he touched disappeared and light flooded the hallway. Inside was a small chamber with several workstations, each holding computer terminals, but only one was occupied. Jackson introduced her to the desk's occupant, Maxim Brevin.

"What is this place?" Leea looked around in wonder.

"Welcome to Sanctuary."

"Sanctuary?"

"It's a little dramatic, we know. But it seems fitting to our cause."

"What cause is that?"

"We are a small group of about fifty, and call ourselves the Watchers," Jackson explained. "This group was formed about forty years ago. It was an idea first envisioned by Farrell's great-great-grandparents, Becca, and Jamie, who felt many of the leaders were hiding things from the people, but couldn't prove it. They voiced their concerns to some friends, and twelve people conspired to keep watch and document anything out of the ordinary. Should something seem out of place, their plan was to inform the rest of the population. The effort grew over the years, and now we have members strategically located within the corporate world to keep an eye out for unusual activity."

"You think something is going to happen?"

"We've been noticing some things lately, but not sure if they mean anything. There is a little-known group of high-ranking officials who we know have a secret agenda, but not exactly what. All has been quiet for the most part, until about two years ago, when we noticed increased activity swirling around this little circle. There has been lots of unusually long absences and sudden changes in personnel. We believe their network is branching out, but no idea who else might be involved, or what the end game is, so we've stepped up our efforts to try and figure it out.

"When Farrell told me about your conversations with Bettina and the questions she's asking you, it seemed to indicate there is something to our speculations."

"What do you know about Bettina?"

"Not much. She does work for Admiral Shaw, but in what capacity, I don't know. I've seen her on two occasions in the test lab, in areas off-limits to non-military personnel, so the admiral must trust her."

"I asked her once what she did," Leea told them. "Her answer was, 'Whatever they tell me to do.' I pushed her a little, assuming she was joking, but all she said was that she did freelance work for different things. She also mentioned at another time that her job required a lot of travel. But like I told Farrell, all she's interested in is my life, or more accurately, the Zantians."

"The government must be collecting information to further their plans; whatever they are," Farrell speculated.

"So why are you showing me this?" Leea spread her arms.

"Because Nethas said it was time," Jackson said with a sly smile. "She stated in the message you gave me that something has changed."

"Like what?"

The couple looked behind her, and Leea turned to find Tellia.

"Something you did yesterday has set everything on a different path," the Morodon said.

"I don't understand."

"Nethas has known for some time that a shift would begin with the coming of a stranger," the Morodon said. "After your arrival, all indications pointed to you. But not much else changed in the prediction until yesterday. Something you did yesterday has caused a shift."

"Our trip to the airfield?" Farrell gave her friend a questioning look.

Leea shrugged, then told them the reason she went to visit Mearos, and about the message she recorded for Yaran.

Tellia raised her eyebrows. "Among other information, the crystal you brought from Zantia contained this message: 'Once the communication lines are restored, the time for planning must begin. Do not hesitate; the danger is greater than anticipated.' We assumed that the communication lines meant the crystal you gave us. But in light of what you have said, maybe it actually means your recording to the Zantian."

"You think so? I'm not sure Yaran will even get it."

Tellia smiled. "The change indicates he will, and will answer as well, thus opening the communication lines."

Leea couldn't help but smile widely.

# CHAPTER 16

# The Storm

Yaran looked at the red tree and drew in a deep breath. He often thought about seeking out Mearos, wanting answers, but realized that no matter what the captain could tell him, it would never relieve the pain and guilt he felt about letting Leea go. His rational mind knew it had been the right thing to do, but he couldn't forgive himself, so he vowed never to come back to this room. But Mearos had asked to see him; for what reason he couldn't imagine.

As before, the room was empty except for the captain sitting at his desk concentrating intently on his terminal. Without looking up, he said, "I wondered if you'd come."

"So did I." Yaran closed the door behind him.

"I'm sorry to ask you come to my office. I—"

"That's all right. I had business here today anyway," Yaran interrupted.

"Give me one minute. My first day back barely leaves me time for a meal, much less anything else. But I wanted to talk to you as soon as possible."

Yaran pulled over a chair from a nearby desk and sat quietly while Mearos finished.

"To be honest, I expected you to come sooner," Mearos finally said, looking up.

"I thought about it several times, but decided what's done is done. I don't need to relive one of the worst days of my life."

Mearos leaned forward, resting his elbows on the desk and concentrated his unique blue eyes on his visitor. "It's easy to second-guess a decision once we've had time to think about it. But most of the time, the first instinct is the right one."

Yaran lowered his head and sighed. "I appreciate that. Maybe I should have come, but I wasn't sure what to ask, or what you would be able to tell me."

"I would have answered what I could."

"Did Leea make it all right?" he asked, his voice just above a whisper.

"Yes. It was a difficult journey for her, but she was determined to arrive in one piece, and I think she accomplished that. She did a lot of second-guessing herself, for sure."

"You spent time with her?"

"Yes. I'm the only one on the ship who knows about the room, so I have to bring the meals. While the men who've traveled with me just wanted to be left alone, Leea wasn't ready for that kind of isolation. I sat with her most days for the evening meal." Mearos smiled. "She talked about you mostly. I feel I got to know you during that time."

Yaran smiled shyly.

"But that's not why I asked you here. I have a message for you." Mearos took out the data-cube and handed it to him. "Leea came to see me just before I left Dekarra this trip… it's a long story. It was important to her that she tell you herself how she's doing, so I suggested she should. On there, you'll find a recording she made, as well as a file she worked on during the journey. She spent most of her time writing about her life on Zantia. She said it made her feel close to you. I think she forgot it was on there."

Yaran's hand shook as he looked down at the rectangular device. "She is doing okay then," he mused softly.

"Yes, I believe she is, but we only had a chance to talk briefly. The Dekarrans keep us pretty isolated at their airfield, and she was taking a risk coming to see me. So, unfortunately, she only had a few minutes to make the recording, but I'm sure she explained as much as she could."

Getting to his feet, Yaran clutched the cube tightly, as if expecting it to disappear. "Thank you for this; you have no idea what it means to me."

"Oh, I think I do, and you are welcome." Mearos stood and walked around the desk. "If you want to send a response, I will see that she gets it," he informed Yaran before he opened the door.

"I thought they keep you isolated?"

"They do. But I know someone who can help me."

Yaran studied him for a moment. "I don't know why you're doing this, but I can't thank you enough. I will be back."

A few minutes later, Yaran excitedly entered his office. Business was finished for the day, so the adjoining rooms were empty, for which he was grateful. He activated his terminal and waited for the files to show on the screen. Within a few seconds, one audio and one text file appeared. He reached up to activate the audio file and found his hand shook almost uncontrollably. He ran his hands through his hair to steady them, suddenly apprehensive about what she might say. What if she discovered a horrible place, or a beautiful place, and glad she went? He pulled in a deep breath and touched the screen.

"Hopefully, I'm doing this right," Leea's voice resonated through the terminal speakers. Yaran's heart pounded fiercely at the sound of her voice. "Mearos can only give me a minute, so I have to keep it short." Yaran heard her sigh in frustration before she continued.

"I hope with all my heart you're listening to this, my love. I can't put into words how much I miss you, Yaran, so I won't try. Just know that not an hour goes by when I don't see something I wish I could share with you.

"I want you to know that I'm safe and doing well. The journey here was hard, but Mearos's kindness helped me through it. I think you would like him. Dekarra is nothing like I envisioned, and trust me, I envisioned many scary places." Leea chuckled softly. "People here are kind and have welcomed me into their society. It's completely different from Zantia, and it's taken some getting used to, but no matter how much I'm welcomed here, this could never be home…not without you."

There was momentary silence, and Yaran feared the recording had ended.

"Mearos told me you're living with Toref now," she finally continued, "and working in one of the mines." She paused again. "I want you to be happy, Yaran. I couldn't stand it if I thought you were miserable because of what happened with me.

"Go home and make amends with your family. I'm sure your mother misses you. Try to live your life as you always have…at least, until we can be together again. I know it will happen. In my heart, I'm surer of it now than when I left.

"How is Julia doing? Do you get a chance to see her anymore? Would you please send her my love and tell her I miss her terribly? I think about her every day. And Marta too—I bet she's grown."

Yaran heard Leea's voice change and knew she was trying not to cry. It was a tone he had heard too much of those last days. She continued with a quivering voice. "I love you so much. You are in my heart and my thoughts every waking moment, as well as many of my dreams. I wish I could feel your arms around me…I miss that terribly.

"I have to go. I don't want Mearos to get in trouble for leaving me here too long. I love you. As always, you are my *A'rinBientS'aan*," she finished with a barely restrained sob.

The message ended and only then did Yaran notice his own tears. But he recognized they were mostly of relief. Hearing in Leea's own words that she was safe and welcomed in her new world seemed to lift a huge weight off his shoulders.

He sat back in the chair, closed his eyes, and let his emotions run their course. He felt a mixture of reawakened pain of losing her, and the relief that she was truly all right. Optimism gripped him. What if it is possible for them to be together again? He had every intention of holding on to that hope.

After listening to the message three more times, Yaran deleted both files from the terminal, took the cube and left the office. He wasn't sure if he would read what she'd written; he didn't know if he could handle it emotionally right now. But he did look forward to preparing a response.

"What's going on?" Yaran poured hot tea from a carafe, and sat down in front of a plate Toref had already placed on the table for him. His uncle seemed preoccupied, which was unusual this early in the morning.

"I got a call a few hours ago from the planetary office. They've detected an approaching sandstorm."

Yaran set his fork down. "We haven't seen one of those in years. How bad is it?"

"Based on their calculations, there hasn't been one of this size since before I was born." Toref handed him a datapad. "See for yourself. These are the orbital scans that were taken over the last two days."

Yaran scrolled through the images three times before handing it back. "It does look bad. According to this, the storm has increased in size ten-fold in just two days. Are they going to evacuate the city?"

"Yes. Preparations are already under way. The only good thing is the storm is moving slow, which is probably why it's getting so big. But it gives us time to seal up the mines, along with whatever else we have time for."

"Is that where we're headed?"

"No, I've already talked to all of the administrators, and they're preparing everything for a shutdown. We may lose some of the power turbines, but that should be the worst of it. We, unfortunately, have a more urgent job to do."

"Oh?"

"With a storm this size, chances are it will hit the mountain lake. If sand reaches up that high and hits the pump station, it could do serious damage to the machinery, which would affect our water supply. So, we're going to shut it down. This is only a precaution, but a necessary one."

"You have been busy this morning."

"Not really. These emergency measures are already in place; it just needs quick coordination with everyone."

"Will it be just the two of us going?"

"No. There will be about twelve of us. Since Alrack will be busy, we're getting help from Emborie. They are sending the administrator, a foreman, several workers, and a few guards. I asked for the extra help because it's been a while since anyone has been up there, and we might need to clean up around the station before we can get to the equipment. And in case you're wondering, the foreman I requested is Roger."

"Oh?" Yaran tried to appear nonchalant.

"It was a logical request," the older man said, giving his nephew a sideways glance. "Roger works with the underground river, and since we're going to the lake, it makes sense to have someone accompany us who is comfortable being around water."

"Yes, I agree." Yaran sighed. "I wish I could have talked to him that day in Emborie, but it wasn't the right time. He seemed instantly uncomfortable when he saw me, and I'm sure he knew that I recognized him too. So, maybe as we deal with our crisis, we'll have a chance to talk. He must be wondering about his family."

"Maybe."

Toref had shown surprise when Yaran told him about meeting Roger. Not exactly surprise, but something closer to unease. His uncle then cautioned him that Roger had been declared dead for a reason, and maybe it was a secret that needed to stay that way. So this arrangement surprised him.

"When do we leave?"

"We'll meet them up at the station mid-morning, which should give us plenty of time to get it shut down before the storm hits."

"Will we come back here afterward?"

"No, we'd have to stay at the mines, and there won't be enough time to get up there and back before they're sealed. We might stay at the pump station, but Haliel offered us accommodations, so most likely we'll head to Emborie. Once it passes, we'll go back up to restart everything. Great way to spend a few days," Toref said, making a face.

After finishing their meal, the two men packed overnight bags and headed to the city office to make sure storm preparations were under way. Once things were secured, Zantian residents would leave and find refuge. Human workers would be put on transports and taken to Emborie, where they would stay in temporary shelters.

"You seem different today," Toref observed once they were on their way to the mountains.

"In what way?"

"I don't know. Your mood seems almost…uplifted. I know you've been sleeping better; so what else has happened?"

Yaran took a deep breath. There was no point in keeping anything from him. "I received a message from Leea," he blurted.

"What? How?"

"She contacted the cargo ship captain for some reason and then ended up making a recording for me."

"What did she say?" Toref's asked cautiously.

"That she was doing fine. That Dekarra is a nice place, and they've made her feel welcome." Yaran smiled. "It's such a relief to know she's okay."

"I'm glad your mind is at ease. Maybe now you can move on with your life."

"What does that mean?"

"You're young, and should stop wishing for something that will never happen. Leea is fine, but she's gone, and thinking the two of you will ever see each other again is unrealistic. You need to move on, find a mate."

"A mate? Are you joking?"

"No, I'm not. Life goes on, and you shouldn't spend it alone."

Yaran studied him for a moment. "Why didn't you ever find another mate?"

Toref frowned and focused on something beyond the windshield. "When Cassa and I mated, I considered myself the luckiest man on the planet. With our population issues, it's hard to find the right person, particularly among those in our position. Finding her was more than I could ever have hoped for. We were compatible in every way that it scared me sometimes. When she died, I wanted to die with her, and I think part of me did. I could never find someone to replace her, and I never had the desire to try."

Yaran smiled knowingly. "You've just explained my relationship with Leea. We've had a connection since we were children. With her, everything is easy and comfortable. She's a strong woman, and loved me unconditionally, as I did her. I can't imagine my life with anyone else. And my situation is different than yours. Leea didn't die…she just went away. I have to believe that someday we'll find a way to be together again. In the meantime, I'll be happy with a few simple messages."

"I hope you're right, Yaran. But don't wait too long to change your mind, before life passes by unnoticed. And one other thing: I wouldn't tell anyone about her message."

"I wasn't going to, except for Julia. She needs to know Leea's safe."

"Just keep in mind, if my brother hears you've had contact with her, he will want to look into it. That could spell trouble for the escape network."

"I promise, only you and Julia."

"Have you ever been to the pump station?" Toref asked.

"No. I've heard it's one of the best trades we've made with Dekarra."

"Probably. A lot of the precious water coming down the mountain was lost because we had no way to control it. But with the pumps, we're able to direct it to where we need it."

"And the dams?"

Toref chuckled. "Our ancestors saw those on Earth. Humans were proud of their ability to control water and showcased them with great pride. When we acquired the pump technology, our engineers felt we should use them in conjunction with the dams to redirect the flow straight to the underground rivers. It was a definite improvement over the channels we used to use."

A few minutes later, Toref indicated toward a body of water about a half mile away. "I'll do a flyover so you can see it from the air. It's quite remarkable. Graeden hasn't made contact yet, so we must be the first to arrive. But first, look over there." Toref pointed to their left across the desert. In the distance, the landscape disappeared behind a wall of hazy red that stretched as far as the eye could see—the sandstorm.

Toref maneuvered the shuttle toward the reservoir for an impressive flyover. Through the cloud-obscured, snow-packed mountain peaks, waterfalls flowed in and out of rock crevasses, ending up in a large, naturally formed reservoir. Before the pump station was built, the water found its way from there through man-made channels, but with no ability to control the amount of flow, about a quarter of the precious liquid dissipated into the hot Zantian air.

Now, the pumps pulled the water from the reservoir and redirected it to another waterfall that emptied into a long man-made lake with a dam at one end. Through there the water was released at a controlled rate, and guided behind other large crevasses that led to the hidden waterways, thus keeping it out of the hot environment.

Toref set the shuttle down on a concrete landing pad about two hundred yards from the station. He contacted Graeden and was told they were about ten minutes away, and then called for an update on the storm. The planetary office informed him it was picking up speed, but had slightly changed direction. The full force was now expected to hit the mountains late evening; sooner than originally anticipated, which meant there would be no time to return to Emborie. The two men gathered their overnight bags and provisions they'd brought and took a narrow path toward the sleeping quarters.

Fifteen minutes later Graeden, Roger, three Zantian guards, and four Human workers arrived. Yaran was taken aback when he saw Marik. Had Graeden brought him because Yaran had wanted to talk to him? The administrator had been hesitant to insist Yaran be allowed to speak with Marik when he was there months ago, and Yaran had quickly assured him it could wait for another day.

But he didn't want to confront the troublesome worker here, around other people. He preferred a quiet room with a guard standing outside the door…more for Marik's safety than his own. Here, he wanted to concentrate on getting to know Roger. Yaran wasn't sure if Leea's father knew what had happened to his family, and he didn't relish the task of telling him, but at least he could assure him his daughter was all right.

They did a quick assessment of the living quarters and assigned tasks. Water and power were turned on and provisions stored. The four workers busied themselves cleaning while Yaran, Toref, Graeden and Roger went to the pump house to begin the shut-down sequence of the three, twelve-foot diameter pumps.

Once completed, the massive machines were covered and secured, and finally, restraining rods were placed within the building's two window frames, and against each of the outside doors. The hope was that whatever sand made it to their level would settle before morning so the cleanup could begin early.

"Did we bring the comm with us from the ship?" Toref asked Yaran once they were all back in the sleeping quarters.

"No, we didn't. Do you want me to get it?"

"Yes. It'll be easier to listen for storm updates that way. And while you're there, double check and make sure the shuttles are secure. Take Roger with you. We've got everything covered here for the moment."

"I hope I didn't cause you any unnecessary concern that day at the mine?" Yaran asked as they made their way along the narrow path. "I tried not to let on that I recognized you."

"I appreciated that."

"Of course. It certainly wasn't the right time, but I am glad we'll now be able to talk. I'm sure you have questions?"

"About what?"

"About your family. You must be curious?"

"I'm not sure what you want from me, Yaran," Roger said with obvious irritation. "I thought it was Marik you wanted to talk to?"

He taken aback by his sharp tone. "I do…but not here. Finding out that you're still alive was quite a shock. I just assumed that after all these years you would want to hear about your wife and daughter."

Roger sighed and looked away. "I've lived in Emborie for the past ten years and in Lutar the years before that. I've had to put my life in Alrack behind me. As much as I appreciate you wanting to bring me up to date, I really would like to keep the past where it belongs."

"You've never wondered what happened to them?" Yaran persisted.

They had reached the landing pad, and Roger stopped in front of Toref's shuttle, visibly shaken. "Of course, I've wondered about them. In twenty-three years, not a day goes by that I don't think about them and what my... death cost them. But it's not a subject I want to dwell on. I've made peace with myself, said my goodbyes, and would rather not open up all those old wounds." He paused a moment seeming to struggle with some inner thought. "I hope you haven't told anyone about me?"

"No, of course not. Only Toref."

He gave Yaran an odd look then moved away, indicating the conversation was over. Yaran watched him for a moment, unable to understand the man's resistance, but what could he do? Nothing. He retrieved the communications module, then they both checked the vehicles to make sure they were secure, and returned to the living quarters in silence.

The howling wind was almost deafening. Sand particles, along with tree branches and loose rocks, pelted against the back of the building making the structure seemed to want to lift off its foundation, but the steel frame held—at least for the moment. The reinforcement rods they had placed in the windows and against the doors strained under the brute force of the violent storm.

The power had failed shortly after the gusts began, but a generator kept several lights on. The twelve men lay on their bunks, some with their eyes closed, a few attempting to read, all trying to ignore the sound, but eventually, weariness overtook them and one by one they all fell into a restless slumber.

An enormous crash woke everyone up. Barely visible in the dim light, a three-foot diameter tree lay across the dining area with the other end still hanging through a shattered window. Sand began swirling in the center of the room like a tornado.

"Everybody up!" Toref screamed over the din, now seeming ten times louder than before. Within a few moments, they all huddled in the sleeping area, looking awestruck at the large obstacle invading their space. The steel table still stood, supporting the trunk, but everything else—chairs, dishes, food supplies—lay scattered and broken. Sand already covered everything.

Graeden grabbed a portable light and carefully angled the beam out the window, but it reflected nothing but blackness. "I can't see anything," he shouted. "There is no way to tell how much more of this thing is sticking out there."

The men spaced themselves on either side of the twenty-foot intrusion, lifted it, and attempted to push it back through the opening, but it wouldn't budge. They tried three more times, but their combined strength had no effect.

"Do we have something to cut it with?" Yaran asked.

Toref gave him a hopeful smile, which quickly faded. "A laser cutter…which is still in the pump house."

"Then we have to go get it," Graeden said. "We have to seal this window, or we'll be buried alive by morning."

"I'll go," Toref declared.

"And how are you planning to get over there without being blown away?" Yaran asked with raised eyebrows. "The pump house may only be fifty yards away, but…."

Toref looked around and pulled a large bundle from behind an overturned chair. "Luckily, we have some rope. I will tie one end around my waist, and it can be let it out slowly as I make my way across." He looked around again and picked up an extra restraining rod, and adjusted it to a comfortable height. "I can use this to brace myself as I go across."

Yaran took the rod and coil of rope out of his uncle's hands. "It's best if I go."

"No—"

"You have far more important things to do here. No more discussion," he added quickly before Toref could protest.

Yaran put on his protective robe and ripped a strip off the bottom. He pulled the hood down, so it covered his eyes and then placed the strip over his nose and mouth, which Toref tied tightly at the back of his neck. This left a small slit he could lift to see where he was going.

"Secure the rope on the other end, and we'll do the same here once you're across. It will make it easier to return." Toref grabbed Yaran by the shoulders. "Please be careful."

Yaran nodded. "Don't worry. I will."

Outside in the mayhem, he turned his back to the wind and groaned as sand and debris pummeled his back. *Maybe I should have worn two robes*, he thought regrettably. The portable light secured to his robe was of little use, so he grabbed the side of the hood, and shielded his eyes so he could get his bearings. It was imperative that he stay on the path. The strong gusts threatened to push him over, but he braced himself on the rod with each sideways step.

Slowly, he shuffled down the slight incline, until finally, the large stone structure loomed ahead. Finding a steel girder, he tied off the rope and gave it three sharp tugs, hoping someone would feel it on the other end.

After a bit of a struggle to remove the door's restraining rod, Yaran was finally inside. He leaned against one of the pumps, exhausted from the strenuous trek and grateful for the momentary reprieve from the wind. He removed his red-encrusted robe, relieved to see it was still in one piece but wasn't sure his back had fared so well. Jagged rocks and pointed tree limbs had relentlessly assaulted his body on the journey over. If the robe spared his skin from lacerations, the bruises would be plentiful. He started to brush sand from his clothing, but soon realized it was a futile effort.

Sand had also made its way through cracks and crevices into the building's interior, covering everything with a layer of red. Turning over unrecognizable objects, Yaran finally located the cutting tool. It was larger than he anticipated and wouldn't fit in his pocket, so he was suddenly faced with the dilemma of how to carry it back and still make his way along the guide rope—knowing he would need both hands for that.

Not immediately finding anything useful, he ripped another strip off the bottom of his robe, tied it around the cutter then hung it across his shoulders. Securing the robe in place, he headed back into the wind. As he hoped, the rope was taut, but he didn't find using it any easier than the rod.

Moving up the incline made the pace slower than before, but eventually, through the swirling sand and flying debris, Yaran caught a glimpse of light seeping through the windows of the sleeping quarters several yards ahead. Suddenly, the ground beneath him started to shake, followed by a loud rumble that seemed to emanate from behind. Fear gripped him, and he tried to increase his speed, but the uneven ground made that nearly impossible.

With another quick glance, he thought he could make out several figures standing just beyond the corner of the barracks. As the sound of splitting wood and rocks crashing together took on a deafening tone, Yaran made one final frantic push and heaved himself toward the building. Several pairs of hands pulled him to safety, just as the mountainside above gave way. Uprooted trees, large rocks, and an endless amount of dirt slid across the area he had just crossed. The guide rope disappeared, taking with it the small tree it had been tied to.

They scurried inside where everyone held their breath as the walls shook around them. The tree that had crashed through their window was partially wrenched out as its roots followed the slide and then with a loud snap, it broke like a thin twig and clattered to the floor. After what seemed like an eternity, everything settled and nothing but the howling wind remained. Exhausted, they did their best to cover the broken window, and then each man fell gratefully onto his cot.

The next morning, sun filtered through sand-caked windows. Tea was brewed, and food was cooked with the supplies they were able to rescue from the sand, then jobs were assigned. Marik, two other workers, and a guard were tasked with cleaning the living quarters. Roger and another worker went to check on the ships while the rest of the group headed out to assess the damage to the surrounding area. If it were minimal, they would begin the restart process.

But the storm had left its mark and completely changed the landscape. Uprooted trees, large and small boulders, and sand mixed with mountain soil now filled in the space between the living quarters and the pump house. The five men cautiously climbed over the newly formed mound, finding the large building completely covered on two sides. But luck was with them—one of the doors faced away from the dirt's path, and except for a large tree, it was clear.

"We'll need the cutter to remove this," Toref said, assessing the partially buried edifice. Carefully, he climbed the mound to the roof and made a further scan of the area. "I was able to see into the gorge," he informed them once back on the ground. "It's filled with rubble. There will be no starting the pumps until we get it cleaned out. But, that will give us time to run a full diagnostic and make sure there's no damage to the underground pipes … now buried deeper under all this mess."

"How do we empty the ravine?" Yaran asked.

"The shuttles could lift the bigger items, but none of us are trained for that kind of work so we'll have to ask Emborie for assistance."

"How long will that take?"

Toref's frown deepened. "I'm afraid we're here for another night. If a crew can come up soon, we should be able to restart the pumps tomorrow morning. I'll put in a call to Haliel's assistant right now. I'll have them bring more supplies too."

"And the rest of this?"

"Once Alrack is back on its feet, we'll send a couple of crews to get this all cleaned up. If the restart goes okay, there'll be no hurry."

The rest of the day went pretty much as planned. Three crews arrived from Emborie by early afternoon but the task of removing several large trees, and countless boulders took longer than expected. It was well past midnight before the men collapsed on their cots.

Marik stood off to the side in the sleeping barracks the next morning, trying not to draw unwanted attention. He had no idea why they brought him here. He would have been much happier staying in his isolation room staring at the ceiling. Here they wanted him to work. He assumed his presence had something to do with Yaran, who eyed him suspiciously whenever their paths crossed. Marik was sure Yaran wanted words with him, and the Human wanted nothing more than to give the Zantian some payback for what he'd done to him. Instinctively, he touched his artificial left eye. Doc had said no one would notice—but he did.

His mind flashed back to his three days in the med-center. The process of fusing his bones had been minimally painful, but the endless hours of laying still, while the machines did their work, were excruciating. And then Doc told him they couldn't save his eye. He had simply nodded as the physician explained how he would adjust while anger boiled his blood.

Upon returning to the house, the other workers had shunned him. Marta was the only one who actually spoke to him but seemed embarrassed to do so. And then the revelation that Leea and Yaran were both gone. Gone where? No one would tell him. Why didn't they understand that for Humans on this world it was survival of the fittest?

As if his time in the House of Alrack hadn't been bad enough, then came the day he was told he was going back to Emborie. Jarock had gone back on his promise for a better life and threw him out like yesterday's trash. But the Desolk of Alrack had failed to mention that he wasn't going back to the House of Emborie, but to its mine instead. His worst fear and a Human's worst nightmare came to fruition in one day.

He had no idea why they sent him to the underground river—harvesting biologicals. He suspected it was his punishment for failing to come between the two lovers, a plan that never could have worked, but Jarock blamed him anyway.

Once in the mine, however, he discovered that he could use his disability to his advantage. At first, he refused to do some of the work they required, claiming he couldn't focus, and then started picking fights with the other workers, which landed him in isolation, a place he preferred.

But now, being here with Yaran was a stroke of luck. Maybe he could finally get the answer he had a burning desire to know: where on this forsaken rock could a Human hide? Where did Leea go?

Quietly, he slipped out of the door unnoticed.

# CHAPTER 17

# Closure

Yaran stood at the base of the small incline waiting for the pumps to start. The gorge around him was comparatively small—a hundred twenty feet at its widest point and thirty at its deepest—having been formed naturally by a hundred years of rushing water. It was bowl-shaped, except for a flat area at the cliff where water funneled through a fifty-foot reinforced opening into the man-made reservoir below.

The fallen trees and large boulders the slide had thrown in were gone, but mounds of red sand mixed with soil remained, which would slowly wash away once the water flowed again. With the exception of several small trees, which had withstood the force of the constant water, and had remained unaffected by the storm, the area was empty.

The crews hadn't dug down into the piles of dirt, so Yaran was there to make sure nothing was hiding underneath that could obstruct the cliff opening. Once the first pump started, the other two would automatically follow in fifteen-minute intervals, which could not be stopped once the process was underway.

He had been waiting about twenty minutes and began wondering what was taking so long. He could use his comm-link to check if there was a problem with the restart, but decided to make the short walk up to the station instead. Coming over the top of the incline, Yaran stopped short. Standing just beyond the rise was Marik.

"What are you doing here?" Yaran demanded, taking a step back.

"I want to ask you something." Marik moved down toward him.

"What? I'm not going to ask you again: what are you doing here? You're supposed to be helping pack up the living quarters."

"They didn't need me, so they told me to see if you needed any help."

"No one would send you down here. You need to go back. Now!"

"Where did Leea go?" Marik ignored Yaran's request.

"What?"

"You helped her escape the wrath of your father. Where did she go?"

"I don't know what you're talking about. Go back to your assigned work area."

"Or you'll do what? Make me," Marik snarled.

"You know what? Stay here if you like, I don't care." Yaran went to move around him, but Marik grabbed his arm.

"I want to know where she went."

"Let go of me!" Yaran gave Marik a push, harder than he'd intended, which sent the other tumbling a few feet down the slope. Yaran paused for a second, watching the pathetic man struggle to get up, and then turned to walk away. He heard the scramble of feet behind him and sidestepped as Marik lunged, causing the Human to tumble again.

Yaran looked down at him. "Do not start with me, Marik, you will not win. I will give you one more opportunity to return to your work area before I call the guard and the foreman."

Marik laughed. "Go right ahead." Once on his feet again, he spoke with a more somber tone. "I can tell you what you want to know."

Yaran stopped short but glared at him. "Tell me what?"

"You want to know what my deal was with your father. I can tell you the whole story."

Yaran studied him for a moment. He had imagined this confrontation differently, but this was probably as good a time as any. Instinct told him to hand Marik over to the guard, but at that moment, the need to know won over. "I'm listening."

"Not until we make a deal."

"Forget it."

"It's only fair. If I tell you what the Desolk promised me, you tell me where Leea went."

"Okay, it's a deal." The smile that crossed Marik's lips almost made him rethink his decision, but he ignored the inner voice again. Yaran moved down to stand at the same level with the blond man. "Why did my father approach you?"

"He didn't. I approached him."

"What? I don't—"

"I overheard them. Your father came to visit Haliel late one evening, and I listened outside the door."

"You listened?"

"Of course, I did. My Zantian is pretty good, so I understand the basics. I only expected to hear them talk about mine business, which was their usual topic, but your father had never visited so late before, so I wondered if something was going on. Immediately he started in about how frustrated he was with his son and that Human girl's relationship, and how he needed to take care of the situation soon. He went into the whole nonsense about your crossover, blah, blah, blah, and about how all of this put him in a bad spot because he didn't want to alienate your mother. He said he was at the end of his rope and wasn't sure what to do and then asked Haliel what he thought about sending Leea to the mines. They both laughed as if it were some inside joke. Jarock then said something about offering her up for exchange, which I assumed meant to another city. After that, their conversation went back to business, and I left."

"Go on," Yaran said through clenched teeth as Marik paused.

"The next day I approached Jarock and told him I could help with his little problem. At first, he was furious that I dared speak to him, and even more so when he realized I had been listening, but I managed to persuade him. I told him my plan about taking Leea away from you, and soon he started to like the idea."

"And why would you do that? What was in it for you?"

"Haliel likes his workers young... if you know what I mean. I knew that my days were numbered, with a few more years at most. My predecessor went to the mines, so I saw this as my way out."

Yaran stared at Marik, thinking the man had gone insane. His accusation against the Desolk of Emborie was ridiculous. "Okay, enough of this. What did my father promise you?"

"While at first, he refused to promise me anything, something apparently came to mind. He said that once I was successful, he would relocate us to a new home far away."

"To where?"

"He didn't explain further. Only that it was all or nothing. We both go, or he would invoke an alternate plan. I assumed for me that meant the mines, but for Leea, I have no idea; obviously away from you." Marik unsuccessfully tried to suppress a smirk.

Yaran felt sick.

"So tell me where Leea went?" Marik persisted.

"I'm not telling you anything. You instigated this whole plan."

"I told you what you wanted to know. Now I want to know where on this rock a person can hide."

Yaran laughed. "You are crazy if you believe for one minute—"

"You said you would tell me if I gave you want you wanted."

"I lied."

Marik's expression took on a crazed look, and he charged forward, hitting Yaran squarely in the chest, and sending both men tumbling to the ground. Yaran attempted to pull Marik off of him, but the worker started swinging his arms and managed to place a forceful blow to the side of his head. Marick then rolled away, and much to Yaran's surprise landed a powerful kick to his ribs.

He was beginning to wonder if he'd underestimated the miserable worker, when Marik energetically sprang to his feet and kicked again, this time connecting with a knee. Yaran found himself silently wincing in pain.

"Tell me where she is, and I might let you live!" Marik seethed, looking down at him.

At that, Yaran laughed. Marik may have the upper hand at the moment, having caught him off guard, but was obviously delusional about his success at beating a Zantian in a physical altercation. As Marik came in for another blow, Yaran grabbed his leg and pulled, sending him crashing backward. This time, Yaran was quicker to his feet and delivered a precise kick to the ribs, causing Marick to groan and roll away. He then lay still, face down.

Yaran leaned over and grabbed a handful of blond hair, yanking upward, but quickly let go as Marik managed to turn—in his hand was a guard's energy pistol, pointed at his chest.

"Ah, weren't expecting this, were you?" Marik waved the firearm as Yaran took several steps back. "I had to make sure we weren't disturbed during our little chat, so I relieved one of the jailers of his gun." He sprang to his feet. "Now, you are going to tell me what I want to know, or I will shoot you."

"I guess you're going to have to shoot me."

Marik fired a warning shot barely missing Yaran's right foot. "Next time you lose the foot. We can make this as painful as you like. Of course, I've never used one of these before, so you might lose a lot more than that."

Yaran stood his ground.

"You're so self-righteous aren't you?" Marik said with disdain. "But who has the upper hand now?"

Yaran slowly reached into his pocket and retrieved his comm-link, but before he could surreptitiously activate it, Marik fired again. The tall Zantian jumped away, but the energy weapon carved a deep groove into his left leg. Blood gushed from the wound as pain seared from his hip through his toes causing him to stumble and fall.

But before Marik could take aim again, a surge of water burst into the ravine from behind them. In their struggle, they had ended up at the sandy bottom, directly in the water's path. As the sound distracted Marik, Yaran scrambled toward a nearby tree with every ounce of effort he could find, clenching his teeth through each painful step. He needed to grab on, or the force of the water would wash him away. With one final painful push, he locked his arms around the wooden base and managed to take a deep breath before the water hit his face. He knew this could only be a temporary refuge. If he couldn't find a way up the incline, the force of all three pumps would send him over the cliff.

Could he survive the fall into the lake? Not likely. Even if he managed to make it through the retaining wall's opening, the cliff-wall angled outward so anything, or anyone, would bounce off the rocks long before reaching the water below. And even if he could survive the fall without major injury, Zantians didn't swim; there was no need in their world. Aside from the mountains lakes, only about one-eighth of the planet's surface had naturally occurring water, which was used to sustain many of the cities, as well as the protein and produce farms. It would never occur to anyone to use them for recreation.

As he expected, the water finally equalized across the chasm, and he was able to take a much-needed breath. Yaran tried to find a foothold, but the pain of his injury shot up through his hip as his feet sank deep into the new layer of soil that had quickly turned to mud. Carefully, hand over hand, he pulled himself up on the sparsely laid out branches until his upper body was above the water and his right foot had found purchase. He looked around for something he could grab and pull himself to safety, but the nearest tree was well out of reach.

Gritting his teeth to keep them from chattering, he felt his pocket for the comlink, but then remembered he'd dropped it during the struggle with Marik. With no other option, he held on tight and hoped for a miracle. After a few minutes, he found a bright spot in his situation: the throbbing in his leg was diminishing. The water was freezing, and while being pelted with the loose rocks and dirt, his lower limbs were starting to lose feeling. He thought about Leea and was suddenly grateful that he had been able to hear her voice one more time. Closing his eyes, he visualized her face, wanting it to be the last thing he saw if he didn't make it through this ordeal.

Marik tried to grab something as the force of the water tumbled him around. In what seemed like forever, he managed to get his arms around a tree stump jutting up through the gorge floor, but when his lungs ached from the lack of oxygen, he was forced to let go. Small bits of debris pelted his body as he struggled to find the surface, and he inhaled deeply when he finally broke through. However, the relief was short-lived; the current was swiftly pulling him toward the opening of the retaining wall. Luckily, he was close enough to grab one side before he was pulled through. Struggling to hang on, he frantically looked around for anything he could use to pull himself to safety, but with only one eye, his limited vision made that difficult.

And then he spotted Yaran. He watched for moment as the Zantian pulled himself up a small tree and partway out of the water. *Of course, the golden boy would manage to get to safety*, he thought sarcastically.

Carefully, he ran a hand around the rock barrier and found it was crudely built, having countless jutting rocks that could be used as handholds. If he pulled himself around, Marik felt confident he could climb to the top of the wall and wait out the pump restart. Stretching his arm, he grabbed a protruding rock with one hand and pulled against the current with every ounce of strength he had. His body slowly eased forward until he could grab with his other hand, and then pulled harder. But just as his hips were struggling to clear the edge, water splashed up in his face startling him, and one hand slipped away. His body jerked back, but he managed to hang on until something hard slammed into his back, and his other hand lost its grip as well.

As he flailed helplessly through the opening, Marik spotted Yaran again with his arms securely wrapped around the tree. His last thought, as he tumbled over the cliff, was how unfair his life had been.

"Yaran, are you there?" Toref called into his comm-link. "Yaran, answer me?"

"Is there a problem?" Graeden asked.

"I don't know. Yaran was supposed to check in, but I can't reach him."

"Could there be interference with the comm?"

"Possibly, but we've talked several times since he reached the cliff area."

"Would you like me to check on him?"

"Thank you, that would make me feel better. I'm sure it is just a problem with the link, but maybe a quick check wouldn't hurt. Take Roger and one of the workers with you."

Graeden pulled out his comlink and held it up. "I'll let you know as soon as we get down there." He motioned to Roger and the worker closest to the door, and the three made their way toward the waterfall. They were about halfway down the rough terrain when the worker stopped.

"What's that?" He pointed to a clump of bushes where a pair of boots protruded from underneath. The group quickly investigated, finding an unconscious guard. Graeden called Toref, explained what they found, and asked him to send help. With a new urgency, they continued their descent.

As they reached the top of the ravine, they found nothing but the partially filled gulf and water rushing over the cliff. Not seeing Yaran, they spread out to scan the area, each with a sinking feeling.

"Over there!" Roger yelled over the roar of the water while pointing to where Yaran could be seen clinging to a tree. He was submerged to his waist, but there was no sign of movement. All three yelled loudly, hoping to get his attention, but to no avail.

"We need some rope!" Roger shouted to Graeden. "I can go out and get him if I can tie myself to those trees." He pointed to a small clump a short distance away.

"Are you sure?" Graeden asked, visibly shuddering.

"Yes. That's why I'm here, right? In case something happens in the water?"

Just then the roar increased as the second pump started. When the water equalized, Yaran was covered to just below his shoulders. What worried Roger was that there was still no movement from the young man. They had fifteen minutes—they needed to work fast.

Graeden ran back to the station to retrieve the rope, leaving Roger to assess his plan of action. When he returned, along with the remaining men, Roger had them tie two lengths of rope around the nearest trees. He did a quick estimate to make sure they would reach, and then tied the other end of one rope around his waist, and the end of the second loosely to the first.

"I'm going to walk down as close as I can before I go into the water," he explained as he removed everything but his underwear. "Once I'm in, I'm counting on the current to take me close enough to reach him. For both our sakes, please keep an eye on me; if I miss, you'll have to pull me back in for another try. I realize we only have a few minutes. Once the third pump starts, the water will cover him."

The shock of the cold water made Roger momentarily recoil, but he pushed the discomfort aside and concentrated on the Zantian clinging to the thin tree. The men were keeping the rope taut, and as expected, the current swept him toward the waterfall. What he hadn't expected was all the debris being washed away or his inability to keep himself upright; the current was strong and wanted to tumble him around.

The current in the warm, underground rivers where he worked was slow and steady, and on those rare occasions when he had to be in the water away from the bank, keeping himself upright was never an issue. Here, his leg muscles complained as he fought against the forceful flow, as well as the icy temperatures.

Soon realizing that his trajectory would take him past the tree, Roger lowered his legs, hoping for a foothold, but his feet only felt loose dirt being washed away. He stretched as far as he could, but before he could make any further effort, his legs were swept away, and he was pulled under. Resurfacing, he coughed up water and revised his plan as he struggled to steady himself. Using powerful strokes, he battled the current which propelled him close enough to grab the tip of one of the tree's branches, but it broke off, and he was pushed further away. The rope pulled him back, then loosened, and with a second attempt, he managed to get a firm grip on a branch just below the surface and carefully pulled himself toward the trunk.

"Yaran!" he shouted. "Yaran, can you hear me?"

The Zantian's eyes fluttered, and his teeth chattered uncontrollably. "Roger? I...I can't hold on any longer...my...my whole body is numb," he stuttered weakly.

"You have to hang on just a little longer. I'm here to help you."

Roger hurriedly tied the rope around Yaran's chest, pried his submerged arms away from the tree then signaled they were ready. The older man turned on his back, grabbed Yaran under the arms, making sure to keep his head above the water, and let the pull of the rope carry them to safety.

They had only made it a few feet when the third pump started, and Roger quickly hooked an arm through Yaran's rope to keep them from being pulled apart. The scarcely consciousness man would certainly drown if he were pulled away. They were tossed around until the current settled, but Roger managed to keep Yaran afloat.

Several minutes later both men lay on dry land, wrapped in multiple blankets, trying to get feeling back into their extremities. Yaran was a little worse for wear, but with his wet clothes removed and the warmth of the coverings, consciousness had returned. Small cuts on his body were tended to, and the large gash on his leg was bandaged, but Toref didn't want to seal it until it could be checked at a medical facility.

"Let's get you both back to the living quarters so you can rest a bit while everything is readied for departure," Toref suggested.

"If it's all the same to you," Yaran said groggily, "I'd just like to lay here in the sun. It feels good on my face, and I don't think my legs are ready to move yet."

Toref crouched next to his nephew and rested a hand on his shoulder. "You scared me, you know?" The emotion was heavy in his voice. "I thought I was going to lose you." He looked over at Roger. "Thank you so much for what you did. It was quick thinking."

"You're welcome, but it was a natural reaction. When you extract the most dangerous element on the planet, which is found in underground rivers, you have to think fast...a lot."

"Well, I'm glad you were here." He turned back to Yaran. "Can you tell me what happened out there? Was Marik with you?"

As they had watched the rescue unfold, Toref noticed the worker's absence and asked if anyone had seen Marik, but no one had. When the unconscious guard came around, he joined the group, telling Graeden someone had hit him on the back of the head and took his weapon.

"I think Marik is dead," Yaran said.

"Dead? Are you sure?"

Yaran told him about how Marik had confronted him, and the resulting struggle. How he was sure Marik had gone over the falls when the first pump started. "He was standing right in the path of the water. If I hadn't managed to grab onto the tree, I would have gone over with him. I don't see how he could have survived."

"Well, I say good riddance," Toref said. "We'll send someone up in a few days to see about recovering the body. I'll feel better once we know for sure." Toref got to his feet. "You two lie here and rest. I'm going to go up and see how much longer before takeoff. Yaran, we need to get you to a medical center and have that wound checked out as soon as possible."

"What? No, I'll be fine. I can treat this at home."

"You should listen to him," Roger said. "That wound looks bad, and not to mention you were in and out of consciousness when I pulled you off that tree. You were exposed to the cold water far too long."

Yaran sighed. "Okay, I am still a little light headed." He chuckled. "And I doubt I'll ever be warm again."

Toref smiled. "Then it's settled. I'll be back when it's time to leave."

"I can go back with you," Roger started to get up. "I can help with the preparations."

"No, you need your rest too. And I would feel better if Yaran wasn't here by himself."

"I, too, want to thank you for saving my life," Yaran said wearily, once they were alone. "I had hoped for a miracle; I guess that was you."

"I'm glad I was here to help."

The two men lay still, eyes closed, trying to recover their strength.

"Yaran?" Roger called out quietly.

"Yes?" he answered, without opening his eyes.

"I want to apologize for the other day. I wasn't trying to be uninterested in what you wanted to tell me."

Yaran turned to look at him. "That's okay. We all have to deal with what life throws us. I assumed you would want to know, so I apologize for the intrusion."

"No, it wasn't your fault. As I told you, I said my goodbye's a long time ago and didn't welcome the thought of having to relive it all over again. But, I have thought about nothing else since we talked, and surprisingly, it left me wanting to hear what you had to say."

"Really?" Yaran tried to sit up, but groaned and rolled onto his side instead. "How much do you know about what's happened to your family?"

Roger grimaced. "I know Kathryn took her own life if that's what you're asking." Roger sat up but didn't look over at Yaran. "She was always a fragile person and had a hard time dealing with day-to-day life. The doctor called it acute depression, but the Zantians couldn't find the right type of treatment to help her.

"When Leea was born, I had hoped the child would give her a new focus, something to be happy about, and for a while, it worked. And when the Desolk sent me to the mines, I hoped again that Leea would sustain her…and I guess it did, but only for a short while.

"Kathryn was okay most days before I was sent away. But sometimes she couldn't get out of bed, and I had to be both father and mother to Leea. My little girl needed her mother, but there were times I couldn't allow my daughter to go into Kathryn's room, which always upset her. The only thing that would calm her was the lullaby I always sang to her."

"Leea was always trying to remember that melody. I guess Kathryn calmed her with it as well after you were…gone. But Leea couldn't remember how it went anymore."

Roger hummed for a few seconds. "Not something I could ever forget."

"Why was everyone told you were dead?"

Roger rubbed both hands over his bearded face before turning toward Yaran. "Because I saw something I wasn't supposed to. And before you ask, I can't tell you what it was." Roger blew out a breath and lowered his head. "I traded my family to keep that secret."

"I don't understand?"

"What I saw, most Zantians don't even know exists. I was sure they would send me out into the desert—"

"They send people out into the desert?"

The older man chuckled. "It's an old story. Workers disappear, and a lot of times it's the troubled ones. So, tales have been created saying they are sent out into the desert to fend for themselves. But I doubt that's really true."

Yaran looked at him wide eyed.

"But instead I was given a choice: keep what I saw to myself and live, or suffer the fate of being in the wrong place at the wrong time."

"This deal was with my father?"

"I doubt the Desolk makes deals with Humans. No, he was told I died in a cave-in."

Yaran looked stunned. "Now that you're in Emborie, don't you worry someone might recognize you?"

"I don't think so. I'm older, and have a nice beard," he stroked his chin, smiling. "And while I'm sure I crossed paths with the Desolk of Emborie a long time ago in Alrack, I can't imagine he even knew I existed."

"True. I am curious, though: how did you find out about Kathryn?"

"I had made several good friends in Alrack, a few in higher positions. After Kathryn…died…word was passed to me."

Yaran shook his head. "What goes on in the mines amazes me every day."

"You don't know the half of it," Roger muttered. Before Yaran could ask what he meant by that, Roger continued, "Tell me about my daughter? Is her grandmother still alive?"

"No, Sara died several years ago. Losing her last family member was a very sad time for Leea. They were very close."

Roger studied him a moment, then made an observation. "I take it you and Leea are also very close."

Yaran suddenly felt uncomfortable and lowered his eyes. "Yes. Our friendship started the day of her mother's remembrance and grew with each passing year."

"I see. So that explains your need to tell me about my family. How did your family accept that?"

"They didn't," he chuckled. "At least, my father didn't. And that's the reason we're having this conversation."

"How so?"

Yaran spent the next hour giving Roger a condensed version of Leea's life, the love that had developed between them, her hasty departure for Dekarra, ending with the message he had received. Roger listened intently, his expression remaining stoic.

"Marik," Roger said with disgust. "I always knew there was something wrong with that man. He spent more time in confinement than actually working. So I take it the reason you wanted to see him that day in Emborie had something to do with what happened to Leea?"

"Yes, it was. He made a deal with Jarock, and I wanted to know what he was promised."

"Did Marik give you any answers before the water came?"

"He came looking for me, demanding to know where Leea went. I tricked him into telling me about his deal with Jarock, and it was pretty much what I expected. When I refused to tell him what he wanted to know, he pulled a weapon on me. The rest you know."

"Well, at least, you won't have to worry about him anymore."

They sat in silence for a few minutes, and then Roger made a request. "I want to thank you for everything you've told me today. It does feel good to know my daughter had a happy life thanks to you. But I do have one favor to ask."

"Of course, anything."

"When you send your reply to Leea, don't tell her about me, at least not yet. I don't want to upset her life any more than it already has been."

"Are you sure?"

"Yes."

Back in the city, Toref took Yaran straight to the medical facility, where he was examined, and his wounds cleaned and sealed, then sent home with orders to rest for a few days. The healer said Yaran was lucky. The blast wound, while deep, missed any major arteries, but had he been in the icy water much longer, hypothermia would have claimed him.

Cleanup in the city was well underway by the time they returned. The citizens had immediately gotten to work repairing damage and hauling the desert elements back where they belonged.

Alrack had fared better than the pump station, but fine red sand covered everything in the metropolis and the outlying villages. The house on the hill received the least of the impact, but would still need some cleanup. More wind turbines were lost at the west mine than expected, so work there would be on hold for possibly a week until they could be repaired or replaced.

Toref left to assess mine damage and insisted Yaran stay home and rest, and there was no arguing with the large man, who scowled at him kindly. But once alone, Yaran realized it was the perfect opportunity to start his message to Leea.

Sitting at his home terminal, he brought up one of the many images of Leea he had stored there and moved it up to into the right corner then activated the video mode. He smiled, but his well-organized words were suddenly gone. Drawing strength from Leea's happy face, he started over.

"My darling Leea," Yaran said and smiled lovingly at the screen. "It's hard for me to express how happy I was when Mearos gave me your recording, but it was as if my life suddenly had meaning again. He didn't clearly explain why he's taking this risk, but I'll be eternally grateful to him for bringing you back to me...even in this small way. I love you so much and miss you horribly every minute of every day. Hearing your voice and being able to talk to you again is more than I ever hoped for, and I'm sure this is a sign that we truly aren't lost to each other."

"While I was fairly confident you would make it safely to Dekarra…Mearos had assured me of that…I am relieved you didn't find any of those horrible places you imagined." He chuckled softly. "I don't know much about the worlds we trade with, but I've never heard that any of them are terrible places, and would hope that the network isn't sending workers to a worse fate than what they had here. I know your message had to be short, but maybe at some point, you'll tell me about Dekarra, but only when you're ready."

"Yes, I am living with Toref now. He's been very supportive, and a great teacher. He's helping me learn everything I need to know about working in the mines, and strangely it's not as bad as I imagined. I'm actually enjoying the challenge as it keeps me occupied, for which I'm grateful. Toref has also been a great shoulder for me to lean on. While Cassa's death isn't the same as you leaving, he understands the sadness I'm going through. It's been a relief to be around someone where I feel comfortable discussing any topic, knowing he won't judge me.

"I take every opportunity I can to visit my mother, but only when Jarock is away, so, unfortunately, it's not as often as I'd like. I do see Julia on occasion and will pass on your love as soon as I can."

Yaran went on to tell her about the sandstorm, and what happened at the reservoir with Marik. While it didn't make this situation any less painful, Yaran did feel a sense of closure knowing Marik was gone and couldn't cause any more trouble—he hoped Leea would feel the same. He didn't mention Roger, respecting the man's wishes, but felt that his daughter was being cheated out of a wonderful addition to her life.

"Well, my love, I'm going to stop for today, but I'll be back tomorrow, and every day after that until I have to take this to Mearos." Yaran rested a hand against the monitor. "I love you so much, Leea, and my arms long to hold you. Until they do, *Er'ShaltMee'Sarn*."

He stopped the video, closed his eyes and visualized how she would sometimes rest a hand on his cheek while she reassured him his heart was safe with her.

He never doubted it was.

The day before Yaran went back to work, Toref sent a maintenance crew to the pump station, where they recovered Marik's partially submerged body near the dam. He was taken to the medical facility, where it was determined he died from the trauma of hitting the rock wall as he tumbled into the reservoir.

Despite Toref's objections, Yaran went to see the corpse. It was the only way to know for sure that Marik was gone forever. He had never seen a dead body before, and this one was badly damaged, not to mention what the water had done. But he held onto his resolve, as well as his morning meal, and looked down at the man who had taken joy in trying to destroy his life and that of the woman he loved.

What surprised him, as he looked at the battered remains, was the sense of pity he felt for Marik. What a waste of a life. To purposely cause others misery, and in one final act of desperation end up broken on a hard slab. But the sympathy was short-lived. Marik had made his choices, and for that, he got what he deserved.

Leaving the medical facility, Yaran made his way to Julia's. He wanted to tell her about Marik personally.

"He's really dead?"

"Yes, I just came from seeing the body."

"You saw his body?!" Julia exclaimed, making a face.

"I had to be sure. Is that weird?"

"No, not really," she smiled reassuringly. "Is it bad of me to say I'm glad?"

"Well, then we're both bad because I'm glad too."

Yaran gave her a wide smile, and she looked at him quizzically.

"Is that smile because of Marik?"

"No. I have something for you." He extracted a data-cube from his pocket and handed it to her.

"What's this?"

"A message from Leea."

"What?!"

"Mearos, the cargo ship captain, called me to his office just before the storm. Evidently, Leea went to see him before he left Dekarra, and he had her record a message for me, so I brought you a copy. She wanted me to pass on her love to you, but I thought it would help if you heard her voice yourself."

"She's okay then." Tears welled in her eyes.

"Yes, she is. Mearos said he would get a message back to her, so I knew you'd want to send one too."

"Oh, Yaran, this is the best news ever. Of course, I want to send one back."

"Mearos is leaving in about two weeks. I'll call a day ahead so you can have it ready."

"Oh, don't worry. I'll start on it as soon as you leave."

# CHAPTER 18

# Revelations

"**I** was beginning to think you weren't going to make it before I left." Mearos looked up briefly as Yaran entered the office.

"There has been so much going on lately, getting everything back in order after the storm, that I haven't had much time for anything. But nothing could stop me from getting this to you on time." He handed the cube over. "Can I ask you a question?"

Distracted by something on his terminal, Mearos held up a finger.

"I'm sorry if I'm interrupting."

The captain sighed and shook his head. "No, I'm sorry. What's your question?"

"Remember the device you used to open the doors the day Leea left? Is it specific to the ones around here?"

"Yes. But there are ones that can open any entry. Why?"

Yaran hesitated. "Do you know where I can get one … for any door?"

"Planning an unauthorized access?" Mearos gave him a crooked smile.

Sinking into a chair, Yaran shrugged. "I'm not sure what I'm planning, but I might have a reason to need … such an item."

Mearos retrieved an oval object from the storage room, about the size of his palm, and handed it to him.

"You won't need it?"

"No. You can give it back when you're done with it."

Something beeped on the terminal, and Mearos immediately returned his attention to it.

"I did interrupt something."

"No, I just seem to have a mystery on my hands that I can't solve."

"What is it?"

Mearos waved him around the desk, and Yaran leaned over the captain's shoulder. At first glance, the screen looked to be covered with randomly scattered lines and curves. But on closer inspection, they actually formed loosely connected groupings, running vertically and horizontally along the page. A sense of familiarity surfaced.

"What are those?" he asked.

Mearos raised his hands, palms up. "I have no idea. I've been trying for weeks to find out what these symbols mean. I've searched every code database to no avail. The language database said *inconclusive*. Whatever that means. I have rerun them in every way I know how. Do they look familiar to you?"

"I think they might."

"Really?" Mearos exclaimed with surprise. "From where?"

"If I can have a copy of the file, I'll try to get some answers for you, but I'd like to verify if my suspicions before I say anything."

"Of course. Can I ask where you're going to find the answers?"

"From the one person I trust most."

Yaran walked through the door of his family's home and paused at the familiar sounds and smells. The evening meal had ended a few hours ago, but the inviting food aromas still lingered. It felt good to be here. Jarock was away dealing with a crisis, and wasn't expected back until tomorrow, so Yaran's visit was well timed.

He looked in his mother's sitting room, finding it empty. Doubting he would find her there, he walked to the kitchen to check anyway. He could hear sounds coming from the workers' common-room, but the kitchen was dark.

He checked Lauranna's sleeping quarters and found those empty as well. Had she gone with the Desolk? She never traveled with him on emergent business, unless it was to Calthena, so it was unlikely. Maybe she went to visit a friend. Before he could decide what to do, Greta, Lauranna's personal assistant, came into the room and stopped short when she saw him.

"Yaran," she said with obvious surprise, "how nice to see you."

"Hello Greta, I didn't mean to startle you. Is my mother away?"

"Oh no, she's taking a walk in the gardens."

"She is?" It was his turn to be surprised.

Greta smiled. "She's kept up the evening walks you both took during your extended visit."

Yaran chuckled. "And here I thought she was only taking them to humor me."

"No, I think she really enjoyed them. She rarely misses an evening now."

"Does she always go this late?"

"She likes it when it's cooler, and the gardens are lit."

"When do you expect her back?"

"Twenty minutes or so. I was just coming to prepare her room. You should go out and join her."

"No, I'll wait until she gets back. I have something I need to take care of first."

Yaran walked into the library and approached the glass-enclosed cabinet. As it had for centuries, the white artifact hovered on the center shelf while groupings of its facets brightened and dimmed. It was an amazing thing to watch, and he had spent many hours as a young boy trying to discover the hidden secret it was attempting to reveal. Jarock had always disapproved and insisted the object served no purpose. He reiterated many times that the only reason it was here, was because the ancestors deemed it too extraordinary to leave behind on a deserted planet.

Removing the datapad from his pocket, Yaran activated Mearos's file. He held it up next to the glass and compared the two. They weren't exactly the same, but the similarity in style was uncanny. The three-dimensional facets of the sphere gave a different perception than the flat screen, but the arrangement of each grouping, and how they connected, was unmistakably similar.

The symbol arrangement on the pad could easily represent writing. Like musical notes, there was a rhythm to their layout, and watching the artifact randomly shift the groupings made him finally believe without a doubt that this was an alien language. And now more than ever, he wanted to know what it was saying.

Yaran had barely made himself comfortable in his mother's sitting room when Lauranna entered. A big smile crossed her face.

"I wish I had known you were coming today." Lauranna gave him a hug after he rose to greet her. "I would have waited to take my walk."

"I haven't been here long, and I had something I needed to do first."

"I'm glad. Did you finish what you came for?"

"Yes and no." Yaran handed her the datapad. "Have you ever seen these symbols before?"

Lauranna studied the screen for a moment then handed it back to him. "No, they don't look familiar."

"Are you sure?"

"Yes, I am sure. Where did you get this?"

"Someone found them on an old terminal and showed them to me."

"And you told him you'd seen them before?"

"I said I might have. Come with me." Yaran led her to the library, and again, he held the tablet next to the hovering orb. "If you look closely, you can see how the symbols on the pad, and the artifact, could easily be the same."

Lauranna moved closer and studied both variations. "Are you sure you're not just trying to make them the same?"

"I don't think so." Yaran removed the sphere and cradled it in both hands. "This piece has spoken to me my entire life, no matter what Jarock tried to tell me. Seeing these symbols on a two-dimensional plane proves to me that it is a language. And since you're the best language expert I know, I'd like you to try and translate it."

"Yaran, I don't know—"

"Please."

Lauranna looked at the object he held, then hesitantly reached out to pick up the pad he'd laid on the shelf. "Okay, I'll give it a try, but I can't promise anything. Translating a language can be easy if you have a good starting point or a key. I'm not sure I'll be able to find either."

"That's okay. If nothing comes of it, then so be it."

"And you know I can only do this when your father is away. He would never approve." Almost as an afterthought, she added, "And he can never know about this file."

Yaran gave her a hug. "Thank you."

Lauranna lay in her bed unable to sleep. She was struggling with a decision she knew she had to make. Looking over the data file, she had scrutinized the text closely in the hope she was wrong. But no matter how long she studied it, there was no doubt of its true origin.

What was she going to do, help Yaran in his quest, or follow the unspoken laws to keep their peoples' secrets? How could she reveal what most people didn't know, without turning all their lives upside down? But she couldn't lie to her son, or keep from him the knowledge his birthright granted him, so what choice did she have?

This decision would give her many sleepless nights—of that she was sure.

# CHAPTER 19

# The Network

With a pillow propped behind her back, Leea sat stretched out under a blanket on her living room sofa, trying to concentrate on the latest book Farrell had recommended, but was finding it impossible. After reading the same sentence three times, she lowered the reader and closed her eyes, listening as the wind picked up outside. She loved the sound of rustling branches, but not as much as listening to the forest creatures as they went about their daily lives. They were all silent now since the weather turned cold. She suspected they had retreated to whatever they called home, the same as the people had.

The raining season had ended about a month ago, making way for the approaching winter, and snow. It still made her chuckle when she thought about the first time she'd seen it.

She had woken up before dawn one morning confused at how light it was and gone to the window. What greeted her was something books couldn't accurately describe. Between the bare branches, large fluffy white flakes fell softly from the sky which had completely blanketed the ground during the night.

Anxious for a closer look, she had quickly dressed and stepped outside, bracing herself for the cold, but was surprised at how mild the temperature felt, even though she could see her breath when she exhaled. Pausing under the roof overhang for a brief moment, she had watched this new form of water glide effortlessly to the ground before stepping into its path. The white crystals stuck to her clothes before disappearing, and stretching out a bare hand she let the intricate, weightless snowflakes fall into her palm, smiling as they melted on her skin.

Something else she remembered vividly about that experience—the complete silence. As if the falling snow was an imaginary barrier keeping all sound at bay. Before going back inside, she had walked around the yard, listening to the white ground cover crunch under her feet, chuckling the entire time. She had hoped no one was watching, or they might have thought she'd gone mad.

Since then, a gray sky hovered above most days like a fluffy blanket expelling its heavy filling about two or three times a week, leaving the ground under a constant cover of white. Leea wasn't sure she would ever get used it. Some days, there weren't enough sweaters or blankets to warm her bones. Farrell laughed when she'd complained and reassured her that many people felt the same way.

The weather report said it was supposed to snow again today, but at the moment, there wasn't a cloud in the sky, for which she was grateful. Bettina had called yesterday and asked if she wanted to join her in the city for an early dinner, and she was looking forward to it. Although her friend checked in regularly by phone, they hadn't seen much of each other lately, so she hoped the momentary reprieve would hold out.

Leea loved going into town, especially in the evening when people wandered about on some unknown adventure. It made her smile when she thought of her first stroll down the city's main street, and the apprehension she'd felt that day—now completely gone. She had spent many evenings in New Haven with Farrell, but her favorite outing was when she and Jackson had taken her to the theater. She had been mesmerized by the acting on stage and became totally engrossed in the story, which she found surprisingly easy to follow.

On Earth, people had spent evenings at home watching television or going to movies, but on Dekarra, they had yet to reinvent that type of entertainment, even after a hundred years. They had old movies, brought by the colonists, which were available to watch on a computer, or at a few venues where they were played on a larger screen. Mary had helped her access the library, and Leea found them interesting.

Returning to her book, Leea finally managed to lose herself in the story. Anxious for the heroine to find her way out of the dark basement and elude a murderer, Leea jumped when there was a knock on her front door. Bettina wasn't due for several hours, and Mary was away visiting her grandchildren, so, intrigued, Leea rose to greet her first unexpected visitor.

Opening the door, she found a tall, older woman standing at the edge of the porch. She was slender, with short dark graying hair, and large dark blue eyes. A white car at the curb told her the stranger wasn't from the neighborhood.

"Can I help you?" Leea asked.

The woman smiled shyly. "Are you Leea?"

"Yes."

"I apologize for showing up on your doorstep unannounced, but I thought this would be better."

Leea looked at her in confusion but waited for her to continue. The woman stepped forward and extended a hand, which Leea took.

"My name is Tamera Jennings. I am Mearos's mother."

Leea's eyes went wide, and her mouth dropped open, but she quickly recovered. Tamera chuckled at her reaction. "You see; this is why I thought the phone would be a bad idea."

Leea regained her composure and nodded. "Yes, I agree. Please, come in."

Taking Tamera's coat and hanging it on the rack behind the door, Leea noticed a pendant hanging around her visitor's neck. It was an elongated triangle filled with tiny colorful stones—a design she recognized.

"I like your necklace," she said.

"Thank you." Tamera took it in her hand and studied it reflectively. "I bought this from a young boy at our outdoor market this past summer."

"A young boy?"

"Yes. It was the strangest thing really. He stood by himself at the end of an aisle and held this out as I passed. Told me, he and his father made them, and as soon as he sold this last one he could go home. The funny thing was, he wasn't in a booth, and I didn't have the impression he'd been there very long. But, I felt sorry for him, so I bought it."

"May I take a look?"

Tamera pulled the chain over her head and handed it to her. The object was about two inches long and made of fused glass like her *jarkut*. But why would someone sell this at a market? She pulled her pendant from under her shirt and laid the triangle on top—perfect fit. It could easily portray a part of the *remdalar*.

"Has it ever warmed in your hand?"

"No. Should it?"

Leea made a fist around both pieces. She wasn't sure what she was expecting, and she didn't want to concentrate on anything specific and possibly scare her guest, so she simply thought: *I hope I have a pleasant, uninterrupted visit with Tamera before Bettina gets here. I also don't want Bettina to know that I've met Mearos's mother.* Leea thought the pieces warmed slightly but assumed it was her imagination. As she opened her hand, a soft pop sounded behind her and another one from the kitchen.

"What was that?" Tamera asked, looking around.

"I have no idea. Maybe some snow fell off the roof." Dismissing the strange moment, Leea handed back the pendant and offered her visitor a seat and something hot to drink. After they were comfortably seated, Leea studied Tamera a moment. Her blue eyes explained Mearos's own unique color, even though everything else about him seemed genuinely Zantian.

One question rose immediately to the forefront: how did Tamera come to be on Dekarra? Leea suddenly realized she was staring, something she regularly seemed to do when confronted by the unknown. "I am so sorry!" she apologized, horrified.

"No apology necessary." Deducing the young woman's reason for staring, she added, "Mearos looks just like his father, except for the eyes, of course."

"Why didn't Mearos tell me about you? We spent many hours talking on the ship, mostly me pouring my heart out to him," Leea frowned, "but he had plenty of opportunities to tell me about his family."

"You will find that my son doesn't think much about his divided heritage and prefers not to dwell on the subject."

"I'm sorry, that must be difficult."

"Our relationship is still a fragile one, but gaining strength every time we meet. My hope is that someday he'll forgive me for leaving him."

"I'm sure he understands that you did what you had to. I don't know Mearos well, but he seems to have a kind heart."

"He says he doesn't blame me, and I'd like to believe that. I try to visit with him whenever I can, but with his seclusion at the airfield, our time is limited." Tamera reached down and removed a data-cube from her bag and handed it to Leea with a smile. "He asked me to give you this. He said it was a message from Yaran."

Leea's heart began pounding wildly. Gingerly she took the storage device and cradled it in her hand as if she held a delicate flower. A big smile formed on her face as she put it in her shirt pocket. "Thank you. Thank you so much for bringing this to me. I assume Mearos told you who Yaran is?"

"He said he was the Zantian you left behind."

"Yes. But I don't think of Yaran as someone I left behind. I think of him as someone I'm separated from for the moment. I will never stop believing we'll see each other again." Leea sighed. "I assume you left someone too?"

"The only one on Zantia I cared anything about was my son."

"I'm sorry."

The older woman smiled warily. "It was a long time ago, and all those feelings are long gone. But enough of that. Along with the cube, Mearos asked me to tell you my story."

"He did? I'm certainly curious, but I wish he would have told me himself."

"He doesn't want me to tell you his story. He wants me to tell you mine." Tamera rose and walked to the front window. "Dark clouds are rolling in. It's going to snow soon," she commented absentmindedly, then returned to the chair, retrieving her cup from the table and cradling it in both hands. Leea waited patiently.

"There was a change in Mearos when I saw him yesterday. I'm not sure how to explain it, and it might have only been my imagination, but he certainly seemed more at ease. He also feels a connection to you ... a friendship."

"I wouldn't have survived the trip here without him. I definitely consider him a friend."

"I'm glad." Tamera looked into the cup, swirled the contents a moment. "Like you, I fell in love with a Zantian who was a member of a ruling house. Sithan was the nephew of the Desolk of Finetig."

"One of the produce farms."

"Yes. The Finetig family was a large one. The Desolk had two brothers and two sons, who all lived in the main house along with their families. Each of the brothers had two sons, Sithan being the youngest child of the youngest brother. Each family member was in charge of a portion of the farm. I worked in the greenhouse that Sithan started managing shortly after his transition training. Our relationship started about six months after that.

"About a year later, I found out I was pregnant." Tamera grimaced. "I had read all the statistics on how we were biologically compatible with the Zantians. But truthfully, I never believed it. I missed two of my cycles, but still assumed something else was wrong, until there was no mistaking the reality that I was going to have a child.

"At first, he wasn't too concerned, but something must have happened that made his attitude change. About six months into the pregnancy I started having medical issues and had to stop working, so he sent me to live with Nira, one of his old instructors. He visited regularly, and shortly after Mearos was born, he said he wanted me to give the baby to her, so things could go back to the way were."

"Abandon your baby?"

"He said I could tell everyone the baby died in childbirth." Tamera paused and seemed to collect her thoughts. "Sithan became a complete stranger to me. Everything I had loved about him disappeared."

"I'm so sorry."

"I told him I could never give up my baby. He said if I insisted on keeping him, Mearos and I would have to leave. At first, I thought he meant to another city, but then he explained he meant off Zantia. He said it was too risky to move us anywhere else because someone still might find out who the baby's father was. And the fact that my son was more Zantian than Human would raise far too many questions. I quickly realized there was no other choice, so reluctantly I agreed to his plan."

"So he contacted the underground network?"

Tamera's brows narrowed in confusion. "What underground network?"

"The secret network which helps workers escape from Zantia."

"No, there wasn't anything secret about it. Sithan explained that the Council had an agreement with Dekarra, and they often sent workers there."

"So you're saying the Council knows there are Humans here on Dekarra?"

"Yes, that's what he told me. Isn't that how you got here? I assumed as much since you were involved with a Desolk's son—"

"No, that's not how I ended up here at all," Leea interrupted. "Mearos didn't tell you about the secret underground network I escaped through?"

"No."

"I don't understand. I was trying to escape the wrath of the Desolk of Alrack, who found out about my relationship with his son, and wanted me gone. My sister had a connection to a network the Zantians *supposedly* don't know about. But now you're telling me they do."

"If I learned one thing while living among Zantians, it's that they are people with many secrets, and it's hard to understand why they do the things they do."

Leea nodded in agreement. "One thing I still don't understand, though: if Sithan arranged for you and Mearos to come here, why did Mearos stay on Zantia?"

Tamera lowered her head. "I left him there," she said, her voice barely above a whisper.

"May I ask why?"

"Because it was the right thing to do. Contrary to what I might have wanted, Mearos would never have been accepted here among Humans. So for his sake, I left him behind. It was the hardest thing I've ever done. Sithan promised to make sure he was taken care of, so I agreed."

"I can't even imagine how hard that must have been. But I agree you made the right choice. Some people here still seem to hold a strong grudge against the Zantians for what they did to Earth."

"I think it's only the government that feels that way. I believe most people don't give our home-world a second thought anymore. We've made a good life for ourselves here. The need for retribution has diminished with the generations."

Leea thought back to her first conversation with Bettina, who had clearly given the impression that all Dekarrans wanted the Zantians held accountable for what they had done. Nethas had told her things on Dekarra were not what they seemed. Could Tamera be right in her assessment? Then why would Bettina have given her the wrong impression?

"How did you and Mearos make contact with each other again?"

"About seven years ago Bettina Reese contacted me, told me my son was on Dekarra and asked if I wanted to meet him. At first, I thought she was someone playing a cruel joke. I knew I'd never see him again, and had made peace with that a long time ago. I imagined the only reason he would want to see me, was to tell me how much he resented what I'd done. But either way, I needed to hear what he had to say. The next day I met Bettina in the airfield's parking garage, and she took me to see him."

"In the parking garage? You didn't go through the front entrance?"

"Oh no, I always take the elevator from below."

"I'm surprised Bettina is involved in your meetings. I thought all she did was escort escapees off the ship, after that they were on their own?"

"I don't know why, but she seems to want to know when Mearos and I see each other. She always acts like it's a hardship on her to make the arrangements." Tamera made a face. "She calls and says he's here, even though I already have the schedule, and we set up a time to meet. At the last minute, she'll call and say she can't make it then give me the elevator code. I'm not sure the point of it all. How did you get in? Mearos said you visited him the last time he was here."

"I did. I didn't tell anyone I was going. Since I still have the robe from the day I arrived, I used it to disguise myself at the airfield. Once in the elevator, it took a couple of stops before I found the right floor."

"Mearos wanted me to tell you he'll take a message back if you can get to him tomorrow morning. I know it's not much time—"

"I'll make it," Leea blurted. "I'll stay up all night if I have to."

Tamera smiled. "Why don't I give you the code? That way you can go through the garage and won't have to worry about running into anyone."

"Will it be the same tomorrow?"

"It's always the same. Bettina must think I don't remember the cipher from one visit to the next, but I do. In all the years I've been visiting Mearos it's only changed once."

Both women laughed.

They sat and talked a while longer, Tamera telling Leea about her husband and children. Her family knew about her past and encouraged her visits with Mearos. Leea shared some of her life in Alrack, and then Tamera said she needed to go. They hugged goodbye, with a promise to see each other soon.

Leea wanted nothing more than to cancel the day's plans with Bettina. She longed to listen to Yaran's message but knew it would have to wait. Resigned, she checked the time and saw that her dinner companion was due in less than an hour, so she needed to get ready.

Opting for full water, instead of the usual sanitizing steam, Leea stood and replayed her conversation with Tamera. Now that she knew Mearos had a Human mother, several things about him fell into place. Leea had assumed that the reason he'd been so nice to her was that he felt sorry for her. But now, she wondered if he imagined her situation the same as his mother's.

But their situations were completely different. While Leea thought nothing could be more painful than leaving Yaran, she couldn't even imagine leaving a child—a part of her. What a horrible decision that must have been.

But the one thing Leea still couldn't wrap her mind around was that the Council knew about Humans on Dekarra. She had been led to believe, by Julia and Mearos, that the network was a secret kept from the Zantians. While she doubted Julia would know, she was sure Mearos did. Being the network contact in Alrack, and knowing his mother's story, made that obvious. So she questioned why he had deceived her.

Thinking about how all this might fit together made her head hurt. But she would see the captain tomorrow, and she had every intention of getting some answers. Finishing her shower, Leea put on a warm bathrobe and lay down on the bed. A new question came to mind. Should she tell Yaran what Tamera had told her? Mearos had cautioned her from revealing too much about this world, but what about revealing things she learned about Zantia? Did she want to burden Yaran more than this situation already had? No, she didn't want that responsibility, so for now, she would say nothing.

"It's me," the associate said.

"I'm busy. Can't this wait?"

"We have a situation. You better make time."

He heard a deep intake of breath. "So what is it that you can't handle?"

The associate smiled at the jab. He was used to the short temper and always added it to the cost breakdown for his services. It was almost a joke between them.

"Well, let me put this in a nutshell: the cameras in the Dennison girl's house stopped working."

"Both of them? Why?"

"I have a feeling that's beyond my pay grade. It had been a pretty quiet morning, but then she had a visitor."

"Who?"

"I have no idea. Tall, older woman. They had a brief conversation on the porch which I couldn't hear and more conversation inside at the door. Leea had her back to the camera so I couldn't see what they were doing, but I have a feeling they were looking at something. Their voices were low and muffled so I couldn't understand much. Then, poof, the cameras went dark, both of them."

The associate could feel his employer seething through the voice-link.

"Well," came a surprisingly calm tone, "see what you can do to get them back up, otherwise go in tomorrow and replace them." The line went dead.

Leea was barely dressed when Bettina knocked. Her visitor rushed through the open door, snow clinging to her clothes, and handed her a large bag. Leea instantly smelled the food.

"It's really starting to come down out there," Bettina said, shrugging out of her coat and hanging it on a hook. "If it gets any worse, I may end up sleeping on your sofa."

Although Leea chuckled and assured Bettina it was no problem, she almost broke into a cold sweat. She had hoped for a friendly dinner and then the rest of the evening to herself. If she was going to get her response to Mearos in time, she needed to catch the first bus in the morning, but if Bettina ended up stayed the night, that would be impossible.

"What's in the bag?" Leea asked, taking a cautionary peek inside and then inhaling deeply.

"Since the weather's not the greatest," she explained, pulling off her boots, "I thought we would have dinner here instead of going out. I hope you don't mind?"

"No, of course not, I think that's a very good idea. I'm surprised you came. We could have postponed this for another day."

"I thought about it, but it wasn't so bad when I left my house, so I took the chance."

In the kitchen, they unpacked warm pasta salad, fish, and yellow beans. Leea placed what needed to be warmed on heat trays while Bettina set the table and poured each a glass of wine.

"So, how has your day been?" Bettina asked once they sat at the small dining table with full plates in front of them.

"Pretty uneventful. I spent most of the morning reading a book Farrell recommended."

"It's a perfect day for that."

"It is. Too cold to do anything else. I can't wait until the snow is gone and I can get out of this house more often."

"Agreed. How is work? Have you settled in okay?"

Leea chuckled. "You should have told me that running errands and managing record storage can be overwhelming some days. My feet were complaining so much, that I had to buy better shoes. But, I like it a lot, and the people I work with are great."

"I'm glad. Are you making friends, besides Farrell?"

"Oh, a few. But I'm still a little shy about people knowing where I come from. The guys in my office know, of course, and they're really nice. They tease me sometimes about my alien ways, but it's all in fun. I assumed since Kent was so eager to tell them about me, the whole lab would know by now. But if they do, no one has said anything."

"You might be overreacting on how people will judge you."

"Maybe." Leea took a bite of the pasta salad. "This is great."

"Thanks. There's a small restaurant near my house where I order dinner several times a week."

"Well, you're a busy person, I'm sure that makes things easier."

"Yes, it does. Not to mention, I don't know how to cook."

Leea chuckled. "I've spent most of my life in the kitchen. Although cooking wasn't my main task, we all had to be able to fill in for each other, so I guess cooking comes easy for me."

"Was there a restaurant where the workers could go eat?"

"We didn't go to the city very often, but when we did, there was a restaurant called Man's."

"Man's?"

"Yes, simply Man's. It's run by a Zantian."

"Really?" Bettina failed to hide her disdain.

"Fortal prided himself on offering authentic Human food. Being around Humans now, I can honestly say he did a pretty good job, considering that all protein in Zantia is grow."

"You couldn't go into the city whenever you wanted?"

"We had free time. But walking into town and back took half the day, so we usually waited until the Desolk was away on business. His mate, Lauranna, didn't mind, as long as we finished our tasks."

"I can't imagine living such a restricted life."

"Well, when it's all you've ever known, it doesn't seem so unusual."

"How does Alrack compare to New Haven?"

"They're not so different. Alrack is much smaller, but they both have tall buildings, with people going about their daily lives. Of course, color wise, Alrack is a drab city. There are no tree-lined streets, or pops of color wherever you turn. But Zantians pride themselves on their architectural designs. For them, it's art, like everything else they create, so the cityscape is cohesively laid out, the flow almost musical, like their voices."

Leea couldn't identify the look that crossed Bettina's face, but it almost seemed like boredom.

"Did you ever see any other races, besides Human, in Alrack?"

Leea thought back to that day she encountered the Morodon in the alley. "No, only Humans. I heard there might be some elsewhere on the planet although I can't say for sure."

"Well, I'm sure what they did to Earth, they must have done to other planets...abducted their people. As such an advanced race, they probably approached many helpless planets, making unreasonable demands. I just don't like thinking that they looked at us as so weak that they could take whatever they wanted."

Leea tried hard to hide her irritation. "Well, unfortunately, there's no way we'll ever know. All those involved in the attack on Earth are dead now, so I'm not sure why it matters."

"You are absolutely right," Bettina agreed with a nervous chuckle. "Well, no use speculating, so let's change the subject before we get too depressed."

"Can I meet some of the other escapees that came from Zantia?"

Bettina looked wary. "Why?"

"I thought it might be interesting to see what their lives are like."

"That's not a good idea. The one thing all those men made clear to me was that they wanted to forget where they came from."

"You don't keep in touch with them?"

"We know where they are, of course, but I respect their wishes."

"I guess I can understand that too. When you've lived your life in horrible conditions, and then find yourself in this beautiful place, it's easy to want to forget."

"No one wants to relive a devastating past."

"No. I suppose not."

Having drank two glasses of wine, Leea excused herself and went to the washroom suddenly wanting to be done with this particular conversation. When they finished their meal, Bettina helped clean up and then looked out the window and checked the weather report.

"There seems to be a momentary reprieve so I should probably go before I really do have to stay on your couch."

"I'm really glad you came. I hope we can do this again soon."

"We'll wait for better weather, though," she chuckled.

They said their goodbyes, and with a sigh of relief, Leea closed the door behind her. Without wasting a moment, she hurried into the office and uploaded the cube, surprised to see a folder titled *Yaran* and a video file titled *Julia*.

She longed to open Yaran's but decided to watch her sister's first.

"My sweet little sister," Julia said, her face beaming through the monitor. A waving hand suddenly shot up from behind, and Marta's smiling face came into view.

"Hi Aunt Leea," she called.

"Hey, go away, you'll get your turn," Julia chastised her daughter lovingly, then returned her attention to the screen. "I can't believe you found a way to let us know you're all right. But I should have known if there was a way, you would find it. You have no idea how happy this makes me. Yaran let me listen to your message, I hope you don't mind, but he knew I needed to hear your voice. Things aren't the same around here without you. I miss you so much."

She went on to tell Leea how Yaran had arranged for her and Marta to move into the workers' complex, and now Tim was able to come home every week. She talked about her new home and warehouse job, which she thoroughly enjoyed. Julia was excited that Marta was being schooled with other children and already had several new friends. After hearing a few words from her niece and Tim, Julia said her goodbyes, promising to send a longer message next time.

Leea wiped away her tears. She was so happy for her and proud of Yaran for finding a way to give her and Tim more time together. With great anticipation, she opened the folder and laughed out loud when she found fifteen video files. "Oh Yaran, I love you," she said out loud, then activated the one titled 'Open me first.'

"My darling Leea," he began with a big smile.

"Pause," she commanded, and for a few moments stared longingly at the man she missed so much. His smile not only brightened his handsome face but also radiated through his steel-gray eyes. She hadn't seen much of their natural color those last days on Zantia, recalling only the dark despair they had both felt. She reached out and traced a finger over his lips, wishing there wasn't a piece of glass and billions of miles between them.

She watched with joy and astonishment at the news Yaran relayed, and visibly shuddered at the thought of what he had endured at the hands of Marik. While she had never wished any harm on the troublemaker, she couldn't help the feeling of relief that he was gone. She had to agree with Yaran that it did give her a sense of closure.

At the end of this first video, when he laid his hand against the monitor, she did the same. And when he said the phrase she knew he would, *Er'ShaltMee'Sarn*, she gave the response she did each time, "Always."

Working hard to keep her emotions in check, Leea watched his initial message again before she could bring herself to turn it off. He said he would record one every day until he had to take it to Mearos. She would listen to them the same way—one every day.

For this brief moment, she was happy. Now, she needed to record a reply.

Leea woke up to her alarm but lay quietly for a moment before opening her eyes. She'd been up late making her recordings, and it had been an emotional task, both for Yaran's and Julia's, but indeed a labor of love, one she hoped to make many more times to come. Leea stuck her feet out and sat on the edge of the bed, suddenly wide awake with excitement—she finally had something to look forward to.

After making a cup of coffee, she washed and dressed, double checked the contents of her bag and hurried to the bus stop where she stood with her back to the wind trying to keep her teeth from chattering. Leea had made the trip to the airfield by bus several times as a test. She wished she could call Farrell for a ride, but wouldn't think of disturbing her this early on a day off. Leea had looked forward to a quiet weekend of reading and watching movies, but it hadn't turned out that way, for which she couldn't be happier.

The bus was five minutes overdue, and Leea began to worry it might not come. Maybe it had been canceled because of the weather. But before panic could set in, lights appeared at the end of the street, and she gave a sigh of relief as she stepped into the transport. Welcoming the warmth, she took a seat three rows behind the driver, surprised to see ten other seats occupied, but then remembered that some people did work on weekends.

In less than an hour later, Leea exited in front of the airfield terminal and made her way carefully through the snow to the parking garage. Upon entering the almost-empty space, she walked around until she found the elevator Bettina had escorted her down that first day. She put on the robe, pushed her bag into the shadows of a secluded corner, and pushed the up button on the elevator. When the car arrived, a code panel appeared on the wall, and Leea tapped in the numbers Tamera had given her and then held her breath. Lights flashed briefly then disappeared as the door slid open. Inside, Leea depressed the button for the docking floor, and the car pushed its way silently upward.

# CHAPTER 20

# Mearos

**S**canning the corridor as she exited, Leea was relieved to find it empty. There were still two hours before the ship's scheduled departure, but she hoped the Dekarrans were gone. She made her way over the familiar bridge and into of the ship. During her last visit, she had immediately encountered one of the Zantian crewmen, but today the area was empty. She could hear activity in the distance, and wondered what she would do if Mearos weren't around. She couldn't very well wander around the ship looking for him.

Luckily, he sat in the cockpit alone, studying readouts on a datapad.

"Mearos," Leea called quietly from the doorway.

Startled, the captain turned in his seat. He studied her for a few seconds before a brilliant smile crossed his face. "Even with that robe, I can tell it's you."

"Well, I'm a lot taller than Bettina, so I doubt it's hard to tell us apart," she retorted, pulling back her hood just enough to show her face.

"True, but Bettina isn't involved in ship's business. There are three Dekarran men who we deal with, and they're probably your height."

"Well then, I'm glad you can tell the difference between a man and me," Leea laughed.

"Most definitely," Mearos joined in the humor. "Not to mention, none of the Dekarrans call me Mearos."

Leea glared at him with a crooked smile and took the seat next to him. "Are they still around? I didn't see anyone on the way in."

"No. Everyone left about an hour ago. We're just starting the takeoff prep." He paused, studying Leea wearily. "I take it you had a visitor?"

"Yes, I did. Thank you so much for sending her."

"Did you two…talk?" he asked, averting his eyes.

"Of course, we did," she said with surprise. "We had quite a long conversation. I was under the impression it's what you wanted."

"I did. I thought you might have things in common."

"And we do. But she made a huge sacrifice by leaving you behind. I'm not sure I could have been that strong."

He set the pad aside and nervously adjusted the seat controls without looking at her. "We all do what we have to. Sometimes it's hard to understand unless you know the whole story."

"Is that why you sent her to me? Because you wanted me to know the whole story, about the networks?"

"And more…"

"Why was my leaving Zantia such a big secret when the Council knows it exists?"

"They don't, because there are two different escape paths. The Council has secret agreements with other worlds where they have sent workers. They—"

"Other than Dekarra? I didn't know Humans lived on other worlds?"

Mearos pursed his lips. "They don't," he raised a hand before she could ask further. "I don't know anything more than that. And truthfully, I don't want to know more."

She nodded in understanding.

"The Council is aware of Humans disappearing on occasion, but not how. For some reason, it doesn't occur to them that workers might be helped off the planet the same way they do it. They would never consider the possibility that a Zantian would help a Human, that's what makes it so easy. The one network is the secret of the Council, the other, the secret of the people."

"Which explains why you were so adamant that I would be safe here."

He nodded.

"How long have they known about Humans on Dekarra? I take it no one else on the ship does, or there would be no reason for the robe."

"Correct. I'm the only one, and I swore an oath never to tell. But the Council found out shortly after the Earth ships arrived here."

"I understand a freighter spotted one of them and followed it here."

"Yes, that's true."

"Bettina said they've always kept themselves hidden from the Zantians."

"They have. But the settlers underestimated the Zantians' persuasive powers. You see, those who attacked Earth had seen the ships on their moon but chose to ignore them, thinking that the less-advanced race was still decades away from exploration outside their solar system. When my people spotted their ship only a few years later and followed it, they were quite surprised to discover them here, a planet they were familiar with. A handful of the newly-named Dekarrans entered into negotiations, but the Zantians turned to tables, making them accept a deal they couldn't refuse if they wanted to survive."

"And you know what that deal was," she stated.

"Yes. But before I explain, I would like to tell you how I got to this point."

"And why you sent your mother to me?"

"I sent Tamera because I wanted you to know that you weren't the only woman to ever come here. And also because, if I'm to get your messages back and forth, I need someone to help me, and I hoped she would. While I do enjoy your visits, it is much too dangerous. If you're discovered ...."

"I understand," she agreed sadly. "So how are you involved in all this?"

The Zantian captain looked thoughtful for a moment. "I won't bore you with all the details, but I was raised by one of my father's old teachers, Nira, and with most of the typical Zantian traditions. I celebrated my transition but managed to avoid the formal crossover. I didn't meet Sithan, my father, or even know who he was until my transition year, and since then, our relationship has been tenuous at best.

"When I was twenty-six, Nira died. She was old, so it was not unexpected, but for the first time, I struggled with the purpose of my life. By then, I was a trained pilot, and part of my training had taken place in Alrack, so I decided to move there and start a new life.

"I had a few short-term piloting jobs, but nothing sustained my interest for long. Then one day, I was offered the position as captain of this ship, which I assumed my father had arranged because I knew the previous captain was loyal to the Council. For that reason, I wasn't sure I would keep this job long, but eventually decided to stay; a decision I've come to regret."

Leea smiled reassuringly. Knowing how the Council operated, she doubted Mearos had any choice in whatever they had him involved in.

"I'm sure you're wondering why I'm telling you all this." He pursed his lips. "I make these trips across space on a regular basis. They are routine, which in most cases is an advantage, and I guess I've never given much thought to wanting it any other way. But having you on my ship was a refreshing change and has made me rethink my life and what I might want out of it. And one thing during my reflection has become very clear ... I'm tired of keeping secrets. Secrets of people who are deceiving an entire planet for no other reason than their fear of change. So, I'm going to tell you something I've never told anyone, not even Tamera. And what you do with that information is entirely up to you."

"You're scaring me."

He got up and laid a hand on her shoulder. "It's nothing scary, just incredibly sad. I hope you won't judge me too harshly."

"Living in the House of Alrack gave me a pretty good perspective of what the Zantian Council is capable of. I will not judge you."

Mearos blew out a breath then turned to look out the forward viewscreen which showed nothing more than a massive concrete wall. "Sithan came to me the day before my first trip to Dekarra as full captain and told me that my leading this particular ship came with added responsibilities. He went into a council's rhetoric on how we needed to preserve our way of life, no matter the cost…and so on.

"He carefully insinuated that it was in my best interest to accept these responsibilities, and never speak of them to anyone. At the time, I rationalized it couldn't be as bad as my inner alarm was telling me it was, so I accepted. Two years later, I was tasked with my first *assignment*. I was told I would be receiving special cargo before departing New Haven.

"We had already begun our departure prep from here when I was summoned to the cargo bay and found four hooded Dekarrans standing alongside a large rectangular box on the tarmac. I was told to clear the area, and once I did, they led me to the secret room…it was the first time I saw it."

"Inside, they anchored the box to the floor, refused to answer any of my questions, re-sealed the entry, and were gone." Mearos chuckled and returned to his chair. "I'm not sure if those men thought I was incapable of unsealing a door, but during the first sleep cycle, I was back, looking down at the strange container. It had a domed lid with a leather cover attached, which I removed to find a small, lifeless alien laying in some sort of green gel. Lights flashing on an attached instrument panel told me this being had to be alive. I tried unsuccessfully to open the dome, so I replaced the cover and never returned to that room the entire trip.

"The moment we landed in Alrack, even before we completely powered down, a city cargo hauler approached and removed the box. After I had finished the routine business, I went and found Sithan, demanding he explain what was going on. At first, he refused, but I swore I would find a way to tell the entire planet about Humans on Dekarra, and the secret the Council was trying to keep. Even though at that moment, I didn't know what it was."

"Did Sithan tell you why the Zantians are smuggling this strange alien?"

"I gave him no choice. I'm sure he could have ended my life at that moment, thus removing the threat, but he chose to tell me instead. I guess being his son does have its advantages." He chuckled grimly. "You know about the energy shield surrounding Zantia?"

"Yes, of course."

"Do you know what creates it?"

"I assume a power station of some sort."

Mearos shook his head. "It's not mechanical. The aliens, who are called Morodon, create it."

Leea grimaced. "I don't understand. How?"

"They have a special ability, which enables them to generate the shield. Twenty-five of them are positioned around the planet to form a grid. Their effort projects a barren world to anyone looking down from space."

Seeing the pain on his face, Leea took both his hands. "None of this is your doing. The Zantian Council operates under its own rules with no regard to anyone else."

"I know. And I will never do it again, no matter what they do to me."

She hesitated a moment. "I've met them … the Morodons."

"You have?"

Leea gave him a brief account of her first encounter in the Alrack alley, as well as her meeting with them in New Haven. "Nethas told me they had hidden this planet many centuries ago to protect themselves from the Zantians. I guess I never made the connection, but now it all makes sense. It turns out what the Morodon in Alrack gave me was a message crystal. It's the first time there has been any contact from those who were taken to Zantia."

"How did a Morodon make contact with you? They're kept in a semi-conscious state. And how did he know you would be coming here?"

Leea shrugged. "I have no idea. But he was very real, and like you said, they have special abilities. Somehow he knew I would choose to escape the Desolk's wrath even before Marik's attack … which happened later that day." Leea paused and reflected briefly on events leading to her departure before formulating her next question. "So when a Morodon on Zantia dies … ."

"They are replaced, which was the case for the one I transported. Somehow the Zantians communicate that they need one, and then somehow the Dekarrans manage to deliver. I guess the only good thing is that Morodons are long-lived, so replacements aren't needed often."

Just then the flight deck door swung open. Leea jumped to her feet, glad her back was to the door, and that she hadn't removed the hood; the quick motion made it fall across her face. The crewman said something to Mearos in Zantian, to which the captain replied, "Give me a few more minutes." The door closed quietly behind him.

"I'd better go," Leea said, "I've taken up enough of your time. Thank you for telling me all this. I'm sure it's a heavy burden to live with, but as you said before... we all do what we have to."

"Thank you for understanding."

"That's what friends are for." She gave Mearos a hug, holding on for a moment, and then handed him the data-cube. "Thank you for this. You have no idea what it means to me."

Brightness returned to his blue eyes as he smiled. "Oh, I think I do. The joy on both your faces makes it worth it."

"By the way, did you ever figure out what those files were?"

He shook his head. "No. I've had no luck with them at all. The one written in Zantian was a part of one of my logs, but with added embellishments. The ones with the symbols are a complete mystery. I've spent many hours trying to research them, to no avail. But I am getting some help."

"You are?"

"I showed them to Yaran when he brought me your message, and he said he knew someone who could help. I'm anxious to get back and see if he found anything."

Leea exited the elevator and quickly retreated into the corner where she'd left her bag. She wrapped the robe tightly around to ward off the cold and slid to the floor. Then she did something she hadn't done in months—she sobbed uncontrollably. As happy as she had been to watch Yaran's recording, it broke her heart anew to hear Mearos talk so matter-of-factly about seeing him when he returned, something she dreamed of daily. It brought the pain of her loneliness back to the surface.

But her tears were not only for herself. They were also for the Morodons, who were experiencing something far worse than she or any of her Human kinsmen had lived through. She had to do something but had no idea what. Of one thing, though, she was sure; in her next message to Yaran, she would tell him everything she had learned today. He needed to know, and maybe he could do something on his end.

# CHAPTER 21

# Safe Haven

*L*eea ran giggling through the Alrack garden, bright-colored flowers brushing against her ankles as she passed. She turned and saw Yaran chasing her, and giggled louder—she couldn't have been happier. Just then, her foot caught on something, and she went down on all fours. Two strong arms lifted her and held her close, making her feel safe from anything that might harm her.

He guided her inside, to where once again, the familiar door loomed ahead. She went to reach for Yaran, but he was gone.

She'd been to this forbidden room before and reached for the door release, expecting someone to pull her away, but it clicked open. She hesitated. This suddenly felt wrong; she wasn't supposed to go in. A hand on the small of her back made her turn to find Nethas.

"Everything will be all right. It is time for you to go in. You are ready."

"I'm afraid."

"There is no need. Nothing inside can hurt you. You can step away at any time."

Leea moved inside, finding herself in the washroom with the opaque bathtub standing on the opposite wall. She scanned the otherwise empty room, and Nethas urged her forward. Looking down into the oval tub, Leea saw the brown haired woman—her mother Kathryn—and dropped to her knees.

"Mom," she whispered in a small, unfamiliar voice. "Mom, wake up."

Kathryn lay on her side facing the wall. Knees pulled in. Her hands were tucked under her head, causing her face to turn slightly upward. Leea looked at the troubled woman's expression—peace. Wherever she had gone, she was no longer sad. The sound of trickling water made her look up to see the slow *running faucet. She wanted to turn it off, but it was too far away. Instead, she reached down and moved a stray strand of brown hair out of her mother's face then brushed the back of her hand lightly against the cold cheek.*

*"I'm sorry Mom."*

*Two strong arms lifted her and took her away from the scene. Looking up, she stared into green eyes much like her own. She laid her head on his shoulder while he wrapped his arms around her, enveloping her in a cocoon, and quietly hummed the melody that instantly soothed her.*

*Suddenly confused, she pulled back, but the man was gone.*

*The sun was making its final descent beyond the horizon as Leea approached the bluff. She looked around for Yaran but instead saw a vaguely familiar figure looking out over the ridge. She moved to stand next to her.*

*"I'm sorry, my baby," Kathryn said. "I didn't mean to hurt you. I was never strong… certainly not enough to care for you by myself. I hope you can find it in your heart to forgive me."*

*The young woman reached over and squeezed her mother's hand. "There is nothing to forgive," Leea assured her through fresh tears. "I love you, Mom."*

*Kathryn turned and stroked her daughter's hair. "I love you too. I'm so proud of you." Her eyes took in her daughter's face, then she smiled and was gone.*

*"NO!" Leea screamed, trying to reach for her.*

Lingering at the kitchen table, Leea poked through the remnants of her breakfast flakes while replaying the latest dream. It had felt so real—so final. Tears dampened her cheeks as the image of her mother in the bathtub played in her mind. *Was that what happened that day? Were these dreams trying to help me remember?* She had woken up grief-stricken as if her mother had died yesterday. Bundled in a warm robe, she'd started her daily message to Yaran, and told him about the dreams. She wished he were here, more so than usual. He always had a way of comforting her, and the feel of his strong arms around her would ease the turmoil. She sighed.

Coffee cup in hand, she moved to the back door and studied the sunshine as it lit up the world outside the window. The last snowfall had been almost two weeks ago, and the sun had stood brightly in the sky almost every day since. As the rays angled their way through the glass, brushing warmly against her face, Leea had a sudden urge for a walk. It was Saturday, and she had no plans for the day.

She had tried several times to take a walk in the snow but never made it more than fifteen minutes. The numbness would seep into her bones, and she'd make a hasty retreat to the warmth of her home. But with most of the snow melted away, the outside was calling her.

Once she'd cleaned the dishes, Leea went back to her room where she washed and dressed: lined pants, long sleeve shirt, thick sweater, waterproof jacket, and comfortable boots. In the kitchen, she packed her rucksack: four bottles of water, several protein bars, and some fruit. After double checking everything, she made her way outside, but when the cold air hit her face, she returned for a hat and gloves. Five minutes later she stepped onto the trail.

While sun filtered through the mostly bare tree branches, not much reached the path, so a thin layer of white still clung to the ground. While her boots were made for such terrain, Leea still stepped carefully. Everything was quiet. Animals, large and small, were still in hibernation, and colorful buds and leaves were still dormant.

After about thirty minutes, Leea realized she was traveling in the same direction she'd taken months ago to Nethas's cave. She wasn't sure if this was an unconscious choice, or if something else was driving her. *A visit to the Morodon's home might be in order,* she thought. *If I can find my way through all the twists and turns, that is.*

As if on cue, chirping sounded from above. There on a low branch sat her greeter.

"Well hello, haven't seen you in a while. Guess you've been keeping out of the cold just like the people have, huh?" It flew ahead as if leading the way. A noise behind her made her turn around, but the trail was empty. *Must be the eerie silence,* she rationalized and continued on her way.

She made her way slowly, still finding a few ankle-deep pockets of snow, and eventually came to the same clearing near the river where she'd rested before. Deciding it was a good time for another break, Leea brushed away a thin layer of snow from the log and made herself comfortable—as comfortable as she could be on the cold, hard surface. She retrieved a second bottle of water and a protein bar then raised her face to the sun, trying to soak in some warmth.

Movement on the log caught her attention. Glancing over, she found her greeter perched a few feet away. "Hello again." Leea admired the unique creature's black breast and long multi-colored feathers. "Wish I knew if I was supposed to give you a name. I tried to find out something about greeters, but you know, nobody knows much about you.

"You are clearly an elusive species, which some find frustrating. Why do you connect with babies? Why did you connect with me? Where do you go when no one sees you?" Leea chuckled. "Here I am asking questions of a bird. But you know what? It beats talking to myself."

Leea broke off a tiny piece of her protein bar and held it out. "Hungry? I don't know what you eat, but—"

Before she could react, the bird thrust out its beak and snatched the morsel from her hand. In the next instant, it spread its wings, brushing one across Leea's hand. The feathers were soft and warm as the full weight of the wing slowly caressed her skin, and then the greeter fluttered, almost leisurely, to the tree top.

"Is that some new form of greeting?" she called up surprised. "Well, I'm glad to see you too." She finished her snack and packed up. "Time to go."

The sound of the approaching river put her nerves on edge, but the dread doubled when she came upon the violently rushing canal that looked close to overflowing its banks. Plumes shot high into the air as water, crashing into large rocks, sent a cold spray misting against her face.

Pulling up her hood and cinching it tight, Leea hunched her shoulders and made her way to the right. As the raised bridge platform came into view, her heart almost stopped—the center of the crossing disappeared in the rushing swells.

As she stood debating whether to turn around and go back, the greeter landed on the railing flapping its wings and chirping as if telling her to continue.

"Great. Are you encouraging me forward so I can fall in?" She grabbed the roped sides, took a deep breath and slowly started across. The bridge swayed from the force of the current and her weight, making her clutch the rail as tight as she could.

"You can do it," a voice inside her head encouraged.

"I'm not sure about that," she replied aloud. "Great, now I'm answering myself." She looked up at her feathered friend, now perched further ahead, its wings slightly spread. "I hope you're good at water rescue. If I fall in, you'll have to pull me out." Leea chuckled nervously.

Setting one foot carefully in front of the other, a death grip on the ropes, she made her way through the submerged part of the bridge. The cold spray was painful against her face, and the water seeped over the top of her boots, but she ignored the discomfort. A sigh of relief escaped as she passed through the middle, and could see the wooden slats again. But three steps further, both feet slipped away, and she fell back hard on the wet boards.

"Don't let go of the ropes," the voice inside urged. The sides flailed wildly and letting go was the furthest thing from her mind. Once the movement settled a bit, she tried to pull herself up, but couldn't find a sure footing. Her erratic gyrations, added to the water's force, made it hard to keep a firm grip on the riggings, and she feared she might not be able to hold on.

A black shape fluttered in front of her. "Concentrate! Find a foothold before you pull yourself up."

Leea wasn't sure if the shock came from realizing where the voice was coming from, or the icy water soaking through the bottom of her pants, but now determined, she wedged both heels between two boards and hoisted herself up. Once confident of her footing, Leea focused on the opposite platform and moved cautiously, pausing between each step to let the swaying calm.

On the other side, she wanted nothing more than to sit, but water sprayed over the platform, so she opted to find someplace dry. A short distance down the path, she appreciatively collapsed on a large tree stump.

A small hooded figure peered around a tree and observed as the associate watchfully entered the clearing. The boy knew his assignment—he had done it several times before. When the burly, black-clad Dekarran reached the center of the meadow, a six-foot *rasaile* emerged from the path at the other end. Dekarrans called the *rasaile* a bear, something they feared, as it presumably resembled an Earth creature. But a *rasaile* was as docile as a greeter and would never hurt a living thing, although its roar disguised that fact, making it perfect for this task. The Morodon had no intention of hurting the Human, just slowing him down.

The man-sized furry animal reared on its hind legs at the sight of the stranger and roared until the nearby tree branches shook. Leea's pursuer stumbled back and then fell over the log she had used as a resting place, landing with a hard thud. The *rasaile* bounded forward like a playful pet then sat back on its haunches sniffing at the legs sticking up in the air. Terrified, the man scrambled backward on all fours, not quite managing to get to his feet.

Watching the comical exchange, the boy snickered silently but calculated he needed to move on. He'd made sure the associate's firearm was unusable, and knew the animal would quickly lose interest, so it was time to make sure the next phase of his task was complete. He took a shortcut to the river that only a person of his stature could traverse, just in time to see the Human woman step off the rope bridge and disappear down the trail.

Once she was out of sight, the hooded figure closed his eyes and concentrated on the crossing. He visualized the length in his mind and let his spirit surround it. Pounding footsteps resonated in the distance, but he blocked them out. His mind enveloped the span, and then methodically pulled it together, end over end, until there was nothing left. Opening his eyes, all that was visible was the rushing water and plumes of spray shooting in the air. In reality, the bridge remained, and his mind could only mask it for a short time, but that would be long enough.

The frustrated man ran past, and the Morodon waited. Five minutes later the other returned, shouting loudly into his comm. "I don't know where in the hell she went… I thought she went toward the river, but I can't be sure. I lost sight of her some time before that, so it's hard to tell if she even came this way… Yes, I've looked everywhere possible, but there is nothing here but freezing water, rocks, and trees… No, I'm done here, I'm coming back… You don't pay me enough to hang out up here. Why don't *you* come up here and deal with huge animals? I'm going to be lucky to find my way out of this damned place." He ripped out the ear bud and shoved it into his pocket.

Carefully making his way through the trees, the Morodon followed the associate until he was well on the other side of the clearing before returning to the river and restoring the image of the bridge. He then crossed it and made his way home.

"So you were in my head?" Leea asked, looking incredulously at her feathered friend.

The bird chirped a response.

"What, you want me to believe I didn't hear what I did?"

It tweeted briefly and flew out of sight.

"Fine, fly away!" Exhausted, she deeply regretted making this trek today, but there was no turning around now, so she forged ahead. Shivering, and trying to ignore the squishing sound in her boots, Leea knew it was imperative to reach the cave soon. A minute later she stopped short. Up ahead stood Tellia.

*Where did she come from?*

The Morodon approached, handing her a bulky wrap, which Leea gratefully accepted. She peeled off her wet jacket, wrapped herself in the thick cloth, and felt the instant warmth.

"Thank you."

Tellia smiled. "Come. We need to get you out of those wet clothes."

Once in the crystal cave, Leea was taken to a small room off the main chamber where she happily removed her soaked garments. Wearing only the short robe, and a pair of slippers several sizes too small, she was escorted to the same room she'd visited before where Nethas handed her a cup of hot, spiced tea. It was pungent, yet lightly sweet, and seemed to travel all the way to her toes when she took a sip.

"I am pleased you are finally here," Nethas said when they were seated.

"You knew I was coming?"

"Of course, Tellia told me you were in peril at the bridge and was going off to help," Nethas smiled, causing the lines around her amber eyes to deepen. "But I knew you would come again, although not exactly when."

"And here I thought you could see the future?" she quipped, taking another sip.

Nethas chuckled softly. "As I explained before, I do not see the future as you understand the term. Seeing specific events, like when you would visit again, is not how it works."

"But you just said you knew I would come?"

"Oh yes. I knew your curiosity would eventually bring you back. I do not need to see the future to know that."

Leea gave her a sideways grimace then smiled. "I felt like a walk today, and before I knew it, I was on my way here, and my greeter seemed to encourage me along. Had I known how treacherous the river was going to be, I would have waited for another day."

Nethas nodded. "The melting snow will fill the rivers, sometimes to overflowing for a while."

"Good to know." She paused. "Tell me about the greeters."

"What would you like to know?"

"Are they telepathic? It communicated with me...in my head. It's never done that before."

"Greeters are not telepathic...they are...a conduit."

"A conduit? To you? Was it your voice I heard?"

"Greeters are attracted to intelligent life, and not only form a bond with them but can also connect them."

"How?"

"To establish a connection, the greeter must touch you. I assume this has happened?"

"Yes. Today when I stopped to rest, it...he brushed his wing across my hand."

"Actually, your greeter is female. Now that *she* has made the connection with you, it will always be there. Only death can break the bond. We are telepathic by nature, so the birds can communicate with us without the physical contact. She connected with us when you were in trouble, so Tellia projected telepathically through her. She was our eyes, and we were her voice. It would do no good for you to be injured, or become ill."

"So you can't communicate with them?"

"No. We can speak through them, and they can convey certain things to us, and even for us. But nothing more complicated than that."

"What attracts them to people?"

"No one knows. Something draws them to a particular person. And do not believe what you might hear about them bringing luck. Many good people in this world do not have one. What we believe is that they are here to help. Somehow they sense if a child is strong and can deal with the world on their own, but others, for some reason, might need a little guidance. As an adult new to this world you would certainly need some guidance, which might explain why one connected with you."

"Well, whatever the reason, I'm glad she was there today." Leea snuggled deeper into the warm wrap and took another sip of the hot liquid. "This is incredibly comfortable. The chill is almost gone."

"The fabric reacts with your body heat, and the tea contains special herbs that should ward off any illnesses."

"I'll have to take some of this with me for when I return home."

"There is another path that will avoid the river. It is a longer walk, but a better choice at this time. Tellia will lead you back."

"Thank you." For a few moments, Leea absentmindedly studied the contents of her cup.

"You have something on your mind… something you want to tell me?" Nethas said.

"I talked to the Zantian captain again. He brought me a message from Yaran," she smiled shyly, "just like Tellia predicted. Mearos also told me why the Zantians want your people. It was a devastating story."

Nethas laid a hand over Leea's and gave her a reassuring smile, "Do not be sad, Leea." Her voice had a calming effect. "Life is full of devastating events. It is up to us to make sure we use them to grow, and not allow them to hold us back. You brought us the greatest gift; proof of life for the ones we thought were lost."

"I don't know how you can stay so positive. You may never see them again."

"That is a possibility. But now we know they live, and the other information the message contained will prepare us for any future attempts by the Dekarrans to abduct more of our people."

"What is the green gel they're transported in?"

"We are not sure. But most likely, it is a technology the Zantians acquired from another species. The message contained its chemical breakdown, but so far we have been unable to decipher what it is. We will not give up until we are successful."

Again, Leea sat silent for a few moments.

"Something else troubles you."

Leea took the still-warm cup in both hands and looked inside reflectively. "My mother took her own life when I was five. I was the one who found her, but the trauma made me block it from my mind. Ever since I've been on Dekarra, I've had dreams about it. Certain parts always change, but the overall event is the same. Then last night, it seemed to reveal what happened that day."

"Dreams are a powerful window into the soul."

"But they're usually just gibberish. I can never remember them after five minutes."

"Yet you remember this one in great detail. The gibberish is your mind's energy refocusing itself. But sometimes your…being…has something it needs to convey, and that can result in dreams that seem to speak to you."

"So you're saying I'm trying to tell myself something?"

"That is partially correct, in simplistic terms. But a more accurate interpretation is that you have unresolved issues that your spirit is trying to make right."

"You were there. You showed me what happened the day my mother died."

"Most likely I represented someone neutral; someone who had no ties to your past and could guide you to where you needed to go."

"You did encourage me. In my past dreams, everyone else held me back, but you pushed me through." Leea lowered her head into her hands. "This all makes my head hurt."

"As I explained during your last visit, everything in this world is connected. The *remdalar* shows us this. What it does not show is that the past, present, and future are also intertwined. Our experiences of the past affect the present, and the present will shape the future. I know it is much to absorb, but I guarantee if you remain on this world you will eventually understand."

"What do you mean, *if* I remain on this world?"

"It is fortuitous that you chose today to visit," Nethas said, ignoring her question. "I was about to have Tellia gather the Watchers."

"Has something happened?"

"Not yet. But a significant event is approaching. The Human government is moving up its timetable to attack Zantia."

"Really? Bettina said this might happen in the distant future. Are you sure?"

"Yes. Going to Zantia has always been the Dekarran government's plan, now there is a substantial time shift for their endgame. The vision is still in flux, but hopefully, in a day or two, more will be revealed. One thing is imperative; the test captain needs to focus on the activities on the third moon. The one they call Sirius."

"Where the last Earth ship orbits?"

"Yes. Whatever the Dekarrans are hiding up there, their attempts at secrecy are failing."

Two days later, Tellia called a meeting of the Watchers. Jackson, Farrell, Leea, and Max met for a quick dinner then made the careful trek to the sanctuary cave where twenty other members were already waiting. Leea was quickly introduced to those she hadn't met, then they all settled at a large rectangular conference table.

Tellia relayed the same information Leea had heard from Nethas a few days earlier. The Morodon did caution that the visions still hadn't solidified, meaning there were still disagreements on the final plan of action by the government.

"So this is truly going to happen?" someone asked.

"It would seem your military officials have found a way to advance their efforts against Zantia. To what extent, we are not sure."

"Then we need to figure it out."

"Yes we do," Jackson agreed. "This would explain why there has been a big push to complete the fighters. I've been making some final adjustments to the software while the factory has been producing them. We've tested some in the desert this past year, and now they're ferrying all of them up to the moon base to test them in a zero-g environment. I never thought much about their motivation, but suddenly it all makes sense. So yes, I agree that we need to find out what those on the top floors are planning. But unfortunately, none of our members has an office up that high."

There was overlapping discussion around the table, ideas were presented, but most were discarded. It was eventually decided to plant a listening device in the admiral's office.

"Now the question is … who's going to do it?" Jackson looked around the table with raised eyebrows. "It'll have to be someone who works in the labs, so that narrows it down to only five of us."

"I'll do it," Leea offered.

"No, we can't ask you to do that," Farrell objected.

"Why not? An attack on Zantia affects me more than anyone around this table. Not to mention, I've been to the admiral's office, I know the layout."

"You've been in his office?"

"No, only to the reception area. Bettina took me up there once before I started my job. She wanted to introduce me, but he wasn't available."

"It's too dangerous. If you get caught—" Farrell protested.

"If she gets caught," Tellia interrupted, "it will be less damaging than for any of you. Farrell, due to your lineage, you have a position in this community. If you are caught, you will be seen as a traitor, and bring shame to your family. Jackson, we do not want to lose your connections to the military operation. Max, your technical skills are invaluable. It will be a terrible blow to this effort if you end up in jail. Renee, you have children. I'm sure you do not want them to see you there. Leea is the logical choice. She has the least to lose."

After a few more minutes of debate, mostly from Farrell, it was decided. Leea would plant a listening device in the admiral's office at the first opportunity.

Dressed in black, Leea entered the tower building at 2:00 am through a service entrance using a fake access card Max had provided. It had taken a few days, but early this morning the computer genius was finally able to access the admiral's schedule and found that the military leader would be away until tomorrow evening; this was the moment they'd been waiting for.

A short hallway led into a storage area, and she listened for voices. The work schedule had shown that the cleaning crew was finished by midnight, but she wanted to make sure there weren't any stragglers.

"I'm in."

Farrell, Jackson, and Max sat in a car about a block away monitoring the building from Max's computer. While they didn't have the capability to scan for current occupants, they could monitor all the entry points and let her know if anyone came in after her.

"Be careful," Max said into her earpiece. "There are a few lights on here and there, but it could be that someone just forgot to turn them off."

"I certainly hope there's no one crazy enough to be working at this hour."

"Except you," Farrell quipped.

"Yes," she smiled, "except crazy me." Leea exited the storeroom and made her way down the dimly-lit adjacent hallway. She had never been to this part of the building, but she'd studied the floor plans, so knew which way to go. Within a few minutes and down several hallways, she found herself in front of an interior set of three elevators. The admiral had a private lift on the other side of the building, but there would be no way to duplicate his personal access card.

"Made it to the elevators."

Stepping off on the twenty-fifth floor, she looked around at the posh decor and listened for voices. Hearing none, she followed the equally spaced floor lights along the wide corridor. Creaks and other unidentifiable sounds made her stop every few yards to turn and listen.

"It's so quiet up here... kind of creepy," she said in a hushed tone.

"Would you like us to sing to you," Farrell joked.

"Um... I think I'll take my chances with the creaky building."

"You're no fun."

Leea chuckled softly. "I've been accused of worse. I've almost reached the hall to the... uh oh."

"What's wrong?"

"I hear voices. Someone's coming," she whispered frantically.

"Can you find a place to hide?"

Leea scanned her surroundings. "I think so." Offices were kept locked at night, but several yards back, she'd passed the recessed door to the washroom. Quickly, she retraced her steps and pressed herself into the corner of the small alcove just as the voices became more audible. Luckily, the low lighting and her dark clothing allowed her to blend into the shadows.

She didn't listen to the conversation as it got closer, but instead concentrated on her breathing, keeping it shallow and willing herself to stand perfectly still. But as the figures passed, Leea's breath caught at one she recognized—Bettina. *Why was she here at this hour?* As the group receded down the hallway, Leea took a careful glimpse after them and saw Bettina, the admiral, and a third person whose hair she would recognize anywhere.

"Kent Madigan," she whispered, receding back against the wall.

"Kent is there?" Farrell asked incredulously.

"He and Bettina are with the admiral."

"The admiral's back a day early. I can't say I'm surprised that Bettina's there. She seems to be the admiral's shadow these days. And I guess this explains Kent's absences."

In the distance, a door opened and closed, and then all was silent. She cautiously stepped back into the hall, and noticed a sign that read 'Stairs.'

"What's going on?" Jackson asked in her ear.

"They're gone. They took the stairs. Why would they come this way and use the stairs instead of the admiral's elevator?"

"They must be going up to the government offices. The admiral's elevator doesn't go beyond the twenty-fifth floor. Interesting. You'd better hurry."

With new urgency, she soon found herself at the military leader's office-suite door. "I'm here." Leea inserted the access card and held her breath as the door swung open. She stepped into the outer office, and scanned the empty space, then moved swiftly to the dark wooden door on the opposite wall, only then seeing that it stood slightly ajar. "The door's open."

"Open? Are the lights on?" Max asked.

"Yes."

"That means he'll be right back," Jackson warned. "Place the bug and get out of there."

Leea took out the recorder and ran her finger along the flat bottom, activating the inconspicuous device. The bug, as Jackson called it, was an enhanced data-cube, no bigger than her thumb, black, and slightly wider at one end. It was voice and motion activated, and would relay the audio and video to Max's computer.

A tall bookshelf stood across from the large desk. A few dozen books lined the center shelf, held upright on each side by several large, colored glass containers. She placed the bug between two of the bookends and moved back to make sure it wasn't visible.

"Okay, it's in place. Is it working?" Leea pushed the tiny button on her ear-piece to turn it off, moved behind the desk and waved. "Can you hear me? See me?" She pushed the button at her ear again.

"Yes. Just move it a tad to your left and it'll be perfect."

"Okay, done. I'm out of here."

"Hurry."

Leea stood behind the dark paneled door and held her breath—she was hiding again. With her hand already on the door handle, she heard the outer entry to the office suite open. There was only one other door in the room, so she quickly stepped inside hoping for a closet but found a washroom instead. She hoped no one would need to use it.

A rustling sounded through the door, but no other voices.

"He's alone," Max whispered as if someone could hear him.

"Hey, it's me," said the deep voice of Admiral Shaw. "We got back a couple of hours ago… Yes, everything is on schedule, so we came back a day early… No, we haven't discussed that yet… We're not going to go over this again… I said no!"

A loud thump resonated through the door.

"Look, we took a vote, and it was decided… It didn't need to be unanimous. We live in a democracy, majority rules."

For a few moments, there was silence. Leea wondered if he'd hung up.

"Stop. This is no longer up for discussion. The plan will go forward as discussed... Yes. We went to his office a little while ago. He's up to speed, and will take care of things on his end. Look, you should stop worrying. Nothing is going to go wrong... Our new friend said he'll be ready when we are... We haven't given up on our planet's latest addition, but I think that's a dead-end." The admiral gave a hearty laugh. "No, not that dead... We'll make that decision when the time comes... I don't want to know. I leave those petty details to the experts... Okay. I'll see you at the meeting tomorrow. And relax, this is all going to work out as planned. We have nothing to worry about."

After a minute, she heard the solid thud of the office door and breathed a sigh of relief.

"He's gone, Leea," Jackson said in her ear.

"I know. I heard the door close." She hesitated a brief moment. "Am I the new addition he was talking about?"

"We don't know that. Let's not jump to conclusions, okay?"

"Okay."

"Wait a minute to make sure he's gone, and then get out of there. We'll talk about all this later."


On the sixteenth day of listening to the monotony of the admiral's daily business, Farrell approached Leea's desk late in the afternoon.

"Max called," she whispered. "We're going to sanctuary tonight. Jackpot!"


*Admiral Raymond Shaw sat behind his desk admiring the 3D schematic of the Starship Atlantis's upgrades when his inner office door flew open.*

*"You are here." Bettina sauntered in and slid into the chair across the desk. "Your aide is away, so I took a chance."*

*"Don't you know how to knock?" he said with irritation and closed the 3D viewer.*

*"Why? Would you tell me I can't come in?"*

*He stared at her for a moment, then raised his eyebrows and shook his head. "Why have you graced my office today? Thought you wanted to lay low until we leave?"*

*"Rumor has it you're going to ask Jackson Owens to pilot the Atlantis?"*

*"Since when do you believe rumors? But yes, although I haven't told him yet."*

*"Don't you think that's risky?"*

*"How so?"*

*"He's friends with the girl from Zantia. Not to mention, romantically involved with Farrell Reynolds."*

"So? He's one hell of a pilot and his insights in the fighter designs were invaluable. Who better to have on board during the first, and most important, operation? As far as his friends go, it doesn't matter. We've gotten pretty good intel from Belag, so your failure to get anything more out of the Dennison girl doesn't change anything. And Farrell Reynolds is probably an asset. Her family led the charge to rescue our people. I doubt she'll have any objections to this mission."

"I don't like it. Leea would never be involved with anyone who might do her precious Zantians any harm. I think letting him anywhere near that ship is a mistake."

"You're being paranoid." He snickered. "But I guess that's what I pay you for, isn't it?"

"And I appreciate the generous compensation, but it's all for naught if you don't take my advice."

"I always value your advice, but this time, I'm going with my gut."

"Let's hope your gut doesn't get you into trouble."

Admiral Shaw made a dismissive wave. "It rarely does."

"When are you going to tell him?"

"As soon as all the upgrades are complete. I'm going to have him do the final tests. No reason to get him involved too early...just in case."

Bettina nodded in agreement. "So, when will our benefactor be back?"

"Belag will tie up loose ends on Zantia...whatever those are. He'll come back on his own ship and go straight to the Atlantis, which should hopefully coincide with our approximate departure."

"What about the special cargo?"

"Already aboard. Doc will monitor the inter-link and let us know if something goes awry."

"And the VP?"

"Nothing to worry about there. He and his aides have everything under control. Once we return victorious, he will announce his longstanding support for us, and then we can finally unseat that useless commander-in-chief. Not sure how that woman got elected in the first place."

"Is that because you don't like her politics, or because she's a woman?"

"I have a great respect for women," he said indignantly.

Bettina snickered. "Even outside the bedroom?"

The Admiral glared at her but then smiled. "I respect you, don't I?"

"Don't confuse fear with respect, Ray. The only reason we have this relationship is because you need me—need me to take care of all those things you find so distasteful. And since I know where all the bodies are buried...literally...you feel safer keeping me close."

"I've done what's necessary to move this project forward. This opportunity fell from the sky… literally… and I wasn't about to let it slip away. Obstacle's had to be removed; they were justifiable sacrifices."

"You might have a hard time convincing other people of that."

"Good thing no one will ask." The Admiral leaned back, laced his fingers behind his head, and let a toothy smile spread across his face.

"Why do you suddenly look like the cat who swallowed the canary?"

"Oh come on, all this nonsense aside, you've got to be feeling it. The adrenalin rush in knowing we're almost there. With Belag's help, the ship is nearly complete: new engines, new shields, new fuel cells, and new fighter planes. And then the second phase begins." He closed his eyes, and the smile widened. "To think the ancestors' objective will be achieved on my watch." His large barrel chest visibly swelled. "Once we destroy the Zantian cities and take control of their mines, we'll come back having secured an unimaginable future for ourselves… we'll be heroes."

"How are you going to justify the sacrifices you plan to make on Zantia?"

"Nobody's going to object to our treatment of the aliens. It's what they deserve. And that's not a sacrifice… that's justice."

"I'm not talking about the Zantians; I'm talking about the Humans."

Raymond Shaw leaned forward on the desk and spoke in a low tone. "I'll be doing everyone a favor. The men who work in those mines were raised like cattle. You know personally that they have no social graces, so they'll never fit into our society. It's best they just stay where they are, doing what they were bred to do." He laughed softly. "But this time, they'll be working for us, so it'll be a step up. We'll bring enough of the city workers back to prove our commitment to the rescue, which will appease the masses, and over time, we'll selectively bring over those we want."

"You're an evil man, Admiral. It's a shame you're squeamish and can't do your own dirty work. I'd love to be out of this quagmire you're creating. I truly believe you're putting your trust in the wrong places, and I don't want to be sucked down with you when this goes wrong."

"Which it won't. But I promise you, when this is all over," he smiled at Bettina sarcastically, "and I control the government as well as the military, you'll get your wish. Until then, I'll still need your counsel." Admiral Shaw got to his feet. "Now, as much as I enjoy these in-depth talks with you, Bettina, I have real work to do."

At the end of the video, the two dozen Watchers sat back in their chairs, staring at each other wide-eyed, stunned by what they'd just seen.

"This is worse than I thought," Jackson finally said breaking the silence. "These people are insane."

"Who is Belag, and what did he mean when he said the opportunity fell from the sky?" Max asked.

"I have no idea. And I haven't heard anything about all the upgrades he mentioned either. But we better find out."

"Leea, what is it?" Farrell noticed her friend deep in thought.

Leea glanced over at Tellia. "They have a Morodon on board," she said barely above a whisper. All eyes turned toward her.

"How do you know?" Farrell asked.

"Bettina asked about the *special cargo*. That's how Mearos referred to the Morodon he once transported."

Jackson turned to Tellia. "Wouldn't you be able to sense the abduction of one of your people?"

Tellia shook her head. "Whatever alien technology is being used to subdue them is impenetrable to our abilities. We have no idea how they are doing it."

"We have to get on that ship," Farrell said. "We have to stop them. They not only want to destroy the Zantians, but they want to keep the workers enslaved for their own personal gain." Farrell got to her feet, her chair almost falling over. "We can't allow that to happen!"

"We won't," Jackson said comfortingly. "We'll find a way to stop them."

# CHAPTER 22

# The Beginning

Approaching the east mine, Yaran slowed his air-shuttle as the landing pad came into view. As expected, it was empty. He had made this flyover several times in the past few weeks, always finding the area deserted. Today, he planned to land and find out what the mystery of this place was all about.

Slowly, he guided the ship further up the mountainous terrain, wanting to keep it out of sight, in case someone did, by chance, come to check on things. It took a few minutes, and several passes, but eventually he spotted a flat area between the trees that would obscure his vehicle.

The hike down took about ten minutes. He had dressed for this eventuality in sturdy shoes and appropriate clothing. He had learned quickly in the mines that solid shoes were essential, and that there was no place in the dirty, sometimes treacherous environment for the loose fitting attire that he typically wore at home.

As the grand entry loomed ahead, Yaran fingered the unlock device in his pocket, but surprisingly, the gray metal doors slid open as he approached. Automatic lighting illuminated the space inside but except for an empty desk against the far wall and a single door to the right, the small reception area was empty. Taking a closer look, he could tell that nothing had ever occupied this area.

"What are they trying to hide here?"

Approaching the interior door, he was surprised to find this one locked. Affixing the electronic key above to the release mechanism, it instantly adhered, and he manipulated the small screen as Mearos had shown him. Red lights circled the center, their speed increasing until it flashed green and went blank. The door swung open, scraping the floor, and Yaran stepped into a narrow corridor. The air was stuffy and smelled as if it hadn't been recycled in weeks. Unlike the reception area, his presence didn't trigger any lighting, so he could only see about ten feet in either direction.

"Which way?" he pondered, then took a step back as the passage to the left illuminated in dim light. "Well, I guess I'm supposed to go this way," he said hesitantly.

Taking a deep breath, he cautiously strode along the five-foot wide passage that had rough walls and a rounded ceiling that barely cleared his head. At the end of the long hall, under the last indistinct light, an elevator door opened as he approached. While his nervousness increased, he stepped onto the lift, and it immediately pulled him upward.

After several long moments, the door opened to reveal another room carved out of the solid rock about twice the size of the reception area. Two closed doors stood on the opposite side.

"Now what?" Yaran waited, wondering if the room would respond as the corridor had, but nothing happened. He opened each of the two doors, finding nothing but darkness. Activating his palm-light, Yaran entered the first room and surveyed more solid rock walls but found nothing out of the ordinary. Expecting the same in the second room, he was surprised to find one wall constructed of tightly stacked stones. *Why would anyone go to all this trouble?* he wondered.

Yaran extinguished his light as he moved out of the room, but before the door closed, a blue hue, seeping between cracks in the stone wall, caught his attention. He ran his hands over the equally-spaced rocks until he felt a defined ridge running floor-to-ceiling. Reactivating the light, he tested the rocks on either side until one came loose in his hand and revealed a metal plate.

He placed the unlock device in the opening and as before, lights danced within, then went blank. After a brief hesitation, a low rumble started from beneath the floor and grew in intensity. Ever so slowly, a cut section of the stone wall began to move outward, forcing Yaran to take a step back as it slid to the side.

Blue light emanated from within, and Yaran's heart thumped in anticipation as he stepped through the opening. Stale air enveloped him, and he wondered when the last time anyone had crossed this threshold. The walls and ceiling were made entirely of light blue crystal that gave the sense of being outside. The space was about the size of a large bedroom, and devoid of anything except a rectangular box sitting on a raised platform at the far end.

*Could this be the room I dreamed about?* he wondered astonished. *It seemed so much bigger.*

Yaran approached the platform and studied the container. It was about six feet long, three feet wide, with a three-foot-high glass dome running the entire length. At first, the glass had appeared milky, but at closer inspection, it was an actual mist swirling inside. He scanned the exterior, looking for a way to open it, but found nothing. He tried the unlock tool—still nothing. The glass nestled securely in a deep groove and no amount of pushing or pulling made a difference.

As he stood back contemplating what to do, an instrument panel on the wall began to glow. Before he could approach for a closer look, a small figure appeared in front of him. Yaran jumped back, almost losing his balance. It wore nothing but a long thin shirt that couldn't hide its frail form.

"Wh… where did you come from?" Yaran inquired cautiously, unable to take his eyes off the deeply grooved wrinkles covering a hairless body.

"Do not be frightened, I mean you no harm."

"Who are you? Why are you here?"

"My name is Genad. Why I am here, is a long story, Yaran."

"How do you know my name?" Yaran took another involuntary step back.

"Because I am the one who summoned you here."

"Through my dreams. Why?"

"Your world is at a crossroads and needs your help."

Yaran laughed. "My help? I think you summoned the wrong person."

"You underestimate yourself."

"I don't understand. Why are you locked in this facility?"

"It might be easier if I start at the beginning."

Yaran nodded in agreement.

"My people are called Morodon, and we come from the world you know as Dekarra. We encountered your species after they settled on this planet about a thousand years ago."

"What do you mean, a thousand years? We are indigenous to Zantia." Yaran looked down at Genad confused.

The alien shook his head. "The environment here is too hostile for life to have evolved naturally. During their darkest time, your ancestors found this world and made it their own.

"It took them a few hundred years to build their cities and start their mining operations before they began exploring the galaxy. Eventually, they found our rich planet and attempted to enslave us and take our world. But as a combined entity, our mental abilities were much stronger than their brute force. After years of hostilities, we were left with no choice. We projected an image around our world that showed its destruction. We led them to believe that we destroyed our planet and moved on."

Yaran stared a moment in stunned disbelief. "But they found you again?"

"Yes. We let our guard down too soon. The Zantians hadn't visited our system in several hundred years, so we made the assumption they had given up. About two hundred years ago, we abandoned the efforts to mask our planet to prepare for another's arrival. About fifty years later your people returned, figuring out what we had done.

"Visions showed us their return, and their impending attack, so we fled to the mountains to hide. But this time, your people were not so easily fooled. They sent a global transmission, stating that if we didn't surrender to them, they would destroy us. A well-placed projectile destroyed one of our larger islands, proving they meant what they said."

"But they didn't take your planet?"

"No. They did not want it anymore. The mining operations here are much too profitable for them. What they did want, however, was the masking technology. It seemed that the many enemies they'd made were joining forces and seeking retribution. When they learned the shield was not technology, but rather the ability of our minds to create the false image, they demanded the appropriate number of Morodons be brought here to hide this world. In return, they would spare the rest of our people, and our planet."

Yaran wished there was a place to sit. His legs felt weak, and he didn't know if they would hold him upright much longer. Surprisingly, anger welled up inside him. He was certain the council members knew his people's history, and no doubt so did their families. But no one had told him. Was that because they didn't want him to know, or didn't trust him to know? He pushed the emotion away. There would be plenty of time for that later.

"So you're saying there are chambers like this one all over the planet, keeping a Morodon in a ... ?"

"Stasis pod."

"How many?" His voice shook with sudden outrage.

"Twenty-five."

"And they've all been here as long as you?"

"No. We are of varying ages and have been here different lengths of time."

"How does it work?" In truth, he didn't want to know, but it seemed an obvious question.

"A green substance inside puts our bodies in a state of suspension. The mist you see creates a unique electronic field that allows our minds to maintain the planetary shield." The alien pointed to the raised box. "This has been my home for over sixty years. My body no longer functions, but my mind is still able to communicate with you."

Yaran felt sick. "You're trapped in a body that doesn't move?"

"Yes. But it is no longer a concern. My lifespan has come to an end. The energy I expelled to give Leea the message crystal sealed my fate. I have only held on for your visit."

Unable to stand on his own anymore, Yaran abruptly leaned against the stasis chamber. His stomach churned, and sweat beaded on his forehead. He was dizzy and longed for fresh air.

"You approached Leea in the alley?"

"Yes. An opportunity finally presented itself to make contact with our home. We could not let it pass."

Yaran's eyebrows arched in surprise. "How did you know that she would be leaving?"

"I am afraid there is not enough time for me to explain."

"What is it you want from me? What makes you think I can help you?"

"You must warn your Council that a war is coming, and they must prepare. A seeker has infiltrated this world and joined forces with a new enemy."

"They will never listen to me. I'm not exactly on good terms with them. And why would you want to save my people after what we've done to yours?"

"We do not pass judgment on others. We all have a path to follow, regardless of which direction. But rest assured, if there were nothing but evil in this world, it would never have survived this long."

"The leadership members are set in their ways. They won't listen."

"Then you must convince them. All those you love will depend on it."

"Well, there's not many of those left," Yaran muttered sadly.

"I am not just talking about people in this world."

"I don't understand."

Before Genad could say more, his image started to fade. "I am sorry. I can no longer hold this form. No matter what happens, your people will move on, but there will be unnecessary loss of life if you do nothing." And then he was gone.

Pulling both hands through his hair, Yaran rested on the case trying to decide what to do when an alarm sounded, and the pod began to vibrate. He pushed away and watched as the white mist dissipated, and the green gel-like substance disappeared through unseen vents. When the inside was clear, the glass surround retracted into the box where the Morodon lay in the center; looking incredibly small in the oversized container. Yaran didn't have to wonder what the alarm meant—Genad was clearly dead.

He was sure the alert would rouse whoever knew the alien was here, and Yaran calculated he had about fifteen minutes before that someone arrived. He hurriedly retreated, resealed the door, and retraced his steps to the main entrance. On his way out, he looked around for signs of recent activity but found none. Of the few rooms he looked in, most were empty. What little furniture he found was covered in thick layers of dust, as if no one had touched them in decades.

Was this facility solely to hide the prisoner? It sure seemed that way. Did Toref know? Of course, he did. He ran all four mines and knew exactly what went on in each one. And this certainly explained why he steered them away the day of the tour.

Yaran checked the time and saw he'd lingered long enough. Outside, he barely rounded the corner of the building when the unmistakable sound of a shuttle engine resounded in the distance. Quickly, he ran to the opposite side and found a hiding spot within a nearby stand of trees just as the vehicle's lights cut through the darkness and landed on the pad.

As expected, the administrator hurriedly disappeared inside. Yaran waited a few minutes, making sure the overseer was well on his way to the crystal room, before leaving the security of the trees. He traversed barely twenty feet when a second craft came over the treetops, also setting down on the landing pad.

Back within the trees, Yaran watched as Toref disembarked and disappeared inside. He waited a minute before attempting another retreat, but changed his mind—he wanted to know what was happening in the blue room.

As he stepped off the lift, he could see the two men busily working through the open doors, unaware of his arrival. Yaran leaned against the stone doorframe, crossed his arms over his chest, and waited while they tended to the pod, still oblivious to his presence. The alarm had been turned off, and the administrator worked busily at the control panel. Toref was attaching a red cover to the dome, now back in place.

"Where should we put him until the next ship departs?" the administrator asked.

"Yes, what do you do with a Morodon, once he's dead?" Yaran tried to keep the sarcasm out of his voice but knew he was unsuccessful.

Both men froze then turned to face him.

"Yaran, wh… what are you doing here?" Toref stammered.

Yaran moved into the room. "I could ask you the same question… but I already know the answer."

"There is an explanation for this."

"No need. Genad explained everything."

"Genad?"

"The Morodon you're tucking back into his prison box. We had a long conversation." Yaran approached the platform and lifted the corner of the leather cover and took one last look at the being who opened his eyes to so many things. He re-secured the corner and rested a hand on the dome. The administrator, although intently listening, proceeded to attach the control panel to the side of the pod.

"That's not possible," Toref replied in disbelief.

Yaran laid a hand on his uncle's shoulder. "I'm not questioning your involvement in all this. I'm aware there are many things in this world over which we have no control. Finish here, and then I'll tell you about my conversation with Genad… then we can decide where we go from here."

Toref paced across the living room floor as he listened to Yaran repeat the conversation he had had with the Morodon. It all seemed surreal. It was common knowledge that these beings had powerful minds, but Toref doubted anyone was aware of just how much. But one thing puzzled him, after almost a hundred fifty years: why now? And why Yaran and Leea?

He looked at his nephew and saw something there he'd never seen before—determination. Unfortunately, it had replaced the look of innocence Toref found so endearing about the young man.

"I'm sorry," Toref said when Yaran finished. "I'm sorry you had to find out this way. I'm sorry you had to find out at all, even though I knew it was inevitable."

"Then why didn't you tell me before?"

"Because it wasn't my place."

Yaran closed his eyes and rubbed his temples. "Who knows about them?"

"Only the Council and the administrators who manage their environment."

Yaran chuckled without humor. "Manage their environment? What do they do…change out the green goo once a month?"

"You're angry."

"Of course, I'm angry! Is there no end to the devastation we can inflict on other cultures? Is there nothing sacred except our own survival…no matter the cost?"

Toref slid into his overstuffed chair but said nothing.

"Well, I guess for now there is nothing we can do, and we will debate this at length another time. But there is one thing Genad said that we should worry about now. Who, or what, is the seeker who has supposedly infiltrated our world, and who is this new enemy he has joined forces with?"

# PART 3

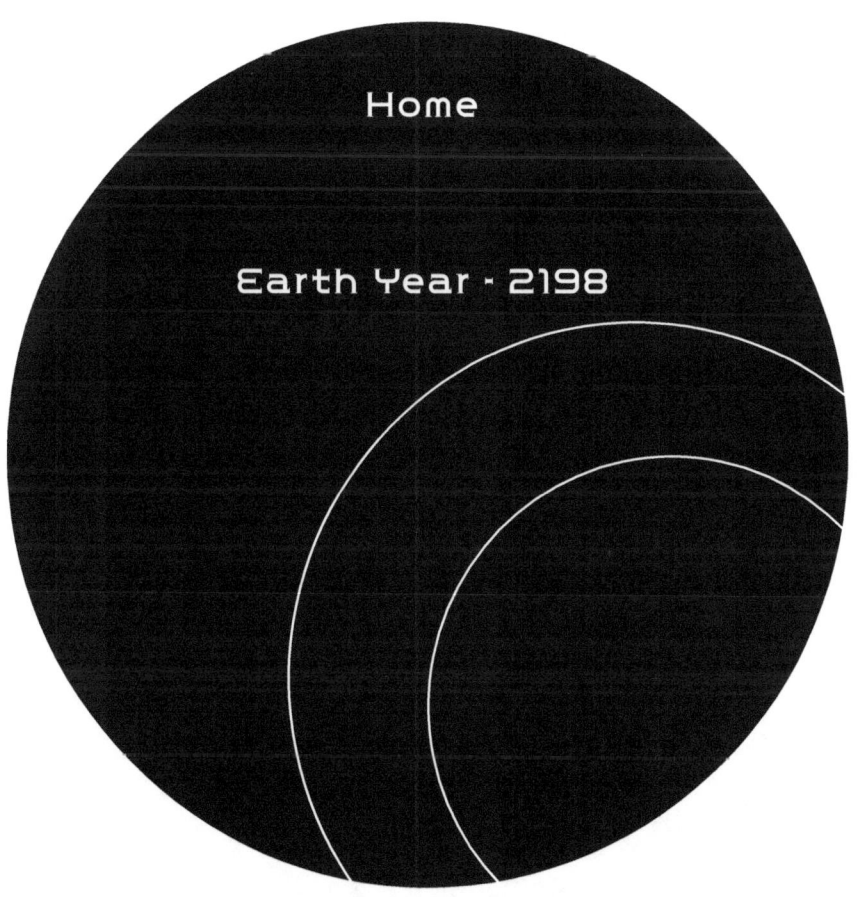

Home

Earth Year - 2198

# CHAPTER 23

# The Zantians

Mearos sat at a corner table of an almost deserted café waiting for Yaran. It was late in the evening, and most of the city was either closing up shop or already at home with their families. A few establishments, such as this one, stayed open late for those who didn't fit into either category. Two other patrons, a man, and woman sat in an opposite corner in quiet conversation.

His ship had landed four hours ago, and once the critical scans of crew and cargo were complete, he informed Pindac that he had personal business to take care of and would be back in the morning. Pindac had looked at his longtime friend questioningly. It was unlike the captain to leave the airfield before all the ship's data was entered, but the copilot didn't pry.

Mearos could have met Yaran in the office and given him the data-cube as they had done before, but this conversation was going to take a while, and he didn't want any interruptions, so he'd left word for the son of the Desolk to meet him here.

Four months ago, he had bared his soul to Leea about his involvement with the Morodons, and had to admit it gave him a certain amount of relief to have shared that horrible secret. Now he needed to tell Yaran the same story. When Tamera had brought him Leea's latest message, she said Leea had explained everything to Yaran, but Mearos wanted to do it first.

It had never occurred to him that participating in what amounted to trafficking of a sentient species weighed so heavily on his conscience, so he hoped this final revelation would ease his burden a little more. What he had done he would never forget, or forgive, but it was time to put it behind him.

The proprietor set a drink in front of him and retreated. It was a small glass filled with a thick, steaming, bright red liquid—a potion discovered on one of their trading planets. It wasn't hot; the steam was a reaction between the liquid and the air. The sweet-spicy brew would warm the esophagus as it slowly traveled to the stomach, and within seconds of hitting its destination, an extraordinary feeling attacked the brain. It was as if something reached deep into the core of one's being, but instead of disconnecting from reality, as a mind altering drug would, it reinforced the connection and brought about complete clarity and understanding—the importance of life itself almost within reach.

The magical moment was over in less than a minute, but a feeling of wellbeing would last for a while longer and increase exponentially with a subsequent drink. How the precise timing worked was a mystery, but the result made difficult moments easier to manage.

Mearos threw it back, closed his eyes, and enjoyed the moment as it worked its magic.

"That bad?" Yaran asked, sliding into the seat across from him.

The captain opened his eyes and picked up the glass. Wisps of residual steam wafted from within the empty container. "*Bouskadian* Elixir. There is a reason they named this drink *to find peace*. It's the best thing to boost courage and provide necessary acceptance. By the time this evening is over, I'll probably need a whole bottle."

Yaran raised his eyebrows. "I take it this isn't the typical exchange of Leea's message?"

"No." He slid two data-cubes across the table. "Leea has a disturbing story to tell you, but I want to tell you about it first."

"Well, after the last few days I've had, if this is more unpleasant news, then I'd better join you in that bottle." Yaran raised his hand toward the proprietor and indicated two drinks—one for himself, and one more for Mearos.

Over the next three hours and six drinks apiece later, the two Zantian men each finished their stories and bonded in friendship. At some point, they had both switched to whiskey, finding the clarity of the elixir too much to handle.

"It's interesting to me that your father is so involved with this," Yaran said, "but then I suppose they all are. I don't know him, but I know who he is. Those times when Jarock made me attend council meetings, I always found Sithan to be less serious than the rest of them."

"Yes," sarcasm bled through Mearos's slightly altered speech, "he is quite the humorist."

"Will there be anything else?" The proprietor asked, approaching the table. Yaran looked at the time and saw it was well into the morning. Mearos raised his eyebrows questioningly at his new friend.

A sly smile tugged at Yaran's lips. "Yes, I think we'll have one more, but make it the elixir this time."

The owner looked less than pleased, but he had recognized the son of the Desolk, and couldn't very well turn them out. He retreated to fulfill their request.

"I believe he wants to go home," Mearos admonished with a twinkle in his blue eyes.

"I know. I'll make it worth his while." When the drinks arrived, Yaran ordered one more whiskey, promising it would be their last, then lifted his glass. "Here's to unraveling all the secrets our world is trying to suppress." He downed the liquid and inhaled sharply as it hit his stomach.

"Let's hope there aren't much more like this to come," Mearos said, following suit.

Yaran absentmindedly fingered the data-cube he still held in his hand. The one for Julia he'd put in his pocket earlier.

"You're anxious to watch that, aren't you?"

"I am, but it can wait."

"You're a lucky man. Her love for you was something I find unprecedented. Not many Zantian women give their heart so completely, but I guess Human women are different."

"I am a lucky man. But believe me, Zantian or Human has nothing to do with giving your heart to someone you love if it's the right person. It sounds like you've had a bitter experience? Someone broke your heart, and you never got over it."

"Yes on all counts. Her name was Selane. And let's just say I don't think she liked what I was made of. Packed her bags while I was away, and was gone without as much as an explanation. But I know why she left. A week before my run I told her about my mother and who my father was. She said it didn't matter, but her actions spoke otherwise." The last drink arrived, and Mearos downed it before it even came to rest on the table.

"I'm sorry."

"Nope, nothing to be sorry about. It was a long time ago. Did you find out anything about those symbols yet?"

"No. Unfortunately, my father has been staying close to home, so I haven't had a chance to go back and see my mother."

"Your mother?"

"Oh, yes, I guess I didn't mention that. I took the file to Lauranna. She is an exceptional linguist."

"You said you thought you'd seen them before?"

"Have you ever been to your father's home?"

"No."

Yaran shook his head and grimaced. "Every ruling house has an artifact room. It's a place where they showcase items we've plundered from other worlds. They are a collection of art, and literature, ranging from the strange to the beautiful. In my father's collection, there is a unique sphere that has projected random sets of symbols for centuries. They are very similar to those in your file."

"And you think your mother can decipher what they mean?"

"If anyone can, she can."

"She's never looked at it before?"

"According to Jarock, the sphere represents nothing. He claims they found it on a deserted planet and kept it because of its uniqueness."

"But you don't believe him?"

"No, never have. The piece is too methodical, too precise in its arrangements. It has to be trying to tell us something."

"What does your mother believe?"

"She claims the same as Jarock. But when I showed her your file her demeanor changed. She strongly objected when I asked her to translate it, but my persistence finally convinced her. I believe the Council meets in Finetig in a few days, so I'll go over and see if she's made progress. I'll let you know what I find."

The next evening, Toref was busy entering information into his terminal, which sat on a desk in a corner of the living space. He had moved it there to provide room in the second bedroom for Yaran—a sacrifice he'd happily made. Yaran sat slouched on the sofa, engrossed in something on his personal pad. Unable to see what it was, he surmised his nephew was once again studying the symbol file Mearos had given him, trying to find a pattern.

Yaran had shown him the file after the Morodon's revelation and voiced his speculation about the connection to the artifact. Toref was no language expert, but they could be the same. The next morning, he had contacted Lauranna and told her about Yaran's discovery in the cave and she confirmed his suspicions about the text.

The door chime sounded.

"Would you mind getting that?" Toref asked over his shoulder.

Yaran eased out of his comfortable position. "Are you expecting someone?"

"Yes," he said hesitantly. "For both of us, actually."

"Mother, it's so good to see you," Yaran said with surprise, as he opened the door. "Toref didn't tell me you were stopping by."

"Must have slipped my mind," Toref mumbled, joining them in the small foyer.

Lauranna pulled the older man into a warm embrace, holding tight for a long moment. "I wish it wouldn't be so long between visits."

Toref smiled at her warmly. "I completely agree. But, for now, I have your son to keep me company, and it has been a joy to have him here."

She smiled at Yaran. "I envy you for that."

"Did you just stop by to say hello?" Yaran asked as they moved into the living room.

"No. I need to share some things with you, and I wanted Toref's moral support."

"Has something happened?"

"I am on my way to Calthena because your grandfather is ill. I'm hoping it's nothing serious, but I plan to stay with them for a few days. Your uncle, Danloc, and his family are there, of course, but I think it's more chaotic with them around." She paused and cut a glance to Toref. "So… I wanted to do this before I go."

She removed the datapad Yaran had given her months earlier from the folds of her robe and laid it on the small table. She then removed her cover-up and draped it over the back of the seat, and without invitation sat down on the sofa.

Yaran picked up the pad as he sat next to her. "Did you decipher the text?"

Her expression clouded, but she held his gaze. "Yes… I did. And I must apologize. It took me a lot less time to do that than it did to find the courage to tell you. There are things I need to explain before we discuss what's on the pad."

"I'm not going to like this, am I?" Yaran speculated, noticing his mother's nervousness.

Lauranna pulled in a deep breath. "Toref told me about your encounter with the Morodon. I've wrestled many hours with my decision to tell you what you should already know. But the time for secrets is over. You are the son of a Desolk and have every right to know the truth about our people." Lauranna straightened the front of her white shirt, lining up the ends of the side-button front, and focused on some unseen spot on the gray tile floor.

"The Morodon was right. Our people settled here about a thousand years ago. I feel that was a dark time in our history, although I'm sure those in charge of our world now would disagree. We came from a beautiful blue and lavender planet in another galaxy named Kree'Lan, and our people were called Ma'Kree. The Ma'Kree were a peaceful race who traveled the stars in exploration.

"But like any society, some weren't happy with the status quo and wanted more. I believe they became complacent in their perfect world, and encounters with other races showed some that a more exhilarating existence was possible. Eventually, a civil war ensued. After years of senseless fighting, the insurgents called a cease-fire and proposed a solution. Those unhappy with things on Kree'Lan would leave to find the thrills they were craving, and let the rest of the population go back to the way things were and rebuild their once beautiful planet. Approximately ten thousand people gathered in hundreds of ships and left their heritage behind.

"Unfortunately, those who spearheaded the revolution were an angry bunch, and out to prove they could conquer whatever came their way. And conquer they did. The more they terrorized harmless races, the stronger grew their resolve to be masters of the universe. They eventually found this planet, barren but habitable, and rich with minerals. They settled here, and christened this world Zantia, and themselves Zantians; *Z'an'Tin* is the Ma'Kree word for powerful.

"After leaving Kree'Lan, one hundred of the most committed loyalists formed a Council. They ruled with an iron fist, instigated the wars with others, and insisted on enslaving alien races to do their bidding. They created laws and decrees, and one such proclamation was that only the offspring of the one hundred would ever be allowed to rule in the new world. They made quick examples of those who tried to stand against them, so the remainder of the new race had no choice but to comply.

"It took a few centuries to cultivate the environment here, using other species they forced into servitude. Once the cities were built, and the mines excavated, they went back to the stars. Partially to establish trade, and partly to once again prove they could take whatever they wanted.

"Centuries passed and the people again became divided. New generations wanted to be like their ancestors. They were tired of the constant conflicts and wanted a peaceful existence.

"To avoid a possible uprising, the Council decided to honor the peoples' wishes, under one condition; all references to the Ma'Kree were to be erased from the official records so there would be no more pining over a place to which they could never return. They did this strictly for self-serving reasons, of course. The city rulers needed the population to continue managing the alien races who worked for them, but they kept this to themselves, so the people agreed.

"That was over four hundred years ago. References to who we were, and where we came from, were removed from the official texts and replaced with fictional accounts. Now our ancestry is forgotten…except by the Council. Council families are raised in the traditions laid out by the extremists, and they alone are the keepers of our history. And that history is stored in a sphere…ours hovers on the center shelf of the library cabinet.

"When the Zantian race was formed, they also modified the structure of the Ma'Kree language. They changed it from a symbolic language to a phonetic script."

"So, the symbols in the files I gave you were Ma'Kree?"

"Yes. The time during transition training where all this is revealed to Council children was something you missed because I kept you at home, and for that, I apologize. And please don't think less of me, but I later agreed with Jarock to not tell you. Not because I didn't want you to know, but because I didn't want to burden you. You never fit into the Council's way of thinking, so there was no reason to tell you something you might feel compelled to reveal. You, too, belong to that part of the population who want to live a different life from what the Zantians started, and not a person to keep its dark secrets. And there is no fault in that."

"So that explains the disappointment my father feels toward me."

"You're not the first child of a council member to reject the old ways," Toref interjected, "but the first one in this family. We've held the leadership title for several generations, and as you well know, Jarock has taken our ancestors' decree seriously. When he and I were young boys, he dreamed of leading our people. But his vision was always to lead them back to the old ways. When our parents died in the shuttle accident, he got his wish. Now, he's allied himself with the more radical leaders, and it's only the rest of the Council that keep his plans at bay."

"But we've still attacked other worlds, as recently as a hundred years ago."

"I can't make excuses for what we've done," Toref said apologetically, "but we still look for ways to increase our trade. And when we find compatible worlds, it is difficult for the Council to take no for an answer when they discover other things they want. They're used to getting their way."

"And species like the Morodons and Humans paid for that mentality with their lives."

"Sadly, yes."

Yaran ran his fingers through his hair and lowered his head for a moment in silent thought. "Thank you both for telling me all this. It's almost too much to take in, but it does explain a lot. So what does this have to do with the files Mearos gave me?"

"You were right about the symbols being the same as the sphere; they are Ma'Kree. The spreadsheet file was an account of payments made, but to whom specifically, it didn't say. The other one is an accounting of our people, written by someone called Belag, but it's probably not his actual name. We're familiar with a race known as Belag. They are mercenary hunters who will do anything for the right price...and they never stop until they find their prey, even if it takes their entire lifetime. If we've been infiltrated by one of them, as this seems to suggest, it's only a matter of time before whoever sent them comes looking. Since this is written in Ma'Kree, it stands to reason this went to them. I can't imagine why they would be looking for us after all these years. Only desperate people align themselves with the hunters. Which makes me wonder….'

"How can this Belag have infiltrated us without our knowing? I thought the shield protected us from anyone entering our atmosphere?"

"They are shape-shifters. They can take on any form, no matter how small."

"Genad said the seeker has joined with a new enemy. Who could that be?"

Lauranna shook her head. "I have no idea. There was no reference in the files to an alliance with anyone. But they did suggest that the hunter has been here for almost three years. If the Morodon is to be believed, I would imagine that whatever the Belag's plans are, they are already in motion, and we will find out soon."

They spent another hour answering Yaran's questions. Lauranna promised that once she returned from Calthena, she would sit down with him and the history sphere, and they would look at some of the old stories together. Then she excused herself, saying she needed to go.

Unable to sleep, Toref made his way to the kitchen to brew some tea and was surprised to find Yaran already sitting there, cup in hand.

"Can't sleep?" Toref asked, pouring himself a cup from the carafe.

"No, and I'm not sure I ever will again."

Toref sighed and nodded in understanding. "Send a message to Cashon and tell him you won't be in tomorrow."

"That's not necessary, I—"

"Please. I want to show you something."

"What?"

"It's connected to all this, but it's better if I show you." Toref picked up his cup and started back toward the bedrooms. "Sleep as best you can, and when we're ready tomorrow, we'll head out."

Yaran raised his eyebrows. "Okay."

Yaran managed to get a few hours of fitful sleep, as strange yet beautiful places plagued his normally dreamless night. He showered, dressed, and then shuffled to the kitchen where Toref already had tea and their meal prepared.

"I don't think I've ever been up before you," Yaran stated lightheartedly.

"I heard you get up, so I came to start the meal." He set a steaming cup in front of his nephew that was soon followed by a plate of bread, meat, cheese and fruit.

"You'd make someone a great mother."

The burly man burst into laughter. "Why, thank you." He bowed appreciatively.

"Are you going to tell me where we're going today?"

Toref took the chair across from him with his own plate. "It's a place out in the desert where we hide another piece of our past. You'll understand when you see it. But like everything else you've learned these last few days, it's a place few Zantians know exists."

"Well, what's one more secret?"

"I'm sorry."

"No need. I've come to realize it's part of the world we live in."

Toref's voice took on a serious tone. "What are you going to do with all the information you've heard this week? Especially what Lauranna told you last night?"

"I'm not sure. My first instinct is to do nothing. There's a reason for everything that's happening here. The Morodons protect us, although I wish I could wipe that knowledge from my mind. And why would I tell anyone about them? It would likely cause chaos, and to what end? Bring unrest among the people again? I won't be responsible for that.

"And the same goes for the revelation about the Ma'Kree. Four hundred years ago, the people agreed to forget where we came from. Who am I to say that was the wrong decision?"

Toref studied him across the table with interest.

"What?" Yaran asked uncomfortably.

"You're a different man from the one who showed up unannounced on my doorstep a year ago. So lost and unsure of himself. It hasn't come without consequences, though, has it? But I must say, you're handling all of this the way any ruler would. Jarock would be proud."

Yaran grimaced. "I appreciate the words. I don't feel much different than I did then, but my entire perspective of the things around me has certainly changed… which I'll get used to in time. But I doubt my father will ever see me as anything more than a disappointment."

"You're wrong about that. He doesn't."

"Well, I think if we're going to get to where we're going, we should go." Yaran got up and cleared the dishes. He appreciated Toref's words, but too much had transpired between him and Jarock. Too much to ignore so easily.

In under an hour the two men were in the air, heading out over the desert. They passed over the solar fields, and then Toref pointed the small craft into the open sea of crimson and set it to full throttle. He kept the shuttle close to the ground, and it kicked up dust as they skimmed along.

The mysterious journey took fifteen minutes before the shuttle started to slow. Yaran couldn't determine their destination because nothing but desert loomed around them, until finally, he saw it; a small red structure, about ten-foot square, slowly rising from the ground. Toref set down a few yards away.

"That's what you wanted to show me?" Yaran asked lightheartedly.

Toref chuckled. "Almost there."

An unlock device gave them entry, and automatic lights lit up the small space. Toref's fingers manipulated a screen on the far wall and then the entire structure pulled them downward. Within several seconds, the doors reopened.

Stepping onto a concrete floor, Yaran stopped short as lights rhythmically illuminated a massive cavern that seemed to have no end. The air was stuffy, and he discerned the scent of metals and old engine fluids. As far as the eye could see, ships of varying sizes stood side by side along the outside walls.

Black ones with seamless shiny hulls; dull gray ones with protruding portholes and engines; white dimpled vessels with extended wings and a topsail, were just a few he could see down the line. About a dozen close by were a mix of scout ships meant for combat, and cruisers designed for comfortable travel. Marred surfaces and visible scorch marks told of their difficult journey.

Equally spaced pillars, similar to those in the mines, rose floor to ceiling with the vehicles parked between them. Portable stairs stood by each ship. Yaran moved under the nearest scout with a dark gray hull. Stopping next to the landing skids, he looked up at the underbelly, fifteen feet up, and saw countless signs of battle. "What are all these?" Yaran asked Toref, who stood gauging his nephew's reaction.

"These are the ships our ancestors traveled in when they left Kree'Lan."

"After all these years? Why are they here…underground?"

"This seemed the best place to preserve them…out of the elements. This cavern was built soon after they settled on Zantia, and many of the ships stored here, especially those that were no longer in the best condition. Once the history of the Ma'Kree was erased, most of the others were brought here too."

"And those we used after that…until the shield?"

"When we stopped seeking out other worlds, we told everyone they were being parked in the desert. We couldn't very well leave them in orbit if we wanted to hide. So, we added the remainder here and sealed this place."

"Yes, that certainly makes sense. How many are there?"

"Down here, two hundred thirty-one. And each ruling house stores its family cruiser in a bunker beneath their homestead."

"I take it this one has seen conflict?"

"Yes. The scout ships are always first in any situation. Come."

Toref led Yaran behind the elevator where he removed a four-person cart recessed in the wall. They climbed on, and he steered it slowly between the ships. Passing countless configurations, Yaran sat in awe of each ship, marveling at how some still stood. Many he surmised had at one point been elegant and sleek, now reduced to a battered form, while others were sturdy freight haulers that looked as if they could withstand the test of time. Yaran couldn't even imagine the journey they must have taken or the trauma they had obviously endured.

They passed, at least, a hundred before stopping by four vessels, each the size of a small city where the cavern had been built out to accommodate them. Exiting the cart, they looked up at the behemoths that were over a thousand feet long and three hundred feet wide. Each one held up by two dozen pilings, thicker than Yaran was tall.

"These are the vessels that traveled to Earth," Toref explained. "They'd been to other worlds, of course, but were never filled to capacity as when they returned from the Human world. Each one can hold two thousand passengers and crew."

The ships were slightly wider at the aft end which supported two massive engines, one on each side, with their cowlings blending into the main body's framework. The bulk of the vessels had five tiers, rounded at the edges, each one slightly smaller than the one below it. With the exception of the largest bottom section, each consisted of two or three stories, indicated by the arrangement of small windows which grew exponentially in size moving up the levels.

The forward end was rounded, and the top three levels displayed the recessed command center that could be seen behind a glass enclosure that encompassed almost the entire width. The hull was black and smooth, and while no armaments were visible, Yaran surmised they were hidden there somewhere.

"How did they get these large ships down here? They didn't land, did they?"

"No, these were only designed for space travel. From what I understand, over a dozen large freight haulers, tethered at various points, guided each into the atmosphere and carefully eased it on its resting place."

"That must have been quite the synchronized event?"

"I imagine it was."

"Was there ever a plan to do something with them … with any of these?"

"Not that I know of. How would the Council explain where they came from?"

Yaran shook his head as he took in the enormous ships. What the abductees on board must have endured he couldn't imagine, and as much as he hated what they represented, he couldn't be upset that Humans were brought here. He would never have met Leea otherwise, and he wouldn't change that for anything. He sighed deeply at the conflicting emotions.

"Do any of them still fly?"

"I'm not sure. They are all well over a thousand years old, but most haven't been in space since shortly after they arrived here. Every few years they send a team of council children down to service them. Jarock and I had that unpleasant duty once." Toref groaned. "It took five of us three weeks to go through every ship; start the engines, run the system diagnostics, replace what was needed. Dreadfully boring task."

"When is the last time that was done?"

"Two years ago, I believe."

"Maybe we should check the service records and see which ones are flight-worthy and if their weapon systems are operational…just in case."

"In case of what?"

"In case we have to defend ourselves against an unknown enemy."

# CHAPTER 24

# The Plan

Leea sat at the edge of the dock, feet dangling in the cool lake water while she watched Farrell and Jackson swim about unhindered. She loved the water but still wasn't brave enough to throw caution to the wind and jump in. She had taken swim lessons, and although she understood the basic concepts and had done well in shallow water, the exercises had been full of trepidation, and she finally had to admit, she preferred the comfort of solid ground under her feet. Maybe someday...

Two weeks ago was the one-year anniversary of her arrival in New Haven. The day had coincided with Tamera bringing her another beloved message from Zantia. Leea had taken the day off work and met Mearos's mother in the city, as she had done before, where it was more convenient for both of them.

After their short visit, Leea had returned home and curled up on the sofa, datapad in hand, and viewed pictures and videos. She watched, and re-watched the current and past messages from Yaran and Julia, and enjoyed them all, along with a bottle of wine. Although the intense pain of leaving them was now reduced to a dull ache, not a day went by that she didn't long to return.

Late that afternoon, Farrell and Jackson interrupted her melancholy mood and stopped her from opening a second bottle, then insisted she wipe the tears away, and join them for dinner.

Farrell had pulled her into a comforting embrace before they'd left the house. "I know you want to be sad today, but I'm happy you're here. I can't imagine your loss, but you need to know we're here for you...you don't have to do this alone." Leea was more than grateful for her new friends, but her heart would never stop yearning for her old ones.

The day of Mearos's departure, she left work a little early and took a bus to the airfield. There, she stood a short distance away and watched the cargo ship make its slow ascent into space—taking a small piece of her heart with it—until it was nothing more than a speck on the horizon. She missed not seeing Mearos but understood it was too risky.

Leea's musings were interrupted by what felt like a bucket of water thrown at her. She screamed and jumped away from the edge. "HEY!! What was that for?" She burst out laughing as she shook water off her clothes.

"You should come in. It's great." Farrell pushed off the dock and floated on her back.

"Maybe next time."

"That's what you said last time."

"Okay…then maybe next year. Are you guys ever going to get out?"

"I'm not sure. I think Jackson is trying to burn off some energy before his meeting with the admiral tomorrow."

"Can't wait to hear what that's all about."

"Me neither." Farrell dove under the water and Leea held her breath until her friend resurfaced.

"This is an impressive ship," Jackson commented to Admiral Shaw as they left the engine room. Jackson had ferried himself up to the Atlantis a few hours ago for a private meeting that he hoped would give him answers about the upcoming mission. "A lot of technology I've never seen before."

"Yes, we've added a lot of experimental equipment." The admiral chuckled. "It's about time those researchers earn their pay."

Jackson joined in the humor but knew what he'd seen had not been invented at the research lab. Having worked there for several years on the design and functionality of the small fighters, he knew the lab techs loved talking about their discoveries. Innovations passed through the tight-knit rumor mill like wildfire.

After they had heard the conversation between the admiral and Bettina, he had cautiously asked around about new fuel or shield upgrades and was assured that the lab was still years away from those kinds of breakthroughs. But one of the techs had mentioned that some independent work was being done off-site, although he didn't know where.

Now having seen the upgrades first hand, he had to wonder where this advanced technology came from. It certainly seemed alien, and if it was, then the Watchers were way over their heads.

The admiral continued the tour, extremely proud of the refit accomplishments and Jackson was surprised by the amount of activity everywhere. They visited the bridge, the crew quarters, the mess hall, and now entered the fighter bay. There, stood dozens of the small single-seat fighter planes—his babies. He was proud of their sleek design and knew firsthand their maneuvering and firepower capabilities. He ran a hand along the underside of the closest ship, marveling at the smooth metal.

"Impressive pieces of machinery," the admiral complimented.

"Yes, they are," Jackson nodded. "It's amazing to see so many of them all neatly lined up."

"Fifty-five. More wouldn't fit."

"Why so many?"

"We have to be prepared for every possibility."

"Such as?"

"Come," the military leader said turning toward the door. "Let's go back to the bridge where we can talk privately."

Adjacent the command center, the admiral guided him into a large empty conference room and offered him something to drink, which the captain graciously declined.

"Amazing vessel, isn't it?" the admiral remarked once they were both comfortably seated.

"It is. Too bad it's hidden up here."

"I would gladly show off this extraordinary ship to every person on Dekarra, but of course, that wouldn't be feasible."

"Then why go to all this effort?"

"Our people have had one specific goal since the day our ancestors landed here."

"Rescue the captives from Zantia."

The admiral smiled. "I'm glad that answer came so quickly for you. I fear it's a goal many people have forgotten."

"Oh, I don't think anyone's forgotten. People are just caught up in their daily lives, that's all."

"Yes, I'm sure you're right. That's why we in the military try to keep that goal at the forefront. We've been working hard to retrofit this ship and ready our troops so we can finally honor the ancestors' wishes."

"Really?"

"Yes. We now have a sustainable number of troops, and their training has been ongoing. With some lucky technological breakthroughs, this ship is almost ready for battle. And that's why you're here. I'd like you to make the shakedown runs."

Jackson's eyes lit up. "Are you serious?"

"Yes."

"That's quite an honor. I have to confess; I've logged many hours in the old simulator."

"I know. That's what brought you to my attention. Your scores were always in the top ten percent, but it was some of your unorthodox maneuvers that intrigued me. That's also why I wanted you on the fighter program, and you've proven beyond my greatest expectations what a good choice that was."

"Thank you, again."

"We've upgraded the simulator with the new helm modifications, and I'd like you to spend the next week familiarizing yourself with them. Put in as many hours as you need; the schedule is booked exclusively for you. We're anticipating that by the end of the week, the Atlantis's final adjustments will be completed, so I want to start the shakedown runs next week."

Jackson's eyebrows shot up. "So soon?"

"Why wait? Everything is ready. Fighter pilots have completed their training and have been performing successful practice runs up here for the last month. Ground troops have been doing maneuvers on the southern continent to get accustomed to the heat. Once we know this ship is sound, we can finally accomplish what our ancestors set out to do."

Bile threatened to rise into Jackson's throat, but he forced his stomach to calm. How could this military man, someone who swore to protect the people, be so willing to condemn those on another world for his own personal gain? But Jackson had to play along if the Watchers were to have any chance of intervening.

"And just to be clear," Admiral Shaw continued. "I want you on this mission. I'd like you sitting at the helm when we reach Zantia."

"I… I don't know what to say. *I'm honored* seems so trivial."

"Nonsense. You've earned your place on this team. I plan to set up a meeting sometime this week with the entire bridge crew so you can all get acquainted."

"What kind of timeline are you looking at?"

"It's going to depend on the shakedowns, but if all goes without any major revisions, I'm going to say three to four weeks."

"That's a sporty schedule."

"I know, but it's been over a hundred years, I'd say it's about time." The admiral got to his feet, and Jackson followed suit. "Unfortunately, we're still a little in the dark on the Zantians' military capabilities. We were hopeful the new girl would have had some intel for us."

"Leea?"

"Yes. You're friends with her, aren't you?"

"Yes, we're acquainted. She works in the records office." Jackson prayed that the admiral wasn't on a fishing expedition to see if he would lie.

The burly man laughed. "The records office … working with your more-than-friend, Farrell Reynolds."

Jackson shook his head and gave a sly smile. "Admiral, you should know better than to believe everything you hear. Farrell and I are friends, yes. But I have lots of other friends as well."

The admiral slapped him on the back. "That's what I like to hear … a man who keeps his options open."

"Always."

"Let me give you some advice: hang on to Miss Reynolds. She's well connected, and will do wonders for your career. No reason to give up on your other friends of course … but keep them at arm's length."

Jackson wanted to punch him. Instead, he smiled and nodded in agreement. "I'll keep that in mind. Can I take another look at the helm before we go?"

"Of course." he chuckled. "Already anxious to get into that seat?"

"I am," Jackson replied with a broad smile.

The two men reentered the bridge and Jackson looked around. He had been to the ship once before, on a tour during his pilot training, and had to admit the original design was as remarkable as the upgrades. Against the back wall were six separate workstations where the various bridge and other ship's systems were monitored. The forward wall was almost entirely a viewscreen, currently showing an image of the planet below. Directly behind the display, were two separate seats, each surrounded by a curved console, one for helm and navigation, and the other for weapons.

In the middle of the room stood three large connected chairs; the center one being the largest. Although currently not visible, each chair had a pullout control panel and screen nestled in the left armrest.

The captain slid into the helm's anchored chair. "Surprisingly comfortable," he said to the admiral who stood back as if gauging his reaction. He turned his attention at the dark displays, running a hand over the smooth surface of the horseshoe-shaped console which also curved upward, making the readouts easily visible.

Jackson ran a hand over the top of the station, and stopped when he felt a sharp edge, but then remembered Leea's speculation that there was a Morodon on board." He had an idea.

Bracing himself for the pain, Jackson quickly ran his left hand across the sharp edge. "Ouch!" He jerked his hand back, blood already dripping from the index finger.

Admiral Shaw scurried into the conference room, returning with a small thin towel which he handed him. "What was that?" he asked.

"I don't know. Something sharp on the console."

The admiral walked around for a closer look. "Yup, there it is. Difficult to miss with all the blood on it."

"And part of my finger probably," he quipped. Blood was already soaking through the cloth.

"I'll get someone up here to fix that right away. So, I guess your tour wouldn't be complete without a trip to the medical bay. Let's get that finger looked at."

Dr. Will Bennett, a short, bald, black man in his mid-thirties examined Jackson's finger that was still oozing. "That's a pretty nasty cut, Captain."

From the nearest cabinet, the doctor pulled out a dispenser of healing spray. He applied a cleaning solution and then administered a thin stream directly into and along the wound. Almost immediately the bleeding and the throbbing stopped. The spray not only promoted instant healing but also provided antibiotics and a pain suppressant.

"Now, let that sit for a moment, and you'll be good as new."

Jackson got out of the diagnostic chair, precariously holding his hand. "This is an exceptional facility. Mind if I look around?"

Without waiting for an answer, Jackson started to roam around the room. Two dozen cabinets lined the walls, filled with medications, first-aid supplies, and many things he couldn't identify. In the far corner was a dark alcove. Jackson sauntered over for a quick look.

"Wow, a regeneration bed. You are equipped for any eventuality." He glanced back, showing a big smile, but noticed the worried look on the doctor's face. With one more fleeting glimpse into the alcove, he saw a door in the back corner standing ajar. A soft green hue emanated from the dark space.

"This is great." Jackson gave the two men as big a smile as he dared. "It looks top of the line, just like the rest of the ship." He wiggled the fingers of his left hand. "Good as new. So, I probably shouldn't take up any more of your time." He extended a hand. "It was very nice to meet you, Dr. Bennett, thanks for fixing me up.

I hope you won't be offended when I say; I hope I don't need your services in the future."

The doctor laughed, accepting the hand. "No offense taken. That's the sentiment of all my patients."

Jackson quietly entered Farrell's apartment. It was almost midnight, but he showed only mild surprise to find her stretched out on the couch with a reader.

"Hey you," she said getting to her feet. "I didn't expect you back until tomorrow." She kissed him, then noticed his clouded expression.

"It didn't take as long as I thought it would." Walking into the small kitchen, he pulled a glass and a bottle of whiskey from the cupboard. He poured a shot, threw it back, and then had another.

Farrell laid a hand on his arm before he could pour a third. "What's wrong?"

"I hate this!"

"Hate what?"

"Having to smile at that pompous ass!"

"Ah, the admiral. Did something happen?"

"No." He grabbed the bottle again, but Farrell took it away from him, replaced the cap and set it back in the cupboard. "I was the perfect minion. 'Yes, Sir.' 'No, Sir.' 'I completely agree with you, Sir.' Ugh!"

"Do you want to tell me about it?"

"No. The more I think about it, the angrier I get."

Smiling, she took his arm and then pulled him toward the bedroom. "Well then, let me help you clear your mind of all that unpleasantness."

A sly grin crossed his face. "What did you have in mind?"

"That's for me to know... and you to find out."

Farrell rested her head on Jackson's shoulder and listened as he calmly told her about his visit to the Atlantis. He left nothing out.

"Sooo," Farrell pulled out of his embrace and rested on an elbow, tucking her golden brown hair behind her ear. "Who are these other friends?"

His eyebrows shot up. "Out of everything I just told you, that is what you focus on?"

"I have my priorities." She tried hard to suppress a grin. "So, out with it… other friends?"

Jackson sighed. "Oh, you know… the harem I keep in my apartment. Why do you think I'm always over here?"

She grabbed a pillow and hit him in the face.

He barely defended himself but then grabbed her and rolled her to the other side of the bed and lay on top of her, pinning her arms above her head. "You have a problem with my harem?"

"No. I was just wondering if I should come over and join in. We could make it one big family affair."

He nuzzled her neck. "No. I have other plans for you, sweetie."

"Sweetie, eh? You must be aiming for some severe punishment."

"Promises, promises."

She disengaged her arms, lovingly pushed him away, and slid out from underneath him. "There'll be no more of that… at least not right now." She sat on the edge of the bed. "Seriously, why would the admiral bring up Leea?"

"I'm not sure. I half expected him to ask me to talk to her, but for some reason, he let it drop. He was more interested in telling me how I should deal with you?"

"Very funny."

"Actually, it wasn't. But I hope I convinced him that my loyalties lay with the mission."

"Did you drool sufficiently over the Atlantis?"

"Yes, I did. But I wasn't lying when I said it was impressive. I'm just worried where this new technology came from."

"You really think it could be alien?"

"It has to be. Belag isn't exactly a Human name. And I asked around the lab; no new technology there. So the bigger question is, if this Belag is alien, how did the military find him without anyone else noticing? And why would an alien species help us in our effort to attack the Zantians?"

"Well, Leea did say they have a lot of enemies. Is it possible that one of them found out what's going on up on the moon and offered to help?"

"Hmmm…. Maybe."

"And you think you saw the Morodon stasis pod?"

"I'm not sure. Leea said they were kept in a green gel. There was a definite green glow coming through the door behind the regen-bed. And the doctor seemed nervous when I walked over to the alcove." Jackson laced his fingers together behind his head, then stared at the ceiling.

"What?" Farrell asked with a frown.

"All of a sudden I'm not comfortable with you being a part of all this."

"Excuse me?"

"We're dealing with an unknown element now. I would never forgive myself if something happened to you."

"Listen, buddy," she poked his bare, muscular chest. "I am more than capable of taking care of myself. Whatever we decide to do, you're not doing it without me. Is that understood?" She narrowed her eyes. "Cause if you try, I will turn your whole harem against you by the time you get back."

"Is that so?" He grabbed her and pulled her down on top of him, enclosing her in an embrace.

Farrell ran a hand through his short brown hair. "I love you. And where you go, I go. Understood?"

"Understood. But I love you more."

The next day, Jackson recapped his Atlantis visit to the fifteen Watchers gathered in the cave.

"Three weeks!" several exclaimed in unison.

"I know. It's crazy." Jackson agreed. "I spent five hours in the simulator today, and must say, the admiral's timeline doesn't seem all that unrealistic. By the end of the week, I should be ready for the real thing. So, we need to come up with a feasible plan of our own, and quickly."

"Any suggestions?" Devon Greene asked.

"Yes! Stop them!" Farrell cried. "If they are allowed to succeed, what's next? Are they going to take that newly designed warship and start roaming the galaxy like the Zantians did? I can't even fathom how someone who is considered a leader of our planet can be so self-centered. And we know our traitorous VP is in on this plan as well. It's unconscionable, something—"

"Farrell, calm down," Jackson said soothingly, laying a hand on her arm. "We'll figure this out."

She drew in a deep, calming breath. "It just makes me so angry... claiming this is what's best for our people."

"What is the firepower of the Atlantis, and the fighters?" Ben McAdams asked.

"The fighters are equipped with two missiles, each with automatic targeting that can be fired from a high orbit, and two laser guns with self-recharging battery packs. The Atlantis has fifty laser cannons mounted on its exterior. Their range is twenty times that of the fighters, but still only useful in a space battle. However, they have twelve rapid-reload missile tubes, which could wipe out an entire city from orbit, and I believe they have two hundred warheads in stock. And I can't even assess the amount of firepower the ground troops will be carrying."

"So what you're saying," Max said, "is that there is nothing we can do to stop them…at least not from here."

Jackson shook his head. "We'll have to be on board. And even then I don't think we'll be able to sabotage their efforts completely. We're simply outnumbered. The most we can hope for is to slow them down."

"Do you have a plan?"

"I designed those fighters, so I know their vulnerabilities. There is an external kill switch that will deactivate the missiles' firing mechanism. It's there for maintenance purposes only, but it is something we can use. We'll have to get five to ten people aboard, and once the ship reaches the Zantian system, they would deactivate all the fighters. It's not great, but will limit them to lasers only."

"What about the Atlantis?"

"Well, that's a bigger problem. The weapons system has several redundant backups. Short of officially shutting it down, there's no way to covertly make them inoperable. I haven't quite figured out how to deal with that," Jackson grimaced.

"I might be able to deactivate them," Max said. "With my own equipment and couple weeks' time…should be no problem."

"You don't have to do this, Max. Since I'm part of the bridge crew, I'll figure it out."

"Are you kidding? I wouldn't miss this for anything. And it sounds like you need all the help you can get."

"Yeah…that, and a whole lot of luck."

"We could make sure the workers are safe if we had help from the other side," Leea murmured.

All eyes turned toward her. "From the Zantians?"

"Yes. We can't rain this devastation down on them without warning."

"And what's to stop them from just blowing us out of the sky?" someone asked.

"One of the things Bettina was always asking me about was the Zantian military presence. What kind of weapons they possessed? What kind of troops they had? I never saw any evidence of such things, but that doesn't mean they don't exist. If I can get a message to Yaran and let him know what's happening, what we're doing from our side to minimize this, he could talk to the Council. Give them a chance to protect the people."

"Will they listen to him?" Farrell asked.

Leea shrugged. "I don't know. He's not on good terms with his father, their leader, but maybe some of the others will listen."

Farrell looked around the room. "We have to consider this. I don't like the idea of dropping bombs on an unsuspecting society. And how many of our own will they kill in the process? You heard the admiral; they're anticipating Human fatalities and are okay with that. This mission should be about bringing our people home, not making them acceptable casualties and enslaving them further. It's unacceptable, so we need to take the chance."

"But won't they see us coming, and then take preventative measures, if they do have weapons?" someone else asked.

"They believe the shield hides them, so they won't consider an alien ship a threat. But since the Atlantis has a Morodon on board, it must have something to do with bringing the barrier down. Once the attack starts, there may be no way for them to defend themselves... that I know of."

"Well, for me then, I see no other choice. We have to warn them. Then hopefully they can at least defend against the fighters." Farrell looked around. "Does everyone agree, or should we take a vote?"

After thirty minutes of weighing the pros and cons, and a final vote, eleven of the fifteen members agreed to warn the Zantians. Eight volunteered to go aboard the Atlantis, including Leea, Farrell, and Max.

"Can we still send a communiqué to Mearos's ship?" Leea asked Max minutes after the group dispersed.

"Yes. They're almost a week out, so still in communications range. Our equipment here won't let us establish a direct link, but I can send and receive a message. I'll send it audio only to make it faster. I just need to find the frequency." He activated a nearby screen, made several entries and after a few seconds, numbers started to scroll vertically. "This will scan for energy signatures or active communications, and return the frequency in the direction I indicated." After a few moments the scrolling stopped, and a set of numbers flashed red. "That's it."

Max handed Leea a data-cube and guided her into a small room off the main foyer. "I figured you'd want some privacy, so record your message in here. Once you're done, I'll have you record a short message for the captain, and send them on their way."

"Thanks, Max."


"Yaran, my love, I hope Mearos can get this to you in time. So much has happened here in just the last few days that I'm not sure where to begin, so I'll just say it: The Dekarran military is launching an attack against Zantia, and could be on their way by the time you get this. Although their official mission is to rescue the workers, we've learned their real plan is to destroy Zantia's cities and take over the mines for themselves. Their warship will have fifty-five small fighter planes and approximately 350 troops, and their armaments are massive.

"They've converted the last Earth ship, Atlantis, with technology that Jackson has never seen before, and doesn't believe it was developed in the research lab. We've also learned that the military is being helped by someone named Belag, who we suspect might be alien. Could this be someone looking to harm the Zantians? One of your old enemies?

"This person seems to know your location and a way to penetrate the shield. We are pretty sure they have a Morodon on board and believe that's how they plan to get through. I realize this is only an assumption, but they wouldn't go to all this trouble if they weren't sure they could succeed.

"As of yesterday, the admiral wants the Atlantis underway in about three weeks, and with all its upgrades, it will take, at most, three weeks to get to you. So we will probably be on our way by the time Mearos arrives home."

Leea paused, not knowing exactly how to tell him the next part. He wouldn't be happy that she was putting herself in harm's way, but if this was a way back to him, it was an acceptable risk. She was glad there would be no time for him to respond.

"I'm going to be on the Atlantis when it arrives. A group of the Watchers I told you about will be smuggled aboard just before takeoff. We're going to try and disable the ship's bombing system, as well as the bombs on the fighters just before we reach Zantia. It won't prevent the attack, but we're hoping without bombs, it will lessen the damage. Luckily, Jackson is the pilot, so with him as part of the bridge crew, we might have a better chance of succeeding."

She paused again and pulled in a deep breath. "I'm scared Yaran. Scared something could happen to you or Julia since you both live near the city now. You have to warn the Council. I know it's a lot to put on you, but you have to make your father listen. If he won't, maybe some of the others will, so please try. Evacuate the cities, if possible, just as a precaution."

"Please don't worry about me. I'll be careful. I know this is a horrible situation, but I can't help feeling happy knowing I'm on my way back to you. Stay safe, A'rinBientS'aan, and I will do the same. I love you."

She gave the cube to Max and then recorded the message to Mearos.

"Mearos, I'm sending you a message that Yaran needs to get as soon as possible. As incredible as this may sound, the Dekarrans are planning to attack Zantia and will be leaving in about three weeks on an upgraded ship. The enhancements will allow them to get to Zantia in three weeks. A group of us are going to stow away on the Dekarran ship and try to do a little sabotage, but it won't be enough to stop this. I have no idea how this is will end, but please take care of yourself. Once again, I'm in your debt."

"Okay, the message is away," Max said. "It's going to take several hours for him to get it and respond."

"Thank you, Max." Leea walked back out into the main hall where an intense conversation was still taking place.

"Message away?" Farrell asked, moving off to the side.

"Yes. I've done what I can." Leea looked at her friend and smiled sheepishly.

"What?"

"I realized something while I was recording the message for Yaran. It's not me."

"What's not you?"

"When I first met Nethas, she told me that the arrival of a stranger would change things on Dekarra. She thought it was me. But it has to be the Belag. He's the one who helped the admiral upgrade the ship, which has moved up the time-table to rescue the people of Earth. So it's not me."

"You could be right."

"I am right. And I'm so relieved!"

"Except for one thing."

"What's that?"

"For sure it's the alien who is helping the military. But you're the one making it possible to save the Humans and Morodons, and bring them back to Dekarra. The message you just sent is the reason for that."

"Well, that's okay. I'll take responsibility for that bit of it."

Farrell laughed softly. "What? You don't want to be solely responsible for changing the course of an entire planet?"

"NO!"

Mearos sat behind the small desk in his quarters and studied the container readouts on a small screen. Generally, he only performed this task once a trip, but his crew was shorthanded this run, so he'd volunteered to do the checks himself. It didn't take up much of his time, but it was incredibly boring, and he was having a hard time keeping his eyes open. A knock on his door saved his head from hitting the desktop.

"Come in."

Pindac entered and laughed as he looked at the captain. "Are you awake?"

"No. I've been staring at this for the last half-hour, and don't think I've registered one thing." Mearos touched the corner of his screen, blanking it out. "Thanks for the interruption."

"Well, don't thank me. Thank an incoming message from Dekarra. I sent it to your terminal. For your eyes only and audio only. Since when do the Dekarrans send messages a week after departure?" Pindac turned to leave.

"Don't go." Mearos reactivated his screen, retrieved the incoming communication and listened to the short piece. Concern clouded his face.

"What is it?"

"According to this, the Dekarrans are planning an attack on Zantia."

"Are you serious? Who sent that to you?"

"Well, maybe I should start from the beginning." The captain sighed and slouched back in his chair. "Have a seat. This may take a while."

Mearos waived his captain's oath of confidentiality and confided in his friend. He held nothing back: the secret room and its purpose, the true identity of the Dekarrans, Leea, and about aiding in the communication between her and Yaran. He told him about the files Leea had found, the translation Yaran had shared with him, along with what Yaran's mother had explained. Pindac listened quietly, only interrupting to ask for clarification.

"I don't know what to say," Pindac finally commented once he had had a moment to organize his thoughts.

"That's all right. I know it's a lot to take in. I would say I'm sorry for not telling you all this sooner, but there was never a reason to involve you in all the secrets and deceptions."

"Don't apologize. I'm just sorry you've had to handle this all by yourself."

Mearos shrugged. "Sadly, it's part of the job."

"You've told me your mother is Human … she's on Dekarra isn't she?"

"Yes. She visits me when our schedules allow."

Pindac chuckled. "That explains a lot of your disappearances."

"Didn't think anyone noticed."

"I don't know that anyone did, except me."

"And, you never said anything."

"No, didn't think it was any of my business."

"You're a true friend."

"A friend who wants to help. What can I do?"

"I have no idea."

# CHAPTER 25

# Council

Effortlessly, the tiny ship climbed into the atmosphere and penetrated the cloaking barrier, too fluid to raise the alarm in the planetary office. The lone occupant gave a sigh of relief; his time on this arid rock was complete.

Of all the missions that had come his way, the Belag had to admit this one was the most distasteful. Most of his jobs were clean. Find the target and carry out the assignment: eliminate, capture and return, or relocate to the edge of known space. But this one was different: find the rebel Ma'Kree, observe, and report back. Where was the fun in that? Finding them had been easy. His peoples' reputation in the universe ensured that information was readily available, so discovering the newly-named Zantians had been no problem.

Once he had located their cloaked planet—another easy feat—it took very little effort to ascertain how to penetrate the barrier, and for the first time in his life, he was mildly impressed with the enigmatic nature of his prey. He had stored his ship in a small cave at the base of the Alrack Mountains so he could observe the head of the planetary Council, and then assumed the identity of a Zantian citizen. He lucked into the job on the cargo ship, which was the perfect cover to send his updates on the rebels; this saved him from having to leave the planet regularly, which would have been an unnecessary risk.

He had thought the plan to hide his communications on an old pad in the storage room was a clever one, until the day he found the device missing. But he believed it was meant to be because it led to the discovery of the Human in the hidden room. He would much rather have toyed with the creature for a while, which would have relieved his boredom, but he rationalized it was a bad idea. The captain would have been alerted to a traitor, and the completion of his mission might have been in jeopardy. But she was being smuggled to Dekarra for some reason—a mystery he'd intended to solve. He had searched the ship's logs, as well as the captain's personal ones, but found no reference to her, so he let it go. After all, he had a reputation to consider, and a directive to obey.

Now he was on his way to meet with his new allies. Discovering the Dekarrans, who turned out to be Human, was a stroke of luck, and a revelation that still made him smile. What a marvelously devious, yet easily influenced, race. After his first delivery run to Dekarra, and their forced seclusion at the airfield, he had to check out their world for himself. He feigned an illness at the next run and took his ship to investigate the city of New Haven. Again, taking an unsuspecting form, he found his way to the government building and accessed their systems. Dekarrans were technologically primitive compared to many other species, so he had no trouble finding the secrets he was hoping for.

He had barged into Admiral Shaw's office and convinced the large man he could help them move up their timetable against the Zantians. That was the best day of this whole mission. Per his directive, he wasn't allowed to harm the rebels, but no one said he couldn't help someone else do it for him.

The admiral had eagerly showcased the moon's orbiting ship, and together they had devised a plan to refit the vessel into a warship and proceed with the attack. Now the upgrades were complete, and the most exciting part of the scheme could begin.

And then there was Bettina. What could he say about her except that she reaffirmed the reason he preferred the humanoid form. He looked forward to spending three weeks on board ship with her. It might actually relieve his boredom for a long time to come.

"I need to speak with Toref concerning one of the shipments," Mearos informed Alrack's airfield controller. "Can you have him contact me as soon as possible?"

"Is it something I can help with?"

"No. This is just something he needs to prepare for, so it's better I talk to him directly. But thank you."

"Okay, I'll have him contact you on this frequency."

"Many thanks."

In less than fifteen minutes, the console chimed, and Toref appeared on the screen.

"Mearos, is something wrong with the cargo?"

"No, the load is fine." The captain hesitated. "I apologize for asking, but are you in your office?"

"No, I'm at home."

Mearos gave a relieved sigh. "Again, I apologize—"

"Mearos, stop apologizing, what's going on? Aren't you still over a week out?"

"Yes. We just came into communications range."

"What's the problem?"

"Several days out of Dekarra I received a dispatch from Leea. It's for Yaran, but I thought you could get it to him faster. She briefly explained what it was about. The Dekarrans are launching an attack against Zantia."

"Attack?" Toref sat up straight in his chair. "What are you talking about?"

"That's all I know. I'm sending the message through. I'm sure she gives a more detailed account."


Yaran and Toref listened to Leea's warning for the second time and then looked at each other in disbelief.

"Can this be real?" Toref said trying to digest what they'd just heard.

Yaran shrugged. "She went to a lot of trouble to get this information to us, so they must believe it. And she knows about the Belag. Genad said the seeker aligned himself with a new enemy. The Dekarrans … Humans … would certainly qualify as such."

Toref nodded. "I can't believe that after all this time, it only took a single alien to uncover our whereabouts, and then reveal it to someone who wants to do us harm."

"One alien whose species specializes in finding what's well hidden."

"True. So if we're to take this seriously, then we have some work to do."

"Yes, we do. If Mearos is seven days out, then by what Leea said, we should have four weeks or so to prepare. I'll need to inform the Council as soon as possible. Where is the next meeting?"

"In Alrack, next week. I'll go with you to talk to them. You don't have to do this alone."

"Thanks, but if they throw me out, there's no reason for you to get on their bad side as well."

"I fear they will dismiss this as a hoax."

"Maybe Jarock will, but hopefully, some of the others won't."

"Let us hope." A look of pride crossed Toref face.

"What?"

"For someone who wanted nothing to do with mining, leadership, or Zantian traditions, you are taking on this challenge without hesitation. I'm proud of you."

Yaran tenderly rested a hand on his uncle's arm. "Thank you. But to be clear, I can do this because I had a good teacher."

"No, all I did was point you in the right direction, the rest is all your doing. Going up against the Council is not something I would readily take on."

"It won't be easy, but that's not going to stop me from trying. Genad said if I didn't warn the Council there would be unnecessary loss of life, and now Leea is saying the same thing. I can't ignore both their warnings."

"The leaders believe we are safe and secure behind the shield."

"Foolish old men," Yaran mumbled.

"There is a question I need to ask, though, and I don't mean to offend," Toref said.

"Oh...."

"Are you being so forceful about this because you know Leea is on that ship?"

Yaran pursed his lip and stared at the floor.

"I'm sorry if—"

Yaran waved a hand dismissively. "No, it's a valid question. I wish I could say with certainty that it didn't influence my motivation. The truth is, when she told me she was going to be on that ship, a bit of panic set in. What if something goes wrong? I can't let that happen. However, make no mistake, I will do whatever is in my power to save our people from this unwarranted attack. And if it comes down to a choice...I hope I'll have the strength to make the right one."

"Yaran, why are you here?" Lauranna embraced her son. "I'm happy to see you, of course, but with the Council here, I'm just surprised."

"Actually...I'm here to address the Council."

"You are?" She looked at him with surprise. "Why?"

Yaran told her about Leea's message. "It corresponds with what you discovered about the Belag and substantiates what Genad said to me. Those three things can't be coincident. So, I have to make them understand the urgency of what's coming."

"You will be fighting an uphill battle. You know how the membership feels about our cloak," she frowned, shaking her head.

"Well then, I'll need to change their minds."

Yaran made his way through the foyer and entered the atrium. The din of the meeting wafted through the now-open wall that typically separated it from the dining room. Yaran made his way past the fountain and looked into the modified space. Two rows of stadium seating had been pulled from the far wall, now full with seventy-six members. Forty-five more sat around the large, extended dining table. One hundred city representatives sat in attendance. Although only one family member was required at the monthly meetings, all future Desolk's were welcome—today the house was full, which was typical when the meeting took place in Alrack.

He ran his hands through his hair and pulled in a deep breath, attempting to settle his nerves, then crossed the open divider. Jarock sat at the head of the table and behind him, a large viewscreen showed statistics for one of the cities.

Not by choice, Yaran had been to these meetings on more than several occasions and knew they went city-by-city discussing mining outputs, production schedules, shipping exports, and imports at a minimum. As Yaran made his way to the front of the room, Jarock stopped in mid-sentence and then the rest of the room fell silent.

"Yaran, are you here to join us?" Haliel, the Desolk of Emborie, sitting to his father's right, asked.

"No, but I would like to address the Council."

"Yaran, we're rather busy, maybe another time," Jarock said with irritation.

"I'm afraid this can't wait. Something has come to my attention that everyone needs to hear."

The council leader leaned back, amusement replacing his annoyance. "Well, what is so important you had to interrupt these proceedings?"

Yaran clasped his hands behind his back to hide their trembling, then faced the room. "I have it on good authority that the Dekarrans are launching an attack on us and will be here in about three weeks."

"Ummm...I'm sure you realize how ridiculous that sounds," Jarock said.

"What I also know," Yaran ignored the interruption, "is that a Belag has infiltrated our planet." A low rumble resonated around the room.

"No one has infiltrated our planet," Jarock said with a condescending tone. "We have sensors and backups to those sensors. Every meteorite that hits our atmosphere is monitored and recorded. If an unidentified ship were to pass through the shield, every alarm on the planet would go off. Now, I don't know what this is about, but you've taken up enough of our time."

"Jarock, let him finish," Mearos's father, Sithan, chided from the stands.

"Fine." Jarock crossed his arms over his chest. "Say what you have to say."

"I know that people from Earth settled on Dekarra. A Belag infiltrated our world a few years ago for some unknown reason, but has now aligned himself with the Humans and is helping them plan an attack against us."

This got everyone's attention.

"The Dekarrans are looking to avenge our workers, and they seem to have found the perfect ally."

"Yaran, this reads like one of your mother's fantasy stories."

Yaran's anger rose but pushed it away. It would do no good to let his father throw him off balance. "This is not a fantasy, and—"

"And how do you know what the people on Dekarra are planning?" The committee's leader gave his son a bemused smile.

"It doesn't matter how I know."

"Oh, but it does matter."

"Yaran, what specifics do you have?" Danloc, his uncle on his mother's side, asked from the other end of the table.

"Someone named Belag, but I understand that's actually the name of its race, helped the Dekarran military upgrade their last remaining Earth vessel to improve weapons and engines. They will be bringing several hundred troops and an unknown amount of firepower. They also have something on board that will help penetrate our shield. The ship is scheduled to leave any day, with an estimated travel time of three weeks."

"They don't have anything that fast," someone from the audience said.

"Well, evidently they do now."

"And how did you acquire this information," Jarock persisted. "You're wasting this assembly's time with nonsense. You expect us to believe you, but you give no evidence that anything you say is true."

Yaran had hoped to avoid this question, but all eyes were on him waiting for an answer. "I received a communication from … Leea."

"WHAT?!" Jarock jumped out of his chair. "You come in here with some dire prediction, all based on the word of a troublemaking worker? One who mysteriously disappeared, I might add. And now you're saying she's on Dekarra and claiming there'll be an attack against us. Well, how convenient." Jarock addressed the room. "Maybe she's the one helping the riffraff on that world plot against us, and using my gullible son to make us do something rash."

Yaran balled his fists. The only other time he could recall feeling this much anger was the day he'd punched Marik—but he let the calming voice of reason take over. It would do him no good to provoke a confrontation, knowing the men in this room would quickly side with their leader, and then his effort would be for nothing.

"You're being ridiculous. What reason would she have to fabricate such a story? If she was helping them, why would she send a warning?"

Another smirk crossed Jarock's face, and Yaran knew he was being goaded. "Maybe it's a ploy. I don't suppose you'll let us listen to the message she sent you?"

He glared at his father anew. "No. I've told you everything she said."

"I bet you did...," he mumbled, retaking his seat, the grin again visible.

Yaran turned his attention back to the room. "I implore you to listen to me. People went to a great effort, and not just Leea, to get this message to me so I could warn you...something they certainly didn't have to do. There is a group on board the approaching ship, trying to stop things from the inside, but we have to prepare. You, the leaders in this room, are the best way I know how to do that. So please, don't ignore what I've told you."

"This is a waste of time," Jarock said with renewed irritation. "You've taken up enough of our time with your fantasies. Every person in this room knows our shield protects us from invaders, as it has for a century and a half. No one is looking for us; no one has found us. Now, I'd appreciate it if you would let us get back to the important business we're all here to do."

"That's how you deal with everything unpleasant, isn't it? 'I don't agree, so I close my ears, and my mind, and POOF, it no longer exists.' Typical in every aspect of your life." The sarcasm in Yaran's voice as he imitated his father's, brought a few muted chuckles.

"ENOUGH! I will not listen to any more of your insubordination."

"Oh please, spare me your indignation. I've heard a lot worse in these meetings." Yaran placed his hands of the tabletop and leaned in. "You won't listen just because it's me, right?" he seethed. "And by the way, I am NOT one of your subordinates." Yaran turned on his heel and made his way back toward the atrium.

"I do have one question," Sithan called, before Yaran was out of the room, and then grimaced at Jarock. "What makes you believe a Belag managed to find his way here?"

Yaran turned to face Mearos's father and chose his words carefully, not wanting to implicate the man's son. "On one of the cargo ships almost a year ago, incriminating files were found on an unused datapad. The files were in an alien language, which I had translated. They were accounts and locations of our cities, our leadership, and our mining activities. The addressee was unknown, but the files clearly indicated someone named Belag composed them, and also showed they were sent from the cargo ship during its scheduled runs.

"Two months ago, one of this ship's crew members failed to return to work, and further investigation revealed he had no history in any of our cities."

"What alien language?"

Yaran hesitated then finally said, "The language of the Ma'Kree."

"Impossible!"

"That can't be!"

Shouts rang throughout the room, dispelling Yaran's revelation. He glanced at Sithan, who pursed his lips and nodded briefly. Yaran took one last look toward the front of the room and thought for the first time in his life he saw fear in Jarock's eyes. He made a quick exit before anyone could ask anything further and headed for Lauranna's sitting-room, where he found her waiting with Toref.

"I am so proud of you," she pulled him into a big hug. Yaran felt the tension leave his body in the welcoming embrace and the reassuring hand his uncle laid on his shoulder.

"You heard?" Yaran asked once she let go.

"Of course. We both did. Toref arrived just as you entered the meeting." Lauranna chuckled. "I had to restrain him a few times from barging in."

"Thank you," he said to his uncle. "There were a few moments when I wasn't sure I could keep it together."

"I am so sorry you had to go through that."

Yaran rolled his eyes. "Why do I let him get to me?"

Lauranna laid a hand on her son's cheek. "You did the best you could. You knew this wouldn't be easy and that your father probably wouldn't listen."

"I know, but this just seemed spiteful. It's like he was making this about me instead of the impending attack."

"Then you'll find another way to ensure we're prepared."

"How? I can't single-handedly save the whole planet, and I wouldn't even know how." Yaran's shoulders slumped in defeat.

She smiled at him lovingly. "You underestimate yourself. And you don't have to do this alone. I can help you."

Yaran recalled the same words Genad had spoken to him and returned a wary smile. "How?"

"Not everyone in that room is sympathetic to Jarock. They show him respect because he's their leader, but they don't all agree with his tactics or principles. I know who a few of them are. You could talk to them, and I'm sure they would be willing to help you. No one wants to see this happen. And even if it turns out to be nothing, it's better to be prepared."

"You truly believe some of them might help?"

"I'm sure of it. And you can start with my brother."

"Danloc?"

"He never cared much for Jarock, even back when neither was involved in council business."

"And that never bothered you?"

"No. I love my brother, but I wasn't going to let him chose a mate for me. I was attracted to your father, and Danloc had no right to object."

"Well, I'm the last person to judge what attracts two people to each other. You really think he'll help me?"

"Well, you are his nephew after all, even if you don't see much of each other. But if nothing else, he can tell you whom on the Council you can trust. And fortunately, Danloc isn't leaving until morning. I'll see if he'll meet with you in the city tomorrow."

"Anytime, I'll be there."

Jarock sat with nine of his closest advisors in the dining room, now otherwise empty. The ten men represented the leadership's inner circle, each of them loyal to the original Ma'Kree vision, and he trusted them implicitly. While others on the Council were trustworthy, the men seated here were his confidants.

It always angered him how so many had turned away from what their forefathers had sacrificed. He had no doubt some members wanted him removed, considering him too radical for the current feelings among the populous. But luckily the remaining majority was undecided as to their society's future. And as long as he could fuel that indecision, he would continue to lead as he saw fit.

"So, what's the plan?" Haliel eyed him at the table. "Do you believe what Yaran said?"

Jarock grimaced. "About the Dekarran ship being a threat? No. Others have tried to find us and failed; this won't be any different. But it can't hurt to be cautious." He grinned. "We haven't used the planetary defense system in a long time. I think this is a good time to test it, make sure it still works, and the perfect target seems to be approaching."

"Sounds like a good plan. Can never be too cautious." One of the men said mockingly.

"So, if that ship does come, whether it knows where we are or not, I want it blown out of the sky."

The Zantian leader entered his mate's sitting room and eased into the chair next to her. The hour was late, but he didn't seem surprised to see her there.

He smiled. "You told him, didn't you?"

Lauranna studied him, still handsome even with the fine lines that now creased his forehead and the frown which was his usual expression these days. They had mated over forty years ago, and his smile could still warm her heart, which she had no doubt he knew. He always smiled brightly, as he did now when he wanted to make sure their unpleasant conversations went smoothly. "Yes, of course, I did. It was time."

"Why?" He tried hard to keep his tone pleasant.

"Because he has a right to know."

Jarock took his mate's hand and squeezed it gently, then sighed. "I will agree he was born with that right, but I don't agree it was the right thing to do."

"Why? Because you don't trust him to keep our most guarded secrets?"

"I'm not sure what I believe Yaran to do or not. Up until this point, he hasn't proven that our way of life ranks high on his list."

Lauranna tried to pull her hand away, but Jarock held it tight. She glared at him. "You base everything he does, on the mere fact that he has no interest in leadership."

"Among other things."

"And because he fell in love with a Human. When are you going to accept that there is nothing you can do to change that? And that it has nothing to do with how he feels about his responsibilities."

Jarock pulled in a deep breath. "I don't want to get into another endless discussion about the merits of our son. Tell me what you know about the Belag."

"Me?"

"You translated the text for him, didn't you?"

"So you believed him?"

"About communication from a Belag? Of course. He couldn't have made that up."

"Then why did you—?"

"If Yaran wants to dabble in the real world he needs to stand up for himself. And I have to say; he held his own fairly well."

"So it was all an act to see how he would handle himself?" she asked incredulously.

"Oh no. He had no right to address our meeting without talking to me first."

"Would you have listened to him?"

"About the Ma'Kree, yes. However, the rest of all that nonsense…no. No one is going to attack our planet. This Dekarran ship, if it does come, won't be the first to wander into our solar system looking for something, and it won't be the last. The others all went away empty handed and this one will too."

"But what about the Belag?"

"If the Belag wants to send them here, let him. He can't know how to disable the shield. Until we choose to relinquish it, the Morodons are under our control; so the shield will remain."

Lauranna lowered her eyes. "Yaran spoke to a Morodon."

"What are you talking about?"

"The one from the east mine. He somehow managed to summon Yaran and spoke with him just before he died."

Jarock's golden-brown complexion went ashen. "That's not possible."

"Evidently it is. *He* told Yaran a war was coming, and that he needed to warn our people. *He* told Yaran about the hunter, which was only substantiated by Leea."

The Zantian leader looked down, eyes darting side to side as he tried to process the information. Finally, he looked up, smiled and gently stroked her arm. "Not to worry, precautions are already in place. Now, tell me about the message."

"It was written in the old language. It was an accounting of our cities, the council structure, some of the mining operations. But nothing in any great detail. More like an overview of who we are and what we're doing."

"Who was it addressed to?

"It had no name and was only signed Belag. But there was a destination code." Having had years of practice with her mate, Lauranna hoped her face wouldn't belie the fact that she was keeping something from him. He wouldn't be happy to learn that she had given the code to Toref, who had already charted the solar system.

Jarock didn't seem to notice. "Will you give it to me?"

"Of course. Do you want all the files?"

"Yes, I think that would be a good idea." He leaned over and kissed her, lingering a moment. "How long are you going to be here?"

"I was just about finished when you walked in."

He smiled. "Good. I have a quick call to make, and then I'm turning in as well."

She simply smiled, and he left the room.

Yaran sat at a small table across from Danloc, in the same café where he'd sat with Mearos, in what seemed like a lifetime ago.

"I'm glad Lauranna suggested we meet," Danloc said. "I was hoping we would have a chance to talk. It was a brave thing you did; barge into the council meeting and stand up to Jarock in front of everyone."

"Not one of my finest moments. I feel I should have done more...said more."

"You did fine. I don't mean to make light of it, but that was the most exciting meeting we've had in, well...a very long time. I have to apologize that none of us stood up for you. There seemed to be a lot of deeper issues there, and no one wanted to interfere. Your parting words derailed any further business and forced Jarock to adjourn the meeting to douse further speculation of the Ma'Kree. However, that's not why you asked me here. Your mother said you have a plan and are looking for help."

"Let me ask you first. Do you think I'm overreacting?"

"No, not at all! Personally, I like to err on the side of caution. If this turns out to be nothing, maybe it'll be a good exercise for the people. Maybe shake everybody up a bit."

Yaran laid a pad on the tabletop. "I would have shared this with the Council, but Jarock would have torn it apart, so I didn't see the point. But I would like you to listen to it...prove that I'm not making this up."

Danloc smiled reassuringly and pushed it back toward his nephew. "There's no need. I have no doubt you're relaying everything you know."

"Will you help me then? Or at least, tell me which of the city leaders might?"

"What's your plan?"

"Toref showed me the old ship storage in the desert. I think the first thing we should do is figure out how many of them might be flight-worthy and what the status of their weapons are. We can then send them out to protect the cities before all this craziness starts. After that," he shrugged, "I don't know."

"That's a good place to begin. If we still have three weeks, we might be able to return some of them to flying status. We do regular maintenance, so it is possible. As far as trusted council members, I would start with Sithan from the House of Finetig."

Yaran chuckled. "I'm not surprised."

"Do you know him?"

"Not personally, but I know who he is. I'm friends with his eldest son."

Danloc gave him a questioning look, which quickly changed to recognition. "Mearos…the cargo ship captain."

"You know about him?"

"Although Sithan is a few years older than me, we still took some of our transition training together and became friends. He confided in me about his son when Mearos was about five. I knew his mother was Human, but he never said what happened to her."

"Sithan always struck me as someone who thought that council responsibilities were a joke."

Danloc chuckled. "That is a pretty accurate assessment. His family delegates these meetings to him, even though they know full well he hates them. So in turn, he refuses to take any of it seriously."

Yaran laughed. "I like him already. Do you think he'll help us?"

"Leave that to me. I'll talk to him. He and I will figure out whom to take into our confidence, and then get everyone together. I would say we meet at the desert depot in two days and start assessing the state of the ships."

"That's perfect. I know just the two people who can help us with that."

# CHAPTER 26

# Preparations

Bettina reclined in her overstuffed home-office chair, her tiny frame looking even smaller in the large piece. Sleep often came to her while relaxing there, and today was no different. Tucking in her legs, she closed her eyes. Scanning the videos of Leea's boring life was taking its toll on her and she'd only been at it for two hours. Typically, she delegated this chore to her hired hand, but she had sent him off on another delicate matter, so she was stuck doing it herself. Luckily, these investigations were almost at an end.

The arrival of the Belag had given the military new purpose, and now the preparations to attack Zantia were almost complete. The best part was, when they returned from this mission, she could finally go back to the private sector and let the military bask in its own glory. It's not that she didn't enjoy the perks the contract gave her and wasn't the least bit squeamish about the tasks she was required to do, but she missed her anonymity and her ability to be selective about the jobs she did.

The comm jingled on her monitor, and she activated it. "What can I do for you, Ray?"

The admiral smiled. "Never any pleasantries with you are there?"

"Pleasantries are overrated. Did you call to reprimand me on my etiquette?"

"Wouldn't waste my breath. I just wanted to let you know that I got word from Belag, and he'll be here tomorrow."

"Is everything on schedule?"

"Yes, it is. We finished loading the armaments late this afternoon, and tomorrow we'll transport the rest of the crew and the remaining provisions. And then the following day we're on our way."

"You've worked hard for this day."

"We all have, and now the dreams can be realized. How's the surveillance coming?"

"Boring as hell, and so far, nothing. The aliens have to be aware of our plans, and must be worried about their own people on Zantia, so I assumed they would enlist her help. We know she's in contact with them, but so far, nothing."

"Well, maybe they won't. This mission spooled up pretty fast so there's no way they could stop us even if they tried."

"You're probably right, but I'll keep watching until the last possible moment. Wouldn't want to miss any opportunities."

"Sounds like a good idea. I'm sure not all opportunities have passed. There will be plenty of time to continue once we return."

They disconnected, and Bettina sat back into her plush chair. 'Not all opportunities have passed.' She let the admiral's words play over in her mind. Maybe he was right. Maybe she should give it one more try. But she had to pick the precise moment, and if Leea still wouldn't give her the information she wanted, she would make sure everything came to its appropriate end.

Jackson inserted a small disc into a tabletop slot and after a swipe on an inlaid screen, a 3D image of the Atlantis floated above. He touched the hologram, and it slowly rotated, giving the eight members of the Watchers a complete view of the entire gray ship with four massive rear engines.

The top and bottom were slightly rounded and blended into straight sides that narrowed at the forward end at a bridge dome. On both sides, hundreds of portholes, arranged in five rows, took up the top three-quarters and along the bottom portion were three equally spaced maneuvering engines. At the aft end were two hangars open to both sides. The upper would hold the fifty-five fighters, the lower, transports, and shuttles. Large doors closed off the bays while in normal flight, but during battle or flight maneuvers, a force field held the atmosphere in place.

Along with the Atlantis's system upgrades, was the addition of several dozen laser cannons, scattered about the rough, riveted surface, partially retracted into the hull.

Jackson touched a flat plane at the top of the image, and the right side fell away, showing a cross section of the interior.

"A thousand people occupied these rooms during the long voyage from Earth." He indicated with a stylus to the crew decks lined with small rooms. "I can't imagine it was a comfortable trip, but it was a sacrifice they were willing to make. Luckily for us, the current mission is taking less than four hundred—all of whom believe they are on a humanitarian rescue mission. However, there is a security squad that only answers to the admiral, and who I'm sure know the true objective.

"On the top level are the command-crew quarters and various ship's stations, and the remaining four levels are the standard crew accommodations. Only the top two will be used for this operation so you can stay on the lower deck without fear of detection. Max, I'm going to give you the access codes to the ship's systems. Each level has its own code, so you'll need to disable those sensors before you can enter the level, as well as activate the environmental controls for whatever area you decide to occupy."

He swiped away the image of the Atlantis and replaced it with a black fighter with short, blended wings and a rounded sloping nose. The ship had one laser cannon on either side of the cockpit, and one missile under each wing.

"As we discussed before, your mission will be to disable the weapons through a port outside each ship." Jackson rotated the image to give them a bottom view. "Just forward of the cockpit is a two-inch square access port used for maintenance."

"Two inches?!" several voices chimed in unison.

"Isn't that the proverbial needle in a haystack?" Devon said.

"It's not as bad as it seems. The port is centered between the forward edge of the cockpit and the forward landing strut, which is only a difference of three feet. It is slightly recessed so shouldn't be too hard to find.

"You will each have an ultrasonic wrench that the maintenance crew uses. There is a unique frequency that will open the hatch, and then it's a simple matter of inserting the other end, locking it into place, and giving it a quarter turn. The implement is retractable so will fit in your pocket, or somewhere on your person."

"Won't the pilots notice that the missiles are deactivated when they're performing the flight prep?"

"Well, there is a small light on the control panel that indicates the weapons are active...but I might have failed to add that to the manual."

Snickers resonated around the table.

"Now, go home and pack your bags. The day after tomorrow we sail."

Leea opened the door, surprised to find Bettina. "What brings you here?" she asked cautiously.

"Did I catch you at a bad time? You look like you're getting ready to go out."

"Farrell is picking me up in a little while for a trip into the city," she lied.

"This won't take long." The tiny woman pushed her way into the house.

Leea tried to stay calm, unable to imagine what Bettina wanted from her at this point. She'd assumed the admiral's confidant would already be on the ship. Farrell and Jackson were due to arrive in twenty minutes so she hoped her visitor would stay true to her word.

Resigned, she sighed and closed the door. "What can I do for you, Bettina?"

"Well, here's the thing; I'm leaving for an extended business trip and will be gone for a few months."

"I hope it's somewhere exciting."

Bettina chuckled. "Probably not. But as long as the outcome is successful, it'll be worthwhile."

"Did you need me to take care of something for you while you're gone?"

"Um...no. I need some information from you."

"Oh?" Leea tensed. The only information Bettina ever wanted had to do with the Zantians. She had told her over and over that she didn't know anything— which was mostly true.

Bettina wandered into the middle of the living room. "You see, my trip...it's taking me somewhere where I'm going to need some better information on the Zantians."

*Yup, there it is.*

"Really? Where would that be?"

"That's not important. What is, is the information I need. We all know the Zantians once foraged the galaxy and took what they wanted, from whoever they wanted, with no difficulties...and you've confirmed that. But they didn't do that by simply asking; they did it by force. I find it hard to believe that they destroyed all their armaments once they decided to go into hiding. And since you worked for the head of their Council, you must have heard things."

Leea's heart began to race. Bettina's normally calm and friendly manner was now replaced by a harsh tone, plus a determined look that told Leea she wasn't going to be so easily put off with 'I don't know.' But nervousness was replaced with irritation. She had enough of these ridiculous questions.

"And as I've told you, repeatedly, I worked in that house...in the kitchen... as a servant. I did not sit in on their meetings and certainly wasn't privy to their conversations."

"But you shared a bed with the ruler's son. He must have told you a few things."

Leea chuckled sarcastically. "I did not share a bed with Yaran. And even if I had, I'm sure the state of the planet's firepower would not have been a topic of conversation. Be serious."

Bettina glowered at her. "This couldn't be more serious. Influential people on this planet want the information we know you have, and they've asked me to get it any way I can."

"What does that mean? It's going to be a little hard to force information out of me that I don't have. What about the other escapees? None of them had any answers for you?"

"The others…they were just a bunch of ignorant men who got what they deserved."

"What do you mean…got what they deserved?" Leea took a step back. "Why would you never allow me to meet them?"

"I had no choice," Bettina replied, ignoring her question. "You have no idea what those men were like…brutes, all of them. I have no doubt the aliens let them leave so they could push their problems on us."

"That's not true. The workers came here looking for a better life."

"Well, they should have been happy with the one they had." She chuckled. "One of those misfits thought he could grope me right there in the car. But he wasn't so smug when I took off my hood and plunged a knife into his heart. My Human face was the last thing he saw."

Leea felt the blood drain from her face. "S… So if I hadn't worked in a ruling house, you'd have what…killed me too?" Leea walked over to the half-wall between her living and dining room, suddenly needing something to hold on to.

"No. Those other men were fools and troublemakers, neither applied to you. You were the first woman to come through the escape network, and when we found out where you had lived, it was a bonus."

Leea shuddered. "I've told you everything I know…that's the truth."

"It's unfortunate you think so." Bettina pulled a small pistol from her pocket along with a thin, slightly curved metal strip with what looked like tiny bulbs along one edge. "But I have a proposition for you. While I'm sure you know more about the Zantians than you're telling, I'll take some other information you have instead."

"What would that be?"

"Tell me where the Morodons' home is."

Startled, Leea pause for an instant. "Who? I don't know who you're talking about."

"You're a horrible liar, Leea. But it doesn't matter. You should know that I've been conducting surveillance on this house since the day you got here, as well as had you followed. I've seen your comings and goings. I know you've been up to the mountains and visited with them… more than once. They are the most valuable export this planet has, but also the most elusive. Tell me where they live and everything else will be forgiven."

"You've been watching me?"

"Of course. Did you really think we're going to let someone who lived among our enemy roam free without making sure there wasn't some ulterior motive?"

Leea glared at her. This was Marik all over again. Why couldn't crazy people just leave her alone? "You're insane. I'm not telling you anything."

"Then I'm afraid I'm going to have to try a little persuasion before I decide what to do with you." She held up the metal strip. "This won't kill you, but I can't promise it'll be pleasant. It's only meant to loosen up the memory cells, but there have been some unexpected side effects."

As panic slowly rose inside her, she inched a few steps toward the kitchen and grabbed the *jarkut* around her neck. "You can prod me all you want, but that's still not going to get you any answers."

Bettina laughed humorously. "Don't waste your time with that trinket. It doesn't work on me. And, I'm not going to kill you… at least not yet."

Leea let the necklace fall back into place. "Why doesn't it work on you?" she asked hesitantly. She remembered Nethas's words when the Morodon had given it to her: '*Beware of those over whom the* jarkut *has no power.*' She had never asked for an explanation, thinking she would never need the talisman anyway.

As if reading her mind, Bettina continued. "Your friends apparently failed to mention that the *jarkut* cannot counteract evil intentions. While I don't consider what I do evil… only necessary… those rocks seem to have a different interpretation."

"Why are you doing this?" Leea was no longer able to hide her trepidation.

"Because that's what they pay me for. Quite nicely, I might add, so I hate to disappoint."

"And again I ask; how are you going to get me to tell you something I don't know? Do you want me to lie and make something up? Earth was one of the last planets the Zantians plundered. Since then, they hide behind their shield. Whatever they did with their armaments or their ships, I have no idea. As far as the Morodons go, I don't know what you're talking about. If you had me followed, then you know that I spent time in the woods alone… nothing more."

"You're lying again. You were gone far too many hours to be hanging out in the woods all by yourself."

"The facts are not going to change just because you, or someone with power, thinks they should. And why this dire need to know now?"

"That's nothing for you to be concerned about," Bettina said curtly.

At this point, Leea had managed to back up far enough to stand next to her small dining table. *If I can get out of here, and make it to the woods, I can get away from her,* she thought desperately. She cut a glance to the tabletop and eyed the datapad she'd set down earlier. Before her brain could even form a cohesive plan, her hand plucked up the pad and flung it at Bettina, slicing it through the air like a saucer, and then ran for the door.

Bettina cursed behind her and discharged the laser pistol. The energy stream barely missed Leea's ear, as she dashed through, slamming the door behind her. She ran as fast as her long legs would carry her until she was well past the tree-line and stopped behind a large trunk. Catching her breath, she waited.

"Leea, you're only making this more difficult for yourself. I promise not to hurt you if you come out willingly." The short blond woman took a few steps further into the woods and listened intently. "Look, let's go back inside and talk this out. There is no reason to be afraid. Hiding in the woods is silly. You'll have to come out at some point, so why waste any more time for either of us."

Leea didn't believe one word Bettina said. Like Leea herself, Bettina wanted to be on the Atlantis when it departed, so she would eventually have to leave. *Can I wait her out? Farrell and Jackson will be here soon. Will they be able to help me?* It was now a waiting game.

"Come on, Leea. I don't want to come in there looking for you."

"Not that you'd have any chance of finding her. So why not give up now?"

Startled, Bettina turned her head toward the familiar voice. "Mary, what are you doing here?"

Mary wiggled a pistol. "Well, a greeter came chirping at my window excited about something, so I came out to see what the problem was. Imagine my surprise when I saw Leea rushing into the forest and you chasing after her. It's a good thing I own one of these," she thrust her gun toward Bettina and took a step forward. "You see, I don't share Leea's love for this forest, and have this in case I need to defend myself from some wild animal. And now here we are in the woods, and you hunting my friend. I guess the animals I should have been afraid of were the two-legged kind."

"Mary, you don't know what you're getting involved in," Bettina snarled. "You need to go back into the house and let me take care of my business."

"But I'm already involved. You moved Leea next door to me under the pretense that she needed a friend. Which I was happy to be after I met her; she's a sweet young woman who's been through a horrible ordeal. But then you continually came to my office, as well as my home, asking all sorts of questions about what we talk about. And when I asked you why, you evaded my questions. So you've made it my business. I won't stand back and let people hurt my friends."

"You don't want to go up against me."

"Hmmm… Maybe I do. You see, my gun is aimed at your head, and yours is pointed at a tree. Did I mention I'm a pretty good shot?"

A hard object pressed into Mary's back. "Toss it away," the deep voice of the associate said menacingly behind her. Mary hesitated but did as she was told.

"What took you so long?" Bettina scolded her accomplice, but he didn't answer.

"Run and hide, Leea, run!" A painful jab into her back sent Mary to her knees. "I suggest you shut up before I make you." Again, Mary did as she was told, a slight smile playing on her lips.

"Guard this one," Bettina ordered her companion. "Should we get any more visitors, shoot them. I've had enough of this. I'm going to go find our troublesome girl, and then we'll clean up this mess." She disappeared into the trees.

The associate roughly pulled Mary back to her feet, stuck his gun into her ribs, and then clamped a hand tightly on her arm as they waited in silence.

"Leea, are you out here?" A voice shouted from the back door a minute later.

"Be still," the man whispered behind his captive, forcing the gun deeper into her back and digging his fingers into her arm. The sun was waning fast, so they were well hidden in the shadows.

Mary paused a moment. "I don't think so." With one swift motion, she kicked back as hard as she could with her right foot, finding her intended target—the man's knee. She jumped out of the way as he doubled over in pain, discharging his energy weapon wildly.

"We're over here!" Mary called, "just inside the tree-line." Before the man could recover, she scrambled for her gun, turned, and shot him in the right arm. He looked at his wound incredulously.

"Yes, that's right," she said with a chuckle. "Bullets. Genuine, old-fashion bullets. None of that laser stuff for me."

Leea ran deeper into the cover of the trees. Inky blackness descended over the forest as the sun slipped away. But she wasn't worried. It had been a cloudless day and within a few minutes, the full Sirius moon would lighten the sky over New Haven. The animals had taken refuge with all the noise the people were making, so the rustling of the underbrush not far away told her Bettina was in pursuit.

A shot rang out in the distance, and Leea felt her heart sink. *Mary.* She silently prayed that her friend was all right. But if Bettina was following her in the woods, that meant she had accomplices—Leea wondered how many. *This has got to stop,* she thought, *Bettina is right, this is just a waste of time.* Not that she was afraid to go deeper into the trees; she actually welcomed that option, but was worried about her neighbor and what would happen when Farrell and Jackson showed up. She didn't want to put anyone else in danger. She stepped out into the open.

She heard chirping and looked up to see her greeter agitatedly rocking on a branch.

"The *jarkut* will protect you," a voice resonated in her head. She found the intrusion into her mind disconcerting but welcomed it just the same. Leea wrapped her hand around the mysterious pendant.

"I wish it hadn't come to this," Bettina said, emerging from the trees fifteen feet away, gun in hand, seeming genuinely sad. The light of the moon played on her almost white hair.

"This is your choice. You don't have to do this."

"Unfortunately, I do, and I'm out of time." She fired.

Leea clutched the *jarkut* and raised her other hand defensively. The talisman burned as it had done the day it bonded with her, but she held tight and concentrated. Suddenly, everything moved in slow motion. The minimal sound of the discharging weapon echoed loudly all around as she focused on the energy beam. The light-stream glided slowly from its openings on a path aimed at her chest. About two feet from her outstretched hand, its forward trajectory stopped, as if hitting an invisible wall. Leea willed it back in the opposite direction, catching Bettina off guard.

In what seemed like minutes, but could only have been a fraction of a second, the beam struck the weapon, causing it to explode. Bettina screamed and clutched at her scorched hand, before dropping to her knees.

Regaining a sense of reality, Leea walked over and looked down at the writhing figure. "Well, the *jarkut* may not have any power over you, but it does on your weapon."

"Leea!"

"Over here," she called, relieved at the sound of the familiar voice.

Farrell and Jackson appeared through the darkness behind a portable light. Each took in the groaning figure of Bettina, then Farrell rushed to her friend, pulling her into a grateful hug.

"Are you all right?"

The fear and dread that Leea had ignored suddenly bubbled to the surface like a volcano, and she burst into tears. "I was so scared," she sobbed, finding comfort in the embrace.

"It's okay. It's over." Farrell rubbed her back reassuringly.

"Is Mary okay? I heard a loud bang."

"She's fine. She's guarding Bettina's friend." She then explained what had happened at the tree-line.

"What are we going to do with her?" Jackson asked, pointing to the whimpering figure on the ground. "We really should get her to a doctor."

"If you will allow, we will take care of her." Emerging from the trees was Tellia, followed by four hooded Morodons.

"How did you get here so fast?" Leea asked, wiping at her wet cheeks. "I only heard your voice a few minutes ago."

Farrell and Jackson looked at their friend quizzically then back to Tellia, who simply smiled but offered no further explanation.

"We will attend to her wounds, and that of her accomplice, and then turn them over to the authorities at the appropriate time."

"That would be wonderful. We have to hurry before the admiral starts wondering where I am. What's that?" Jackson pointed to the three-foot container with several cutouts that Tellia carried.

"We would appreciate it if you would take this with you." She handed it to Jackson.

All three peered inside as Jackson opened the picnic-basket style lid to reveal a small greeter, and then looked at Tellia confused. "I don't understand," he said.

"Set it free on the ship. It will find a hiding place and observe. Food is in the bottom compartment, just be sure there is available water. We have asked her to communicate with our brother once you have freed him from the stasis chamber. If it becomes necessary, she can find our missing people the others have lost contact with on the Zantian surface."

"But how can she survive on Zantia?" Leea asked.

"She is not asking to survive, only to help."

"I don't suppose you could tell us if we'll be successful?"

Tellia smiled and shook her head. "What I can say for certain is that no outcome has been revealed. In this type of situation, the result may not be known until the final moment."

"We have to go," Jackson urged. "I guess you'll miss your ride," he said sarcastically as two Morodons pulled Bettina to her feet.

"You'll never get away with this," she sneered. The portable light showed that her fair complexion had changed to a pasty pallor as she clutched the injured hand to her chest."

Jackson smirked. "I think we already have."

With Leea in the lead, the group quickly made their way out of the forest. They gave a brief explanation to a shocked Mary, and then Leea gave her neighbor a big hug, promising to explain everything once she returned.

The refugee hoped with all her heart that she would be able to keep that promise.

Jackson maneuvered the large shuttle into the lower hangar deck, parked it tail-end into an empty spot next to five others, and powered down the engines. Once the vehicle was secured, he made his way to the back where the eight occupants sat in awe of the journey they'd just completed—he recognized the look.

"Space, the final frontier...."

He laughed at the baffled faces looking back at him, then shrugged. "Never mind, I saw that in an old movie once. The shuttles on this deck won't be used again until we reach Zantia, so everyone should be safe down here. A stairway, and elevator, at the other end of this wall, will take you up to the crew quarters." He pulled two containers from under a bank of seats. "I grabbed these boxes of uniforms and maintenance overalls. Hopefully, everyone will find several pairs of each in their size.

"Max has all the codes for the lower level as well as a security badge for everyone. Now, these badges are fake. NEVER let anyone scan them. Clip them to your pocket, and you should be able to blend in as long as you keep your presence around the ship to a minimum. Find a quiet time to venture up to the fighter deck and take a look at the layout.

"We'll be departing in about three hours, and I'm sure the admiral is already in a panic because I'm not there," he chuckled. "I'll get word to you once we're two days out from Zantia so you can finalize your plans. Good luck."

Jackson opened the shuttle's side door and waited for the steps to lock in place, but then jumped past them down to the hangar floor. He waved for Farrell to follow him, and the couple disappeared behind the rear of the small ship. They held each other tightly and lost themselves in a deep kiss.

"Be careful," Jackson said breathlessly, looking deep into her blue eyes. "I'll never forgive myself if something happens to you."

She stroked his cheek. "I'll be fine. I have no intention of putting myself in harm's way. But the same goes for you. Don't let the pompous ass assimilate you into his new world order."

Jackson smiled. "If that happens, I'll just shoot myself… save you the trouble of doing it for me."

"You know me so well," she grinned. "That's why I love you."

"I love you more."

She took a deep breath and pushed him away. "Go, get out of here."

Jackson moved to the front of the shuttle, then out into the open bay. He looked around, determined all was clear and rapped on the shuttle's hull three times. He gave a final wave to Farrell, who stood watching him, and disappeared.


"I was beginning to think you got lost," the Admiral's deep voice resonated as Jackson stepped through the automatic doors, hurrying to the helm.

"Sorry. I had to stop by my quarters and drop off my stuff."

"Did Bettina come up with you?"

"She never showed. I waited as long as I could, per your orders, so I thought maybe she caught an earlier flight."

The burly man rose out of the center chair and disappeared into one of the conference rooms

"Well, Captain," one of the science officers whispered loudly, giving him a sideways grin. "Looks like we're going to start this journey on a sour note. Not sure what the admiral will do without his sidekick."

"Well you know, her hair appointment probably ran late, and she just expected I'd wait for her."

Snickers resonated from the bridge crew. Jackson had spent the last weeks with the ten-member crew, as they had all been part of the shakedown runs. He liked them all which made it hard to comprehend how a group of seemingly decent people could have sold their soul to the egomaniac in the center chair.

# CHAPTER 27

# The Ship

Leea slipped into the stairwell and headed up to the command level. She needed coffee and hoped the mess hall would still be empty. She hadn't slept well the last few days, attributing it to their nearness to Zantia and the upcoming effort to sabotage part of the admiral's plan. Tomorrow evening, she would be home. It amazed her that she still considered it home, but she knew she always would.

On deck five she exited the stairs—right into the arms of a man in a security uniform. She wore her maintenance coveralls, and her auburn hair was pulled up, keeping with the standard style of all the women on the ship, but she had gratefully left her badge in the room.

"Oh, sorry, not quite awake yet," Leea smiled moving around him, but he held out a hand to stop her. He was a couple of inches shorter than her and his uniform strained over the bulge of his muscles. She couldn't tell the exact color of his close-cropped hair, but his hard brown eyes were unmistakable.

"Excuse me, who are you?" He cast a look over her body, taking in the uniform, eyes resting on the emblem sewn over the left breast pocket.

Dread immediately coursed through her. "Part of the maintenance crew. Sir." She pointed to the logo matter-of-factly, hoping the confidence she was trying to project came through in her voice.

"I don't recall ever seeing you before."

"I signed on just before we left," she said nervously. "Guess you can't be expected to recognize everyone."

He looked at her menacingly. "Actually, I can. You see, I command the security unit. It's my job to know all the ship's crew. Maybe not by name, but certainly by sight, and I've never seen you before. And to be clear… *no one* signed on just before we departed."

"Well, you're obviously mistaken." Leea attempted to push past him again, but he grabbed her arm.

Leea wished she had her *jarkut*. The amulet was tucked away with her things, not appropriate with the military uniform, but she wasn't even sure it would work away from Dekarra. She tried to pull out of his grip, but the commander forcefully twisted her arm behind her back and pushed her forward. "Maybe the brig will help you remember who you are."

*How could I have been so stupid?* she chastised herself. The man led her aft, past the mess hall and into a small annex that held three eight-by-twelve cells. He unceremoniously shoved her into the first one, activated an electronic field, and left without further comment. Leea gingerly raised a hand to the invisible barrier. A few inches away her fingers started to tingle, and she quickly pulled back.

"Stupid! Stupid! Stupid!" She yelled at herself and dropped onto the narrow cot, resting her head in her hands. It wasn't bad enough that she was a prisoner, but she had left Farrell asleep so no one would know what happened to her.

Within the next half-hour someone came and took a DNA sample, and shortly after that, the first of two interrogators arrived.

"What's your name?"

"Sara Miller." It was the name on her ID badge.

"We can't find anyone with your DNA in our system. How do you explain that… Sara?"

"Maybe you should keep better records."

He ignored her flippant remark. "How did you get on this ship?"

"On a shuttle, just like everyone else."

"Enough of this. I talked to the maintenance lieutenant and showed him your picture. No surprise, he's never seen you before."

Leea shrugged and smiled. "Okay, you're right, I'm not part of this crew, but I did find my way onto a shuttle."

"Why?"

"Because I've always wanted to go into space. Thought this was the perfect opportunity."

"How did you hear about this ship?"

"Hmmm… I think it involved soldiers, a bar, and lots of alcohol."

"Where did you find the uniform?"

"I took it from someone's room."

"You're making all this up aren't you?"

"I don't know, am I?"

He asked the same questions a hundred different ways, but Leea managed to keep up her nonchalant attitude until visible anger took over the man and he stormed out.

The second man came about an hour later. The questions were the same, but this officer was threatening, claiming she would never see the light of day again if she didn't start telling the truth. But Leea held to her story, and eventually, he too went away, although with a little more grace than the first one. At some point, someone brought a tray of food, but Leea had no appetite and left it on the small table by the door. Instead, she lay down on the cot and closed her eyes, suddenly tired. It had been a long morning, and she never got her coffee.

A buzzing sound brought her out of the fog. It wasn't a constant buzz, but a random beat. She opened her eyes, looked around, and abruptly sat up. On the other side of the barrier, someone stood watching her, tapping a finger against the energy field.

Fear gripped her as she studied the bald visitor. Its facial features were distinct: eyes, nose, mouth, ears, but somehow they didn't form a cohesive look. It was as if they'd been placed without much thought to their exact location. The figure didn't wear the standard black uniform, but instead, a green mesh jumpsuit with fibers that shimmered in the light.

"Who…who are you?" She got to her feet and moved back to the end of the cot.

"The more intriguing question would be," came a soft, whispery voice, "who are you?" The alien face smiled, showing small white teeth. "But then, I know who you are. Should I tell them?"

"I… I don't know what you're talking about."

"Oh, come now, no reason to be coy. My friend Bettina, who for some unexplainable reason missed this trip, told me all about you…the girl from Zantia. But she never mentioned you came off a cargo ship." Its eyes fluttered almost indiscernibly. In the same instant, the facial features seemed to go fluid as they rearranged themselves, shimmered, before solidifying into the face of a Zantian. His body was now muscular, and he stood about six inches taller than before. The green jumpsuit was replaced with a dark gray one, similar to the one Mearos had worn. "Maybe this form will explain better?" A deep voice resonated as the gray eyes drilled into her.

"Who…how…?"

"You don't recognize me? Did my captain *really* never let you out of your little cage except to look at the stars?"

"You were on the cargo ship?"

"Yes. And you took my datapad."

Realization set in. "You wrote the files I found?"

"Imagine my annoyance when I went looking for that pad and found it gone. I was getting ready to leave the storage area when my *captain* came down the stairs. And imagine my surprise when I watched him open your door. I stayed back to observe, and moments later he came out with you, and then you made your touching little visit to the porthole.

"I almost took my displeasure out on you. I desperately wanted to come into your cell after he left…have a little fun. But as much as that excited me…the consequences wouldn't have been worth the momentary enjoyment. Mearos would have realized he had a traitor on board, and that would have led to an extensive investigation. Sadly, I still had some work to do. And not to mention, my mission directive specifically states 'no harm will come to anyone during my observance.' So, lucky for you, I wasn't ready to cross that line just for sport. And now here we are again. I made the right choice to leave you alone that day…this is so much better."

Leea felt the blood drain from her face. "Are…are you here to kill me?"

Dejected, he lowered his head. "No, my directive stands." Then his eyes brightened. "But no one said I can't have a little fun." As he had done a minute earlier, his eyes seemed to lose focus for a brief moment before the Zantian was replaced by Leea herself. Her hands flew to her mouth as a cry escaped her lips. Her duplicate looked just like she had on Mearos's ship, even the same clothes.

"How…how is that possible?" She felt dizzy and sank onto the cot.

The alien shrugged. "The mysteries of the universe are hard to explain." The duplicate glanced down at her attire. "I guess your look has improved."

Leea laughed with a touch of hysteria. "I don't think you'll fool anyone with that voice." It was still the male voice of the previous form.

"Oh, that is so easily fixable." He lifted his right hand, palm out, and concentrated a moment before stepping through the energy field. "You see, to replicate you, all I need is to absorb your DNA from something you've touched. To get more specific details, like your voice, and even your language, I have to touch you."

Leea jumped off the cot and scrambled to the far corner of the cell. She screamed for help.

"Don't waste your breath. There's no one around to hear you. But as I already told you, I'm not here to hurt you."

Pressing herself into the corner, Leea closed her eyes, tears escaping the corners.

"No need for tears."

She opened her eyes and flinched. The alien stood less than a foot away, presenting a bright toothy smile. Her duplicate leaned in, cupped her face and kissed her on the lips, its tongue trying to push its way into her mouth. Leea squirmed and unsuccessfully tried to push the alien away.

The Belag laughed out loud. "That wasn't so bad, was it? Bettina never complained, no matter what form I took." Her own voice now emanated from the shape-shifter and it wore her current uniform as well.

Leea shuddered and was grateful she'd left breakfast by the door. "Why are you doing this? Why would you want to be me? I'm in jail."

"Yes, you do seem to like being in a cell." The other chuckled. "But you see, unlike the fools who interrogated you, I know you didn't get this far by yourself, which means you have accomplices. And with this form, I can find them and put a stop to whatever your grand plan might be. You see, I went to a lot of trouble to organize this little adventure. You and your band of rebels are not going to spoil the fun I have planned."

"I'm not here with anyone. It's just me. Yes, I came from Zantia and wanted to go back. I have friends and loved ones I want to see again. I would do anything to see them again, even stow away on this ship. That's the only reason I'm here. You're wasting your time looking for anyone else."

The duplicate cupped Leea's face again and gave a mournful groan. "My dear, I think your rambling protests reveal a different truth." It kissed her gently on the cheek. "Stay safely tucked in here while I go ensure that what I've arranged stays on track. It shouldn't be too hard to find what lonely corner of this ship your group is hiding in. There are only a few places where the crew doesn't go."

The alien walked back through the energy field and out the door.

Leea slid to the floor and let the tears flow freely. *What have I done?* When her tears dried, she calmly took stock of her situation, and an idea started to form.

They had searched her for weapons but hadn't gone so far as searching her bra, where she had hidden the ultrasonic wrench. The Watchers had all kept the tool on their person, in case they couldn't return to the rooms for some reason.

Leea removed the implement and extended it to its full length of about ten inches. The ultrasonic feature wouldn't do her any good, but the other end of the tool could be used for small jobs. It was light weight, so useless as a weapon, but maybe she could dismantle something to use instead.

She checked outside her cell, making sure all was clear, then scanned the small room. The cot was securely bolted to the floor, and trying to disassemble it would be too risky, but there was a partition in the back that hid a toilet and sink. Moving behind it, Leea examined the fibrous material of the far wall, finding it pliable enough to damage.

Taking the wrench in both hands, she stood sideways and slammed the pointed end as hard as she could into the wall. It made a dent but didn't break through. After several tries, a small hole formed. Periodically checking to make sure her efforts weren't attracting attention, Leea continued working until she had an opening big enough to put both arms through.

Inside were pipes that plumbed the sink and toilet, and she gave a sigh of relief when she spotted two fittings within reach on the drain line. Checking the annex one more time, Leea set to work removing the pipe. She wished she had a laser cutter instead, but with a little work, the narrow teeth of the wrench began loosening the joints. She made a mental note to thank Jeffrey next time she saw him for teaching her how to use basic tools.

She only had to stop her efforts once, when someone brought her a dinner tray, but finally, the two-foot section came loose. She retracted the wrench, returned it to its hiding place, and carefully took another peek around the partition. Now the hard part. She'd solidified her plan while she worked, something she'd seen in one of the old movies, and hoped she could pull it off as well as the on-screen actress had. Now it just required her to wait.

After nervously sitting on the cot for what seemed like hours, the annex door opened. Quickly she lay down facing the wall, clutching the pipe to her chest and pulling up her knees. When she heard the distinct sound of footsteps outside her cell, she moaned. The person stopped, and she moaned again…this time louder.

"What's the matter?" the guard asked with disinterest.

She moaned again, then as weakly as possible said, "I'm sick, you guys are trying to poison me."

"That's ridiculous. There's nothing wrong with the food." He looked over at the empty plate.

Leea moaned again and curled up as best she could. "I think I'm going to be sick. Can you help me?"

When the guard hesitated, Leea groaned louder. After a brief moment, she heard the buzz of the force field go silent. As the guard turned to reactivate the barrier from inside, Leea leaped off the cot, pipe in hand, and hit him across the back of the head. Startled, he spun around. Leea hit him again, and he slumped to the floor. She quickly grabbed his access card and weapon, putting both in her pocket, then struggled to pull the unconscious man onto the cot, finally managing to roll him over and face the wall.

After reactivating the force field, she cautiously stuck her head out the brig door and looked both ways. The corridor was clear. She slipped out and headed for the stairwell.

She flew down the steps to the lower crew deck but found all their rooms empty. The only other place the Watchers would go was the shuttle bay. With the big event approaching, they were most likely planning their strategy for the fighters.

Entering the large area, Leea made her way slowly along the wall behind the shuttles. Rounding the last one, she heard muted voices and peered cautiously into the open area. Four of the Watchers stood with her duplicate.

"We were so worried about you," Farrell said, giving the shape-shifter a big hug. "I can't believe you got locked in a storage room."

"Me neither," the alien lied, rolling her eyes. "It was the stupidest thing… going in the wrong door and having it lock behind me. I was lucky the guy who let me out wasn't too bright. I told him if I didn't get to the bathroom soon we would all drown. He laughed as I rushed by."

They all joined in the laughter.

"So, what's the plan? Have you figured out all the details?" the impostor asked.

"Well, we've been so worried about you, we haven't had a chance to decide anything. But now that you're here—"

"STOP! Don't tell it anything!"

The Watchers stared in disbelief as another Leea hurried out from behind the shuttle.

"What the…?" they all seemed to say at once, looking from one to the other.

"Don't say anything, she's an imposter," Leea urged.

"WHAT! NO! It's me, guys, she's the imposter," the Belag implored.

They all took a few steps back, leaving the two standing alone.

The duplicate looked at the four stowaways. "It's me, how would I have known where to find you?"

Leea pointed to the alien. "This is the Belag. It wants to know what our plans are. Listen to me—" At that moment, fluttering sounded above their heads. They all looked up as the small greeter descended and floated over Leea's shoulder.

"Leea?"

"Yes, it's me," she said relieved, running to her friends. "It's a shape-shifter, who's helping—"

"Look out!!" Max shouted, but it was too late.

"You had to spoil my fun," the whispery voice said with a touch of annoyance.

Leea turned just as the alien changed to its original form and a split second before she heard the click of a weapon.

And then she was spinning.

Farrell seemed to scream from miles away as arms grabbed her and eased her to the floor. Only then did her brain register the excruciating burning sensation in her left shoulder. Her arm was on fire, and so was her chest. Looking down, she watched with detachment at the dark stain that slowly spread over the fabric of the coveralls. The edges of the world started to turn black, and she looked up questioningly into the horrified faces that hovered above her. She had one final thought before it all completely disappeared—*I was so close, Yaran.*

"Oh God! Leea!" Farrell was on her knees.

"MOVE!" Ben McAdams gently pushed her out of the way and knelt over the unconscious woman. He ripped open the maintenance uniform and examined the gushing wound. "We have to stop the bleeding." He took off his shirt, wadded it up, grabbed Farrell's hand and pressed it to the wound.

"Where did everybody go?" Ben surveyed the empty cargo hold.

"They went after the other…Leea…or whatever that was."

A few minutes later, Max and Devon Greene reappeared.

"It got away," Max said before anyone could ask. "We went as far as we dared before turning back, but it disappeared into the fighter bay." He knelt beside Leea. "How is she?"

"We have to get her to the med-bay," Ben said with urgency. "There isn't much I can do with a wound like this. By the sound, I think it was an energy-bolt weapon. If the bolt makes its way to her lungs, we're already too late."

"We need to contact Jackson," Farrell said, trying to keep her voice steady. "He could get help for her."

"You know we can't do that," Max said. "If we blow Jackson's cover, all this will have been for nothing. We're so close."

"We have to help her; she's losing a lot of blood," Farrell pleaded, her voice rising. The shirt she pressed against Leea's shoulder was already soaking through.

Max ran to the information panel near the stairwell and touched the screen. "Medical," he demanded when the screen lit up. A map appeared, showing the medical facility on the upper deck, just above the fighter bay. "Damn," he swore under his breath. "Well, looks like we're going to have to kidnap us a doctor."

The three men made their way along the empty corridor. The hour was late, and the crew was most likely getting their last restful night's sleep before the attack. The Watchers had carefully moved Leea into a storage room off the hold, not knowing how long it would take to find the medical personnel. Her pale complexion told them they needed to hurry.

"It should be up ahead," Max said to his two companions.

Devon, being the only experienced marksman in the group, fingered the guard's weapon in his pocket that he'd taken from Leea. With Ben in the lead, they moved through the automated doors into the stark white room.

"Can I help you?" Dr. Will Bennett sat at a nearby desk hunched over a computer busily entering data. He wore a white coat over his black uniform but didn't look up. The new arrivals made a quick survey of the facility finding it otherwise empty.

"We need to see the doctor," Ben said.

"That would be me." The physician still didn't look up.

"We have an injured friend."

This finally got his attention. "Where is he?" The doctor scrutinized the three men. "Why didn't you bring him here?"

"The injury is too extensive. We didn't think it would be a good idea."

"Why didn't you call?" He got to his feet. "What do you expect me to do from here?" He reached for the communications console sitting on the desk, but Ben grabbed his arm.

"No. You're not going to call anyone."

Will Bennett looked at them suspiciously. "I need to call a nurse and get a gurney."

"Just you. Bring your medical kit and come with us," Ben said impatiently.

"That's not how this works."

Devon moved forward and withdrew the pistol but stopped short of pointing it at him. "You're going to have to make an exception this time."

"Wh… what is this?"

Ben ignored the question. "You'll need a trauma kit, a portable regenerator, and blood enhancers."

"What are you… a want-to-be doctor?" the physician said sarcastically.

"I'm a paramedic, so I know what we need." Ben turned toward Devon. "Keep him here. I'm sure I can find what to bring."

"Hey, wait a minute! I don't want you rummaging around in my things… even for a *paramedic*. And why should I help you?"

"Look," Ben turned back. "We need your help. We have no intention of hurting you, but we'll do whatever we have to."

The doctor studied him for a split second. "Fine. Let me pack my bag."

The ship's medical officer ran the scanner over Leea's shoulder, along her arm and chest area. He moved it back to her shoulder, then manipulated something on the scanner's screen. After a moment, it beeped. He looked at it quizzically and made another adjustment. When it beeped a second time, he still seemed perplexed.

"So, I have good news, bad news, and worse news. First, you should have told me this was an energy-bolt wound. The good news is the bolt missed her lung. The bad news is it still did a lot of damage before lodging in her shoulder joint."

"But, she'll be okay, right?" Farrell asked hopefully.

"The worse news is, she's lost too much blood and has gone into shock, and I can't seem to deactivate the projectile. Meaning, the blood enhancers won't be enough to help her. She's going to need a direct transfusion, but we don't have a blood supply on board, so someone will need to donate. Don't suppose any of you know your blood type?"

"You can check that, right?"

"If you give me your name I'll look at your chart." The doctor watched them all exchange glances. "But no matter, I can do a quick scan. So, now the other thing: removing the bolt and repairing the damage can't be done with any portable equipment. Look, I don't know what's going on here, and I don't want to know. But if you want your friend to live, I need to get her to the regeneration bed soon, or nothing we do will matter."

They all seemed to ponder the decision.

"What? Are you afraid of ending up in the brig?"

They looked at him questioningly.

"Look, I may only be a doctor, but I do recognize a guard blaster when it's pointed at me," Will said, misinterpreting their silence. "I don't know how you got it, probably the same way you got me, and again I don't care, but what I don't understand is why you have a blaster, but your friend was shot with an energy bolt. I didn't realize we had any of those on board."

They all remained silent.

The doctor rolled his eyes. "Why is everyone on this ship so anxious to start shooting people?" he muttered, more to himself than the others.

"You don't approve of the impending attack?" Farrell asked cautiously.

Fear flashed briefly across his dark face, but he returned his attention to Leea without commenting.

Max blew out a breath. "We appreciate your help, but we have a mission here that's not quite complete. Nothing can stop that from happening."

"Look! We all have a mission here. I'll make you a deal. You help me get her up to the med-bay so I can treat her, and I won't report any of you. Deal? That way none of you will miss out on the festivities."

Farrell wanted to tell the doctor, whose name no one had bother to ask, that he was wrong about them, but now wasn't the time. Maybe she was reading him wrong, but she had the feeling he wasn't overjoyed with the attack about to happen either.

Dr. Bennett sent Ben to the med-bay to get a backboard, saying it would be less conspicuous than a gurney, then patched up his patient as best he could, injected her with the blood enhancement serum. When Leea was ready to move, the four Watchers carried her to the medical bay using a rear service elevator.

Once they had her on an examining table, Max, Devon, and Ben retreated, but Farrell refused to leave, saying she would stay until she knew her friend would be okay. None of the four had the correct blood type, so the doctor searched his database and summoned two crew members to donate.

While he waited for the donations to complete, the doctor removed the energy-bolt from Leea's shoulder. He showed it to Farrell, and she was amazed how something so small, no more than a sixteenth of an inch long, and no thicker than the tip of a sewing needle, could do so much damage.

"The problem isn't the small projectile," the physician explained, "but the energy it's charged with. This causes it to spin and rotate inside the body for as long as the charge lasts. Which, depending on the weapon, could be up to five minutes. Killing the victim long before help can arrive."

She shuddered.

"You know what else I can tell you about this piece?" He held the minuscule object with plastic coated tweezers. He moved some boxes aside on a metal table and dropped it. Hitting the surface, it sparked and jumped an inch off the table before coming to rest. "This bolt is still active, even though I should have been able to deactivate it."

"I don't understand."

"For obvious humanitarian reasons, energy-bolts have a deactivation code which is programmed into all medical scanners. But it didn't work on this one because we didn't make it."

"What do you mean?"

"I think you know exactly what I mean. The look on your face is a dead giveaway, and that's why all the secrecy. We acquired energy-bolt technology from the Zantians decades ago. But we've never been able to produce something that holds this long of a charge. And it doesn't have a known deactivation code. I don't suppose you want to explain that?"

Farrell shook her head. "I wish I could. I want to, but it's not up to me."

The physician sighed. "Well, to say the least, your friend was lucky. The bolt lodged in her shoulder joint, probably when you moved her. They're not designed to go through bone. Although it had already done considerable damage, the regeneration chamber will repair it."

"Thank you, Doctor, for everything. By the way, what's your name?"

"Will Bennett."

Her wound temporarily sealed, two fresh pints of blood, and Dr. Bennett said Leea would recover, but wouldn't regain consciousness until after her procedure. They transferred her to the regeneration bed and adjusted it to fit her six-foot frame, then waited for the conductive gel to mold to the contours of her body. A six-inch-wide gel strip was laid across her naked shoulders and covered with a heavy plastic sheet. Each end was fastened to the side of the bed to keep her from moving while the lasers did their job.

From the side of the bed, a multi-directional arm with a five-inch-diameter plate attached rotated over the wound. A piece of the sheeting was cut away, and the plate lowered to adhere directly to the gel. A readout on the top of the arm glowed, and an endless stream of text cycled through as the doctor entered data into a hand-held device. In less than a minute, the round disc started to glow.

"What's it doing?" Farrell asked.

"The plate heats the gel, which activates the micro-lasers. I have entered the parameters, and uploaded the internal scans I took, and the lasers will repair the damage."

"Thank you, Dr. Bennett. I know you didn't have to do this. But we appreciate your discretion. We'll be back tomorrow to collect our friend."

The doctor nodded, then scrutinized Farrell a moment. "You look familiar to me. Have we met?"

"No. But I'm sure we've passed in the hall or something."

"No, not from the ship...from somewhere else."

"I'm sure we've never met."

"Hmmm...I'll remember eventually."

# CHAPTER 28

# Leaders

"The Dekarran ship will come this way." Yaran indicated a path above two planets in close proximity, known as the Twins, on a large 3D view of the solar system hovering in front of him. Behind him, at the elevator end of the desert depot, stood 120 pilots, mechanics, and flight crew. "The remote sensors we sent out a few days ago verified their trajectory, and by their estimated speed, they should be here within one to two days. One of our pilots has agreed to find an orbit around the right Twin where he'll be able to monitor their approach and give us an exact accounting of their movements."

Seventy-three ships had been brought back to flight status before time ran out, and now sat on the desert floor above. Most of them were scout ships and cruisers. Along with Jeffrey and Tim, trusted Zantian engineers and mechanics were tasked to help, but many of the ships had been inoperable for far too long and the repairs too extensive.

"He will also act as bait. I want to ensure the Dekarrans establish their orbit over Alrack. Some of the ships here may not be able to fly, but many of their long-range weapons still function. If we can lure their small fighters over our city, we might be able to disable some before they can leave the area. Unfortunately, our large ships won't be able to out-maneuver theirs in close combat, but maybe they'll give the Dekarrans pause for a moment.

"In the meantime, we've selected the most vulnerable cities to protect. Everyone has their assignments, but before we go, I want to thank each and every one of you for your commitment to this effort and wish you success for what's to come."

"Well," Mearos said to Yaran as the assembled group began to disperse. "I guess I better gather my crew and be on my way to the Twins."

"Thank you for doing this. I wish I could go with you."

"I know you do, but you're needed here." Mearos saw the dejected look. "You can't do anything for her up there. Not to mention, what I'm doing could be dangerous. How do you think she'll feel if something happens to you?"

Yaran smiled. "I know. But I can't help feeling that I should be doing more."

"You are doing everything you can. And this plan of yours will succeed, as long as you let others help you."

"I appreciate all the help I can get. So, do you feel comfortable with these weapons system?"

"I think so. They are a bit different, but the test runs went okay."

"Good luck." Yaran squeezed his friend's shoulder and returned to a fray of activity behind him.

Sithan fell into step with his son as he made his way to the elevator. "I would like to accompany you on your flight."

"That's not necessary," Mearos said curtly.

"I would still like to."

Mearos studied his father for a brief second and shrugged.

"Well, what do you think?" Mearos asked Pindac, as the command-class cruiser approached the right Twin planet. "Orbit or land?"

Pindac made an input on his screen and studied the readout. "I think we can land. The northern pole will almost give us a continuous line of sight between the planets."

"Good. I wasn't looking forward to the tight orbit we'd need to maintain otherwise."

"Agreed."

Working together, the two Zantians expertly maneuvered the cruiser onto the barren rock, barely large enough to be considered a planet, and found a relatively flat area to land.

"Well, this is better," Mearos said, propping his feet up on the seat behind him. The flight deck was larger than on his cargo ship, with five large seats, but it was still a limited space. "We can relax until they arrive. The proximity sensors are set to raise an alarm if anything passes between here and the left Twin, but I'd feel more comfortable if someone was here when that happens."

"No problem. I'll set up a shift rotation as the time gets closer."

"Great, thank you."

"And I'm glad we're spending the time on this classy vessel," Pindac smiled. "Even as old as it is, it's still nicer than that heap we're always flying."

"Hey, nothing against our cargo ship, there are many more passages on it in your future."

"Let's hope. So…" Pindac hesitated, "what does it feel like having your father on board?"

"Strange. I'm not sure what to make of it. He was insistent on coming along, but I'm not sure why."

"Maybe he feels it's time to get to know you."

"I'm forty-four years old… why now? Except for a short time after my transition, he hasn't paid much attention to me. Since I became captain, we've only talked when it was business related."

"Well, this whole situation has brought about some interesting revelations. Maybe he's rethinking his choices. He has other children, doesn't he?"

"Yes, two boys. Seems to be the requirement for the Finetig family. There hasn't been a girl born to them in over a century."

Pindac raised his eyebrows. "Have you met any of them?"

"Oh no. I may have been *born* a member, but that doesn't qualify me to *be* a member."

"I'm sorry."

"What?! Don't be. I don't give them a second thought, never have."

"Well, I'm sure changes are on the horizon."

"As far as it concerns me, probably not. As far as it's going to affect the people of Zantia, I don't even want to think about it. If this attack indeed happens, it's going to change everything, and all the well-kept secrets will be revealed." Mearos frowned. "I can't imagine what it will do to our way of life."

"Our current way of life will be over… but we'll find a new one. Everything the Council did hundreds of years ago will be undone." Pindac looked out the forward viewer. "You know… it could all be avoided if Yaran sent all the ships here and we destroyed the Dekarrans before they get close to Zantia. Then no one would ever know."

"I think enough people already know, so those secrets can no longer stay hidden."

"True."

"Besides, if the one person you loved most in life was on that ship, could you order it destroyed, just to preserve your people's way of life?"

Pindac paused reflectively. "No. I suppose not. We will adjust."

"Exactly."

"I wonder how much longer this is going to take," Sithan said absentmindedly as he and Mearos monitored the empty space around them. They had been parked now for thirty hours. Father and son made small talk in their second four-hour shift, the first one having been awkward and uncomfortable. Mearos knew he was to blame for their lack of communication, but somehow he felt indifferent to the man sitting next to him, so the wall between them remained.

"We brought three days' worth of provisions. We'll be fine here as long as their projected arrival isn't too far off."

They sat quietly for a while longer, the tension in the small room growing exponentially.

"I'm sorry for sending your mother away," Sithan finally murmured.

The sadness in his voice took the captain by surprise, and he studied his father for a moment, then sighed. "I don't blame you for that. Staying here with me would have made things difficult for her. And taking me with her would have been the same. It was the right thing to do. But, I do blame you for letting it all happen. Unwanted pregnancies are unheard of in our world, so I take it, it's something you disregarded?"

Sithan hung his head in silence.

"Having your fun with a Human is one thing, but doing so without regard to the consequences is unconscionable."

"That was uncalled for," Sithan came back indignantly. "Yes, I was careless and let it happen, and I know there's no excuse for that. But I did care for your mother, and did not take our relationship lightly."

"But not enough to make it work."

"That's not fair either. Our traditions are complicated so it would never have worked."

"Yes, our traditions. Not every Zantian follows them so closely."

"Ah…you mean Yaran. He's paid a high price for his choices."

"A price he would pay again ten-fold to get Leea back."

"Of that I'm certain. But he is obviously stronger than I was at that age. I'm not trying to make excuses, but you have to understand my position within the family. I was the youngest nephew of the Desolk. At that time, everyone was telling me what to do. I was barely twenty-two and had just begun managing one of the greenhouses and a bit overwhelmed by the responsibility.

"When my relationship with your mother started, I didn't hide it but was constantly reminded by my brother that these relationships never end well. So, when Tamera became pregnant, I was out of my element. I needed help. My brother said if I didn't remove myself from the situation, the family would do it for me. He wouldn't explain what that meant, so I did what I thought was best to protect her… to protect you both. I was young and stupid, which is my only defense."

"You're right, I don't understand the complicated dynamics of ruling families, and I must say, I'm glad for it. I prefer the mundane existence I was given."

"Not too mundane, I hope."

"No, I guess not. And in case you've ever wondered, Tamera is well and has made a good life for herself on Dekarra."

"You've met her? How?"

"A few years after I transported the *special cargo*, I was approached by the woman who sees the escapees off the ship and asked if I wanted to meet my mother. How she knew who Tamera was I didn't ask, but I assumed this little introduction was her way of ensuring my further cooperation, should it be needed.

"While I was a bit reluctant, I was curious, so I met with her. Since then, she comes to see me at the airfield whenever our schedules allow. Our visits are never long, an hour or so at most, but we've managed to build a relationship, if still somewhat cautious. It wasn't easy at first, but I've come to enjoy my time with her. She was the one who delivered Yaran and Leea's messages back and forth to my ship."

Sithan smiled. "I am happy for her. She deserved a normal life. It's more than anything she would have found here."

"True. And if it eases your mind, she doesn't blame you. While not right away, she said she eventually came to understand that leaving me here was the right thing to do. And I was raised as I should have been."

"What eases my mind, is knowing that in spite of your unconventional heritage and upbringing, you turned into an exceptional man. And while I know it doesn't mean anything to you, I couldn't be prouder. I hope someday you will be able to forgive me as well."

"When I moved to Alrack, did you arrange the captain's job?"

"No. That was my father's doing. The captain you replaced had been a confidential operative for the Council ever since he took the job. He was there at the beginning with the Morodons. But I convinced the Council that you would do what's right for our planet concerning the shield, and you did. However, I was surprised when I discovered you aided the underground network."

"How did you find that out?"

Sithan chuckled. "It was only with Leea's leaving. Jarock had made special arrangements to send her to Karba. We've sent Humans there before, and before you ask, I don't know why. Only the inner circle knows those secrets. But I overheard a conversation between my father and uncle. They talked about Jarock having to make a trip to Karba to ease their ruffled feathers since Yaran's Human lover had disappeared on her own. So, I did some investigating. It didn't take long to find out that you were involved."

An alarm sounded on the ship's console. Mearos swiveled his chair back into place and brought up the 3D viewer. "They're here."

Mearos put in a call to the airfield tower, where Yaran and the rest of the supporting leaders would be, and gave them the news. He could almost hear their collective sigh.

"Okay. Keep them on your scanner, and follow when you think it's safe," Yaran advised.

After an hour, Mearos was back with an update. "They've established an orbit around Aru. Could they have the wrong planet?"

"No. The Belag went to too much trouble to get them here. He knows where we are, but I wonder what they're waiting for?"

"We'll head for Alrack's moon. From there we can monitor their movements."

"Okay. Our ships are already on their way to their designated cities, so everything should be ready once they make their move."

"I'll let you know as soon as that happens."

"Entering the Zantian system," Jackson announced. A map of the solar system ahead appeared on the forward screen. The sun was slightly to their left, and five of the eleven planets currently held a position on the nearside.

"Reduce speed to one-quarter full, Captain Owens, and take us in between the two closest planets. Establish an orbit around the one down to the right."

"Aye, Sir."

"Ensign Berringer, scan the planet slightly to the left and search for a beacon at 147.52 MHz."

"Aye, Sir. Scanning. Got it. Adding location to the forward map."

Admiral Shaw moved to the large viewscreen as if needing a closer look, then turned to his audience and pointed to the flashing red icon. "This is the city of Alrack where the leader of their ruling Council resides. Here we make our stand. We take out the ruling seat, and the resulting turmoil will give us an even bigger advantage than just catching them by surprise. What time of day is it in Alrack?"

The flight officer studied his station's readouts. "Should be close to sunset."

"Perfect. We can get everything ready here."

"Open—" The console on the admiral's chair chirped and he looked over at it annoyed. He pointed to the communications officer, but before he could get another word out, the chair chirped again…then again. With a growl, he returned to the seat. He stabbed at the comm button. "What!" Upon seeing the face on the armrest's screen, he immediately inserted his earpiece before anyone could hear a response.

"I need to see you," the whispery voice said.

"Now?!"

"Yes. Unless you'd like me to come to the bridge, so we can discuss it there."

"Fine." He disconnected and got to his feet. "There is an urgent matter I need to attend to, but it shouldn't take long. Captain Owens, I'd like you to assist the flight squad in getting the fighters ready, then retake your post for our final approach. Ensign Berringer, contact all the department heads and let them know we've arrived. When I return, I'll make a ship-wide broadcast, to let our troops know victory is at hand."

Admiral Shaw entered Belag's quarters without knocking. "What was so—?"

"Come in. Take a seat." The Belag sat in a chair, legs crossed, in his original form, grinning widely.

"There isn't—"

The alien stood, and transformed into the shape of a Human male.

"I hate it when you do that," the admiral said, frowning.

"I know. That's why it's so much fun."

"I don't have time for this. We are—"

"You have stowaways on board."

"What?"

"Stowaways. You know…people who don't—"

"I know what stowaways are! How do you know?"

"I may have killed one. But the bigger question you should be asking is: why no one told you they had one in custody. And, that she escaped."

The large man stared at him dumbfounded. Without another word, he turned on his heel and stormed out of the room, slamming the metal door behind him.

The Belag returned to his original form, sat back into the chair, crossed his legs and smiled. "Hmmm… Guess he didn't want to know who she was."

"Why wasn't I told about the stowaway?" The admiral glowered at the shorter Commander Reese, head of security.

"I apologize. I thought we had it under control."

"Well, obviously you didn't. I want to be informed about *everything* that happens on my ship! Is that clear?"

"Yes, Sir. Very clear."

"Good." His tone softened. "So, tell me about the prisoner. How did she escape?"

"Tricked the guard. Gave him a pretty good lump on the head with a pipe she managed to remove from behind a wall. But he'll be all right, and I'm sure he's learned his lesson. Other than that, not much to tell." He relayed the answers Leea had given over and over during the interrogation. "Also, her DNA wasn't in any of our databases."

"How is that possible?"

"I don't know, Sir. Possibly, someone erased it."

"Which means, she's here for a particular reason. I have it on good authority that she's not alone."

"Are you sure?"

"As sure as I can be. I want every one of your teams on alert, and I want this ship searched from top to bottom. There's got to be traces of them somewhere." He started to turn and quickly added. "And when you find them … if they don't come quietly … shoot them."

"Yes, Sir."


"Attention all hands; this is Admiral Shaw with an update on our mission. As I'm sure you already know, we've entered the Zantian system and are orbiting the fifth planet. We are waiting for nightfall in the city of Alrack, and then we'll take out the head of the Zantian ruling Council. The vision of our ancestors, who made the perilous journey to Dekarra with the intention to free those enslaved, will be realized today. The time for retribution is here, and I am honored to share this victory with every single one of you who have chosen to stay true to our grandparents' dreams.

"You've all had three weeks to relax. You know your assignments. Let's go free our people."

The comm panel chirped on the center seat's armrest. Admiral Shaw inserted his earpiece before answering. "Did you find anything, Commander?"

"We found where they were staying, but everything is cleared out."

"How many?"

"We can't be sure. We found four rooms that were occupied on the lower crew deck, but it's hard to tell how many were in each room."

"Well, keep looking. Only so many places they can hide."

"Yes, Sir."

"Well, I guess that's our cue," Ben said after the admiral finished his speech.

"Can I throw up first?" Max rolled his eyes.

"Nope, no time for that."

"Killjoy." Max got to his feet.

After the attack on Leea, the stowaways had moved to the storage room off the shuttle bay where they had hidden their wounded friend. It was a large room, containing odd machine parts, but had plenty of space for all of them to remain undetected.

"Okay, well, I'm going to set up my equipment in the shuttle, but I need to wait until we're on our way before I can start the process. If I disable the backups too soon, someone might notice."

"The rest of us should change into our coveralls and make our way up to the fighter bay."

"What about Leea?" Farrell asked.

"Come with us for a while, and then go get her. We'll all meet back here when we're done with the ships."

The seven Watchers took the stairs to the fighter bay. One by one, they carefully slipped into the large area, already teeming with activity. Personnel in flight suits and maintenance overalls hurried from one end to the other.

"Busier than I'd hoped, but this could work to our advantage," Devon said, looking around. "We should be able to blend in, as long as we act like we belong." He removed the retractable wrench, extended it, and held it up. "See, we even come with tools."

"I'm going to go check on Leea." Farrell moved back to the stairwell. "I don't like the idea of leaving her. This ship is getting too busy. Someone might realize she doesn't belong."

"Okay, that's probably a good idea. Take her back to the storage room, and then join us."

"Will do."

Leea's eyelids fluttered heavily. As soon as she could focus, she looked at her surroundings. Where was she? How did she get here? Then it all came rushing back; the shape-shifter, and the excruciating pain in her shoulder. She tried to move, but something held her in place.

"Whoa, you can't get up yet. Your treatment isn't done."

"Where am I?" Her voice seemed far away. "Who are you?"

"I'm Dr. Bennett, and you are in the medical bay. Your friends brought you here after your... accident."

"Is Farrell here?" Her voice slurred.

"Farrell?"

"My friend, Farrell."

The doctor looked at her quizzically. Then recognition spread across his face. "Farrell... Reynolds?"

"Yes...." Leea felt something press against her neck, heard a hiss, and the world went dark again.

"Dr. Bennett, I'm here to check on my friend. Dr. Bennett, are you here? I'm sorry it's so early." She looked around, but the facility was empty. She walked around the corner to where the regeneration bed stood, and came face to face with two security guards pointing weapons. She glanced over at the bed—empty.

Leea was gone.

"Why are you here?" Admiral Shaw looked at the two women behind the security barrier.

"No reason," Farrell retorted, giving him an icy stare.

"Don't play games with me. Whatever your plans were, you've failed. So, why not tell me what you were planning, and where your accomplices are."

Farrell laughed sarcastically. "If you must know, we have no agenda. My friend here wanted to go home, and I thought I would go with her and see what Zantia has to offer since New Haven is full of megalomaniacs!"

The large man glowered, but then burst out laughing. "No wonder Owens likes you. You have spunk. Too bad you're both traitors. But don't go away; let me bring your other half right up."

"AAAAAAH!" Farrell yelled once the outer door closed behind him. "Jackson wasn't kidding when he called that jerk a pompous ass!"

"I told you so! I told you so!" Bettina's sarcasm screamed in Ray Shaw's head. Why hadn't he listened to her? Well, he had to say this much for Captain Owens: he was a good actor. He had completely fooled him. Now, the joke would be on the traitor. Once he had them all in custody, he would line them up at the forward viewscreen and let them watch as he took out their precious Zantians. That thought lifted his spirits. He activated his personal comm.

"Commander Reese, arrest Captain Owens."

"Excuse me, Sir?"

"You heard me…I want Captain Owens in the brig. It seems he's not the friendly we thought he was."

"Yes, Sir."

"Oh, and commander…don't be gentle."

The Watchers had devised their plan and gone to work. Locating the access port on the first ship took longer than Devon was comfortable with—it looked much easier on the 3D image Jackson had shown them. He pulled over an unused ladder and climbed two rungs to reach the underbelly at the forward end. The sonic frequency released the cover, and Devon inserted the other end of the tool, engaged the bolt and gave it a quarter turn, feeling it click into place—done.

He was moving away from his fourth ship when an alarm sounded. Everyone in the bay came to a standstill. On an upper observation platform stood a security guard holding the intercom.

"This is a security check," he announced. A low murmur swept the room. "I want everyone to stop what they're doing and stand in front of your respective ships. My men will come around and verify your identification." At that moment, all four access doors opened and a dozen guards, weapons drawn, filed in.

*Oh, crap!* Devon thought. He looked around and made eye contact with two of his companions. They all shrugged. He looked around trying to devise an escape plan, but quickly realized it would be a futile attempt. All four doors, as well as the two stairwells, were now guarded by armed security. His shoulders slumped. They had done what they could; hopefully, it would be enough.

"Well, the accommodations are horrible," Farrell quipped, pacing in the small cell. "At least, they could put a coffee machine in here, or something."

"No! No coffee. That's what got us into all this mess." Leea sat on the cot, wearing a white doctor's coat, her hair cascading over her shoulders, having lost all its pins.

"You're going to give up coffee?"

"No, I'm just cranky because I haven't had any."

"Don't be so hard on yourself," Jackson said quietly, sitting beside her. "We all knew this had a fifty-fifty chance of succeeding. We did the best we could."

"We should have gone sooner," Devon added from the next cell. "There were too many people around."

"Well, we tried." Jackson rubbed his sore chin, where a purple bruise was already forming, but at least his split lip had stopped bleeding. He didn't blame the commander; had the roles been reversed, he would have done the same.

The five Watchers had been quickly arrested once the security sweep began. There was no point resisting, and none of them did. The only thing they could hope for now was that Max could still deactivate the weapons system before getting caught. The group wasn't sure if their activity in the brig was being recorded, so they said little to each other about the specifics of the mission. Devon had furtively held up two and then seven fingers, letting Jackson know they had deactivated twenty-seven of the fifty-five fighters.

The outside door to the brig opened, and Dr. Bennett entered. He walked to the cell where Leea, Farrell, and Jackson sat, anger clearly visible on his face.

"How's the shoulder?" he asked Leea curtly.

She lifted her arm and rotated it in a circle. "A little sore, but not too bad. Thank you for what you did."

"Uh huh. Try to rest it for the next few days." He turned to leave.

"Wait." Farrell got to her feet and stood at the barrier. "Why did you betray us?"

"Why do you think?" His anger rose. "You are all traitors. We're on a rescue mission and you…," he looked at her with disgust. "You're here to stop it."

"No, that is not why we're here." Farrell paused and considered her words. "We're here to stop the slaughter of innocent people."

"The Zantians aren't innocent."

Farrell shook her head. "Of course, they are. There is not one of them alive today that had anything to do with what happened on Earth. And that aside, how do you justify the abduction of a Morodon to further Admiral Shaw's cause? Don't they have rights either?"

The doctor's angry eyes wavered, and he hesitated. "Sacrifices are necessary."

Leea joined Farrell at the barrier. "Your admiral is lying to you. He only plans to save a handful of Humans to bring back to Dekarra, just enough to make himself look like a hero."

"You're lying."

"No, she's not," Farrell said, glancing at Leea, who gave a quick nod. She hoped they were thinking the same thing. "We have proof."

"Let me guess… I'll have to let all of you out so you can show me."

"No," Farrell said. "Just me."

"Farrell," Jackson called cautiously, but she gave him a reassuring smile.

"Doctor, if there is any chance that what I'm saying is true, don't you owe it to yourself, and everyone else, to hear it? I saw your hesitation in the cargo bay. I got the impression you don't like the idea of going there, guns blazing, either. Was I wrong?"

The doctor hesitated a moment. "No, you weren't wrong. But if this is a trap—"

"I assure you, I only want to show you what we have. If you still don't believe what you see, you can bring me back."

He studied her for a long moment, then resigned, deactivated the energy field and let Farrell step out. She smiled back at her cell mates. "I'll be right back."

Max sat on the shuttle floor, legs crossed, his computer system spread out on the bench. Sweat dampened his curly blond hair, cut short so he could blend in, and now dripped down his face, blurring his vision. His back was on fire from the bad posture, and his hands were beginning to cramp; he wasn't sure he could make it to the end.

His fingers flew over the screen and keyboard simultaneously; a second, smaller screen, showed several levels of colored bars across. As Max manipulated the data, the bars slowly diminished. He had to work fast. The backups to the weapons system would reactivate if they sat idle. This was the drawback for not having the specific access codes. Without them, the system suspected it was being hacked. But as long as the data was being manipulated it couldn't distinguish between a legitimate request or unauthorized access. It would have to wait until the input flow stopped and then sort it out. If he successfully removed the backups first, there would be nothing left for the computer to sort out, and it would accept the deactivation as correct.

He gave a quick glance at the second screen. Three more levels to go. He had removed five, which had taken him about thirty minutes. At twenty-seven, he had hacked many systems but had never encountered one as complex as this one. He would love to meet the person who programmed it.

Two more levels to go.

"Max. Max, are you in there?"

NO! No, no, no, no, no! Not now! Max ignored the calls. He willed the muscles in his hands to relax.

"Max, it's me, Farrell."

"Give me a few minutes, Farrell. I'm almost done." He forced his concentration back to the inputs. They were repetitious, and he didn't want to lose count of the strokes and clicks.

Final level. He concentrated with every ounce of effort he could muster. He heard voices outside the door and they were distracting his tired mind, but his hands suddenly seemed to move on their own. Finally, the last one-inch-high bar flashed red, slowly changed to green and disappeared. The system beeped, and then 'BACK-UP DEACTIVATION COMPLETE' scrolled across the screen. Max had one final task, to deactivate the system itself, which only took another two minutes. He moved his stiff fingers away from the equipment and stretched out on the shuttle floor. Every muscle in his body ached.

"Max? Are you okay?"

"Be right there." He got up slowly and unlocked the shuttle door. Farrell rushed in, followed by Dr. Bennett.

"Farrell, what's going on?"

"How did it go?"

"Just as it was supposed to." He wiped his brow and looked at the physician's dark face, trying to read the hard look.

"Max, I need you to play the conversation between Admiral Shaw and Bettina for the doctor."

"Why? Why would you bring him here?"

"Max, don't argue. I'm trying to show him what his fearless leader is really up to."

He looked doubtfully. "Okay, if you're sure." He pulled up the video recording and played it on the larger screen.

"This can't be real," the doctor said in disbelief when the video ended. He slumped onto the opposite bench.

"I'm sorry, but this is as real as it gets."

"This is not what we signed up for. It was never about personal gain. It was to reunite our people…all of them. How can he do this?"

Farrell sat down next to him. "I know more than anyone what this should have been about, and I'm sorry. But you had to have suspected something?"

The doctor sighed heavily. "I turned a blind eye to the things I found odd. I rationalized that he knew best how to accomplish our mission. When he brought the stasis pod and explained what was in it, I objected, but he convinced me it was the only way to lower the Zantian shield. He promised once it was done, he would set the Morodon free, along with the rest. But he probably won't do that, will he?"

"I don't know, but my guess is…no. And now the question is: if you believe what you've seen, how can we stop him?"

Will Bennett shook his head. "I have no idea. We would have to organize a coup, but we don't have time to convince everyone."

"I have an idea," Max said. "What if we broadcast the conversation over the ship's intercom?"

"You can do that?"

"Of course, that's easy. I'm already linked into the system. Give me some time so I can crop the recording to just the good parts."

Farrell turned her attention back to the physician. "I think you should be out there when the broadcast happens. You would be someone they trust, and can start organizing people. I also hope you will release my group from the brig. If we can take over the bridge, Jackson can assume command of the ship…but only if that's okay with you."

"I've met Captain Owens a few times. I think he's a good choice to get us out of this quagmire."

"How much time do you need, Max?"

"I should have it ready to play in about half an hour."

"Okay, we'll get things started and let you know when to start transmitting."

# CHAPTER 29

# The Return

The doors to the medical bay swished open and Admiral Raymond Shaw accompanied by the Belag, in the form of a tall, lanky crewman dressed in a security uniform, walked in.

"Where is Dr. Bennett?" the admiral asked a nurse sorting supplies.

"He isn't here at the moment. Can I help you with something?"

"No. Where did he go?"

"I don't know, Sir. He left about a half-hour ago. Would you like me to call him?"

"That won't be necessary," the soft voice of the crewman said and walked toward the rear alcove.

"Excuse me! You can't go in there." She tried to cut him off.

"Actually, he can," Admiral Shaw said, looming over the petite nurse. "On second thought, why don't you go find the wayward doctor while we tend to our business here?"

The nurse hesitantly stepped aside and watched suspiciously as the two men passed through the door on the far wall and closed it behind them.

The Belag walked to the stasis pod and activated the attached control panel. He entered several commands before a small door next to the panel opened. Removing a cylinder from his pocket, he inserted it into the opening and made several adjustments until the door closed.

"I'm introducing commands into the inter-link that will clear the mind of the pod's occupant and keep him from receiving any communications from the ground," he explained. He continued the manual input for a few seconds then removed a disc from his pocket, which he inserted into the top of the panel. "This new data will simulate the brain waves we've isolated, and tell him to broadcast instructions on lowering the shield and how to disconnect from the Zantian program. In other words, we're letting those on the surface know that a rescue mission is here, and they need to disengage the cloak so the rescuers can find them."

"Which is essentially what we are doing," the Admiral said, grinning.

"Exactly."

"We're just leaving out the part that we won't be letting them go. Once we have control of the planet, and all the remaining Zantian men barricaded in their own mines, we'll make them put the barrier back up so the world can keep its anonymity. And this one," the burly man lightly patted the chamber, "will replace the one who recently died. How long before this takes effect?"

"It shouldn't take too long once we reach the planets orbit. I suggest we go witness it firsthand."

As the two men entered the bridge, curious eyes took in the tall, thin stranger who eased into the chair next to the admiral. No introductions were made, so the crew went about their business.

"Lieutenant Fuentes, take us out of orbit and set a course for the enemy's planet."

"Should I call Captain Owens back to the bridge?"

"No. Captain Owens has been relieved of his duties."

"Sir?"

Bridge activity came to a standstill as everyone looked to their leader for an explanation.

"Captain Owens has proven himself unworthy to sit in that chair." The large man pointed toward the screen. "Now Lieutenant, one-quarter full…that way."

"Aye, Sir."

Normal activity returned, but the crew glanced at each other with raised eyebrows.

"Coming up on a Zantian moon," the helmsman informed them as a small planetoid came into view. "The moon has an orbit over Alrack City."

"Perfect. We couldn't ask for a better hiding place. Take us to the moon's far side, but far enough out so we can observe the planet."

"Aye, Sir."

The helmsman expertly maneuvered the massive vessel behind Alrack's satellite and eased the nose around until the forward viewscreen had a full image of the desolate landscape below. Once their forward motion stopped it took barely ten minutes before the planet's appearance started to change. The crater-ridden, storm-filled scenery faded slowly until finally, the twinkling lights from the city of

Alrack appeared, nestled next to the large mountain range. The bridge crew stared with astonishment.

"Well, there it is," the admiral said in awe, leaning forward in his chair. "Take us out of hiding, and ease us toward the planet."

"Aye, Sir."

*"And the VP?"* The voice of Bettina played loudly over the ship-wide intercom.

*"Nothing to worry about there."* Admiral Shaw's familiar voice boomed. *"He and his aides have everything under control. Once we return victorious, he will announce his longstanding support for us, and then we can finally unseat that useless commander-in-chief. Not sure how that woman got elected in the first place."*

*"Is that because you don't like her politics, or because she's a woman?"*

*"I respect you, don't I?"*

*"Don't confuse fear with respect, Ray. The only reason we have this relationship is because you need me. Need me to take care of all those things you find so distasteful. And since I know where all the bodies are buried... literally... you feel safer keeping me close."*

*"I've done what's necessary to move this project forward. Obstacle's had to be removed."*

The bridge crew sat in stunned silence as they listened.

"Turn that off!" the mission commander bellowed having shaken off the shock. He jumped to his feet and rushed to the communication console.

"Yes, Sir," Samuel Berringer said.

*"Why do you suddenly look like the cat who swallowed the canary?"* Bettina continued.

*"Oh come on, all this nonsense aside, you've got to be feeling it. The adrenalin rush in knowing we're almost there. To think the ancestors' objective will be achieved on my watch. Once we destroy the Zantian cities and take control of their mines, we'll come back having secured an unimaginable future for ourselves... we'll be heroes."*

*"How are you going to justify the sacrifices you plan to make on Zantia?"*

"I said turn it off!"

"I'm sorry, Sir, I can't. The feed is being controlled from another source."

"Find a way," he snarled leaning over the ensign's shoulder.

*"Nobody's going to object to our treatment of the aliens. It's what they deserve. And that's not a sacrifice... that's justice."*

*"I'm not talking about the Zantians; I'm talking about the Humans."*

*"I'll be doing everyone a favor. The men who work in those mines were raised like cattle. You know personally that they have no social graces, so they'll never fit into our society. It's best they just stay where they are, doing what they were bred to do."* He laughed

softly. *"But this time, they'll be working for us, so it'll be a step up. We'll bring enough of the city workers back to prove our commitment to the rescue, which will appease the masses, and then over time, we'll selectively bring back those we want."*

*"You're an evil man, Admiral."*

The irate man slammed his fist on the console, activating the intercom. "Launch the fighters. Launch them NOW!" The recorded conversation started to repeat, and he swung around. "Lieutenant Ryan, fire the first barrage of missiles at that city."

The officer at the weapons station looked astounded. "All of them, Sir?"

"Of course all of them!" he roared. "I want it destroyed! I want nothing left but a hole in the ground!"

"But, Sir...."

"That's an order!"

With trembling hands, the lieutenant adjusted the controls, loading a dozen missiles into the defense array. Hesitantly, he activated the firing mechanism, which would launch two at a time in rapid succession. Nothing happened.

"Lieutenant," the admiral seethed. "I said—"

"The missiles aren't firing, Admiral. Something's wrong."

"What are you talking about? Why am I surrounded by incompetence?" Admiral Shaw approached the weapons station and tried activating the missile systems himself, but they didn't respond. "Find out what the problem is or I'll put you in the brig!"

"Aye, Sir."

The bridge doors slid open, and Commander Reese rushed in. "Admiral, what's going on?"

"I thought you arrested all the stowaways?" he said accusatorily.

"We did. They're all in the brig."

"Well, you missed some! Find the rest of those traitors and confiscate this garbage they're transmitting. It's obviously something they spliced together to sabotage our mission." The admiral's conversation with Bettina ended its second playback and remained silent. He looked around, noticing that the three command chairs were empty. The Belag had slipped out unnoticed.

"Aren't you gone yet?" He snarled at the commander.

"Sorry, Sir, I'll find them."

"I want your teams armed and patrolling the hallways just in case anyone decides to sway from our agenda. I also want two of your men in here. Let me know immediately when you find the rest of that riffraff."

"Yes, Sir."

The admiral slumped into the center chair seeming suddenly exhausted. "Ensign Berringer, open a ship-wide channel, I need to do some damage control." But before he could get the first word out, the door opened, and Jackson, Devon Greene, Dr. Bennett, and two armed crewmen entered the bridge pushing Commander Reese ahead of them. The muscular security chief tentatively rubbed the left side of his jaw.

"Get off my bridge!" the indignant admiral roared, jumping to his feet. "I suppose I have you to thank for this theatrical performance, Owens? What did you think you were going to accomplish with all this?"

"Share the truth with the ship's crew."

"Well, unfortunately, you can't just invent something to suit your own needs."

Jackson laughed. "Why would I need to invent anything, when the truth speaks for itself?"

"And what's this? Tell me they haven't duped you, Doctor?"

"I didn't want to believe them, Admiral, but I watched the video…the whole video."

"Nobody is going to take this nonsense seriously. It's a blatant fabrication."

"Is that the card you want to play?" Jackson said. "I can have the complete video streamed to every onboard computer in two minutes if you insist."

"Did you let this traitor out of the Brig, Will?" The burly man's voice seemed to waver.

"Yes, I did. But he's no traitor. On the contrary, he wants to fulfill our true mission. He and his team are here to keep you from committing an atrocity. We are supposed to be rescuing these people, but instead, you want to enslave them for your own personal gain. Not to mention that you find a certain number of casualties acceptable. This is not what any of us signed up for."

"You don't know what you're talking about. I'm doing what's best for the people of Dekarra. You have no idea what your meddling will cost this operation."

"Yes, I do. It will ensure *everyone* gets saved, not just a select few. What you're doing makes you no better than those who enslaved them to begin with."

"You're a fool. You'll never convince everyone to follow you…or them." He indicated the Watchers with disgust.

"Maybe. But strangely, most of the crew I've talked to seemed genuinely shocked by what they heard. These are mostly decent people. They're here to do the right thing; not to take over the Zantian cities or their mines, and certainly not to hold them hostage. How could you possibly think this is what the people of Dekarra want?"

"Well, it's a little late for an intervention," the admiral said with a smirk. "The fighters are away. The takeover has already begun."

The doctor shook his head sadly and motioned to the two guards. "Take both of them to the brig. And by the way, Admiral," he said before they were out the door, "your security force is being rounded up to join you, so don't expect them to come to your rescue."

Once they left the bridge, the doctor turned to Jackson. "Well, Captain, I leave the rest of this to you." He sighed. "I fear you have your work cut out for you."

The tall, lanky crewman moved cautiously down the corridor. Chaos seemed to be everywhere around him. He assumed this was partially due to their proximity to Zantia, and the revelation that their leader had lied about his true intentions for this mission. Humans: so gullible and easily deceived.

The admiral had completely underestimated his adversaries—probably didn't even think he had any—and they'd outsmarted him. The Belag had realized early on that the single-mindedness of the military leader could be the undertaking's downfall, but hadn't expected it to happen so easily. Well, the ruse was up, and so was his time on this ship. The last thing he wanted was to be caught up in any of their internal conflicts.

It did anger him somewhat that all his efforts to help them prepare for this attack had been for nothing. But no matter; he would take his ship around the planet and watch the action at some of the other cities. Not the same as watching what happens to Alrack, but it would have to do.

Up ahead he spotted armed crewmen, and instinct told him it probably wasn't a good idea to be seen in a security uniform. He approached the mess hall and slipped inside. Without bothering to check if anyone was around, he shifted into the form of Leea. He didn't know if she was dead, and at the moment he didn't much care, but her form in the maintenance uniform would be less conspicuous.

Back in the main corridor, no one gave him a second look as he hurried along. Taking the aft stairwell two steps at a time, he moved quickly to his small ship standing in the far corner, obscured behind a large transport. Luckily, both levels of bay doors were open so he would be able to ease out undetected.

Once all the fighters had cleared the bay above, the tiny ship made its way through the force field and disappeared into the blackness.

Mearos directed the cruiser around the Zantian moon as the Dekarran behemoth approached. He hoped they were too busy concentrating on their destination to pay any attention to the small vessel trying to stay out of their sights. But they believed their presence to be a surprise, so probably weren't looking for them at all.

The captain had summoned Pindac to the flight deck, and Sithan had taken a seat at a separate communications console. The two pilots expertly maneuvered their ship around the orbiting planetoid, keeping at a safe distance, and watched as the Atlantis came to a full stop with its nose toward Zantia.

"What are they waiting for?" Pindac asked after a while.

Soon, something began to change on the planet below. Sensors on Zantian ships were calibrated to scan through to the actual surface. But now, the turbulent, uninhabited landscape projected by the Morodons started to fade. Within a few minutes, city lights were in plain view, along with the vast Red Desert.

Once the image was completely clear, the Dekarran ship eased from around the moon, heading for Zantia at a leisurely pace. After it had completely cleared the planetoid, small black ships emerged from each side. Sithan had kept the comm-line open, and was relaying what they were seeing.

"Stay hidden," Yaran's voice came through the console. "We'll deal with them here."

Mearos called two additional crewmen to the flight deck, who quickly busied themselves with weapon systems.

"Sithan, can you manage the communications?" Mearos asked.

"Yes."

"Good. Find the frequency to that ship, and relay it to the surface. Monitor any transmissions between it and the fighters. Grys, I'm going to go around its backside slowly. As I do, scan the exterior and let's catalog their armaments."

"Mearos, a small craft is leaving the warship."

"Heading?"

Pindac studied the sensors. "Away from the planet. Do you want to follow?"

"Is it one of the Dekarran fighters?"

"No, it's much smaller."

"Hmmm… Interesting. Let it go. We don't have time for distractions."

As they neared the planet's atmosphere, the small black fighters dispersed in all directions, seeming to know exactly where they were going and waylaying

Yaran's plan to use the firepower from the desert depot. Only three penetrated the atmosphere over Alrack.

"Pindac, put up an image of Alrack on the screen."

Within a few seconds, the Dekarran ship was replaced with an aerial view showing the entire city and outlining areas. As the three ships descended over the metropolis from the mountains, their lasers arbitrarily carved a path through the city as they headed toward the house on the hill.

Seemingly out of nowhere, an old Zantian scout ship, three times the size of the attacking vessels, moved to intercept. With surprise on its side, it destroyed one fighter, causing the other two to scatter in opposite directions. But they quickly veered back returning fire. The larger craft rocked, but kept its course, attempting to lure them out over the desert which worked for a moment, until one broke off and resumed its original course. Fortunately, the maneuver was enough to pull them away from populated areas.

Continuing over the desert, the two adversaries banked, the smaller one making the turn easy and coming up behind its perceived enemy. It opened fire, but the Zantian pilot had anticipated the move and banked as sharp as the old framework would allow which put him perpendicular to the invader. The Dekarran fired, taking out the Zantian's forward left laser—but it couldn't have anticipated the scout's side guns.

The Zantian opened up, puncturing the warhead beneath the others right wing, and within seconds the ship exploded. The shockwave rocked the larger ship as it turned to pursue the remaining fighter, already bearing down on the large homestead.

The scout discharged its lone laser with no effect as it was well out of range. Expecting the enemy ship to launch a barrage at any moment, the pursuing pilot coaxed maximum speed, causing the old vessel to groan under the force.

But instead of the anticipated missile attack, the sleek black plane banked upward, gaining altitude. A half mile up, it turned back and pointed its nose directly at the estate in an attempted suicide run.

Closing in, the Zantian pilot depressed its firing mechanism—nothing happened. Knowing he only had seconds to spare, he maneuvered behind the craft as it plunged toward the ground, hoping he hadn't been detected and accelerated toward its underbelly. Without hesitation, he rammed the small arrow-shaped fighter, pushing it away before both erupted into a fireball, ensuring that except for falling debris, the house below remained undamaged.

The crew of the orbiting command cruiser watched the drama unfurl in stunned silence, but their mood turned crestfallen as the viewscreen panned back to show the entire city. The south end had taken the worst of the destruction. Two warehouses, one processing plant and an area with shops and lab facilities lay in rubble. Some distance beyond, smoke billowed from doors and windows of buildings partially intact, but where furniture and belongings obviously burned from within. Mearos was thankful that the Dekarran ships had concentrated on the city and ignored the outlying villages.

"What about the other cities?"

They panned through the twelve within their sensor's range. Of those, all smaller than Alrack, two showed massive destruction and one was no longer recognizable as a municipality. The rest looked to have sustained only minor damage if any at all.

"Two fighters are returning from the surface," Pindac informed them.

Anger flashed in the darkened blue eyes. "Well, it's too bad for them." Taking the controls, Mearos maneuvered the cruiser under the Atlantis and opened fire as they approached. The first ship was immediately destroyed, but the second had time for an evasive maneuver before it landed in the Atlantis's fighter bay. The Zantian captain fired after it.

An explosion rocked the large warship, and the atmosphere began venting out into the vacuum of space. Seeing the twisted metal floor told Mearos none of the fighters would be returning home. He instantly regretted the impulsive action and hoped there were no significant injuries. He moved his ship away and braced himself for retaliation, but none came.

"Mearos...we have a problem."

Twenty Zantian men stood in the airfield control room, silently watching as the ten large monitors scrolled through aerial views of all the planet's capitals. One-by-one, almost in meticulous order, their cities came under attack and Yaran's heart ached at not being able to tell if they had been evacuated. *Hopefully, the leaders had sided on caution,* he thought.

"Everyone needs to see this," one of the control technicians announced loudly. Immediately, the large center monitor showed a missile launch platform. Three launch tubes were slowly rising from beneath the surface.

"What...where is that?" Yaran stammered, moving closer to the screen.

"That," his uncle Danloc said, moving to stand next to him, "is the planetary defense system located on the moon. Something we haven't activated in decades."

"Communication is coming in from Mearos. I'll put it up on the right monitor."

"Yaran, we have a problem up here," Mearos said with concern in his voice.

"If it's about the missiles, we've just seen them," he said. "Any suggestions on what we should do?"

Mearos looked dejected. "We won't be able to get there fast enough to stop them from launching. And unfortunately, it only gets worse. Sithan tells me the warheads are shielded, but the Dekarran weapons we scanned will never penetrate it."

"Maybe I can do something," Danloc offered helpfully. "The shielding has a deactivation code in case the weapon misses its target, or for some reason needs to be detonated early. The planetary office is in my city, so give me a few minutes to see if I can find it. Let's just hope Jarock sent my people home and didn't lock them up." Danloc sat at the nearest communications console, and with relief reached the office's manager. Quickly he explained what he needed.

"Yaran, a private word, please?" Mearos asked while they waited.

Yaran moved the link to an empty corner station. "How are you holding up out there?"

"All right. But I did something I shouldn't have."

"Oh?"

"Impulsively, I destroyed one of the incoming Dekarran fighters, and then fired after another one as it landed in their hangar bay. I'm not sure if I destroyed it, but none of their ships will be returning there. They didn't fire back, which surprised me."

"Well, if they didn't retaliate, we can leave it at that." He gave Mearos a weary smile. "However, I will have you contact the Dekarrans with this recent information about the missiles, and you can explain it to them personally."

"Fair enough. As soon as we come up with a plan—"

Danloc interrupted, and Yaran turned away for a moment. "Okay, the deactivation codes are on their way now, along with instructions."

"The timing couldn't be better; the warheads are launching."

Yaran drew in a breath. "Best of luck to you, Mearos, and to your crew. Let me know if you need anything."

"I will."

"And Mearos," he said quietly before the pilot could disconnect, "Bring Leea back to me." Yaran's shoulders visibly slumped as the strain of the last few days momentarily shone through his brave façade.

The captain smiled reassuringly. "I have no intention of letting anything happen to her. Don't worry."

Yaran pursed his lips as the screen went blank. "I'm afraid I'm well beyond that." He ran his hands wearily through his hair. He was so tired—emotionally and physically. He had barely slept the last several days. Stress, as well as anticipation, constantly gnawed at his mind; worse than those weeks after Leea's departure. Back then it had been the weight of despair, and now it was as if the whole planet's future rested on his shoulders.

He mourned the devastation that was happening on the planet, but now it was personal. He didn't want to make this about Leea, but his heart had other ideas. It pounded nervously as he envisioned the destructive force headed for the alien ship and the fact that he could only sit and watch.

"Can we bring up the Dekarran ship on the monitor?" he asked, returning his attention to the room.

"Yes." The image on the center screen was replaced with one of the Atlantis and the moon against a black backdrop.

The floor of the bridge shook and then the whole ship seemed to roll slightly. Ensign Berringer, who was standing at his station, lost his balance and fell backward. Countless sirens and klaxons went off, and red lights on several control panels blinked wildly.

"What the hell was that?" Jackson shouted as he gripped the armrests, waiting for the ship to settle, then jumped up. "Sam, are you okay?"

"Yes…I'm fine," the dark-skinned communications officer said getting to his feet.

The bridge crew had remained intact after Admiral Shaw's arrest, each breathing a sigh of relief that he was gone, after hearing the man's true plan. The remaining Watchers had helped round up the security force and then offered their services where needed. Max had taken an empty station on the bridge and was busy scrolling through data, having just restored the weapons systems.

"An explosion in the fighter bay. One of the force field generators was damaged, and atmosphere is venting into space," the systems officer informed him while manipulating his control panel.

"Cause?"

"Seems to have originated from outside."

"Close the bay doors and turn off those alarms."

"Aye, Sir."

"So, no one thought to scan the outside for ships?"

"We thought we were catching them by surprise," someone said shyly.

Jackson sighed. "Where is the Zantian ship now?"

"Sitting off the port side. Should we return fire?"

"No. We're done shooting at people we don't know." Jackson got to his feet. "I'm going aft to check out the damage. Let me know if anything changes."

"Aye, Sir."

Jackson had barely been able to assess the mangled fighter bay floor when his comm jingled.

"Captain," the communication officer said, "the enemy ship is hailing us."

"Let's refrain from labeling them just yet, shall we? I'll be right up. Oh, and, Ensign Berringer, send a message to all the fighters and tell them there's nowhere to land up here. They'll have to stay on the surface until we can make other arrangements."

He ran toward the bridge as fast as he could and slid into the command chair. "Put it here." Jackson activated the monitor on his armrest and enlarged the surface area to its maximum size, then moved it to arm's length.

He studied the face that appeared on the screen for a brief second. He had seen many accounts of the Zantians in old news feeds, but now looking at one seemed unreal. At first glance, the alien didn't look any different from someone he might pass on the streets of New Haven, but slowly he recognized the pronounced bone structure that gave it a slightly different look from a Human face. He also took in the man's blue eyes and remembered Leea mentioning that the captain of the cargo ship didn't have the normal gray eyes. Jackson suspected this was Mearos.

"I'm assuming you fired on my ship?" Surprisingly, Jackson wasn't irritated with the Zantian. After what the fighters had just done to his planet, he understood the reaction.

Mearos visibly sighed. "Yes. It was a rash decision, one that I instantly regretted, but of course, it was too late to take it back. Were there casualties?" he asked hesitantly.

"No. The pilot was badly injured, but will survive. There were a few other minor cuts and bruises, but nothing serious."

Relief crossed the Zantian captain's face. "I expected you to retaliate."

"No. There will be no retaliations. Our admiral, who sent the fighters to your planet, is under arrest and so are his sympathizers. The rest of us are here to find a more peaceful solution."

"I understand. You must be one of the Watchers Leea spoke about?"

"Yes. I am Captain Jackson Owens. And you are…?"

"Mearos, from the city of Alrack."

Jackson smiled wearily, "Yes, I believe Leea mentioned you as well. Is all this craziness done now?"

"Unfortunately, no. Some of our leaders have launched a reprisal. If you turn your scanners toward the moon, you'll find three missiles headed in your direction."

"Swell." Jackson glanced at one of the occupied stations, and the officer frowned and nodded. "Have them. How much damage will they do?"

"Their destructive power is unlike anything you are familiar with. Two will completely annihilate your ship. I assume the third is for good measure."

"Can we destroy them?"

"They are protected by a shielding which is impervious to any of the armaments we scanned on your ship."

"Is there any good news?"

"Maybe a little. The shielding has a deactivation code, which I'm sending you, but that will not veer them off course. I can lure one of them away, but you will have to destroy the remaining two, which will be coming at you back-to-back. Two cannons for each warhead should suffice, but you must intercept them as soon as they cross into your firing range because even at that distance, the shockwave could put your ship on end.

"The protective barrier will go down ten seconds after you send the code but will reset itself after twenty seconds if you miss. If that happens, you will need to start the whole process again."

"Why are you helping us?"

"We don't all consider you the enemy, Captain Owens."

Jackson smiled. "Understood. But what about you?"

"My ship is smaller and can move faster. I plan to use the moon as my shield."

"I don't know how to thank you."

"Let's just get through this. Good luck." Mearos disconnected.

"Codes are coming in," Max announced. "I'll calculate the timing."

"Can we get the Zantian ship and the missiles on viewer?"

"Yes, Sir," Ensign Berringer said. A moment later the forward image showed the three missile heading away from the moon, and the cruiser moving on an intercept course.

Jackson activated the ship-wide intercom. "This is Captain Owens. There are two high-powered warheads on a collision course with us. We have a plan to destroy them, but the shockwave is going to shake us up a bit. Everybody hold on tight, it's going to get bumpy."

"The Zantian ship successfully pulled one of the weapons away. They're heading for the moon." The bridge crew watched intently as the two objects faded from view.

"You're really going to do this?" Pindac asked incredulously from the copilot seat.

Mearos frowned. "Yes."

"You do know how close that weapon will have to get to us for your plan to work?"

"Yes."

"And there is no talking you out of it?"

"No." He gave his friend a determined smile. "In my training days, I was pretty good at evasive maneuvers."

"And how long ago was that?"

Mearos activated the ship's manual controls and slowed their speed as they rounded the moon letting the weapon gain on them. When the raised launch platform came into view, he dropped the nose toward it until the collision alarm sounded. At almost the same instant the proximity alert rang loudly as the missile closed in from behind.

"Mearos!" The crew cried out in unison.

In the next second, he pulled back hard—the ship's belly barely missing the surface—and banked around the launch tubes, increasing to full speed. As anticipated, the metal structure of the platform confused their pursuer. Unable to adjust its course fast enough, it slammed into the towering chambers, incinerating the entire installation. Mearos kept the cruiser low as they continued around the planetoid, which protected them from the massive explosion.

"Just like yesterday," he said to Pindac with a broad smile.

The copilot frowned and shook his head.

"Fifteen seconds."

"Okay, let's do this. Close the blast shield and fire when ready, Max."

"Weapons launched, and sending codes ... ," he paused for ten seconds, "... now."

The crew watched as their artilleries streaking across the sky, then waited with bated breath until a bright explosion lit up the viewer.

"We missed one!" Max cried studying his monitor.

"What?" Jackson was out of his chair. "Fire again!"

"Hold on. I need to recalculate the sequence and compensate for the incoming shockwave." Max's hands flew over the console. "Done."

A few seconds later the ship shook violently as the first wave hit. Jackson managed to ride the rollercoaster wave by holding on to the back of Max's chair, but several others weren't so lucky and did their best to scramble unsteadily back to their feet. Several alarms resounded loudly.

"What is it?"

"Some of the external sensors went down."

"The second missile exploded, but it's too close!"

It was as if an immovable object slammed into their left side. The ship lifted forty-five degrees and then rotated. The force was too great for Jackson to hold on and he tumbled over the command center and slid across the floor. Catching a momentary glimpse around, he saw that every station-chair was empty before his head slammed against the anchored leg of the helm. While his vision blurred slightly, he managed to wrap his arms around the chair's post to stop his forward momentum.

As he made a fruitless attempt to scan for the crew, an explosion rocked the ship, followed by the worst sound anyone wanted to hear in space—the fire alarm. Jackson tried to get up, but the violent shaking made it impossible. All he could do was hold on tight and pray that the fire suppression system hadn't been damaged—and most importantly—that no one was injured.

Ceiling tiles fell as the structure continued to twist and rock back and forth. Sparks flew as conduits came loose and monitors shattered. Soon, all alarms sounded, and every light on every console flashed red, but, this time, there was no one there to silence them.

The excessive strain finally caused the main engines to fail, cutting power to all systems and thrusting them into darkness. The sudden silence accentuated the ship's agony as it groaned and screamed under the remaining force of the shockwaves. Jackson could feel himself slowly lifting off the floor as the artificial gravity disengaged, but within a few seconds, the auxiliary power took effect.

Then, as violently as it had started, it was suddenly over. The shaking stopped, and the ship seemed to settle, even though the groaning continued. Cautiously, Jackson got to his feet.

"Is anyone hurt?" he called, trying to find his footing as some of the deck plates had buckled.

Moans and weak 'I'm okay's' came back.

He surveyed the bridge. All in all, it had fared pretty well. A dozen ceiling panels lay on the deck, a few more swinging on their hinges, all revealing dangling wires. But luckily, nothing was on fire. The center seating had lifted off its fittings and lay precariously to one side.

"If you need medical attention, please go to the med-bay. After that, we need to get communications back up. Hopefully, some of the exterior modules survived." Jackson manipulated something on the nearest, intact control panel. "Auxiliary power will only last three days, four if we are extra conservative, so let's shut down all non-essential systems and power to unoccupied areas."

Jackson moved to the door but turned back before stepping through. "I'm off to the engine room, and to check on that explosion. I want to thank everyone for sticking with me," he said modestly. "It makes all of this easier... knowing the ship is in good hands. Just sorry it's all such a mess." Before anyone could answer, he was gone.

Wanting to check on Farrell and Leea, Jackson's first stop was the med-bay. After the admiral was arrested, the two women, along with the doctor, had gone to see if they could release the Morodon from the stasis chamber.

The doors slid open to a flurry of activity. The med-bay looked as if someone had picked up the room and given it a good shake. Strewn all over the floor were the contents of every cabinet that lined the walls—not one had been spared. He spotted Farrell helping Dr. Bennett and three nurses returning things to their rightful place.

"Doctor, I need you to grab some personnel and med-kits. We need to check on the crew," Jackson said.

"Okay. As soon as I take care of you."

"What?"

"Jackson." Farrell stepped carefully as she made her way over. "You're bleeding." She reached up and lightly touched the side of his face, pulling away bloody fingertips.

Reaching up, he winced as he felt the gash just above his ear. "I guess in all the excitement I didn't notice."

"Sit," the doctor ordered. He cleaned the wound then examined it. "You'll live. It's not deep." One of the nurses approached, healing spray in hand and applied the thick substance. "Okay, you know the drill. Sit here for a moment and let the stuff do its job. Do you hurt anywhere else?"

Jackson moved his head, rotated his shoulders, and bent side to side at the waist. "Well, except for feeling like I went through a spin cycle and was then forcefully ejected, I'm fine."

Will Bennett smiled. "Good. I'll gather my stuff and be ready in a minute."

Left alone, Farrell slipped her arms around Jackson's neck. "Do you have any more excitement planned for us today?"

"I certainly hope not. Are you okay?" He put his arms around her waist

"I'm fine. We took your advice and held on tight; luckily the beds are bolted down. All we had to do was try to avoid flying scanners." She chuckled then kissed him tenderly. "How did the bridge fair…besides you?"

"Not bad actually. It might take a while for all the equipment to come back online, but the crew seemed okay. But I need to check out that explosion, I hope I won't find a big hole in the side of the ship."

"I'm sure it's fine. This ship has a great crew, so I'm sure everything is already under control. You can't be responsible for every single thing that happens."

"I know you're right, but I can't help it. I'm worried," he said, the strain visible on his face.

"That's just who you are. It's what makes you an excellent captain." She smiled sweetly.

"Were you able to bring the Morodon out of stasis?"

"We were. Luckily, the doctor had been included in the initializing program that put him under and was able to reverse the sequence. We thought about just opening the lid or smashing the control panel but weren't sure what effect that might have.

"His name is Trame. He seems fine and is resting now. Leea is with him. The greeter is there too, as if by magic, of course, and passed along whatever message she was supposed to. We did learn that we won't have to bring the bird to the surface. Some of the Morodons on the planet can communicate with each other and know their locations. They will help find the others."

"That's great." He stared at the floor.

"What is it?"

He pulled her close, needing the comfort. "This is a lot harder than I thought it would be."

She held him tight. "Just believe in yourself and it will all work out. I love you."

"I love you more."

She pulled back and stroked his cheek. "Never believe that for a minute."

The doctor approached with three nurses, all carrying med-kits. Jackson gave Farrell a quick kiss. "Oh, by the way, tell Leea I met Mearos."

"I'll do that."

The explosion was the result of one of the maneuvering engines being ripped from its riggings, and the subsequent fire was the ruptured fuel lines igniting within the ship before the system could shut down. Much to Jackson's relief, the flames had been quickly extinguished before the main engines failed. The riggings for the maneuvering engines were designed to break free under extreme stress without affecting the hull. While they wouldn't be able to assess the exterior damage until later, no hull breach was detected in that area. Sadly, three crew members were burned in the fire, but their injuries could be treated in the regeneration bed.

One of the nurses stayed behind to treat the men while the rest of the group made their sweep of the living quarters. Twenty-nine crew members were found with extensive injuries as they knocked on doors. Most had broken bones, and only a few with deeper lacerations. The captain left the rest of the medical team to tend to the wounded and moved on to inspect the rest of the ship.

The fighter bay sustained the worst damage. The already mangled floor hadn't been able to withstand the strain of the twisting structure, and much of it fell into the bay below, damaging two of the five shuttles and one of the larger transports.

Countless ceiling tiles lined the hallways, and a few doors hung askew. Two bulkhead doors were sealed in the cargo areas, and Jackson suspected there were hull breaches on the other side. These areas would have to be repaired from the outside, but he wasn't sure they had the proper equipment for the job.

Minimal communication had been restored by the time he returned to the bridge. He was immediately informed that the Zantian cruiser was hailing again and that he had a message from Dekarra, addressed directly to him. Deciding to save the long-range communication for later, he took a seat at the only monitor to survive destruction and connected with Mearos.

"It's good to see you survived the ordeal, Captain," Mearos said.

"Likewise. When everything exploded, we were afraid maybe you didn't make it."

The Zantian captain chuckled. "My copilot was none too happy with my maneuver, but luckily, except for a few singed hull plates, we came out unscathed. But we were also concerned for you when our scanners showed you missed one of the missiles on the first try."

"So were we. The first shockwave didn't cause much damage, but that second one was brutal. I see what you meant when you said they would annihilate us. Even exploding at that distance, there were a few moments when I wasn't sure the ship would hold together."

"Rest assured. The Atlantis held up well."

"Our sensors are down, so we haven't been able to check the exterior."

"We expected as much when we saw that your engines were out, so we flew around for a look, and this is what I can tell you: the ship is listing, but not too bad.

You're missing one of your side engines, and many of the sensor arrays and weapon turrets have either been ripped off or are hanging by a wire. Quite a few hull plates are twisted, although none seem to be missing, and there are two hull breaches in what I believe is your cargo area."

"That's better than I was expecting. The area around the breaches was automatically sealed, but repairing it is going to be a challenge. This ship has a triple hull, and we haven't detected any of the interior panels out of alignment, so I don't believe there are any others. The missing engine caused an internal fire but was quickly put out. The floor in the fighter bay fell, damaging a few of our shuttles. Internally, we have a lot of wiring and panels to reconnect, but other than that, we did okay."

"I'm happy to hear that. The coming days will be tense as we all deal with this crisis," Mearos said speculatively. "But once things have settled, I offer the services of myself and my crew to help with your repairs."

"Thank you, that is much appreciated. I'm not sure if we have the expertise or the right kind of equipment to repair any of the external damage."

"We will do what we can. We have a few things we need to do right now, but we'll be back to check on you later." Mearos disconnected.

Max, seated next to him, looked over. "The Zantians aren't anything like I imagined," he murmured.

Jackson sighed. "No, they aren't," He listened to the message from Dekarra, smiled, and got to his feet. "I'm off to make a deal with the devil," he said to no one in particular and left the bridge.

Out of courtesy, Jackson knocked on Admiral Shaw's prison room door. The former commander and his thirty-five-member security force were confined behind locked doors at the aft end of the third crew deck—the admiral the only one allowed a room to himself. Armed guards were stationed at the beginning and end of the corridor, but only as a precaution; the portable locking devices attached to each door could only be accessed from the outside.

Raymond Shaw sat at the small table reading a book. It was one of the few personal belongings he was allowed to bring to these temporary quarters. He looked up briefly and grimaced. "Are you done trying to destroy my ship, Captain?"

"Last I heard this wasn't your ship anymore. And for your information, if it had been, we wouldn't be having this conversation."

"Of course, we wouldn't, I'd have destroyed those bastards."

"Actually, they would have destroyed us first. But instead, they helped us avoid our precarious predicament."

"You're so gullible. That's what they want you to think. They'll pretend to be our friends, invite us down to their planet, and we'll all disappear into their mines, never to be seen or heard from again."

Jackson rolled his eyes. "Do you actually believe the words that come out of your mouth?"

The large man's dark eyes glared at him. "Why are you here?"

"I have some good news for you. I just received a message from Dekarra. It seems your cohorts: the vice president, his aides, Bettina and a handful of other people, have all been arrested for treason. It seems the VP couldn't wait until you got back to start his new job, so he launched a campaign to discredit the president and used this trip as leverage.

"Unfortunately, your minions didn't count on my little group foiling their plans. They exposed your true objective, and then it was...well...game over. The government wanted me to relieve you of command, but I guess I've already done that. So, whatever you think you're still going to accomplish here, won't happen."

The admiral's expression didn't waver.

"I have a proposition for you. The Zantians' weapons did quite a bit of damage. It's nothing we can't fix; it's just going to take some time. I was hoping you would ask your team to help. You have thirty-five able-bodied men and women sitting on their collective asses doing nothing. And, your efforts would be taken into consideration once we're back on Dekarra."

A dark shadow crossed the admiral's face, but then he gave a crazed laugh. "I would rather pilot this ship into the sun than hand it over to the Zantians—which is exactly what you're doing. You'll get no help from me. And as far as my security team goes; they'll never take orders from you."

Jackson smirked. "I always knew you were a pompous ass."

He left the admiral, who had already returned to his book, and went room by room making the same offer to the incarcerated security squad. While there were a few hesitations, in the end, all refused. Jackson shrugged indifferently at each one but gave them the option to change their minds.

He went back to the medical bay to check on the patients, but mostly to see Farrell. He was tired and wanted nothing more than to spend some quiet time with her, but knew that wouldn't happen anytime soon. Inside, all five beds, as well as the regeneration bed, were occupied, and several injured crewmen sat nearby waiting their turn. Dr. Bennett, his nurses, Ben McAdams, Farrell, and Leea were all busy tending to them. Before he could successfully pull Farrell into a far corner, Max stepped through the open doorway.

"There you are," he said looking at Jackson.

"Is there no rest for the weary," he exclaimed lightheartedly, resting his head on Farrell's shoulder.

"Sorry. The Zantian captain wants another word."

"Okay, I'll be right there." He pulled Farrell close and kissed her. "Can all this be over now?"

"You were the one who wanted to come on this trip," she said smiling, then ran her hands over his dark hair. "And it's a good thing we did. Right?"

"Yeah, I'm glad we came too."

"Good. Now go perform your duties. I'll be busy here for a while anyway."

"Can you spare Leea for a few minutes?"

"Sure. Why?"

"I'm sure she'll want to say hello to Mearos."

"Captain Owens, I hope I'm not disturbing you?" Mearos said once they were connected.

"No, not at all," Jackson smiled. "We're not able to do much with the limited power we have, but we're managing."

"I understand."

"But I do have someone here who would like to say hello first." Jackson moved to one side and let Leea step closer. A big smile crossed her face.

"Leea, it is so good to see you in one piece."

"I believe I told you once," she narrowed her eyes, "how I like uneventful journeys."

"So you did." He bowed his head. "My humblest apologies."

She laughed. "It's so good to see you too, Mearos. Although I wish it could be under better circumstance."

"As do I. Captain Owens, the reason I contacted you again so soon is that I've been asked to invite you and your small group to the surface to meet a few of our leaders before the real work begins. Now, if you can spare the time."

"Yes, that should be fine. As far as I know we still have a couple working shuttles; I just hope I can get out between all the rubble." He turned and smiled at Leea. "And I'm sure someone here is anxious to go home."

Leea lowered her head as redness crept into her cheeks.

# CHAPTER 30

# Coming Home

**"Y**ou look nervous." Farrell glanced over at Leea who sat next to her on the shuttle's bench, fidgeting with a button on her shirt. Jackson had managed to maneuver the craft around the debris-strewn bay, and now they were on their way to the Zantian surface.

"I'm terrified."

"Why? I thought you'd be giddy with excitement."

"I am, but …."

"But what?"

"What if we've changed?"

"Of course, you've changed. This situation will change everyone on both our worlds."

"Oh, I know, but that's not what I mean. Yaran changed before this. I could tell in the messages he sent. It's like … it's like—"

"Like he grew up?"

Leea chuckled softly. "Yeah, something like that."

"Don't be fooled. Men, at least Human men, never grow up. Look at Jackson." Farrell adoringly eyed the man in the pilot's seat. "My hero; so focused today; so leader-like; so in charge. But away from the public eye, he's still the twelve-year-old boy I fell in love with in college."

Leea's eyebrows shot up. "He was twelve when you met in college?"

Farrell laughed. "No. But he sure acted like it sometimes. And deep down, he hasn't aged a day. And let me say one more thing. From what you've told me about your relationship with Yaran, I'm sure he's as anxious for this reunion as you are."

"But what if he looks at me differently now? What if I look at him differently …?"

Farrell laughed again and put an arm around Leea's shoulders. "Stop it. You have nothing to worry about. I'm going to bet, the minute you two lock eyes on each other, this past year will be forgotten. And trust me; love is not so easily dismissed. Change is inevitable, yes, but as long as you accept that, and grow with it, you will always be the same two people who fell in love."

Leea hugged her friend. "Thank you, I needed that."

"Eh, that's what I'm here for—the calming influence." This time, they both laughed. "But I have to say I'm a little nervous too."

"About meeting everyone?"

"Well, yes, that too. But I'm more worried about the change in the environment. The Zantian captain said they weren't sure, but it shouldn't be anything more than some lightheadedness, but I don't want to step off the shuttle and faint in front of a group of alien men. How am I going to prove how tough I am if I can't stay on my feet?"

Leea chuckled. "You are a silly person. I'm sure you'll have no problem proving what a hardnosed negotiator you can be."

"I hope so."

Soon the city of Alrack came into view as they followed Mearos's cruiser to the airfield. The only time Leea had seen this city from the air was the day she left this world, and the one thing that immediately caught her attention was the absence of lights. It wasn't completely dark, but no longer the magical vision of a thousand stars she remembered. What lights did illuminate the streets, she realized, came through open doors and windows at ground level.

At one end of the main street, the complex that housed Marta's favorite sweet shop was now a pile of rubble. Leea's heart sank as she saw another path cut through a processing plant and several tall buildings as the shuttle rounded toward their destination. She hoped everyone had gotten out, and pushed away the thought that Julia worked down there somewhere.

Craning her neck toward the opposite window, she searched for the house on the hill, normally a beacon visible for miles, but it too was shrouded in darkness.

When they reached the airfield, Jackson banked the shuttle toward the back of the terminal and landed in front of the only lit hangar. Through the window, Leea immediately spotted Yaran. Her heart raced with anticipation, much like it had all those years ago in the music room when she had declared her love him. She only wished he stood there alone, as he had that day. As much as she longed to throw her arms around him and never let go, she knew that moment would have to wait.

"Well, here we go," Farrell said laying a hand on Leea's arm. "Deep breath."

Leea smiled at her friends. "Can't I just wait here? You guys can go out, introduce yourselves, and then you can send Yaran in here."

"Not a chance." Jackson eyed her expressively. "As a matter of fact, you're going first."

"What? Why?"

"Because they know you. You need to introduce us."

"Well, I had to try," she said dejected, but then smiled. "But just to be clear, I'm a nervous wreck. When I step off this shuttle, my legs might not hold me upright."

"Not to worry, we'll be right behind you to catch you if you fall," Jackson said, pushing her gently toward the door.

"Thanks," Leea chuckled. "But you might want to keep an eye on her," she pointed to Farrell. "She afraid her reputation will be tarnished if she faints at the feet or our hosts."

Jackson smiled. "Babe, you can be as tough as nails if you want to be. No atmospheric pressure is going to get the better of you."

"Thanks for the vote of confidence," she said and rolled her eyes.

"All joking aside, are you sure you're okay with being our spokesperson?"

Farrell took a deep breath and nodded. "I have imagined a moment like this all my life." Her eyes misted over, but she quickly grimaced. "What is wrong with me?"

Jackson pulled her close. "You're going to be wonderful. The Human race couldn't be in better hands."

"No pressure I take it?"

"That's when you do your best work, babe." He kissed her lightly, and they made their way out the door.

The world stood still for Leea as she stepped off the shuttle. She saw no one but Yaran—everything and everyone else around her disappeared in a distant haze, and the only sound she heard was the beating of her own heart. She wanted to run, but her legs felt as if they weighed a ton and she could barely make them move. A hand on her shoulder brought the surroundings back into focus.

"Everything all right?" Jackson asked.

She smiled back at him and nodded, then made her way toward the love of her life, who was already on his way to her.

Yaran took both her hands and pulled them to his lips, looking at her lovingly. She returned his gaze as happy tears welled in her eyes. Her heart beat wildly, and she still wondered if this was real. Her dreams had often included Yaran, only to have their reunion shattered upon waking.

As if sensing her turmoil, Yaran leaned down and laid a cheek against hers. "Welcome home, my love," he whispered.

"*A'rinBientS'aan*, it's so good to be home," she whispered back, trying to keep her voice steady. She deeply inhaled the fresh scent of his favorite soap, and with the feel of his warm skin, she wanted to melt into him. "Why are there so many people here?" she quipped.

Yaran chuckled softly. "I was just asking myself the same question."

She closed her eyes and nestled closer for a moment then forced herself to pull away. Yaran studied her face and smiled brightly before turning back to the group. He kept a hold of her hand, which she clutched tightly for fear he might slip away. All eyes were on them. In what Leea thought was a far-too-brief moment, the remaining Watchers had exited the shuttle and stood nearby, waiting.

A broad smile crossed Leea's face when she saw Mearos, which he returned, and she briefly wondered about the older man standing next him—there was a definite resemblance. With him also stood three other men she assumed were his crew, and the five remaining men in the hangar were Zantian leaders.

Leea introduced her group, and Yaran presented the rest. Although Mearos and Sithan observed the Human custom of shaking hands, the Desolk's, all introduced with their title and city affiliation, simply gave a respectful nod.

"Thank you, Captain Owens, I appreciate you making this trip," Yaran said, glancing at Leea.

"Please, call me Jackson, and it was my pleasure. I wanted the opportunity to meet Mearos and his crew face to face. To personally thank them for what they did for us up there."

"The appreciation goes both ways," the Zantian captain assured him. "Without your efforts, this all could have had a very different outcome."

"I know there is a lot that needs to be discussed," Farrell interjected, trying to appear calm in the presence of the alien men. "I think we should get together soon to determine where we go from here."

"I agree," Yaran said. "Is tomorrow afternoon too soon?"

"Not at all."


"I need a shower," Leea said firmly, gently pushing Yaran away and stepping back.

They were in the Desolk's plush city apartment which had been spared from the attack. It had been Toref's suggestion, stating that as much as he would enjoy their company, he was sure the reunited couple would appreciate some privacy. He got no argument from either of them.

"It can wait." Unsuccessfully, he tried to pull her close.

"Trust me...it can't. In the last two days, I've been shot, imprisoned, and nearly blown out of the sky." She held up a hand as Yaran started to protest. "So, right now, I need a shower. I won't be long." She slowly ran a finger along his cheek. "And then we can catch up."

Quickly, she entered the washroom, closed the door behind her and leaned against it for a brief moment to let her heartbeat calm. A shower was definitely necessary, but it wasn't the real reason she sought this brief escape. While she desperately longed for the man on the other side of the door, her nervousness from earlier had returned, and she needed a moment of calm; she wanted this reunion to be perfect.

A few minutes later, warm water gently flowed from above, washing away the soap and all the unpleasantness of the last few days. Her nerves had settled, and now full of anticipation, Leea smiled and turned her face up toward the gentle spray. Reaching blindly for the shower's control panel, she stopped when two hands gently came to rest on her shoulders. Her breath caught at the familiar touch.

"I couldn't stay away," Yaran said barely above a whisper as his lips lightly brushed against her neck.

"I'm glad." While every inch of her being screamed to touch him, Leea stood perfectly still, enjoying the feel of his lips on her skin. "If this is a dream, please don't let me wake up."

"No dream, my love. We're both here." He reached over to the control panel and set the water on a five-minute delay, then filled his palm with foaming soap. Pushing her long wet hair over one shoulder, and taking a small step back, Yaran began to explore a slow, sensuous path over her body.

She closed her eyes and concentrated as every one of her nerve endings reacted to his slow caress. His hands moved across her shoulders and down her back in small circular motions, stopping their downward route at her waist. With the last bit of foam, he moved down her arms and laced their fingers briefly.

He refilled his hands and moved to her waist, slowly across her hips, and down her thighs as far as his arms could reach, softly massaging her overly sensitized skin. Leea moaned blissfully. As the hands traveled up the back of her legs, they lingered a moment at the well-shaped rise of her buttocks before coming to rest again at her waist.

"I've missed you so much," he whispered hoarsely. "You are more beautiful than I remember."

As Yaran continued to her stomach, Leea placed her hands over his, instantly realizing she wanted more—needed more—and moved them upward. "Please...," she begged, barely recognizing her own voice. With their fingers intertwined, Yaran tenderly massaged her full breasts.

The task took its toll on him as his soft moans grew ragged. The water restarted, and Leea couldn't wait any longer. She turned and placed her hands, fingers spread, on his smooth chest and took in the bronze skin slick with moisture. She wanted nothing more than to stand there and take in every inch of him, but her body had more urgent needs. Finally looking into his lightened eyes, she slowly slid her hands around his neck, pressing her body against his.

He pulled her hard to him. "I need you, Leea," he said, panting.

"Come to me, my love."

Moving his hands to the back of her legs, Yaran lifted her and rested her back gently against the shower wall then kissed her hungrily. After a year of longing to be in his arms, Leea clutched at him in desperation as their bodies joined, her mind still not completely able to grasp the reality of their circumstance. But as it had been since their first night together, completeness washed over her, and she relaxed into the moment, knowing that no dream could bring about this incredible feeling of happiness.

When he finally set her feet back on the tiled floor, she gazed lovingly into his eyes and ran her fingers through his wet hair, pushing strands out of his face. Tears of joy ran down her cheeks. "I love you, Yaran, and have missed you terribly. There were days I didn't know if I would make it through."

"We're together now, and nothing will ever change that again." He cupped her face. "I will never let you go again … no matter what. We always said we would enjoy the time fate allowed us. Well, fate has chosen to bring us back together, and we should honor that decision." He smiled and then kissed her gently for a long moment. "We should probably dry off," he finally said, reaching for the shower controls, but her hand stopped him.

"Oh no," she said seductively, reaching for the panel herself, "now it's my turn."

When Leea woke up the next morning, the feeling of complete comfort enveloped her. She was happier than she could ever remember being. Without opening her eyes, she snuggled deeper into her pillow, pulled the thin blanket under her chin and reached out, only to find the space next to her empty. With slight panic, she sat up looking around but then smiled as she discerned the familiar aroma of sweet herbal tea. Yawning, she let herself fall back and stretched, smiling wider as she felt the soreness of her body. Her heart rate increased with the memories of the previous night—it was good to be home.

Before leaving Zantia, she and Yaran had enjoyed, what she considered, a satisfying physical relationship, although it was always subject to finding the time to be alone. And when they did, it had been a gentle and tender experience. But what happened last night was something completely different. This was a raw, desperate emotion that refused to be satisfied until their bodies collapsed with exhaustion. It was the most incredible thing she had ever experienced.

Slipping out of bed, she pulled out Yaran's shirt from her bag and made her way to the washroom. Leea had never worn it on Dekarra. At first, it was because she wanted to preserve its fragrance. However, time eventually evaporated Yaran's familiar scent and after that, she was afraid something might happen to it. But from the first day, it had occupied the opposite side of her bed, and she woke up many mornings with it clutched to her chest.

In the kitchen, Yaran stood at the small cooking surface stirring the contents in a glass pot. Walking up behind him, she wrapped her arms around his waist, resting her head on his back.

After a moment he placed the pot on a warmer, turned, and with surprise, took in her attire. A slow smile spread across his face. "Where did that come from?"

"My bag. Julia gave it to me the day I left. She wanted me to take something of yours that would make me feel close to you."

"It looks much better on you than it ever did on me." He eyed her again artfully.

"That's a matter of perspective."

"Yes, I guess it is. I wish I had thought to take something from your room, but I found a different way to feel close to you. I slept in your bed a few times when I was home."

"You did? No one saw you?"

"I don't think so. The first time was the first night I was home after my father left for Karba. I was restless and couldn't sleep... too many memories, so I went to the kitchen for some water. On the way back I found myself going up the stairs to the workers' quarters. My intention was just to go into your room for a moment, but I couldn't resist the urge to lay down on the bed. Being there made me feel close to you, and I slipped into a peaceful sleep. The next morning, I waited until everyone was busy with their tasks and returned to my room. I did that several more times whenever I had trouble sleeping. If anyone noticed, it was never mentioned."

"If someone had seen you, they probably would have understood."

"I suppose they would have."

"But I do need to ask: last night... was something completely unexpected... completely amazing," she looked up dreamily at his handsome face and blushed. "Should I be worried where you—?"

"Never. Let me be perfectly clear. There has never been, nor could there ever be, anyone in my life but you. Last night was the result of a year's worth of missing you and wanting to prolong every moment of our reunion. I have always loved you, Leea, and tried to prepare myself for a very lonely life, and well, being with you again I needed to make up for lost time."

"So, I don't have to worry about a seven-foot arm wrestler coming after me?" she said teasingly.

He laughed heartily and pulled her into a tight embrace. "No. No need to worry about that. But, to make a personal observation," he said slyly, "you were full of your own surprises last night. Maybe I'm the one who should be worried."

She smiled and then blushed. "I was only trying to keep up with you."

He eyed her doubtfully. "Hmmm… Are you hungry? Food is almost ready."

"Great. I'm starving." Leea reached past him, picked a few purple berries from a fresh fruit plate before walking over to the large window overlooking the city. She craned her head to the left and could just make out a partially toppled building. The leader's mansion, straight ahead on the hill, glowed in the bright sunlight, seemingly untouched by the previous day's tragic events.

"This is completely different from what I'd imagined," she mused.

"What did you imagine?" he asked, handing her a steaming cup of tea.

"Well, to be honest, I didn't know what to expect. I pictured you picking me up from the airfield, taking me back to the house where I would go back to my old room. I knew you lived with Toref, and I knew I wouldn't be welcome in that house. Guess I couldn't picture it any other way."

"I would never let you go back there. I never want you to be subjected to the bad memories of that place again. We'll be okay here for now. I just wish we could lock ourselves in here for the next couple weeks."

She smiled up at him. "Me too, but I know we can't. There is too much to do out there. We'll have our time, so for now, these moments will be enough."

"Yes, they will. And the best part is, there will be no more hiding our relationship."

"Are you sure?"

"I love you, Leea, and I will no longer hide that from anyone."

She smiled at him lovingly. "I love you too."

After they finished their meal, Yaran double checked the time. "The Dekarrans will be returning in about six hours. That should give us enough time to get some things done before they arrive. As soon as we're ready, I'm going to take you over to Julia's. I want to go see Lauranna, and I also need to check on the status of the cities, so I won't stay long."

"Have you heard how the others fared?"

"Not all of them. Some we haven't been able to reach yet. We've set up a command center at the airfield, where we'll meet with the…Watchers, later today."

"I see it's already been a busy morning."

"I made several calls before you got up." He sighed. "I look forward to all this being over."

"I'm sure everyone does."

He grasped her hands across the table and looked at her meditatively. "I'm not sure how I survived this last year without you. Letting you go was the worst thing I've ever done."

She squeezed his hands. "I was the one who made the decision to go. I thought I was doing the right thing. But I will never make that mistake again."

"From now on, we stay together."

"Yes, we will. In the coming weeks, along with everything else, we'll need to decide where to live. I'm sure Humans are going to want to leave, so things will be in turmoil for a while."

"I'll go wherever you want. As long as we're together, it doesn't matter."

Leea shook her head. "No, this can't be my decision alone. And if you leave it up to me, I'm going to say we stay here."

He raised his eyebrows. "Why?"

"Your family is here: your mother and your…crazy father." She chuckled. "And you and Toref have become close this past year. I don't have a family. Yes, I'll be extremely sad to see Julia and Tim go, and I'll miss Farrell and Jackson, but I won't ask you to leave. It's not like we can't visit Dekarra. We could catch a ride with Mearos. He can drop us off, and pick us up on his next trip. Or," she winked, "we could get our own ship."

"You seem to have this all figured out."

"Actually, I'm making it up as I go along, but I like the idea. And like you said, as long as we're together is all that matters. I don't care if we build a hut on the moon."

He smiled. "Let's hope it won't come to that."

They started to clear the dishes when Yaran asked, "Do you think other Humans will want to stay?"

She shrugged. "Maybe. I'm sure the first reaction will be to go. They'll want to see that new planet where other people from Earth live. But if Zantians make some concessions, like giving the workers complete freedom, especially those in the mines, you might be surprised. Not everyone is comfortable with change."

He looked at her appreciatively. "I would be one of them."

"Well, let's see where these negotiations take us, and then we can decide."

"Agreed."

Through tears of joy, Leea and Julia hugged each other for several long minutes.

"I'm so glad you're back," Julia said after they made themselves comfortable in the small living room. "Ever since Yaran told us you were on your way back I've been so excited."

"I can attest to that," Tim verified. "It's all she's talked about." He smiled at his wife affectionately. "Now, we can finally change the subject."

Julie narrowed her eyes at him and grimaced, before bursting into laughter.

"It's good to see you both together," Leea said. "I'm so glad Yaran could make this happen for you."

"He's been our family's savior," Julia smiled at him. "And, he's been a regular visitor to our humble abode, and we love having him, so you have no excuse."

"As if anything could keep me away."

Yaran got to his feet. "On that very high praise, I'm going to take my leave. I want to check on my mother and then on things in the city."

"Can you drop me off in the city first?" Tim asked. "I want to see if they need help at the processing plants. Since Toref decided to seal the mines until all this is settled, I find myself with nothing to do. And then the sisters can catch up."

"Of course. I'm sure your help will be appreciated."

"So, how does it feel to be back?" Julia asked once they were alone. Marta also left to visit a friend.

"I couldn't be happier. Being back with Yaran is a dream come true."

"I bet," Julia smiled slyly. "How was the reunion?"

"It was amazing. But I will admit, yesterday on the flight in I was extremely nervous. It was easy to tell in Yaran's messages just how much he'd changed. I was worried that things between us would be different. But you know what? I think they're actually stronger now."

"And that probably explains why you both look so tired this morning."

"Well, we had a lot of…catching up to do. Not to mention, the time on the ship is different than here, so it will take a few days for me to adjust."

"That may explain your tired look…but not his." Julia laughed. "I've missed you so much, little sister. Tim was right when he said all I've talked about recently is you coming back. Of course, I was a nervous wreck when Yaran told us what was probably going to happen once your ship got here."

"It was all pretty scary on the ship too." Leea told her about the events of the last couple days.

Julia listened to the recount with wide eyes. "Oh, Leea, what a horrible experience! You must have been so scared?"

"I was." She lowered her head and grimaced. "But the worst part is, because of my actions we couldn't deactivate all the fighters. I'm to blame that bombs destroyed so many cities. How do I live with that?"

"None of this is your fault," Julia said forcefully. "Do you think if your group hadn't overthrown the admiral when you did, he would have worked with Mearos to stop the missiles coming from the moon?"

"No, probably not. Most likely, the admiral would have tried to destroy him."

"Then you would all be dead…Mearos too. How can you blame yourself for not letting that happen?"

Leea pulled in a deep breath. "Thank you. I guess my emotions are still on edge…the lack of sleep doesn't help."

"Put all that stuff out of your head and be happy that you're back with your sister…oh, and Yaran too."

Leea laughed heartily, her trepidation gone. "I am. So, show me your new home and tell me what's going on in your life."

"Mother?" Yaran called as he entered the front door of his parents' home. He walked into her sitting room, expecting to find her sitting in her large chair as usual, but the space empty. Making his way through the atrium, Yaran stopped short when he noticed her on a bench in the far corner with her eyes closed.

"Mother?"

"Yaran," she said startled, opening her eyes. "I'm wasn't expecting to see you today."

"I had to make sure you were okay." He joined his mother on the bench. With everything that's happened…."

"I'm fine," she smiled and laid a reassuring hand on his arm. "The house didn't sustain any damage, but the gardens didn't fare so well. How are things out there?"

"Not as bad as they could have been, but worse than they should have been."

"You did what you could."

"I know. I just wish I could have done more."

"I'm proud of you, Yaran. You followed your heart and saved many lives. Focus on what you did accomplish and don't let that which was beyond your control negate that."

"Even though it went against Jarock?"

"I'm not judging. You both did what you thought was best."

Yaran scowled but stayed silent.

"Is Leea back?"

"Yes," Yaran smiled languorously.

"I'm very happy for you."

"Thank you." He got to his feet. "I can't stay. I just wanted to stop by and make sure you were all right. But since I'm here, I'm going to get a few things from my room." Lauranna got to her feet and hugged him. "I love you, Yaran. I'm glad you came."

"I love you too, Mother. I'll come again as soon as I can."

Yaran made his way down the curved hallway and entered his old room. Little adorned the space except for several ancient instruments, from worlds he didn't know, hanging on bare white walls. His large bed, always freshly made, stood against one wall and a wall-length wardrobe on another.

Behind one of the cabinet's doors hung several shirts and pants he'd left, while the other door revealed a work-desk and storage area. He had taken his datapad with him, but most of his music was still stored on his stationary terminal, so he copied everything to several data-cubes. He would come back for the antiques when he and Leea decided where they were going to live.

It would take some time to get used to that thought—living together with Leea. Unrestrained by traditions and family expectations, they could now live the life they had always fantasized about. He almost felt guilty. With all the tragedy that was taking place on the planet, he felt nothing but happiness.

He went in search of a bag, then filled it with the remainder of his clothes along with a few items from the storage drawers. Taking one last look at the room he would never again occupy, he smiled. The thought that Leea was back in his life made anything in this room seem insignificant.

A bit distracted, Yaran hurried back the way he came and almost ran head-on into Jarock. The two men studied each other a moment, and then the older one walked past his son and entered his office. Incredulous, Yaran dropped the bag in the middle of the hallway and followed him.

"There is nothing for us to talk about, Yaran. Don't waste your time."

"We should have plenty to talk about. Have you seen what's happening to our planet?"

"Of course, I have! But who's to blame for that?"

"I'm not surprised you blame me. But here's the truth, if you had listened to me, taken what I said seriously, or even just as a precautionary measure, some of this could have been avoided. But when I stood in front of the Council to tell you what I knew, you used that opportunity to make me look like a fool. 'My misguided son...how sad,' Yaran seethed sarcastically. "So I suggest you blame yourself."

"Not for one minute," the Desolk snarled in return. "You see; I did take a precautionary measure. Had you and your sympathizers not interfered, that Dekarran ship would have been destroyed and none of this would be happening."

"I wasn't going to let you destroy that ship. These people have every right to come here and demand that we return their citizens. Isn't it enough that we've enslaved them for over a hundred years? Not to mention, there were people on board trying to help us, and you callously tried to murder them."

"Murder? They were attacking our world. We had every right to defend ourselves. And let's be realistic; your only interest in saving those Humans was for one reason...that girl. You lose all sense of reason—"

"Enough!" Yaran balled his fists but kept his anger in check. He had no intention of letting Jarock's affronts distract him. "I find it insulting that you actually believe I would put everyone on this planet in danger for the sake of one person. But then you've always thought the worst of me. As for Leea, she and her friends put their lives on the line to overthrow those carrying out the attack, and they succeeded. So their deaths would have been for nothing. Not that that matters to you. You probably saw this as an opportunity to get rid of her permanently. 'Getting me away from her influence' is most likely what you're thinking, which tells me you've never actually loved anyone."

Jarock stepped forward and jabbed a finger in his son's chest, eyes black with rage. "Don't you dare presume to know what I have or haven't done! Get out! I will no longer tolerate your disrespect."

Yaran forcibly pushed his father's hand away and took a step back. "If you want respect, maybe you should show some. And as I mentioned at the Council meeting, I'm not one of your subordinates; you can't order me into silence. I will have my say, and there's nothing you can do about it."

Resigned, Jarock leaned back on the desk. "Fine. Have your say, and then leave."

Yaran decided to appeal to the leader he hoped was still there. "We should be putting our difference aside and discussing how to put this world back together... if that's actually a concern of yours. The people need leaders who can move us forward, not try to place blame."

The head of the Council stared at his son a moment. "You claim to want what's best for our people. Really? Yet you and your…supporters…took away the one thing that has protected us for over a century: the shield."

"And you find nothing wrong with imprisoning the Morodons to create that shield, do you? No problem forcing them to stay locked in a tiny box for a hundred years, just to keep you safe. Is no one else's life worth anything to you?

"But you seem to have forgotten that someone found us anyway. Or didn't you believe that either? The Belag was on the Dekarran ship and showed them where we were. The shape-shifters are paid seekers. Whoever hired him will come looking for us eventually, and since he knew where we were, so will they."

"And we would have dealt with them as we had all former enemies. But of course, you destroyed the missile silo, so that won't be possible now."

"You consider the Ma'Kree your enemy? They are our ancestors, who for some reason, are looking for us. I doubt they have gone to all the trouble of hiring a Belag so they could do us harm. But then I wonder if the perceived threat from outside is only a ruse to keep the people under your rule."

"Think what you like. But if you have any notion that we're going to roll over because some Humans have gotten the momentary upper hand, then you're delusional." Jarock pushed away from the desk and walked behind it, then looked over with a mocking smile as he sat down.

"But maybe this is an opportunity we shouldn't pass up. While the threat to us has always been real, no matter what you think, your friends may have done us a favor. It might be time for us to stop hiding. Go back to what we were once good at. Everyone seems to have forgotten that at one time we always had the upper hand."

Yaran's stared in disbelief. "You think our people want to go back to conquering other worlds? Then I'd say you're the one who's delusional. Have you looked at the people around you? When was the last time you stepped away from the council floor and looked at what this planet is all about? It's not about conquering; it's about being creative and living a peaceful existence. We're not warriors. We're—"

"We've become complacent! It's time Zantians get back on the right path."

"And what path is that? Stealing the treasures of others and enslaving a new race? And you call yourself a leader? The only thing you lead is the Council. A bunch of like-minded old men who live in the past and should never have been allowed to decide the future of our society. A true leader guides the people. You don't even know who your people are anymore."

Yaran's voice took on a softer tone "This silly notion that we have to adhere to some long-dead philosophy needs to be buried once and for all so we can move forward according to the will of the people."

"Since you've heard the story of our history, let me remind you, the Ma'Kree rebels left the world that had become stagnant for a better, more exciting life. The agreement four hundred years ago should never have been made. Now that we seem to be at another crossroad, I will not fail to carry out the vision of those who built this world."

"But you've already failed—failed the living in favor of the dead. All you care about is keeping your antiquated ideals alive while lying to the Zantian people for centuries about who they really are. While I realize this didn't start with you, you have been more than happy to carry the ruse forward. And to what end? For some ridiculous notion that we're better off living to some ancient principle. After a thousand years, you still believe this is what they wanted for their descendants, never to grow or evolve into something better. This can't continue. I will see to it that everyone knows the truth. And there are those who will help me."

"I will not allow—"

"You have no choice!" With a feeling of Deja vu, Yaran leaned over and rested his palms on the desktop, anger taking control. "While you and your inner circle sit back and plot what's best for you, the rest of us will be doing what we can to move forward once the workers are gone. If that's something you don't want to focus on, then I suggest you evaluate where you belong. Maybe you should do what those Ma'Kree rebels you seem to admire so much did; take your like-minded supporters and leave those here who want to rebuild and run this world in peace."

Jarock rose and contemplated Yaran for a brief moment. "Well, my son, it seems you have quite the array of opinions. Now, you've had your say, and I'm sure we both have a busy day ahead."

# CHAPTER 31

# Final Decisions

"**W**here are we going?" Leea asked, sitting next to Yaran in the airborne shuttle.

"To Emborie."

"And you're not going to tell me why?"

"No." Yaran pursed his lips and sighed. "Only that there's someone there I want you to meet."

"I'm not going to like this, am I?"

"Oh, you will…but…I wish you wouldn't ask so many questions."

"Okay." She looked at him apprehensively. "You're scaring me."

He gave her a surprised look then reached over and rested a hand on her knee, squeezing gently. "There is nothing to be afraid of. I would never do anything to hurt you."

"I know. But the secrecy worries me."

He gave another deep sigh. "It wasn't my idea."

As the shuttle set down, Leea gave him a sly smile. "We're going to the mine? Did you change your mind about keeping me after all?"

He laughed and pulled her close. "No. You're stuck with me."

"Good." She kissed him tenderly.

"Let's do this."

"You're nervous…why? Oh sorry, I'm not supposed to ask any more questions."

He flashed a smirk. "I'm not nervous about why we're here. But Graeden, the administrator, is loyal to Desolk Haliel, who, as you know, is my father's closest friend. When I called him this morning to ask for this meeting, he seemed reluctant to grant my request. Unfortunately, I had to put him in his place. I told him that the Council is dealing with our current situation, and he had no right to deny me anything. But if he wanted to take it up with his Desolk he should, although I believed they all have more important things on their minds and might not appreciate his petty objections." Yaran paused. "And this is a man who, half a year ago, helped save my life."

"During the storm?"

"Yes."

They entered the atrium of the administration building, expecting to be greeted by Graeden, but the only person present was a guard sitting behind the reception desk.

"We have an appointment with Administrator Graeden," Yaran, irritated, informed the Zantian.

"The administrator is attending to urgent matters," the guard returned. "I will take you to where your meeting is set up."

"Thank you."

They walked into an office halfway down an adjacent hallway where a tall man stood at the window looking out at the mountain range. He turned as they entered.

"Yaran, it's nice to see you again," he said, moving toward them. The man had red hair and a gray-streaked beard. Vibrant green eyes studied them, and he pulled in a quick breath as he looked at Leea.

"It is good to see you as well." He placed a hand gently at Leea's back, and she took a step forward. "I've brought you a visitor."

Familiarity washed over her. An image on her holo-ring came to mind. That man was younger and had no beard, but the eyes were the same—the vibrant emerald that seemed to twinkle in the light. She took a few steps closer and studied his face. He smiled at her, and there was no doubt—this man was her father.

She felt herself wobble, and Yaran was instantly at her side putting a steadying arm around her waist. "I'm sorry, I should have warned you."

Her head cleared as she studied the red-haired man. "No, I'm all right. Is it true? Are you my father?"

He smiled sadly and then briefly hummed the tune she'd long forgotten. Tears welled in her eyes as she approached the man she thought long dead, and gently hugged him. Gingerly he returned his daughter's embrace.

"I'm so sorry," his voice cracked as he pulled away and studied her face. "I'm so sorry I couldn't be there for you when you were growing up. Not a day has gone by that I haven't thought about you."

"It's all right. I'm sure whatever your reason, it was the only one you had."

"Please don't blame Yaran for the secrecy. I made him promise not to tell you."

"Why?"

"I didn't want to upset your life any further."

She smiled reassuringly. "I have so many questions." Leea turned to Yaran. "Can we stay for a while?"

"I told Graeden we would be an hour," Yaran informed them. "Roger, when this current crisis is over, I will see to it that you're released from here. Unfortunately, I'm not sure when that will be."

"I understand. I'm just grateful that you brought my daughter back to me."

Yaran smiled. "It was my honor." He kissed Leea on the forehead. "I will leave you both to get reacquainted, and be back in an hour. I'm sure Graeden won't leave you here one minute past."

"You're leaving?"

"I'm just going back to the shuttle to check on a few things."

Leea looked at the closed door as she and Roger sat down in two chairs by the window.

"You care for him very much."

"He's my life," she admitted dreamily. "He's been my rock through all the bad times. Without him, I wouldn't be here...here with you anyway. How did he find you?"

"Completely by accident. He came looking for Marik."

"Marik?" she shuddered.

"He had been sent to my crew a few months earlier. He proved to be completely useless and spent most of his days in confinement. Yaran came here to talk to him, and I was summoned to explain why he was unavailable. He recognized me the same way you did." Roger stroked his beard. "I guess I can hide my face, but the eyes are a dead giveaway."

"Yes, they are."

"From the day you were born, everyone said you looked like me."

"I have a few images of us as a family, and saw the resemblance too."

His eyes misted. "You were the best part of my life, Leea. Don't misunderstand; I loved your mother very much, but she lived in a very sad place. One she retreated into more and more each year. Foolishly, I thought a child would bring Kathryn out of her dungeon, give her something to be happy about, and for a while, it seemed to work. You were such a cheerful baby. Always quick to smile, and she found joy in that. You pulled her back from some of her dark recesses. But when they sent me to the mines, she lost her balance. And when I... died...she couldn't hang on anymore. I'm so sorry."

"None of that is your fault. Zantians didn't know how to help her. Or maybe they didn't want to. We're not much use to them if we can't perform our duties, and well, as you pointed out, mom had her difficult days. But, tell me why you... died."

He settled back in his chair and focused his gaze out the window. "I worked in the south mine, in the area where the train cars bound for the city were loaded and secured.

"One day, a cargo hauler leaving the Alrack airfield had to make an emergency landing in our yard. I don't remember where it was headed, but it had some mechanical problem and set down. Along with one of our mechanics, the pilot determined that the engine needed some new part, which they easily located, but it would take a couple of hours to be delivered.

"The shuttle's cargo wasn't perishable, but because the vehicle needed to be powered down, there was one item the pilot didn't want to leave in the hot sun. It was a strange thing: a large box with an opaque domed lid. We could have gotten an anti-grav hauler from below, but the depot was close, so four of us each grabbed a corner and carried it inside to a secure room, and then returned to our duties.

"A short time later, I realized I was missing my gloves and remembered I had taken them off after we moved the box, so I headed back to the room, finding them inside on the floor. I leaned up against the container for a moment, and suddenly things started to beep, and a panel with flashing lights appeared. Panicking, I made the mistake of trying to figure out how to turn it off and pushed the wrong button.

"What I thought was opaque glass, turned out to be a mist inside the dome that dissipated, and then the glass retracted into the platform. A small, still creature lay inside, and I think instinct made me reach in to check if it was alive. I almost screamed when its eyes opened. It studied me for a moment and then spoke... I think... and told me to leave quickly before someone came. But, before I reached the entrance, the administrator, and the shuttle pilot entered."

Leea sat riveted to her father story. "And then what happened?" she asked as he paused reflectively.

"They kept me in confinement for a few days, where they were obviously deciding my fate, until one morning Toref walked in."

"Toref?"

"He had just taken over mine production responsibilities, so the administrator apparently went to him before bothering the Desolk. I knew Toref, of course, and maybe that's why he didn't do what was expected of him to keep this Zantian secret... even though I had no idea what the alien in the strange box was for.

"So, he offered me a deal: he would spare my life, but send me to another mine. There I could live out my life as long as I never mentioned what I had seen to anyone. Everyone would be told I died, and those that knew what happened would assume the appropriate measures had been taken." Roger lowered his head. "And until this moment I've kept that promise."

"Did Toref tell you why he saved your life?"

"No, and I was too devastated to even care. I'm sure he was supposed to make me disappear, but the Toref I remember was a kind man. Maybe by saving me, he could live with himself."

Leea took her father's hands and held them tight. "Well, I'm glad you made the deal. I'm happy to have my dad back."

He smiled. "I'm glad I did too; although I didn't always feel that way. I was a wreck after they moved me. Once I realized that my family was mourning my death, but I was very much alive, I deeply regretted saving myself. Not that it would have changed anything for you and your mother, but I would have been spared the pain.

"A few years later, Toref got a message to me that your mother had died. That was another low time in my life. I blamed myself for what happened, and how it must be affecting you." His voice trembled. "All I could think about was my baby girl. How was she going to manage without her parents? It took me a long time to finally realize it was all just an unfortunate accident. Maybe that's why Toref spared my life."

Leea choked back tears. "I did all right, Dad. I had Grandma, and Julia's parents treated me like one of their own. They went to another city after Julia married Tim, but by then, I had Yaran, and he's been there for me ever since."

"I'm glad. I was a little hard on him during the storm."

"You were there too?"

"I was the one who pulled him from the water," Roger said with a smile. "He seemed so excited to talk to me about you when we first arrived, but I cut him off, saying I didn't want to open old wounds. He was visibly hurt but honored my wishes. From that moment on, however, I thought of nothing but what he would tell me, so after the incident, I apologized, and asked him to tell me about my daughter. Which he happily did." Roger chuckled. "Not that I said anything, or objected, but I was granted a view of the beautiful, perfect woman he saw through his eyes."

Leea blushed.

"I would ask one favor, though."

"Anything."

"Don't tell Yaran about his uncle's involvement in my disappearance. Since Toref knows Yaran found me and didn't tell him, he obviously has his reasons."

Leea frowned. "I won't lie if he asks me specifically, but I don't see why he would."

"Thank you, that's all I ask. Now, tell me how things are going out there."

They continued their conversation, and as Yaran predicted, Graeden walked into the small office at exactly one hour. Father and daughter hugged for a long moment, whispering promises of seeing each other soon, through happy tears.

The administrator escorted Leea back to the atrium and Roger returned to his duties in the opposite direction. Yaran thanked the older Zantian for letting them come, and in return, Graeden mumbled something about not having a choice.

Yaran had barely closed the shuttle's door when Leea grabbed him into an embrace.

"Thank you, thank you, thank you."

"I feared you'd be upset that I didn't tell you."

"What? Of course not. I understand why he didn't want me to know. But it must have been hard for you to tell me about the storm and not mention my father?"

He smiled wryly. "Oh, yes. And honestly, I didn't agree with his reasoning, but, of course, I respected it."

"You did the right thing. Losing you and Julia was hard enough, but if I had learned my father was still alive, it would have only added to my heartache."

"I guess I understand that." He looked at her lovingly and started the engine. "Did you have a nice talk?"

"We did. I look forward to seeing him again."

"Maybe I can expedite his release. I will see what I can do."

An hour later, they stood in the airfield hangar alone as the Dekarran shuttle set down where it had the night before. The Zantian leaders waited in the temporary command center, still trying to collect data on the status of the remaining cities. Scout ships had been sent out to those they couldn't reach by comm, but some still hadn't returned.

As the group disembarked, Farrell greeted her friend with a hug and a large insulated cup.

Leea's eye grew wide. "Is this what I think it is?" Without waiting for an answer, she removed the lid and inhaled the escaping steam deeply. Cautiously she took a sip. "If anything could make this day any better, this is it." She scanned the group over the rim of the cup, realizing everyone was staring at her. "What?"

Everyone laughed except for Yaran, who studied her with a furrowed brow. "What is that?"

"Coffee. The best drink ever." She held the cup up for him to take in the steam. Taking a whiff, Yaran wrinkled his nose and took a step back.

"That's awful," he said.

Everyone laughed again, and then Jackson handed him a large box. "We pillaged the admiral's command suite and stole his coffee maker, then took coffee from the mess. Leea will be forever in your debt if you can make this work here."

Yaran still looked confused and said quietly, "I know the perfect person for the job. But I need to ask: is this a drug of some sort?"

"For some," Jackson admitted, "it comes pretty close."

"Well, here is something in trade." He handed Jackson a wrapped package. "While not as exciting as…coffee," he cut a glance to Leea, who still held the cup to her lips, "it will counteract any dizziness you may encounter. Brew these herbs with your favorite beverage and have a cup before coming down, then you'll be a step ahead, but there will be a carafe of the special infusion in the conference room for you. Our local healer said two to three glasses a day should be adequate to reduce any ill effects. Everyone's tolerance is different, so you'll need to gauge how much you need."

Yaran noticed the flushed countenances of their guests. "We will also provide each of you with a protective robe. The buildings are cooled, but the heat out here can be overwhelming."

"Thank you." Jackson gave the package to one of the other Watchers who hurriedly put it in their shuttle.

"Are you ready for this?" Leea asked Farrell.

Her friend wiped away a bead of sweat from her upper lip. "I think so. I would like to make a request," she addressed Yaran. "Can our first priority be the release of the Morodons. Trame, the one on our ship, says his communication with the few on the surface is weak."

"That will be as good a place as any to start," Yaran agreed. "But first, let's all go inside."

Tension lay heavy in the room as Humans and Zantians studied each other quietly across the oblong conference table. Yaran and Leea purposely chose to enter last, sitting together at one end, hoping to present a united front. Although some had met the night before, introductions were made around the room.

"I want to thank everyone for being here today," Yaran began. He turned to Farrell, who sat in the middle of the Human assemblage. "Farrell Reynolds will be speaking on behalf of the Dekarran government, and eventually our Human workers. Leea will assist her until she becomes familiar with things here. I know this will be difficult for everyone, but we've made it to this point with mutual respect, so I hope the subsequent negotiations will continue in the same manner. The people in this room are not responsible for the events that unfolded yesterday, but it will still make these proceedings challenging. I hope we can come to an agreement on how we move forward that will be acceptable to both sides.

"However, before these discussions begin, I want to point out to both parties that the outcome here cannot be all-or-nothing for either side. Understandably, the Dekarrans... Humans... have come here with the intention of freeing their people from their servitude to us. But you need to realize," he turned to the Watchers, "we are currently a divided world, so giving you everything you want won't be possible right away. And I hope you'll consider that pulling your people out all at once will put us in great hardship. While I know this isn't your concern, please know, we will work diligently for an acceptable solution for all."

He turned his attention to the Zantian side. "Human is not the first unwilling race we've brought here and then sent away, and we have always recovered. This time will be no different."

As Yaran continued, Leea eyed him in silent awe. The words he spoke were simple and to the point, but the tone in which he said them took her aback because they were almost like his father's. While Yaran's tone was kinder than she'd ever heard from the Desolk, and he gave the assembly a warm smile—something Jarock never did—Yaran made it clear he was not to be taken lightly. The loving and passionate man from the night before, and the kind and gentle man that had taken her to meet her father, was now replaced by someone she hadn't met yet.

Yaran seemed to sense her staring at him as Danloc, his uncle, and senior council member, took over the proceeding, and glanced over. "Everything all right?" he whispered.

"I'm not sure." she mouthed with a smile.

He returned the smile, then gently squeezed her knee under the table before turning his attention back to the conversation, where Farrell had already broached the subject of the Morodons.

"The Morodon on our ship, Trame, has been able to connect with some on the surface. He said that the pods have a built-in program that keeps its occupants just below conscious level and keeps them focused...." Farrell paused, and her cheeks brightened a bit. "But then you already know that." She pulled in a deep breath. "Trame is worried they could be harmed while we conduct our negotiations."

"The program that generated the shield has already been deactivated by the Morodon's themselves," Danloc said with a touch of wonder. "Unfortunately, the substance in the pod that keeps them in a state of suspension, cannot be shut down until we're ready to remove them because it also sustains them. And given their varying ages, the removal will have to be done on an individual basis. Right now, the bigger problem will be getting to them all. Thirteen of the twenty-five Morodons are housed in cities ruled by council loyalists."

"We have something that can help find them," Farrell said.

"Finding them isn't the issue. It's actually getting to them. The city leaders who support Jarock are not going to let us into their regions and remove the Morodons, even though the shield isn't active anymore. Morodons are kept deep within a mine, and I'm sure by now, guarded. We will certainly negotiate their release, but it might take a little time. However, we will free the ones we can as soon as possible."

The remainder of the day was spent defining how these meetings would move forward. Since the Atlantis needed repairs, and the damage to the cities was still being assessed, everyone agreed to hold off on any final decisions. In the meantime, Leea would help coordinate the opening of information centers around the planet where Humans would go and register their intentions.

It was late when Yaran and Leea finally returned to the apartment. The evening meal was shared with the visitors, and while accommodations had been offered, the Dekarrans chose to return to their ship.

"Honey, we're home," Leea announced as they walked through the door. Seeing Yaran's confusion she laughed. "Living on Dekarra for a year has expanded my terms of endearment."

"I see," he said smiling. "Does it feel good to be home…honey?"

"Incredibly so." She moved to the large window overlooking the city. "While my little house on Dekarra was comfortable, and I loved its surroundings, there was always something missing." She looked up at him over her shoulder as he slid his arms around her waist. "But here, in this strange apartment, with you, everything feels right."

"I completely agree."

Leea turned back to the window. "Can we take a walk, further into the city?"

"It's a mess out there."

"I know. I'd just like to take a closer look. From what I saw when we flew over, there was a lot of damage where Julia and I used to shop."

"Yes, there is. It's a bit of a walk but, of course, we can go."

Once on the street, they walked hand in hand in the warm evening. There was no breeze, and the smell of smoke still lingered in the air as well as a slight haze. When they turned onto the main thoroughfare, the sight in the distance could have been from another world. On both sides of the street, cut in erratic patterns were paths carved through the once beautifully crafted edifices. While for some, there was nothing left but twisted metal and large chunks of glass, other's seemed surprisingly unscathed.

Turning around, Leea spotted their ten-story apartment building and realized this was where the carnage ended. Had it gone any further, the residential lodgings would have been gone as well.

"Did Alrack sustain casualties?" she asked tentatively.

"Only one," he said. "Toref made sure the offices, warehouses, and processing plants, were evacuated, and then an announcement was made about the impending attack. Many took refuge in the mountains. But what you see here is probably minimal to what could have happened had the planes actually dropped any of their bombs. It seems the focus of the three fighters that entered Alrack was my parents' house. Luckily, one of our pilots intervened and sacrificed himself to protect it." He sighed. "But not all the cities were so lucky."

Leea stopped and lowered her head. "I can't get past the feeling that that's all my fault."

"What are you talking about?"

"I got caught on the ship, which exposed the Watchers. If that hadn't happened, we could have disarmed all the fighters."

"Oh, Leea." He pulled her into a protective embrace and stroked her long hair. "None of this is your fault. This plan was devised by powerful men who only had their own interests in mind, aided by a powerful alien. You and the Watchers did all you could to minimize the damage, and should be proud of that. What lives were lost in our cities is the fault of their own leaders, not yours, or any of the others. Believe me, my love, you are not to blame."

She looked up at him with a wary smile. "Thank you, but it might take a while before I can really feel that way."

"I understand. But consider this: their plan could have had many different outcomes. One being that the missiles destroyed the Atlantis. I truly believe this was the best outcome."

"Yes, I agree."

They continued, carefully avoiding broken glass that seemed to be everywhere. Transitioning glass was designed to be shatterproof, but obviously, it couldn't withstand this kind of assault. Steel beams lay haphazardly about; some still tethered to the support structure that they eased under, while others lay on the ground that they climbed over.

"Look, it's Man's," she said when they'd reached Alrack's shopping district. It stood alone, surrounded by piles of debris on both sides, but seemed otherwise untouched. While they hadn't passed a single person since leaving the apartment, the door to Man's stood open, and light poured out from within.

She pulled Yaran along and carefully entered the establishment. Once inside, it was clear that the eatery had sustained damage. A portion of the back wall was missing, and more than half of tables and chairs were scattered about in pieces, along with a fair amount of glass.

"Leea?"

She turned toward the soft voice coming from the far corner behind them. Fortal sat at one of the tables covered with decorations. He rose and approached them.

"It is you," he said, a smile brightening his face. He took both her hands and clasped them warmly. "It is so good to see you. I ... ," he glanced cautiously at Yaran, "I heard what happened."

Leea squeezed his hands reassuringly. "It's okay. I made it back. I'm so sorry this happened. But I'm glad you're all right."

"It is amazing how this building still stands, where everything around me is gone. I am very humbled." The emotion was heavy in his voice. "I believe every Zantian suspected a day like this could happen while hoping it never would."

Yaran concurred.

"Please," Fortal motioned toward the corner where he'd been sitting, "let me offer you a drink."

"Oh no, we didn't mean to intrude," Leea said. "We were—"

"No, I insist." He swept his arm around the room. "It is going to be a long time before I can serve guests here again. If ever," he added sadly. "But there is still a fully stocked bar that was spared any damage. Please ... ."

Leea looked at Yaran questioningly.

He smiled. "We would love a drink."

The three sat at one of the empty tables and Leea told the proprietor about Dekarra and some of its amazing sights. After two drinks the young couple excused themselves with a promise to return.

# CHAPTER 32

# Departure

About a week later, soft chiming bells brought Yaran out of his slumber. Disoriented, it took him a minute to realize it was the communications console. He reached over and activated the voice only. "Yes."

"Yaran? Did I wake you?" Lauranna asked quietly.

"Mother? No. No, it's fine." He slipped out of bed, pulled a shirt over his head, and quickly finger-combed his hair. Turning the monitor around, he brought up the video.

"I'm so sorry—"

"It's okay, Mother. Is something wrong?"

"No, I wanted to get in touch with you before your day got too busy."

"Actually, except for an appointment this afternoon, I'm free today. Negotiations are on hold since the Council called their special meeting."

"Then I'm truly sorry I called so early."

"No, it's all right. What do you need?"

"Can you and Leea come by sometime this morning?"

"Yes, of course. We'll be there—"

"No hurry. Wake up first," she chuckled, "enjoy your morning meal, and stop by when you're ready."

"Okay, we'll be there in a few hours." He disconnected.

"What was that all about?"

He looked over at Leea, propped up on one elbow, auburn hair disheveled, and only one green eye open warding off the light of the console. He put the unit on sleep mode and sat on the edge of the warm bed.

"I don't know. She wants to see us this morning."

She looked at him doubtfully. "Are you sure she said me too? I can't be on her list of favorite people."

"Yes, she was very specific…you too."

"When are we meeting Mearos?"

"Since Farrell has been staying in the apartment downstairs, he asked the three of us, and Toref, to join him for the midday meal, and then he'll take us up."

"I'm glad Jackson invited everyone to the Atlantis for a tour. Do you know if those not at the council meeting are going?"

"I think so. The Zantians are curious about the alien ship. Interested in what upgrades the Belag made."

Leea sat up, propping several pillows behind her back. "I'm glad things are on hold for a bit. I'm looking forward to finally being able to spend a whole day with you."

"Me too," he smiled. "We've been so busy lately that there's been no time to think about anything except the future of Zantia. I definitely need a break. Especially since the reality of what's happened…with us…is starting to sink in." He reached under the blanket and caressed the leg Leea stretched in his direction, letting his hand travel up to rest on her thigh, then studied her meditatively.

"What?"

"'One thing we discovered through that amazing experience was that we were truly meant to be together,' he quoted, eyeing her lovingly. 'We both opened our heart, body, and soul and let the other ease in completely as if it were the most natural thing in the world.'"

Her eyes widened, then she blushed. "You read my stories?"

"They were on the original data-cube Mearos gave me. I didn't want to read them at first. But at some point, I wanted to…needed to."

"I had a hard time writing about our first night together, and only finished it with some difficulty. I cried horribly for a long time when I was done, fearing I would never feel you next to me again." Tears welled in her eyes as she smiled. "But I refused to believe our separation was permanent, and that's what got me through the last year—it would have gotten me through as long as I needed."

Laying his head on her lap, Yaran took her hand and stroked each finger individually as if seeing them for the first time, before pulling it to his lips and kissing her palm tenderly. "When I left you that day…on the ship…you took my heart and soul with you, and left my body with an unimaginable void. I've loved you for so long that you've become an extension of me, and I was ill prepared for the emptiness or the pain your absence brought."

Leea disengaged her hand and stroked the side of his face, a tear sliding down her cheek. "I kept it safe—your heart. I held it every day, close to my own, never giving up on us."

"I knew you wouldn't, and neither did I," he assured her, then pulled her down to him.


"I'd like to go upstairs while you visit with you mother. I want to see if anyone's around," Leea said as she and Yaran walked through the grand entrance of the Alrack mansion.

"Okay, I'll come find you later."

She reached up and kissed him. "I'd like to visit the library before we go if that's okay?"

"Of course. Let's meet there later then."

Yaran entered his mother's sitting room, but instead of finding her seated in her large chair with some piece of literature on her lap, she stood at the window studying her partial view of the city. She had on a long white dressing robe, which she rarely wore outside her bedroom.

"Mother," he called softly and went to stand next to her by the window. "Is everything all right?"

"It is a beautiful view, isn't it?" she commented without looking away.

"It is." From this vantage point, none of the city's damage could be seen. Looking out, it would seem as if Alrack was going about its daily routine, but that was far from the current reality.

Lauranna looked around. "Did Leea come with you?"

"Yes. She went upstairs for a bit and will meet up with us a little later. Are you alone here?"

"No, most of the workers are still here. They all put their names on the registry, but most came back … at least for now."

"I'm sorry how this all turned out."

"No, it turned out just as it should have. We will all adjust. But come, I have a surprise for you."

Without another word, she took his arm and guided him to the music room. As they entered, Yaran stared in disbelief. Except for a few instruments, the room was empty. "What happened here?"

"I had everything packed up for you."

"What do you mean … packed up?"

She tried unsuccessfully to hide her sad expression. "Yaran, this is no longer your home…nor will it ever be again. You may want to leave this world now, so I thought you should take your music with you."

"But—"

"It's done. The workers packed it all up yesterday and loaded them on a transport. I sent Jeffrey to the airfield with it this morning. It'll be there waiting for you."

"You didn't need to do that."

"Yes, I did." She smiled. "But I left a few things so I could still hear you play."

Leea entered the room she had called home most of her adult life. Nothing had changed. She had expected a well of emotion when she walked in, but surprisingly, the familiar space with limited décor only evoked indifference. It had remained unoccupied during her year away, so she opened the door to the wardrobe and looked at the drab clothing that still hung there, but then quickly closed it. This was her past, and she was happy to leave it here. She'd brought along a small bag, knowing there were a few things she wanted to take, and hurriedly packed them, suddenly anxious to leave.

"What am I afraid of," she said aloud, "that someone will come and lock me in here?" The thought made her chuckle. No, she just wanted to close this chapter of her life.

A short distance down the hall, Leea stood in front of the door that had haunted her dreams for months on Dekarra. Cautiously, she released the lock and stepped inside. The private washroom looked smaller than in her visions, but what she'd experienced here was over twenty years ago, so the dreams were seen through the eyes of a child.

She knelt on the floor in front of the white tub and ran a hand along the top edge, surprised as tears stung her eyes.

"I'm sorry, Mom," she whispered. "I'm sorry life was so hard for you. I wish I could have known you, could have helped you." She sighed. "I'm happy, Mom. I'm back with the man I love, and my father is alive. The only thing that would make this all perfect would be you. I love you and miss you." Leea crossed her arms over the edge and laid her head down in silent reflection before getting to her feet. "Rest in peace," she said with a feeling of finality. Wiping the tears from her cheeks, Leea walked into the corridor, closing the door to the last of the sad memories generated in this house.

The next hour was spent talking with old friends. They listened in awe to her stories about Dekarra. It surprised her that while some expressed excitement to leave, others seemed to waver. She encouraged them all not to make their decision lightly, no matter which way they decided, and ensured each one she would be there to help in any way she could.

Saying a temporary goodbye, she made her way to the library but lingered a few moments in the atrium to enjoy the moist air. Leea admired the flowerless plants that stood proud in their decorative pots, so different from the bright flora that grew wild on Dekarra. It brought a sudden longing for that colorful place, the woods, and all of its creatures, but she would happily leave it behind to be with Yaran. She meant what she'd told him; she wouldn't ask him to leave his family. And while she made that promise before knowing her own father was alive, she wouldn't take it back. Once everything settled on Zantia, they would have plenty of time to decide on what to do.

Leea entered the empty library and stopped just inside the door as the devastation she'd felt the last time she stood here flashed through her mind. It was hard to encompass everything that had happened since then. Did she wish it never happened? Did she wish everything would have stayed the way it was? In all honesty—no. While she never wanted to relive that kind of heartache again, or the fear of Marik's attack, she wouldn't trade her life today to avoid it.

Pushing those thoughts away, she walked around the library admiring the items stored there as she had secretly done many times before. As always, the books from Earth fascinated her, and she ran a hand along their leather bindings enjoying the feel on her fingertips. She took one off the shelf and wished she could sneak it out as she leafed through the pages. A lifetime of reading stood here and it made her sad to think that it would all be left behind once her people departed.

"Would you like to take some of those with you?"

Clutching the book, Leea spun around to find Lauranna and Yaran in the doorway. "Oh…no… It's just…impressive." She hurriedly replaced it and moved toward them, suddenly nervous at being caught in the sacred room she had never officially been allowed to enter.

"I am serious. There are many books here from your world. I would like very much for you to take some."

"I… Yes, I would love that."

"Good, it's settled then." Lauranna removed over two dozen volumes and laid them on a nearby chair. Then she approached the center, glass-enclosed cabinet, and removed a thin translucent square from her pocket. Opening the door, she pulled out the hinged, center shelf and inserted the small device into the top of the hovering orb. Immediately, it powered down and settled on the shelf.

The young couple stared in stunned disbelief.

"Forgive the deception, Yaran," Lauranna said. "It was your father's wish to never lose sight of where we came from, which meant leaving this active all these centuries." She placed the large artifact on top of the books. "I want you to take this as well. I insist," she said as he started to protest. "Remove the activator and the orb will restart, it will also act as a remote of sorts. I've added a language key that will translate the stories for you. When there's time, listen to some of them and get to know your true ancestors. The relic will teach you about them."

"What will Jarock say when he finds it missing?"

"He hardly comes in here anymore, so it may take a while before he notices. I'll deal with any consequences then. Now, Yaran, take all these things and find something to put them in while I have a moment alone with Leea if you don't mind."

"No, of course not." He gathered up what he could carry and left the two women alone.

As he retreated across the foyer, Lauranna pulled them deeper into the room.

"I'm glad you're back, Leea," she said, smiling warmly. "This last year was very difficult for Yaran... difficult for all of us."

"I'm sorry," Leea said.

"Oh no, none of this was your fault. Actually, I'm the one who needs to apologize for everything you endured in this house. What happened with Marik was unfair to you."

"No reason to apologize, it wasn't your fault."

"I didn't start it, but I was aware it was happening, which makes me equally responsible."

"I don't agree, but I accept the apology."

"Thank you." Lauranna seemed genuinely relieved. "I wish things could have been less complicated for everyone. Please don't take offense when I say that everything would have been so much easier had you been Zantian. But women of our world rarely give one hundred percent of themselves to any man. I know I didn't. Yaran has a tender side, something many Zantian men of ruling families lack; it seems we force it out of them during their transition years. So he needs someone like you. Someone who will allow him to be who he is, while encouraging him to be so much more."

"He's changed a lot over the past year. It surprises me more every day how confident and take-charge he's become. He did that without me."

"Maybe. But he could do it because of you. You always fueled his inner strength." Lauranna grabbed Leea's hands, catching her off guard. "I'm so grateful he has you because I need you to be strong for him again. There will be many struggles ahead, and he'll need you now more than ever."

"I'll always be there for him. I love him very much."

"And he loves you equally."

"I know. Whatever happens in the coming weeks, we'll get through it together."

"Thank you, Leea. I've known for a long time how you two felt about each other, but I needed to hear you say it. It eases my mind to know my son won't be alone."

"This isn't goodbye. We haven't decided where we're going, and we won't make that decision hastily."

Lauranna smiled. "I'm glad to hear that. Well, we should find Yaran before he thinks we're conspiring or something."

"Good idea." Leea chuckled. The two women picked up the remainder of the books and Lauranna held her back one more moment. "Take care of my son," her voice quivered.

"Always."

They found Yaran in the foyer, two containers at his feet, to which they added the rest of the items.

"I was beginning to wonder what happened to you two," he said lightheartedly.

"Oh, just a moment of girl-talk," Lauranna said smiling sweetly. "Now, I've kept you both long enough. I'm happy you could come on such short notice."

"Of course, I'll come back and see you tomorrow," Yaran said.

"Unfortunately, I'm leaving this afternoon to visit my parents; that's why I was hoping you could come this morning," She sighed. "This entire situation is taking its toll on my father's already failing health. I'll be gone for a few days, but will let you know when I return."

Yaran gave his mother a hug and she clung to him for a long moment.

Lauranna watched the young couple from the doorway and marveled at how they slipped into each other's embrace as they walked, even with the load they carried. He opened the small shuttle's passenger door, letting her slide in before setting the items in the back. She said something that made them both laugh. Yaran leaned in and kissed her gently, then lingered close a moment for a brief conversation. Leea caressed his cheek before he closed the door and moved to the driver's side.

Lauranna smiled as she watched their tender exchange. She wanted to remember her son in this happy moment forever.

"Live well, my son," she said aloud as tears dampened her cheeks.

For the rest of the week, Leea busied herself at the information center. Thankfully, her time at the negotiations table had only lasted two days. After that, she helped set up many of the facilities where workers came to learn about Dekarra and add their name to a registry list that would eventually be converted into a departure schedule. Now, she found that talking to people about what they would find in the new world was much more to her liking than negotiating minute details on their release. The center was slow at the moment, so Leea sat in front of the terminal trying to reorganize some hastily entered data, but her mind wandered.

Working here had turned into a family affair. A week ago Yaran had insisted that Roger be transferred to Alrack. At first, Administrator Graeden emphatically refused, but since all the city leaders were off somewhere in secrecy, presumably arguing over the fate of their planet, the overseer had little choice but to comply. Especially once the son of the council leader threatened to bring a security force and take all the workers. Yaran had been visibly relieved that the administrator hadn't called his bluff because he said he had no idea where to find guards if he'd needed them.

Roger moved into the worker-complex and now spent his days here with her. Julia also came as often as she could, juggling her schedule around Tim and Marta and her hours at the plant. Mining production had resumed on a reduced schedule, which meant she only worked a few hours a day, but Marta still had school, and Tim came home every other day.

It amazed Leea, as Humans trickled through, how many were undecided on what they wanted to do, especially among older workers. Julia contacted her parents, who said they wouldn't leave Zantia just yet, but encouraged her to go, and promised to visit once they were settled on the new world.

Leea knew that her father was having the same thoughts, which he'd voiced to her the previous day.

"I am fifty-seven years old, Leea, what will I do in this new world?"

"Anything you want."

"I know how to mine dangerous elements, something I'm sure they don't need on Dekarra. But, I will go wherever you go."

"I'm glad. I don't want to lose you again. But we haven't decided either."

Since her return, Leea was amazed every day at Yaran's transformation. The gentle, unassuming man she'd left behind was still there, but at times, was quickly overshadowed by his new determination and self-assuredness. Living together with him was also eye-opening.

They had lived their entire lives under one roof, but now, sharing the same room—the same bed—was nothing like she'd imagined. She was realistic that this discovery phase between them wouldn't last forever, and that eventually, the routine of daily life would set in, but she intended to enjoy every minute of these exhilarating experiences. And as the days passed, her love for him grew stronger— something she would never have thought possible. Leea had never imagined her life this way, but now, she couldn't imagine it any different.

"Excuse me."

Almost reluctantly, Leea pulled out of her reverie. Before her stood a Zantian woman Leea guessed to be in her forties, with black hair cut just below the ears. Her presence was a surprise because except for Yaran, Zantians never came to the center.

"I'm sorry…daydreaming."

The woman smiled. "It must have been some daydream. You had quite the smile on your face."

Leea blushed and got to her feet, absentmindedly pulling her long ponytail over her shoulder. "How can I help you?"

"I was told I might find Mearos here or someone who could help me get in touch with him."

"I can do that. But may I ask what this is about? He's out on the cargo ship."

"My name is Selane. We are…old friends."

Leea studied the woman Mearos had told her about. She was slightly taller than Leea and had a warm smile. She was impeccably dressed in a light shimmering tunic and white leggings, which complimented her olive complexion.

Selane gave Leea a questioning look. "You know about me?"

"Yes, Mearos told me about you," then quickly added, "but not in any great detail, I assure you."

"With everything that's going on, I needed to come and see him." She lowered her head. "I made a mistake many years ago. I want the chance to tell him that."

Leea heard the desperation in her voice. "Mearos is getting things ready on his ship, but I'll take you out there."

"If you're sure it's no imposition?"

"None at all." She smiled. "I believe we all need the opportunity to set things right."

"Thank you."

Leea borrowed one of the small transport carts, along with a driver, and they made their way to the opposite end of the airfield. Four cargo ships stood on the tarmac surrounded by bustling activity, and they stopped at the bottom of the second loading ramp.

"It might be best if you wait here," Leea said. "I'll go in and get Mearos, and then he can take it from there."

"Thank you again."

Leea walked up the ramp weaving her way around containers, equipment, and people. Walking through the lower cargo area brought back instant memories of her escape, which seemed like a lifetime ago.

The door to her once-hidden room stood open, and she walked in to look around. It was the same as she remembered. She sat on the cot and laid her head against the wall. Closing her eyes, Leea thought about the heartbroken state she'd been in during those four weeks. Now, she was glad no one would ever need to occupy this space again.

As expected, she found Mearos on the flight deck, intently going over the instrument panels, comparing the console's data to the pad resting on his lap.

"How are things going?" she asked, taking the seat next to him.

"Surprisingly smooth," he said without missing a beat of his data entry, then held up a finger for her to wait. When he finally laid the pad aside, he turned and faced her. "What brings you here? I thought you'd be busy at the center."

"It's been pretty quiet today. I think we should be wrapped up in a couple of days."

"That's good. We should have basics loaded by tomorrow morning. We're still waiting for some of the personal items, and after that, I'll be ready for takeoff at any time."

"Great."

"So, is this a social visit? Don't get me wrong; I enjoy your company, but I do have a schedule to keep." A wide grin spread across his face.

"Wow, is that a polite way of telling me to get out?" They both laughed. "Actually, I brought someone to see you."

"You did? Who?"

"I thought it best if we did this outside. Can you take a break?"

"Of course, now that you've spiked my curiosity."

They made their way through the ship, chatting conversationally, but then Mearos stopped short once he stood at the top of the ramp. Leea looked out and saw Selane standing next to the cart with her hood pulled back.

"If you don't want to see her, I'll send her away."

Mearos seemed mesmerized. "No, that's okay, I'll see her." He slowly made his way off the ship.

For the second time in four days, Yaran was awakened in the early morning hours by the communications chime. He reached over and activated the voice only.

"Yes?"

"Yaran, this is Toref. I'm up in the airfield tower. You need to get up here… now."

"What is it?"

"Hurry." Toref disconnected.

Yaran turned to Leea, confusion on his face.

"Go," she said. "Come to the center later."

Fifteen minutes later, taking the tower stairs three at a time, Yaran quickly scaled the five floors. Bursting onto the observation floor, he found all the occupants standing in front of the largest viewscreen.

"What's going on?" he asked, trying to catch his breath.

Toref pointed to the screen, which showed two ships moving away from the planet. "They started leaving about an hour ago."

"Who?"

"The Council."

"I don't understand."

"Remember the day I first showed you the desert storage? Do you remember how I told you that each of the city houses have their command cruiser buried under the house?"

Yaran circled the floor until he spotted the house on the hill through an opposite window. Smoke billowed from behind it.

"Their ship was the first to leave," Toref informed him sadly.

Yaran quickly activated a console in the corner and put a call through to Danloc—grateful when his uncle's face appeared on the screen.

"I'm glad to see you, Danloc. Is my mother there?"

"No. I haven't seen her."

"She told me the other day that she was coming to see your parents."

"I'm sorry, Yaran, she hasn't been here. But I need to tell you—"

Yaran quickly disconnected and flew down the stairs, his feet barely touching the steps.

Landing in front of his parents' home, Yaran scurried from the shuttle, not bothering to power it down. He burst through the front door and was instantly assaulted by acrid smoke.

"Mother!"

He tried entering her sitting room, but it was filled with a thick haze that smelled of burnt paper. He didn't detect the sound of fire, but he couldn't see far enough into the room to be sure. The house's framework and shelves were steel and glass, and the floors concrete tiles. The insulated walls were derived from the glass, so the only thing to burn would be the furniture and the items on the bookcases. In the library across the foyer, he found the same. He imagined many of the paintings, artifacts, books and memorabilia charred in an act of, what—vengeance? He was instantly angry.

"Mother!"

Yaran ran through the atrium and almost stumbled into a crater-sized hole that had once been the back of the house. Gone were the workers' quarters, the music wing, and the greenhouse, along with most of the gardens. Yaran sank to the floor and stared into the void below. He had no idea how long he'd sat there when two hands came to rest on his shoulders. He raised his confused face to find Toref.

"I'm so sorry, Yaran." The older man carefully lowered himself to the floor next to him.

"She knew," Yaran said, looking back into the abyss.

"Knew what?"

"A few days ago…she called me early in the morning and wanted Leea and me to come over…which we did. She had all my music equipment sent to the airfield as a surprise, saying she wanted me to take it for my new home. She gave me the history sphere and Leea some of the books from the library. Obviously, she did that because they were leaving and destroying the house."

Toref patted his arm. "You ran out before I could explain. And you should know they didn't purposely set these fires. This is a result of the ship's engines during taking off."

"So you knew as well?" Yaran asked.

"Not until early this morning. Lauranna called me—"

"She called you?!"

"Let me finish, Yaran."

The young man lowered his head. "I'm sorry."

Toref sighed. "I know this is difficult for you, but let me start at the beginning. Danloc contacted me after the special session of the Council was under way. He told me most of the members were fairly irate, and a lot of blame was laid on Jarock for what happened with the Dekarrans."

"They should have gone against him … protected their cities anyway."

"Very true, and some did, but others didn't. He was accused of ignoring the warning of the attack just to spite you. Late yesterday, by a narrow margin, Jarock was voted out as leader. In his anger, he resigned his position altogether."

"He did?"

"Lauranna called me late last night and told me that after the Council adjourned, Jarock met privately with those who supported him and proposed that they leave this disaster behind and seek new opportunities elsewhere. There are a few races that still owe us favors, so they thought maybe they could start over somewhere else. Or maybe they should go find out why the Ma'Kree were looking for us. The Council has always stockpiled a certain amount of precious metals and gems that can be used as currency in other parts of the universe."

"But why would he give up on Zantia, a place he considered his personal property?"

Toref chuckled softly. "Yes, he did. But the truth is, for years my brother has barely held his control over the membership, and he knew it. He must have suspected that a vote was inevitable and made preparations. Lauranna said the day after the attack he had an engineer come to check on their ship, and that's why she moved the music equipment to the airfield, just in case."

"Jarock and I had another argument that day. I told him he should evaluate where he belonged, but I'm sure he didn't leave because of what I said."

"No. While I'm not surprised that your father didn't lose gracefully, this is most likely a reaction he didn't think through, but now it's done."

"Why didn't Mother tell me?" Yaran said defeated.

"Because it would have been too hard … for both of you. She wanted to remember you the way you were during your last visit. She said it had been a long time since she'd seen you so happy and that made leaving easier; knowing you'd be okay. But I am supposed to tell you that she loves you very much and hopes that someday you will see each other again."

"I would have tried to stop her."

"I know, and so did she."

Yaran pulled in a deep breath, which he let out slowly. "Did they ask you to go?"

"No."

"Would you have … if they'd asked?"

"No. I don't believe in my brother's ideals, haven't for a very long time, and Jarock knew that. As brothers, we respect each other, but that's as far as it goes."

Yaran got up and helped Toref to his feet. "We should have a meeting with the remaining membership and figure out where we go from here. How many ships left?"

"Sixty-three at last count. But we're assuming some of those are for extended family as well, since not that many supported him. I think a meeting is wise. I suspect everyone is a little shocked at the moment."

"I'm going to stop at the information center first. I left in such a hurry this morning, so Leea must be wondering what's going on. Although I'm sure she already knows."

"I'm sure the whole planet does. But yes, you should talk to her, she'll be worried about you. I'll call the meeting and let you know when and where."

Leea exited the transport shuttle that had been provided for the workers to visit the information center, excited to be spending another day with her father. Their relationship was growing stronger every day, and she was at a point where it felt like he had always been a part of her life.

"Hi, Dad." She gave him a big hug then put her protective cover in the wardrobe.

"It's crazy what happened this morning, isn't it?" Roger said.

Leea looked at him confused. "What happened?"

"Oh, you don't know? Half the Zantian Council left the planet. Got into their private ships and headed out."

"What! That must have been what Yaran's call was about this morning. Oh no! Did his parents leave too?"

"From what the news said, they were the first to go."

"Oh, Yaran! He must be devastated. I should—" Before she could finish, the rear door opened, and Yaran stepped in. One look told her everything she needed to know. A few people were coming into the center, so she pulled him behind a partition at the rear of the temporary building before putting her arms around him.

"I'm so sorry." She held him close as his tears silently fell.

"She already knew they were leaving when we went to see her the other day," he said after regaining his composure. They sunk down into two nearby chairs. "She never went to her parents' house."

"I guess that explains why she had us over."

He nodded.

"That also explains what she said to me." She laid an arm around him and pulled his head onto her shoulder. "She told me to take care of you, and that she was glad we had each other because there would be hard times ahead. This is obviously what she meant."

He placed a hand on her knee. "I'm glad I have you too."

"Is everything destroyed? Nothing salvageable? What about the workers?"

"I'm not sure. I assumed the house was empty. The workers' quarters are gone, and there was so much smoke. Toref is going to send a crew over to make sure the fires are out. When it's all clear, we'll go back and look. But you should contact Julia and have her check on Tim's family." He leaned forward and ran his hands through his hair.

"So what happens to the leadership now?" Leea asked rubbing his back.

"Not sure. Toref is setting up a meeting with those who remained, and we'll figure it out."

"I wish them luck."

"I'm not sure where the meeting will take place, so I might be gone for a while."

"Don't worry about me. I'll be fine. Does this mean the negotiations are over?"

"I think we've pretty much covered everything except for a few loose ends, and they'll work themselves out. I understand the repairs to the Atlantis are almost complete. I'm sure once that's done the Dekarrans will want to go home." He paused and looked back at Leea over his shoulder. "I want us to leave with them."

"You do? Are you sure? What about the Council, won't they want you to help rebuild?"

"They don't need me for that. This crisis has given Toref a new purpose and he will do fine helping to pull this planet back together." He chuckled softly. "And if I've learned anything these past weeks, it's that I have no desire, or aptitude, for governing. I'll leave that to those more qualified. So, I think we should leave the bad memories here and make happy ones somewhere else."

"If you really want to, I'd like that. But if you need to come back, we will."

"I love you, Leea." He turned and pulled her close.

"I love you too... we'll get through this."

They shared a tender kiss, and he held her tight for a long moment. "Well, I should go check in with Toref. I'll let you know what the plan is."

After Yaran left, Leea immediately called Julia, who informed her Tim's parents and brother, David, had been at her house since the night before. Evidently Lauranna had insisted that the workers go spend time with family and friends, or just some time in the city. Several empty units in the worker-complex had been put at their disposal so they wouldn't need to return to the main house. Julia said all complied except for Lauranna's personal assistant, Greta, and one of the kitchen workers. They weren't sure what happened to them, but Tim's mom said neither was planning to leave Zantia, so the hope was that they had been on the departing command cruiser.

It was late morning, and Jackson sat in the captain's chair on the quiet bridge. Only two other crewmen occupied their workstations, busily preparing for their impending departure. He was ready to go home.

It had taken a little over two weeks to repair the Atlantis: wiring restrung, ceiling tiles reattached, or repaired; hull-breaches closed inside and out, and engines brought back to full capacity. With Mearos and his crew's help, the fighter bay floor had been replaced, and the twenty-nine fighters that survived the attack were back aboard. The three damaged shuttles would wait for repairs until they were back on Dekarra.

Surprisingly, Jackson found he enjoyed working with the Zantian captain and had gained a great respect for him. He liked most of the Zantians he had met which was something he'd been unprepared for. He had expected a mutual tolerance, not impending friendships. Unfortunately, he hadn't been able to spend much time with Yaran, but Farrell was quite smitten with him. Said she had never met a more charming person.

"You're lucky you're the love of my life, and that Leea is my friend," she had quipped one day, "because that tall-dark-n-handsome alien could easily make my heart go pitter-patter." Typical Farrell—always trying to push his buttons. But he had to admit that he loved that about her. It definitely kept their relationship interesting.

"But," she continued. "He truly has eyes only for Leea, so I doubt he's even aware I'm in the room."

"Oh, I'm sure that's not entirely true," Jackson had replied slyly. "Even if he doesn't see you, I'm sure he can hear you."

That had earned him a forceful punch in the arm, and a threat to get her own room on the trip back. To which Jackson informed her there were no other rooms available, so she was stuck with him, like it or not. He smiled. Yes, sometimes he could give as good as he got.

Only about eighty percent of the workers had requested to leave, while the rest had added their names to a sometime-later list. Many of the Zantian cargo ships had offered to help transport provisions and personal belongings, but it would still take four trips with the Atlantis to transport everyone. Extensive meetings were held in all the cities, and most of the mine workers agreed to continue their work while they waited for their time to go.

Jackson sent and received several communiqués with Dekarra, and the government was scrambling to find accommodations for the influx of thousands of refugees. New Haven was Dekarra's largest city, but couldn't possibly handle them all, so several outlying metropolises were also making space available.

As a sign of a newfound friendship, an open invitation was extended to the Zantians to visit, or relocate. As far as Jackson knew, only Yaran was moving permanently, but several art studio owners said they would like to visit right away and assess possible business opportunities. This excited Farrell, who had visited several Alrack shops and was impressed by their quality and unique craftsmanship.

To no avail, Jackson had tried twice more to entice the admiral out of his room, but then decided it wasn't worth the effort, and left the man to brood by himself. A few of the admiral's security team finally offered to help, and even with the restrictions that were placed on them, the days went by without incident.

Tomorrow evening, they would be on their way back to Dekarra. The supplies were loaded and early this morning they started ferrying the first group of passengers. He would not miss this place. He had spent some time on the surface, mostly to be with Farrell, but also to feel solid ground under his feet. The planet below was hot and uncomfortable, even with the protective clothing they were given, and while the buildings were climate controlled, they could never completely ward off the constant heat.

A few days ago, Yaran had taken their group to the desert depot and showed them the massive ships. With great trepidation, they had boarded one of the vessels and seen the rooms where hundreds of Humans had lived for more than two years. It had been an overwhelming experience, and men and woman alike had shed more than a few tears, thinking of what they must have endured.

Right away Farrell said those were not the ships Becca and Jamie had seen from the moon's observation tower that day. The teenage artist had made detailed drawings of what had passed over their heads, and they looked quite different. Yaran's uncle, Danloc, said he would look into it, but didn't think the old records gave any credit to another species.

Tonight a private, casual get-together was being hosted by Yaran and Leea. All the Watchers had been invited along with the bridge crew and Dr. Bennett, who had been instrumental in the coup, and also spent a considerable amount of time in a Zantian medical facility. The Alrack healers had been more than happy to share some of their innovations and then had graciously helped the doctor come up with a more progressive treatment for the workers who would be coming aboard the Atlantis.

On the planet-side, it would be some of the remaining council members, and friends and family of the hosts—most of whom Jackson had already met. The pseudo-party was actually Farrell's idea, who loved organizing such things, and Yaran and Leea had been more than happy to let her make all the arrangements.

Yaran moved through the crowded room that had served as the makeshift command center for the last two and a half weeks. The small gathering of about sixty Humans and Zantians had finished a late meal and now mingled in friendly conversation. Yaran smiled inwardly as he walked through, noticing that most Humans held one of Zantia's more exotic, brightly-colored drinks, while most Zantians drank the wine or whiskey they imported from Dekarra. He also drank the latter, feeling it calmed his nerves more than any of the others would.

But he didn't need to be nervous since the room seemed completely without tension. Although he would have liked more mingling between the two races, pleasant conversation, and even laughter, could be heard all around. Yaran stopped where Leea, Farrell, and Julia stood deep in conversation, and gently rested a hand on Farrell's shoulder. "Would you join me in saying a few words to the guests?"

"I'd love to."

As they turned away, Yaran winked at Leea, then with a hand at her back, guided Farrell in front of the beverage station.

"I'm not good at making speeches," he said smiling, once they had everyone's attention. "But I would like to express my thanks to everyone here, and to those that couldn't make it, for their efforts these past weeks. Whether you were repairing the Dekarran ship, helping out in the information centers, or, as some were so gracious to do, helping clean up our cities—it is all much appreciated. I would like to thank the Watchers, who put themselves on the line to limit the destruction of our world, and the Zantian leadership for embracing the change our people are facing, and their willingness to jointly come up with the next steps.

"On a personal note, I would like to give a special thank you to Farrell. She drove some hard bargains but was always willing to see both sides. I'm not sure if these negotiations would have gone as smoothly without her." He smiled down at Farrell.

"I also want to thank everyone for coming today," Farrell addressed the room. "Seeing our two races standing together with mutual respect warms my heart." She turned to Yaran with a bright smile. "Thanks to our gracious hosts, and a special thanks to Yaran, my counterpart. Yes, while we were adversaries, in the end, our mutual respect and understanding made these negotiations go smoothly. There will be hard times ahead, on both sides, but we are strong and will prevail. This gathering is proof of that. I believe new friendships have been made here, something that seemed unimaginable just a few short months ago, and I'm honored to have been a part of it." Farrell seemed unable to say more.

"So," Yaran quickly said and raised his glass. "As is the Human custom, I would like to propose a toast. To our continued working relationship and mutual respect for one another."

Mearos and Selane made their way to where a large group stood, including Leea, Yaran, Farrell and Jackson.

"I apologize," he said to the group. "But I need to steal these four away for a moment. I'll have them back shortly."

"Is there a problem?" Yaran asked.

"No, I just want a private word."

The three couples walked out of the large room, leaving the din of conversation as the door closed behind them. Mearos guided them into a nearby office, and as the light illuminated the space, Yaran noticed the red bottle and six small fluted glasses sitting on the nearest desk.

"Oh no," he exclaimed, lightly chuckling.

"What's oh no?" Jackson asked, following Yaran's gaze.

"Yaran and I have some history with a bottle like this." Mearos removed the seal from the bottle's narrow neck and filled each flute halfway and resealed it. Steam billowed as he distributed them all around. "The contents are not hot," he explained. "The steam is a chemical reaction between the liquid and the air. This is not a sipping drink; it must be downed at once. It has a pleasant sweet-savory flavor, but the effect is purely spiritual and lasts for about a minute. It's called *Bouskadian* Elixir, which means 'To find peace.'

"The reason I brought you here is that I would like to make a toast of my own." He raised his glass, and the others followed suit. "I want to toast to rekindled friendships," he smiled warmly at Selane. "To continued friendships," he indicated Leea and Yaran. "And to new friendships," looking at Farrell and Jackson. "Whatever lies ahead, may our friendships prevail."

They all agreed. The six glasses clinked together and in unison, they downed the contents, which was followed by silence as the steaming liquid worked its enchantment.

"Wow!" was the eventual reaction by all. Mearos quickly refilled their glasses.

"Drink up." Mearos picked up the bottle and held it to the light. "There should be enough for one more each."

"So, what is the history you and Yaran have with this?" Leea asked with a wry smile.

"Oh, we don't want to talk about that now." Yaran raised his eyebrows to Mearos. "Do we?"

Mearos shook his head. "Let's just say, unpleasant circumstances brought us together, and a lot of this made these events possible."

Jackson whispered something in Farrell's ear, and a bright smile crossed her face. "Can we take a couple of cases with us when we leave?"

Yaran and Leea stood arm-in-arm at the window of their small quarters on board the Atlantis, watching the planet Zantia recede in the distance. She leaned her head against his shoulder, trying to hide the tears that silently escaped the corners of her eyes. But the emotion did not go unnoticed.

He pulled her in close. "Why the sadness?"

"I'm not sure. The wrongs have been righted, and my people are free … and so are yours, to some extent. But for better or worse, this was our home. We were born here, as were our parents and grandparents several generations back. I feel like I'm leaving them … and their memories." She choked back a sob and clutched at him.

He rested his chin on the top of her head. "Don't you think they would want this for you: to leave this dreary place, and find a better life?"

"Yes, they would, I just wish they could have found it too."

"We will honor their memory and their sacrifices by living the life they would have wanted for us. That's all we can do."

She smiled up at him. "And together, we will make them proud. But …."

"But what?"

"What about your ancestors, the Ma'Kree?"

"I would be lying if I said I wasn't curious. But no, I have no intention of seeking them out."

"Do you think that's where the Council is headed?"

"I have no idea. There was a lot of bad blood between the Ma'Kree and the rebels who left, but that was a long time ago. Since Jarock's ideals correspond to those who deserted Kree'Lan, our former leaders may not be welcome. Unfortunately, we'll never know."

They turned back arm in arm and watched as the planet Zantia faded from view.

"I was talking to your father a couple of days ago. He was explaining some Human traditions to me," Yaran said, breaking away.

"Such as?"

"I hope I do this right," he mumbled nervously, taking a step back and dropping to one knee. He took both of Leea's hands and looked up lovingly into her confused face.

"Leea, I have loved you for most of my life. In all those years I silently wished that we could have been open about our relationship, but at the time, it wasn't possible, and for that, I apologize.

"Even though we made a pack to make the most of the time fate allowed us, and not worry about the rest, I was devastated when you were taken from me. But fate brought you back." Yaran smiled then let his gaze play over her face before looking deeply into her misty green eyes. "I am incredibly lucky to have you in my life. You are a part of me, the best part, and my best friend. I never want that to change."

Tears rolled down Leea's cheeks, but the shock was replaced by a bright, loving smile.

"During our separation this past year, I promised myself one thing: when we were reunited, I would never let you go again, and I would tell the world how much I love you." He took her left hand and effortlessly slipped an intricately carved band, supporting three gleaming blue crystals, onto her ring finger.

"Will you do me the honor of being my mate—my wife?"

# One year later

"**H**old still!" Toref chided as he attempted to fasten a blue boutonniere to his nephew's tunic.

Yaran wore the traditional Zantian dress which consisted of loose fitting white linen pants, a high-collared silk shirt—in this case, a medium blue—and a steel-gray linen tunic, reaching mid-thigh and was fastened at the waist with two ornate silver buttons. All exposed edges of the tunic were trimmed in silver, and a one-inch strip of a silvery fabric was inlaid into the outside seams of pants and tunic as well as on the stand-up collar of the shirt.

Zantians had little occasion to wear the formal dress. The last time for Yaran had been his education's completion ceremony. Celebrating the crossover was also a formal affair, but he and Toref had spent it quietly without any need for official observances. He had told Leea he would gladly wear a tuxedo, but she had insisted he wear this, and he was thankful for it. Toref wore a similar outfit, although his colors were different.

"I don't see the point in all this," Yaran said, rolling his eyes, "but whatever makes Leea happy. She's been so worried these last few weeks that everything isn't going to be perfect, so I don't want to do anything to upset her." He chuckled. "But I still don't understand why we couldn't have just had a Zantian mating ceremony; it would be so much simpler."

"You didn't say that to her, did you?" Toref asked mortified.

"No, of course not. I did mention it to Julia a few weeks ago, though, and she said if I valued my life I would forget that notion. I took her advice."

Toref shook his head but smiled.

"And they expect … dancing," Yaran added with a grimace.

"I thought you took lessons?"

"Oh yes, we did. I have to admit I found it enjoyable, even if it did make me feel awkward. I guess it didn't help that the female instructor was barely taller than Julia."

Toref roared with laughter. "I wish I could have seen that."

Yaran sighed. "Ask Leea. I'm sure she has some images. She found it amusing too."

"I would love to have a look at those," he said, still unable to calm the snickers.

Finished, Toref took a step back and gave Yaran a once over, seeming pleased. "You look very handsome, as Humans would say. I'll go and find out how things are progressing. Be back as soon as I can."

When Toref was gone, Yaran looked at his reflection and smiled at how happy he looked. And why should that surprise him? He was marrying the woman he'd loved his whole life.

It was hard to believe that only a year had passed since the attack on Zantia—it seemed like a lifetime ago. So much had happened since they left there and made Dekarra their home. They had moved into Leea's small house at the edge of the city, and he loved it as much as she did. They spent a lot of time among the giant trees, and every time they went, Yaran discovered something new. He was still a little apprehensive about the animals, but they didn't frighten him as much now as they had at the beginning.

Acclimating to the Dekarran seasons had been a more difficult task, but he hoped with time it would get easier... although he had his doubts. The worst was the winter. The freezing, windy days were worse than the time he'd almost drowned in the icy water of the Alrack pumping station. He told himself that Zantian physiology wasn't designed for the cold, but knew that was just an excuse.

Soon after their arrival, Julia told everyone she was pregnant. Four months ago she gave birth to twin boys and decided her place was at home with them and Marta. Marta, of course, had already taken on the role of mother, according to Julia. Yaran found the little ones fascinating but wasn't comfortable holding them for long, much to Leea and Julia's amusement.

Tim and Roger had taken jobs in one of the New Haven factories, and with their experience, were able to help improve some of the manufacturing processes. According to Roger, there was some resentment at first, but once the others realized the new men weren't trying to take over, everyone relaxed and were happy to listen to their ideas.

Farrell and Jackson were now officially engaged, and their wedding was six months away. When the President was briefed on how Farrell had successfully negotiated with the Zantians, the Dekarran leader appointed her off-world ambassador which required Farrell to travel to Zantia. Three Zantian cruisers had been given to the Dekarran government, and Jackson had seen to their upgrades and retrofit. One was dedicated for Farrell's travels, and Jackson insisted on being her pilot. Yaran and Leea had accompanied them once so Yaran could visit with his uncles.

The Dekarrans' newly elected Vice President had put Jackson in charge of special projects for the military. Jackson was currently negotiating a deal to upgrade the Atlantis for a trip to Earth, and Farrell was doing her part to convince him as well. Word of this had recently been leaked to the public, and the government was being bombarded with support for the mission. Jackson said the VP hadn't given his approval yet, but he was sure the official would; having just been elected by the people he wouldn't want to alienate them so soon.

The Zantian Council had been reformed, and Danloc was elected the new leader. New city leaders were also elected, and this time, the candidates were not restricted to only the descendants of the original hundred. With the absence of enough workers, the leadership had been reduced to fifty until the mining procedures could be reorganized. Toref now focused on trade negotiations for all the cities whose mines were still operational; smaller ones had been shut down and others consolidated under one leader. In this position, he worked closely with Farrell and had also visited New Haven on one occasion.

While Yaran was happy that his friends and family had all moved forward from the upheaval their worlds had experienced, he considered himself the luckiest of them all. His passion for music had landed him a teaching position at the University. Every day he taught young minds how to embrace the beauty of a musical instrument and make it play on its own. He truly enjoyed watching their faces when the instruments did exactly what the student wanted. He didn't think he would ever tire of teaching—something he knew would have made his mother proud.

Their house was too small to set up all the music equipment, so except for a few pieces, Yaran had loaned the rest to the school with the agreement that he be allowed to use them during after school hours whenever he wished. They happily agreed. His music students were enthralled with the unusual pieces and often asked for a private lesson on the weekend. Yaran chuckled. Leea always insisted on accompanying him if that student was female, even if it meant tearing herself away from the engineering studies she was now doing.

Roger stepped into the room, pulling Yaran out of his daydream. Leea's father had made an amazing transformation since his days in the mines. His once scruffy appearance was now replaced with that of a rugged man. His beard was now always neatly trimmed, making their white streaks more pronounced, while the close-cropped red hair had yet to show any sign of gray. The clean cut made it easy to see how much Leea resembled him.

"Jackson called and said he's on his way back from the airfield with Mearos and Selane," Roger informed him. "They should be here in about ten minutes."

"Great. How much longer until the festivities start?"

"Anxious?"

"Something like that." Yaran sighed.

Roger laughed. "Well, just hang in there. It shouldn't be too much longer. Where's Toref?"

"I'm not sure. He went to check on things and never came back."

"Well, be patient, I'll go see if I can find him."

Mearos and Selane had mated shortly after returning to Zantia a year ago. Six months after the first Humans left his home-world, cargo runs had resumed on a limited basis. Mearos still made his regular run, and Selane was now a part of his crew. She refused to be just the captain's mate, insisting she could contribute. In the city of Bragnon, where she had lived after leaving Mearos years ago, she worked at one of the healing centers. Although not officially a healer yet, she did have an extensive knowledge of all things medical. A cargo ship didn't typically need a healer, but she took care of their minor cuts and scrapes, and otherwise monitored the cargo—the task vacated by the Belag.

A lot of speculation revolved around what happened to the shapeshifter, or whether he still lurked about observing the Zantians. However, everyone felt sure that the small ship Mearos had seen leaving the Atlantis, heading for deep space, must have been the alien's, and whatever his objective was, had probably been accomplished.

Ex-Admiral Shaw and Bettina had been interrogated to find out what they knew about him but didn't provide anything of value, both claiming to know nothing. The two head conspirators, Admiral Shaw, and the Vice President, along with those who conspired with them, which included Bettina and Kent Madigan, now called the prison island New Alcatraz their home. The members of the admiral's security force on board the Atlantis who had stood by him during the ship's repair joined the group.

His thoughts were interrupted again by a brief knock, this time, Toref and Roger entered. "Are you ready?" Roger asked. "I have been instructed to get my daughter, and just wanted to make sure everything was ready here."

"I've been ready, just waiting for everything to get started." He hoped his impatience wasn't evident in his voice. But obviously, it was.

Roger smiled and laid a hand on Yaran's shoulder. "My boy, men, aren't supposed to be enjoying this…this is all for the woman." He lowered his voice to a whisper. "But let me assure you, once your bride walks toward you down that aisle, you too will think this was all worth it."

Yaran smiled at his future father-in-law but said nothing. He was sure Roger believed what he was saying.

Yaran and Toref walked downstairs and went to stand in their designated spots in front of the minister. Yaran sighed as he looked out over the hundred spectators sitting there to witness the event—he had met maybe half of them. He understood the concept of extended family and friends, but for Zantians, mating ceremonies were a private matter, shared with the immediate family at most, so this was a bit overwhelming.

He looked to the front rows and smiled at his family and friends. To his left were Mearos, Selane, Danloc and his mate, and surprisingly, Sithan and his mate. To his right sat Tim with Marta, Farrell and Jackson, Mary and her daughter with her family behind them. He smiled inwardly when he saw Tamera and her family a few rows back. He would be eternally grateful to Mearos's mother for helping to get his messages to Leea, but he wondered how meeting Sithan again was going to go.

He saw Tillia and Trame, who smiled, giving him a respectful nod. Many hours had been spent talking with the relatively young Morodon on board the Atlantis. He had chosen to stay with the Dekarran ship instead of returning with the rest of his people, who had left days earlier on a cargo transport. Fourteen of the twenty-five had been able to leave their stasis chambers once it was deactivated, which included Nethas's son Partnam. The remainder stayed in the pods and were tended to here, but sadly, only three of the eleven had survived.

"Do you have the ring?" Yaran asked Toref quietly.

Toref reached into his pocket and pulled out the narrow band that had belonged to Leea's mother. "Right here."

The music changed, and Julia appeared in a long blue dress holding a small colorful bouquet with both hands and made her way slowly to where Yaran and Toref stood. Smiling as she approached them, she moved to her assigned spot.

When Leea—a vision of white—appeared at the other end of the aisle, her right hand resting in the crook of her father's elbow, her left holding a cascading bouquet of bright, colorful flowers, Yaran felt the air leave his body. Her auburn hair was swept up, but long, thin wispy curls flowed over her bare shoulders, and tiny white flowers were scattered throughout.

Father and daughter stood for a moment as the wedding song started to play—a melody he had composed based on the lullaby Roger had hummed to his daughter as a child. Leea looked lovingly at her father, squeezed his arm, and then they started their slow walk toward him.

He had thought, on that day a year ago when Leea had stepped off the Dekarran shuttle that she could never be more beautiful to him. He had been completely wrong.

Sitting appropriately on the groom's side, she smiled as she watched the proceedings from the back of the room. Blending into the crowd had been easy, her friendly manner and excitement over the event gave the impression that she belonged. The happy couple, so obviously in love, said all the appropriate words and received all the appropriate blessings, and now made their way back down the aisle hand-in-hand. They smiled lovingly into each other's eyes, oblivious to their surroundings—not that it would have mattered.

Zantian and Human, who would have thought?

As people milled out behind them, the uninvited guest lingered, and once the room was empty, except for a few stragglers, made her way to the side door. No one gave her a second look. Once outside, she hurriedly crossed the lawn and headed to where she'd parked her vehicle, two blocks away. She desperately wanted to congratulate the bride but knew it wasn't worth the risk. There would be plenty of time for that later, but right now there were more pressing matters to attend to. If her plan were to work, patience would be required.

# Acknowledgements

Writing this book has been a lifelong dream, but wouldn't have been possible without the loving support from my family and friends. I want to thank my children, Marvin Oakcrum, Tamara Gessner, William Bossé and Michael Bossé, who have always encouraged my inner sci-fi geek. Their inputs, ideas, and general helpfulness were invaluable.

Thank you to John Griskenas who read the beginning of my rough draft as this started coming together, and encouraged me forward. A special thanks to Chris Dimm and Nora Lindberg who read my finished draft and made great suggestions on improvements. Thank you to my writing buddy, Jim Johnson who made me believe I could manage this frightening path into publishing.

My writing would never have evolved into this final product without the endless suggestions and critiques from the members of my writer's workshop: Barb, Donna, Gerrit, Jim, and our leader Ariele Huff. Thanks to Marvin and Tammy for their proofreading efforts, however, all grammatical failings, modern rule avoidance, and typos are my own. Thank you to Vladimir Verano from Third Place Press for the wonderful cover and interior layout.

# About the Author

PETRA BOSSÉ has been fascinated with all things science fiction for as long as she can remember, so it was inevitable that when writing became an important part of her life, it would be science fiction. Petra is also a full-time technical designer for a large airplane manufacturer, mother, grandmother, and neurotic cat owner. Born in Berlin, Germany, she now calls the Pacific Northwest home where she lives close to her four children and three grandchildren.

You can connect with her at either WorldsofDeception@gmail.com or on her Worlds of Deception Facebook page.